MW00684959

DEATHWISH

DANA MARTON

Broslin Creek Series

DEATHWATCH

DEATHSCAPE

DEATHTRAP

DEATHBLOW

BROSLIN BRIDE

DEATHWISH

ISBN:1-940627-07-9
ISBN-13: 978-1-940-627-07-6

DEDICATION

My sincere thanks to Sarah Jordan for having my back day after day, Diane Flindt, Linda, and Toni for editing, Kim Killion for the perfect cover, and Kelly Stypulkowski Phillips for giving Pickles his name. DEATHWISH is dedicated to my loyal readers. Thank you for being my friends on FB. I love chatting with you, Kat Hauger, Anna Carbone, Daniela Garza, Helen Dickenson, Laura Sorvillo, Tammy Brandon, Connie Felkins, Cheryl Hunt, Deb Ledford, Riana Rrf, Sandi Robinson Armstrong, Robyn Konopka, Elaine Howell, Jalane Hess Terhune, Debra Knotts, Kimberly Perry, Jane Squires, Shirley Presson Brown, Liz Campbell, Trudy Miner, Susan Jordens, Sandra Key McNees, Altaira TaraWho DatWilson, Mistie Lamb, Tina Bassi Shaar, Kristal Hinds Singletary, Liane Craig, Shy Rask Black, Donna L. Kranz, Linda Kurminczuk, Theresa Campbell, Anita Unami, Valerie Earnshaw, Judy Pflneger, Christopher McMinn, Martha Baca, Nancy Huddleston, Jama Hembree Conner, Marilyn Bateman Hendry, Carle Thorn, Gale D. Sroelov, Ramona Kersch Kekstadt, Brook Ritchie-Oliver, Susan Kulik Dolan, Melissa Adkins, Misty Garoutte Clarkson, Susan Spacek Thomspon, Sandy Swanger Bartles, Natasha Nichole Jaffa, Teresa Ellett Russ, Angie Heavner, Karen Schavrien, Elizabeth Cooper, Arlene Valle, Shirleen Miller, and LauraLea Anderson. Big hugs going out to all my readers. Love you all!

Chapter One

Hunter Bing crept forward in the shadows of the narrow street, moving carefully so the frozen mud wouldn't crunch under his combat boots. Other than a lone dog barking in the night, the small village clinging to the Afghan hillside slept in wintry silence. Hunter and the three American soldiers following him kept low and moved softly, avoiding the Taliban lookouts on the rooftops.

The village resembled the adobe dwellings of the pueblo Indians, efficiently tucked against the hill that protected the backside—the windows and rooftops great lookout spots. The structures had been built with defense in mind, the result of centuries of tribal warfare. Moonlight glinted off the square mud-brick homes that butted up against each other, the flat roofs painted with cold light.

Under different circumstances, Hunter would have put off the rescue op until the moon waned or at least until his team had some decent cloud cover. But their latest intel had to be acted on immediately. If they waited even a day, J.T. might be moved or killed.

Bitter winds swept around the hill and plowed between the rows of houses, but Hunter ignored the chill. The Afghan winters no longer fazed him. And, in any case, he only had to put up with the elements for a few more days. He was going home in a week, and this time he wasn't reenlisting. He was going home and getting married.

As long as he made it out of the village alive tonight.

He ducked, avoiding a low-placed window in the wall he'd been skirting, and from the corner of his eye caught a small, flickering light ahead and above, a guard on a distant rooftop lighting a cigarette. More Taliban soldiers were holed up in the village than the dozen he'd expected—there had to be close to a hundred men.

When the hell did they get here?

Hunter's team had been up this way six months ago, training local police to care for the wounded, aka *Combat Lifesaver Training*. His platoon participated in a number of International Security Assistance Force missions, going on foot patrols through villages to meet the locals and build trust, create connections.

Connections worked. The shepherd who'd brought the intel about J.T. had originally met Hunter's unit during a foot patrol six months earlier. Making friends instead of enemies was one of the most important missions of the international forces in the country, to ensure the safety of NATO forces and turn the locals into partners instead of the opposition.

Sadly, as it often happened, after the US soldiers had moved out, the Taliban had pushed in. They were getting more numerous again in isolated pockets like this, and getting better at targeting some of the peacekeeping missions. They were definitely in the village. And that meant trouble tonight.

Hunter's four-man team had prepped for a difficult extraction, but with each yard they gained, the mission inched closer and closer to impossible. Yet none of them would so much as think about turning around. They'd spring J.T. free or die trying. They'd all understood that, without having to say it, when they'd left the forward operating base.

Hunter stole forward, saw another lookout on another roof about a hundred feet ahead, and gripped his M4 rifle tighter. *Fuck dying.* Last deployment. All he had to do was survive tonight—then he was going home to Pennsylvania, to his girlfriend Cindy and a Christmas proposal.

He passed a rickety gate cobbled together from branches. A donkey brayed in the courtyard inside, the sound impossibly loud in the night. Hunter froze midstep. He gritted his teeth.

Keep sleeping, people. No reason to come outside. He didn't want to have to start tonight by shooting at civilians. One tension-filled second passed, then two. But, thank God, even after a full minute, nobody stirred in the house.

To be on the safe side, in case the rooftop lookouts were checking the shadows more carefully, he dropped to his stomach and crawled to the corner of the street. Then he finally spotted the building he'd come to find.

The single-story dwelling had a flat roof like the others, two chimneys. A guard sat cross-legged between the two chimneys, propped up by his rifle. Moonlight illuminated his wind-chafed face as he slept.

Hunter inched toward the blue-green wooden gate with the broken handle. Just as described by the shepherd who'd brought news of the missing American soldier. So far the intel had checked out. If all went well, the rest of the shepherd's story would be true too, and they'd find J.T. inside.

Black cloth covered the building's small windows; no way to tell if anyone was awake in there.

Hunter held his position until his team caught up with him, then signaled to the three other soldiers to move forward. In a patch of dark shadows, Freddie—a gangly kid from Montana—climbed the wall that surrounded the courtyard attached to the house.

He slithered up like a giant lizard, stayed flat on top while he inspected the territory inside. Then he gave the safe signal before silently dropping down into the courtyard. Ron—a wide-shouldered Texan—went next, then Malik—a rapper who could talk for hours in rhyme. Hunter brought up the rear, making sure no enemy snuck up on them.

When his feet touched down inside the courtyard, he froze, but no Taliban lookout raised the alarm. Good to go.

Freddie stayed in the courtyard to secure their safe exit, ducking behind an ancient KAMAZ truck that'd probably been left behind by the Soviet occupation. Hunter, along with Ron and Malik, hurried forward in a crouch, silently moving from shadow to shadow. They were at the main building in under five seconds. Ron climbed to the roof to eliminate the guard. Malik and Hunter entered the house after a brief, quiet struggle with the lock.

They had no intel on the inside of the house, didn't know which room was J.T.'s prison, how many Taliban guarded him, or how well they were armed.

Malik disappeared left; Hunter silently inched to the right. No matter what waited ahead, nothing could stop him now. He'd been J.T.'s patrol buddy that night three months ago when they'd been ambushed. Hunter's rifle had jammed. He'd grabbed for his backup weapon. Too late. A shot had grazed his forehead, knocked him out, and spilled enough blood that the enemy thought he was dead.

They'd left him to rot but taken J.T. prisoner. And Hunter felt responsible.

When he'd come to, he was so weak from blood loss, he couldn't stand. He'd tried to go after J.T., follow the car tracks. He'd collapsed. In the end, he'd crawled back to base to report the incident so men more able than he could be sent. But those men hadn't found J.T.

And Hunter had sworn that if he ever found him, he'd never leave the kid behind again. J.T. was twenty-one, the youngest member of their unit. Hunter, close to thirty, felt like an older brother.

A silent shadow, he floated toward the room at the end of the hallway, faint voices drawing him forward. He halted in front of the door, caught J.T.'s muffled voice through the scarred wood. He couldn't make out the words, but the voice was J.T.'s. Definitely.

Relief eased some of the tension in Hunter's chest, sheer gratitude filling him. He wasn't too late.

One deep breath. He grinned with sudden optimism. *Party time.*

He kept his finger on the trigger as he kicked in the door and burst into the sparsely furnished space with a loud crash. A series of images registered in a split second: bed, desk, shelf, a map on the wall, some photos tacked up with bare nails. Four men, all wearing the same drab local garb: J.T. and three enemy combatants.

Hunter registered the details, firing at the same time. The Taliban men had their rifles leaning against the wall while they'd been interrogating J.T.—a momentary advantage.

Hunter used that advantage to the fullest. J.T. jumped from his chair. Since he'd been surrounded by armed men, they hadn't seen the need to tie him down, another stroke of good luck. He tripped as he pivoted toward Hunter with shock on his face. But shock or no shock, when Hunter tossed him his backup weapon, J.T. caught it. Even with what injuries he'd sustained in captivity, the kid had reflexes like a circus juggler.

Hunter kept firing the whole time, the men shooting back as they ducked for cover. Bullets buzzed across the room, kicking up dust as metal shredded mud brick. The men were good shots, several bullets coming within an inch of their target, but Hunter was better.

One enemy down, one injured.

While Hunter finished the injured guy, J.T. mentally caught up with the unexpected rescue and took care of the last one of his captors. But he didn't have time to celebrate his sudden freedom. Gunfire sounded outside.

"Go! Go! Go!" Hunter darted from the room.

The sound of gunshots came from the back of the house now. *Malik.* Hunter rushed forward to help, but Malik didn't need backup. He came running the next second.

The three American soldiers were less than a dozen feet from the front door in a narrow, dark hallway when a shadowy figure burst from a room right in front of Hunter. He caught the glint of a gun and fired on instinct. His target folded with a soft gasp. He caught the curve of a breast as she fell.

Shit.

He could barely see in the dark, just a hint of her face. *Too damn young.* And very dead—he'd hit her center mass, a fatal shot. The silver cell phone he'd mistaken for a weapon slipped from her lifeless fingers, clattering to the floor tile.

Shit.

Regret marred his insides like acid, instant guilt, then anger as he paused. Why in hell hadn't she stayed in her room, stayed down, kept out of the fray? He'd had no quarrel with her. *She didn't need to die tonight, dammit.*

Shouts came from outside. The village was waking up. The gunfire was drawing more armed men this way, the odds against the Americans stacking higher with every passing second. He needed to get his team the hell out of here.

Malik cast a glance at the still body, then darted through the front door, gun first, ready to fire. Hunter leaped forward, burst outside right behind him, checking back for J.T., who wasn't keeping up.

Is he injured? A miracle that he was still walking after three months of captivity that had probably included endless hours of torture. But they couldn't stop for an assessment of his injuries. As long as J.T. could move, they had to keep running. And he did come at last, walking stiffly, but moving forward.

Freddie was back on top of the wall, laying down cover. The rest of them kicked their way through the blue-green front gate that splintered into a hundred pieces under their boots. Ron rushed through first, provided cover as they were shot at by a dozen or so Taliban fighters who came running from a narrow alley.

Next to Hunter, Malik was on the radio, calling for extraction as Freddie dropped down next to them and the five US soldiers knocked back the enemy, then melted into the side streets, into the darkest shadows, pushing forward steadily, firing back to keep the Taliban fighters at a distance. Hunter made sure he kept J.T. with him.

He had to wait for the kid a couple of times, but they made it to the hillside goat path without trouble, then hauled ass, up and up to the prearranged rendezvous point.

They could hear the CH-47 Chinook's rotors by the time they reached the small plateau up ahead, then they could see the helicopter at last, outlined against the sky.

On the way here earlier, they'd trucked in from the forward operating base to a safe distance from the village, then they'd snuck in on foot to keep their arrival as quiet as possible. Now, with their cover broken, stealth no longer mattered. And their departure had to be speedier than their entry. Suddenly, the entire Taliban contingency that had been holed up in the village was behind them.

As the gunner began shooting from the chopper, the enemy fighters halfway up the path fell back, ducking every which way, looking for larger rocks to flatten behind.

Hunter pulled J.T. to the safety of a boulder as they waited for the Chinook to touch down. He punched his buddy in the shoulder. "Hey. We made it." He had to shout to be heard over the gunfire and the chopper. "We're going home."

Back to base, then, next week, back all the way to the good old USA. *Cindy. Family. A normal life.* "Ready to go?"

J.T. didn't say a word. He was a tough kid, but at the moment, a tear rolled down his gaunt face as he began shaking.

He was going to need help, Hunter thought, pushing J.T. toward the Chinook, then turning back to lay down more cover fire. He was going to see to it that his friend got that help. He was never going to leave J.T. behind again.

* * *

Three weeks later. Broslin, PA, USA

The welcome home party at his brother's new, fancy log home surrounded Hunter in an exuberant embrace: good friends, good

8

food, good beer. He'd barely stopped by his apartment on his way from the airport before coming here.

Christmas decorations mixed with American flags; welcome home signs covered every available surface. The scent of spruce sprigs and pastries filled the air—more normalcy in one place than he'd seen in the past decade put together.

He couldn't take two steps without someone hugging him or clapping him on the back, or shoving something into his hand to eat or drink.

"Hey, Hunter." Dakota Riley strolled up, her blue eyes sparkling with cheerful determination as she checked him out without bothering to be subtle. Her short dress's neckline dipped dangerously low, her small breasts on full display under the stretchy red fabric. "Want to go out on the deck? It's freaking crowded in here." She smiled with friendly invitation.

He kept his gaze up and away from the dress's low-cut neckline. Last time he'd seen Dakota, she'd been a sweet kid, all legs and teeth.

"How's high school treating you?" He glanced around. Maybe her mother was here, ready to rein her in. But he didn't see Michelle Riley.

He didn't see his girlfriend either. Hadn't seen Cindy in close to a year other than Skype, but tonight was the night. He tried to shake off his restlessness. He enjoyed the party, but he *was* impatient to get to the part he'd been planning for the past week. He wasn't going to wait until Christmas to propose. He was going to ask Cindy as soon as he saw her.

Dakota stuck out her chest. "I'm a freshman at West Chester University. I'm almost nineteen." The look on her face turned uncomfortably suggestive.

Oh hell. Hunter shifted away from her. And here he was almost thirty. *Not going to happen.* And not just because of the age difference. He'd already found the woman he wanted to spend the rest of his life with.

He checked his phone, but Cindy hadn't called, so he set the phone next to him on the kitchen island, then grabbed a soda. As he turned, he caught his big brother's gaze on him. Ethan—Captain Ethan Bing of the Broslin PD—flashed a grin, then moved on to grab a bag of ice.

Sophie, his wife, a petite fairy woman with red Shirley Temple curls, was carrying a tray of bacon rolls, smiling and chatting with every guest she came across. She must have been cooking and baking all week. Hunter's chest swelled with gratitude and warmth. He loved his sister-in-law. Ethan was a lucky bastard.

Hunter nodded *thanks for all this* to his brother, and Ethan nodded back. He put out more plastic forks. Smiled at his guests. But his shoulders were stiff.

Hunter narrowed his eyes. His brother's shoulders wouldn't relax, not even when he moved on through his crowd of friends.

"Come on." Dakota headed for the sliding glass doors that led to the deck, shooting an enticing smile over her shoulder.

Hunter stayed where he was. "Too cold outside."

She smiled wider. "Barely snowed an inch."

"If you spent as much time on snowy mountainsides as I have in the past couple of years, you'd want to stay next to the fire too," he said easily and looked toward the floor-to-ceiling fieldstone fireplace on the far wall.

The combined living room, eating area, and kitchen hosted half the town. Hunter's gaze found his brother again. Ethan was acting the gracious host, but he couldn't settle into any of the dozen conversations. Something was making him antsy, unusual for a guy who was known for being as steady as a professional sniper's trigger finger.

Hunter watched him for another few seconds. Maybe his own restlessness was just his brother's restlessness rubbing off on him. And he could have used some relaxing. *Big night.* He'd come home with a surprise up his sleeve and couldn't wait to spring it.

He'd served his country for the past twelve years, but the wars in the Middle East were winding down. He didn't see himself sitting at Fort-This-or-That, or in Germany, stashed away at some base, patrolling the streets for strudels instead of insurgents.

He was ready for something new—house, wife, and kids at the top of his list. He was hitting thirty in a month. He had high hopes that by that time he'd be, at the very least, engaged. Except, he couldn't enjoy that sweet fantasy at the moment, because the shadows in his brother's eyes kept needling him.

Dakota pushed her chest out, then wiggled her body in a way she must have thought seductive but made Hunter think she was struggling with a wedgie. She was more than enthusiastic—one wrong move and nipples would start popping out. Dollars against demibras her mother had no idea that the girl had left the house dressed like this.

Hunter shifted away, ready to move on.

"Do you want to hang out sometime?" Dakota rushed to ask. "I'm on Christmas break. I'll come over tomorrow."

Hunter didn't want to hurt her feelings. "I have to take care of a couple of things in town. I'll be in and out all day. But thanks for offering."

He glanced toward the front door, willing it to open. Cindy had better hurry up and get here. Then again, the house was getting crowded. Maybe she'd come already and he'd just missed her.

"Excuse me. I have to find somebody." He stepped away from Dakota at last. "Thanks for coming to the party. You look great." He winked at her, not wanting to make her feel like she'd just been brushed off, but then her face lit up, and he thought, *oh shit*. He had *not* meant to encourage her in any way.

As he turned from her, his gaze caught his brother again, who was watching him with a frown, a troubled look on his face.

Something was definitely off. Hunter's soldier instincts were suddenly bristling.

Chapter Two

Hunter automatically scanned the room for any possible source of danger, then caught himself. Insurgents weren't going to pop out from under the couch. Nobody was going to step on an IED while walking from the living room to the kitchen.

Welcome home party, Buddy. He gave his head a slight shake. The kind of professional paranoia that had kept him alive in the service had no place in civilian life. He turned off his soldier radar. He didn't need to be on guard every second of the day anymore. He was home, not on the battlefield.

He flashed Dakota, who still stuck to him like honey to baklava, a carefully neutral smile. "I should go and find my girlfriend."

Dakota wilted, eyes and mouth turning down, her expression so ridiculously dejected, he couldn't leave her on that note. "Hey, you got something going with Brandon Boldini? He's been staring at you for the last five minutes."

She turned to look at the gangly young man in the corner. Brandon tipped his beer bottle toward her in greeting. And while she looked intrigued for a moment, Hunter went AWOL.

He restlessly made the rounds, accepted the hugs and the pats on the shoulder, looked for Cindy but didn't see her anywhere.

Tonight was going to change everything. No more rushed dates, counting the days of his leave. They were going to have time for each other at last, a normal relationship like everyone else had. He couldn't wait to get started. Damn ring was burning a hole in his pocket.

He needed a moment of quiet. He walked out to the deck after all. Peaches the Rottweiler pushed out behind him, then the new dog, Pickles, same breed, then Mango, Ethan's orange cat. Hunter shook his head. Maybe he'd give his brother a hamster for Christmas, just to complete the menagerie.

The dogs ran off to race through the snow, clowning around,

while the cat used the railing for a balance beam, observing them in the moonlight with the superior air of a circus ringmaster.

Hunter set his soda can on the wooden table, brushed the snow off one of the oversize Adirondack chairs, and plopped down. The deck overlooked rolling land, barns and the corrals, and the fields, a patch of new construction, all frosted in sparkling white. His brother's property bordered the town, close enough for convenience but far enough to have some real privacy and peace.

Snow fell gently, slowly, like in a Hallmark movie, the view picture-perfect.

Hunter loved everything about the place: the familiarity, the comfortable silence, that fact that he knew exactly what to expect here. A drastic change—going from being surrounded by enemies to being surrounded by people he loved. He'd come home, and this time he was here to stay. The hard part was over.

When the door opened behind him, he didn't turn to look. He hoped Dakota would see his back and decide to grant him a few minutes of solitude. He cursed Brandon Boldini for lacking the skills to distract her.

But instead of Dakota, Ethan walked up to the railing. He braced his hands on the unpainted wood as he looked out into the night. For a moment, his shoulders relaxed. He drew a slow breath, filling his lungs with cool night air, then blew it out in a visible puff.

He looked right here, on this land, in the house he'd built. He looked like a man who was exactly where he was supposed to be. Hunter hoped someday someone would look at him and think the same.

As his brother turned, their eyes met. They had similar dark, short hair and brown eyes, similar build and height, although Hunter was leaner at the moment, courtesy of the Afghan mountains that made foot patrols physically demanding. They were both strong men who'd spent time and effort building that strength. Nobody would pick a fight with either of them in a dark alley.

The dogs' playful barking broke the silence. Ethan turned to Hunter.

Hunter saluted the land with his soda can. "I'm glad you bought the old homestead back."

Their father, Zechariah Bing, had drunk away the family legacy when they'd been kids. Ethan had spent decades of hard work scraping together enough money to rectify that mistake.

He came over, brushed off the chair next to Hunter's, and thumped down. "I got a couple of acres with your name on it."

Hunter appreciated the more than generous offer, but he shook his head. "You bought it, it's all yours, bro."

He had plenty of combat pay set aside to get something started.

"Half this land should have been your inheritance," Ethan said gruffly. "It's more than I need."

Hunter looked to the south toward the row of new buildings in the distance, in the middle of the twenty acres his brother had sold a couple of months ago. A crane slept in the moonlight among the half-completed buildings. Construction done for the day.

Ethan followed his gaze. "That all right with you?"

"Hell, yeah."

Murph Dolan, ex-Broslin PD, had bought the chunk of property with a partner. They were building a rehab center for returning military, an enterprise Hunter fully supported.

"You know when they'll open?" he asked his brother.

Ethan turned to him. "Probably in the spring."

"I might let J.T. know." He'd already told his brother about J.T., as much as he could say. Most of what he'd done in the army was classified. "I'm worried about him. He was different afterwards."

"I'd imagine." Ethan nodded somberly.

Hunter wondered how J.T.'s homecoming was going. They'd parted ways at Reagan National in DC, J.T. running to catch a commercial flight to Nashville, Hunter hurrying to make his flight to Philly. He would call the kid in the morning, Hunter decided, tell him about the rehab facility.

He sat in silence for a while, then eventually his gaze drifted to the east and settled on a gently sloping hill, the top nice and level, perfect for a house. He thought it over. "If you're selling off more land, I might be interested." Then he said, "I should probably see about a job first."

"You could try the PD," Ethan said. "We're shorthanded. You already have weapons training."

"In spades," Hunter agreed. *Job, house, family.* He couldn't wait to build a new life here in Broslin. He glanced back at the sliding glass doors behind him, at the people milling around inside. Eddie Gannon, the guy who drove the town plow was talking with Robin, the PD's part-time dispatcher. "Cindy here yet?"

Ethan shrugged, muttered something about probably working late.

"You invited her, right?"

"It's not an invitation kind of shindig. Whole town knows you were coming home today."

Hunter watched his brother for a second. He was a fair man. He'd come around. "Just give her a chance, all right? She's a sweet woman."

"I don't know her that well."

Hunter reached into his pocket, pulled out the small black velvet box. He grinned. "You're about to get to know her a lot better."

He popped the box open and turned the ring, let the light coming through the windows reflect off the diamond in the middle. For a split second, hesitation floated over him, a twinge of doubt, but he dismissed it. *Nothing more than nerves.* Every guy probably felt this way since proposals had been invented.

He flipped the box closed. "Bought it in Germany. Going to ask her tonight."

He was alive, at home, at the beginning of something. This was what he was supposed to be doing. He'd seen plenty of death in the past dozen years. He was ready for life with a capital L. He wanted to make new memories, with Cindy, lighter than the dark shadows that had followed him home.

A crumpled body flashed into his mind, that stupid cell phone on the floor, the woman he hadn't meant to kill. He blinked the image away. He was *not* going to think about that today. He wiped the frown off his face.

His brother was smiling, but his smile seemed forced too. Ethan definitely had something on his mind tonight. "Maybe you should wait until you settle in," he said. "You have plenty of time now. You don't need to rush anything."

Hunter shook his head. *My big brother, always looking out for me.* He appreciated the brotherly advice, but he was ready.

He might not feel all the romance and the desperate need like in the movies, but that kind of thing wasn't in the Bing DNA. His own parents' relationship had been rough. His brother's first marriage had been…restrained, although Ethan seemed very different now with Sophie.

Hunter figured he loved Cindy as much as he was capable of

loving, and he cared about her deeply, would give his life for her, which counted for something in his book. He was going to do right by her and spend his life making sure she was happy. They were going to be just fine together.

"I'm thinking a quick wedding, then four boys, all blond haired and blue eyed. Best-looking kids in town."

His brother raised an eyebrow. "They're going to take after the pizza delivery guy?"

Hunter shoved him, but he wasn't too serious about it. Now that Ethan was the police captain, they couldn't have a brotherly, rolling-on-the-ground kind of wrestling match, especially not with half the town watching. His brother was supposed to behave in accordance with the dignity of the office he held or whatever.

Which didn't keep Ethan from rolling his eyes. "I don't know how a person can be such a freaking Pollyanna after three tours in Afghanistan."

"Born that way. Sweet by nature. I can't help it if you got the morose-bastard gene," Hunter taunted him. "In contrast, I'm just an all-around pleasure."

Ethan shoved him back. He was smiling for real for a second or two, before the shadows crept back into his eyes, giving Hunter pause.

Hunter glanced toward the house. "Everything okay with Sophie?"

His sister-in-law had had a heart transplant a few years back. She'd fully recovered, but one infection or germ and things could rapidly turn bad. Ethan would walk through fire for her. If something was wrong—

But Ethan said, "She's doing fine. Better than fine." And there, at last, came a true, unbridled look of pure happiness.

Exactly the kind of marriage Hunter wanted. "How are things at the station?"

His brother scoffed. "No shoptalk at your welcome home party." He looked like he might say more, but then ended up clapping Hunter on the shoulder. "It's colder out here than a witch's tit in a brass bra." He stood and whistled for the animals. "Everybody's here to celebrate you. Come back in."

"You're going to tell me what's wrong?"

A conflicted look floated over Ethan's face before he shook his head. "Later. Right now it's party time."

Hunter picked up his soda and followed. "You have a lot more pets than you used to." He let them go first, before stepping inside. He looked around. "You have a lot more furniture too."

Bing flashed an indulgent look toward Sophie, who was filling up wineglasses. "Word to the wise. You get married, and stuff appears out of nowhere. One minute you have a nice little house with just what you need. Next thing you know, you're living inside a magazine photo shoot with things that have no use or purpose whatsoever. Sophie calls them *decorations*, and *focal points*, and *accents*," he said as if the words were in a foreign language. "I don't see the point." But he was still smiling.

Then one of the kids called him to fix the TV, and he stepped that way.

The buzz of the crowd enveloped Hunter in a warm welcome. Eileen, the diner's owner, came to give him a hug.

New people had arrived since he'd stepped outside. Immediately, he became the center of attention again.

He had food handed to him. He accepted handshakes and hugs, looking for Cindy all the while. She was exactly what he needed, a small-town girl who wanted all the same things he did. She was sweeter than cotton candy drizzled with honey, a petite blonde with the bluest eyes and the biggest heart, a delicate woman in need of someone exactly like him. He couldn't think of anything he wanted more than to take care of her and protect her for the rest of his life.

He glanced back to the deck door. He could propose out there, then they'd come inside and make the announcement. He grinned. Perfect. All their friends were here.

Another half an hour passed before he remembered to check the cell phone he'd left on the counter earlier. In the service, he'd gotten out of the habit of carrying it around with him everywhere. *One missed message.* From his landline at the apartment. Only his brother and Cindy had keys. She was probably there, waiting for him.

He started calling back but then headed for the door instead. He could sneak out, propose at his place with a little more privacy, then bring Cindy back and share their news with everyone. Even better than his original plan.

Sophie caught him. "Do you have everything you need?"

"And then some. Thanks. I mean it. I can't tell you how much I appreciate all this."

She hugged Hunter, a firm, warm hug, her slim arms strong and sure. She made it last. Whatever she did, Sophie put her whole heart into it.

"I'm so glad you're home." She pulled back as two little girls ran up to report a cookie emergency. She glanced back at Hunter. "Let me see about this, and we'll catch up later, okay?"

He headed toward the bathroom in case anyone was watching, but turned in the hallway and made it to the front door without anyone calling after him. He didn't want to spend half an hour making explanations. He snuck out but barely reached the bottom of the steps when the door opened behind him.

Dakota Riley stepped out onto the wide fieldstone porch, dragging on a wool coat that matched her red dress. The coat was weather appropriate, while her high-heel pumps were definitely not, but she didn't seem to care. "Going for a ride? I'll go with you."

She rushed down the stairs and caught him around the waist, her brown eyes filling with expectations. A snowflake snagged on her eyelashes, and she blinked with a dreamy expression as if that fit her movie-moment fantasy perfectly.

The snow was slowing, but it had already dusted everything with sparkling powdered sugar, the house, the driveway, and the young hemlocks that lined it on either side. Their surroundings did look like a movie set.

Hunter extricated himself, refusing whatever lines Dakota had assigned him in her script. But even as he gently pushed her hands off him, Dakota caught his fingers and held on.

He had to take a step back to break their connection. "I'm going to pick up Cindy. You should go inside. Those shoes weren't meant for snow." He moved toward his truck.

"Hunter! Wait!" Tears flooded Dakota's eyes. Then true teenage fury colored her face the next second. "She doesn't even love you. Do you think she waited for you all this time?"

He wasn't going to stand here and fight with a misguided kid. "Go back inside."

He strode to his car, hopped in, and drove away before she could say anything else she would regret later. He wasn't going to let Dakota's temper tantrum ruin tonight. He dismissed her from his mind and focused on Cindy.

One kind of life was ending for him, and another was beginning, full of possibilities. He couldn't have been more excited about the change. Any amount of hesitation or doubt on his part was only because this *was* a big shift.

The town, wrapped in red and green, greeted him, welcomed him home as he drove down familiar streets. Driving his old truck filled Hunter with pleasure. He didn't have to look for IEDs on the side of the road. He grinned all the way to the apartment, enjoying the ride, the peace of the night, the old brick buildings on Main Street, the holiday finery, the palpable presence of town spirit.

He parked his truck in front of the apartment building that Ethan owned as a side business, and suddenly couldn't wait another second. He hurried up the front stairs, down the inside staircase, then just about ran down the hallway to his basement-level unit.

He had his key in his hand, but the doorknob turned easily as he put his hand on it. Cindy had left the door open for him.

He grinned like a fool as he walked in. The loose floorboard in the middle of the living room creaked a familiar welcome as he passed his army duffel bag on the floor where he'd dumped it earlier. Cindy's little pink purse sat on his brown leather couch like a cupcake on a tray.

"Cindy?" He strode toward the bedroom in the back, his smile spreading as he anticipated a private party. If she was waiting for him naked in bed, the proposal would have to wait a little. "Honey?"

But she wasn't waiting for him naked.

She was waiting for him dead.

Chapter Three

Officer Gabriella Maria Flores gripped her cell phone as she drove her police cruiser down Broslin's Main Street. "No."

But the reporter on the other end wouldn't take no for an answer. "Now that the case has been tried in court and everything is out there for everyone, I'm sure you'd like to give an updated statement," he pushed on, his tone all cheerful, all *I'm helping you, here, this is all for your benefit.*

They were like worms, always wiggling forward, pushing, searching for scandal to feed their hungry masses. If she didn't fight them back, they'd chew right through her. She'd lost enough. She wasn't going to give more, dammit.

How in hell had the worms found her new number again? She'd changed her cell number twice since she'd left Philadelphia's Twelfth District.

"Don't you want to tell your side of the story?" the oily voice wiggled through the line. "If you could give me a quote." The reporter wouldn't give up. "Just a few sentences."

"No comment." She wasn't going to give a story to a paper that'd printed baseless accusations of her on the front page. *Daughter from Family of Criminals Becomes Cop, then Returns to Crime.* Weeks later, the news that she'd been cleared of all charges had barely been a footnote in the back of the paper. She doubted anyone had read that.

She turned off her phone and dropped it on the passenger seat.

The past was not going to drag her back down just because Tony's trial was finally over. He'd ruined her professional reputation and broken her heart. But she'd learned from the past. She was going to build her reputation back, right here in Broslin. Forget about love. Love was a sucker's game. Her mother had been right about that.

She'd made good progress on the job front. Her record here was flawless. If she didn't mess up in the next month or so, once Tony's trial buzz died down, she should be able to transfer right back to the Twelfth District.

She drove slowly, looking down every dark alley. No drug dealers in the shadows, no homeless huddled around the heat escaping the sewer covers, not a single prostitute on any of the corners.

She swallowed her homesickness for the city and drove past Broslin Square, fantasizing about a motorcycle gang coming in for a drug showdown. The sudden discovery of a meth lab in the closed travel agency on Baltimore Pike would give her something to do. Or even just a good bar fight. In addition to helping her improve her record, a bar fight would also allow her to work out some of her frustrations.

Not that she wished for anyone to get hurt. But if something bad happened, she wanted to be there to take care of it.

Of course, on the average night, Broslin was as peaceful as a yoga retreat.

Gabi glared at the softly falling snow that looked fake, a pristine white, sparkling blanket that glazed everything to Christmas-postcard-syrupy perfection. In Philly, snow turned into gray slush the instant it hit the streets. She liked it that way. It felt more real.

Here, spruce swags and red bows decorated everything that didn't move, courtesy of the township. Every door, be it a business or private home, had a ridiculously overdecorated wreath. Trees dripped with sparkling mushroom ornaments—Broslin was the mushroom capital of the country.

She slowed at the stop sign at the corner and could practically feel the town's syrupy sweetness giving her cavities. *These people need therapy.*

The amount of energy used nightly for the blanket of Christmas lights that covered the town could have powered Philly.

And even that wasn't enough. The gazebo on Broslin Square was decked out in an explosion of holiday finery, spruce swags *and* wreaths, and giant candy canes, twinkling lights, enormous foam snowflakes, large cutout mushrooms each with a Santa hat, an entire full-size sled on top of the gazebo with full-size plastic reindeer—and so depressingly much more—as if when Santa's elves had run through town, they'd been on speed.

Red bows made her stomach clench. Tony had proposed last Christmas, red velvet box, big red velvet bow on top…and a ring stolen from the evidence room, as it'd turned out later.

Gabi glanced down one of the side streets. Three boys huddled together in front of the closed car wash, thick as thieves. One had a backpack that the other two were showing a lot of interest in.

Some small-scale weed operation, most likely.

She stifled a sigh. Philly PD was probably on their second or third shooting of the day by now.

She turned on the next street, parked behind the car wash, Charlie's Suds, and came up next to the building, stopped before stepping into view, and peeked through the bushes in the narrow strip of landscaping that hugged the wall.

The three boys, around twelve or thirteen, still loitered on the sidewalk, the two taller ones who looked alike enough to be brothers shoving the third, who had a slighter build.

"Are you lost, retard?" bully number one asked. "Why don't you go back to Massa-two-shits?" He chuffed at his own joke, thinking he was so damned smart.

New kid at school, Gabi thought. Christmas break equaled all the kids out and looking for trouble. She stayed back. During her seven years as an inner-city cop, she'd seen more than her fair share of drugs being dealt out of schoolbags. If that was the case here, she wanted to see the goods first.

Bully number two reached for the new kid's backpack and rattled it. "What do you got in there? You got any money, dumbass?" He grabbed the backpack, and the contents spilled.

"Freaking books!" His incensed tone screeched into the night. "Are you kidding?" He lifted his right arm, ready to strike.

Gabi stepped into view and cleared her throat. "Are you boys having any trouble here?"

"Going home." The two bullies immediately retreated.

"How about you just hang around for a minute." She checked the spilled book bag. "What do we have here?"

No little plastic baggies. In her old neighborhood in Southwest Philly, she could have gone through twenty book bags without finding one that had nothing but books in it. She couldn't remember the last time she had to search a backpack and didn't find weed, pills, knives, guns, pipes, or other paraphernalia, or, at the very least, smokes and alcohol.

"Turn out your pockets."

The boys did. All pockets empty.

"Lift up your coats. Turn."

They obeyed. No weapons stuck into waistbands.

Maybe they weren't bad kids. Yet. "I'm Officer Flores. What are your names?"

The brothers were Zak and Zane, the short kid was Gregory.

She thought of her brothers, who chose the wrong path and were now dead. "What are you doing out on the street after dark?"

Zak and Zane looked at each other; the one closest to her shrugged. "Wanted to get pizza. We ain't got enough money."

She turned to Gregory.

"Nobody's home. I wanted to hang out at the library."

She thought for a second. "Come on." She led them across the road to the pizza place.

They went in. She checked the board with the prices, took money from her pocket, divided it into two batches.

"This is how it's going to go. I'm giving you three enough money for a large pizza and drinks. Half to you,"—she handed half to Gregory—"half to you"—she handed the rest to Zak and Zane. "Half isn't enough for anything. But if you can talk to each other nicely and agree to put your money together, you can buy dinner."

The two brothers looked at her as if they didn't believe their luck. Gregory still looked wary.

"You're going to eat that pizza together, all three of you," she told the brothers, "then you're going to walk your new friend home so nothing else bad happens to him."

She pulled a card from her pocket that had her cell number on it. "When you get home safely, you call to let me know." She handed the card to Gregory, who was beginning to look more optimistic. "If I don't get a call, I'll come looking for you."

Her radio went off. "One-eighty-seven."

Homicide.

Gabi snapped to attention. Her adrenaline spiked a notch higher when Leila the dispatcher slash admin assistant added, "Gabi, it's your apartment building. The captain's already there. He's requesting immediate assistance."

"On my way." Gabi looked at the kids. "You behave."

Then she was out of there, barely hearing one of the taller kids call a "Mooch-ass grassy-ass" after her.

Siren on. Pedal to the metal.

Homicide. At her building.

She didn't know most of her neighbors, didn't socialize if she could help it. She wasn't in Broslin to make friends. She was here in exile. The urgency of the need to know who the victim was surprised her.

She thought of her next-door neighbor, Doris Hastings, an elderly widow who'd come to the US from England after the Korean War, following her American GI husband. She had an apartment full of teacups and doilies.

For the past six months, Gabi had told herself the woman was a bother with her invitations for tea and need to chat and the shortbread cookies she'd bring over no matter how many times Gabi had told her that she was staying in shape for work.

But now, she was thinking, *don't let it be Doris.* And not the single mom with the two kids either, even if the girls drove Gabi nuts riding their scooters in the hallways when she was trying to sleep after a double shift.

She pulled to a screeching halt in front of her apartment building, owned by none other than Captain Bing. This would be important to him. If she shined here, she could pretty much count on a good recommendation when she left.

Officer Mike McMorris secured the front entrance, less than a year younger than Gabi, red hair, freckles, good-natured, cop to the bone. Spit-and-polish was his middle name. He wore his uniform like the pope wore his robes, as if the blue cloth was sacred to him. Other than Gabi, he was the only other outsider at the Broslin PD, originally from Boston. He was the PD's jokester, but tonight, he looked grim.

Gabi ran up the stairs. "Who's the victim?"

"Cindy Simme." Mike let her in.

Gabi tried to place the name as she hesitated inside the door, couldn't attach Cindy Simme to a face. "You knew her?"

Mike's head jerked in a nod, and he winced as if the movement hurt, pressed his hand against his side. "Downstairs. Last apartment to the right."

She noted that he hadn't moved the hand and paused by him. "Are you okay?"

"Ate something bad for lunch." He dropped the hand at last.

"Captain's waiting for you."

Things were looking up. This could be just the case to add extra shine to her record. If she handled it right. "Leila said homicide."

"Single shot to the head."

Burglary, domestic violence, drug deal gone wrong, suicide—the options streamed through Gabi's head, but she shut down the ticker tape. She didn't want to walk in there with a preconceived notion. She wanted to see everything fresh. "Her apartment?"

Mike grimaced. "Her boyfriend's."

That painted a story right there. About eighty percent of murder victims were killed by either a friend or a family member, most of the time their significant other. "Know him?"

"Everybody knows him," Mike said darkly. "It's Hunter, the captain's brother."

Chapter Four

Gabi hurried down the drab hallway.

The captain's brother. Who's going to get stuck with that?

The captain couldn't take the case, not when the murder involved family. Detective Joe Kessler, Broslin's favorite son, was standing guard outside the apartment, so he wasn't the lucky winner. Detective Harper Finnegan was on leave to run the family bar, Finnegan's, while his father recovered from a heart attack. That left Detective Chase Merritt as the lead investigator. He was probably inside the apartment with the captain.

Gabi frowned. The captain shouldn't be at the crime scene at all. She didn't envy Chase. Investigating your boss's brother was one of those situations a cop couldn't win. Do the job well, push hard, turn over every stone, and you'd be stepping on toes, turning the boss against you. Or please the boss by looking the other way, and have everyone know you did. Sucked either way.

"Cindy Simme, twenty-seven, local, single, no criminal record," Joe said as she reached him, his face as grim as Mike's. Tall and wide-shouldered, beyond good-looking, the whole small-town football-hero thing just radiated off him.

He handed her a pair of shoe protectors. "Captain wants to see you."

Gabi yanked the plastic bags over her boots. The door was open a crack, so she didn't have to touch the knob and smudge any possible prints.

She pulled a pair of latex gloves from her pocket and tugged them on as she stepped inside, her gaze snapping to Doris. Her neighbor sat white-faced in a recliner in the living room, wearing her pink, flowery robe and matching house slippers. What was *she* doing here? The old woman looked shaken but unhurt, no visible injuries. Gabi relaxed a little.

The captain, on his phone, stood in the hallway that led to the bedroom, talking in a low voice, probably to his wife, judging by the "He's fine," "I'll be home as soon as I can," and "I don't want you to worry," type of comments he was making.

In the kitchen, a younger version of Captain Bing paced like a prize fighter in the ring. Fluid movement, restrained power, live wire. He had to be close to six feet, all sinew and muscle. Not gym-rat muscle either, but muscle obtained by lifting, running, fighting, plenty of it and in all the right places, muscle that had purpose.

The man's mocha-color eyes snapped to Gabi. He measured her up as if she was the enemy and they were about to enter hand-to-hand combat. "So you're the city girl."

On the defensive. He could have called her a city *cop*, at least. Nothing in his stance or eyes showed it, but he was worried about her, needed to put her in her place right off the bat. A subconscious response to a perceived threat.

Because he was guilty?

Gabi measured him up in return, let him see she wasn't rattled. "You must be the soldier boy."

She might be only a grunt on the case, here to take notes for the primary investigator, but Hunter needed to know that he wasn't going to intimidate her.

Hunter Bing, returning war hero.

Investigating him in this town wasn't going to be easy.

She'd heard his name a thousand times during the past few weeks. He'd been awaited more than the second coming of Christ, had certainly been mentioned more often. Some women's do-gooder club had even dropped off frozen casseroles for him at the station. Leila had dutifully saved the containers in the freezer drawer of the fridge in the break room.

"Ever worked a murder case?" Hunter demanded. He had a deep voice, sure, crisp.

"I assisted with a number of homicides." Not that she had to give him her credentials.

His lips flattened. Beyond the warrior body, he had a square jaw— the kind the average punch would glance clear off—sharp eyes, and chiseled lips. Okay, so the captain's brother wasn't entirely unattractive. He might even be as good-looking as Joe, but harder all around, with an edge of danger.

Her gaze hesitated on a scar at his temple. Something had ripped off a chunk of skin there in the not too distant past. The spot was raised and red still, the injury maybe four or five months old.

"What's the scar about?" she asked, out of curiosity and to see if she could throw him a little.

He didn't so much as flinch. "Parting gift from the army."

He was GI Joe from top to bottom: scar, a tan T-shirt that molded to his well-developed pecs, army fatigues, and chunky combat boots. Gabi was a physical person. She appreciated physical excellence, and he was the poster boy for what a male body could look like when properly trained.

His live-wire eyes only enhanced the image.

She imagined women went for him, big-time. Not her. She'd already had a relationship with a cop, and look how that had ended. Gabi refused to so much as acknowledge attraction for a potential suspect. Anyway, what she was feeling wasn't even attraction. It was appreciation. Two different things.

She followed him with her eyes as he kept moving. Her gaze skidded along his corded arms. She couldn't achieve biceps like that if she moved into the gym. The female body didn't work that way.

He was already brimming with tension, and all that pacing was just pumping him up even more. He needed to be still for a minute.

"Why don't you sit?" She liked her suspects in cuffs. Her second choice was sitting. A sitting person needed an extra second to get going, launch into an attack. That extra second could make a big difference for a police officer. "It might help."

He paused, his gaze hardening another notch. His stance said he thoroughly resented her presence in his kitchen. "When I need your help, I'll ask for it."

That'd be never. He didn't look like the kind of guy who asked for help.

Thank God, Hunter Bing was going to be Chase's cross to bear. The detective was probably in the bedroom with the victim. Gabi couldn't see in there. The captain was blocking the hallway.

Hunter shoved his hands into his pockets and went back to pacing, his anger visible in every move.

A lot of murders were committed by angry men. And if there was murder to be done, he was the man for it. A soldier. He'd definitely know how to shoot a weapon.

Beyond the anger, Gabi caught a glimpse of grief in his hard eyes, just as carefully controlled. Of course, in domestic violence cases, the perpetrator often deeply regretted his actions. Not that she would jump to conclusions.

He stared at her with open insolence as if daring her to accuse him of something.

She stared back long enough to let him know he wasn't scaring her. Maybe if she found herself unarmed with him in a dark parking garage in Philly, she would walk the other way. Depending on the circumstances. But right now, right here, she was the one with the service weapon at her hip.

Effectively dismissing him, she moved over to her neighbor and crouched next to the recliner. "Are you all right?"

Doris closed her eyes for a second. Age spots dotted her crinkled eyelids. "I could use a cup of tea. Maybe with a little something. I won't pretend I didn't have a fright."

Doris was known for fortifying her tea with a shot of brandy when the occasion called for it. And sometimes when it didn't. Gabi figured that at Doris's age, the woman had earned the right.

"I'll try," she promised, but the captain was hanging up, and she needed to check with him first. She patted Doris's hand, then stood. "Captain."

"I'm glad you're here." Her boss stepped forward, his jaw muscles tight, his face hard with tension, an ominous look in his eyes.

"I'm putting you in charge of the investigation," he said heavily.

She saw the trap spring beneath her, felt herself falling. *Wait. What about Chase?* She wanted to have as little involvement in this case as possible. "I don't have the seniority, sir."

Not for a murder case. The last place she wanted to be was in the middle of this. She needed to keep her nose clean. She needed a good evaluation to be able to get her old job back. If she pissed off the captain, she could kiss his recommendation good-bye. She was *not* going to get stuck in Broslin with a boss who had it in for her.

But his expression brooked no argument. "You're the only one I have without a conflict of interest."

She couldn't refuse. The trap had closed around her.

He stepped forward, indicating Hunter with a choppy, frustrated gesture. "Hunter is my brother. I can't take the case. The rest of the

PD are some of his best friends. We need an outsider to keep this investigation on the up and up. I don't want some jackass DA questioning any kind of abuse of power."

"No, sir." She could feel the tension radiating off Hunter behind her. If he was guilty, Hunter would be a formidable opponent.

Her heart hammered as she tried to rearrange her swirling thoughts into some logical sequence.

Okay, observation number one: the captain was aware that his brother was the prime suspect until they had evidence to prove otherwise.

Question number one: did he think Gabi would go easy on Hunter to score some brownie points?

She gritted her teeth behind her best cop face. This case could sink her career all over again. The captain had said he wanted everything on the up-and-up, but, behind the scenes, would he do his best to tie her hands?

Maybe he wanted her to be primary because she was the newest on the team with the least seniority, far from her support system, the only woman. Maybe he figured she'd be the easiest to intimidate.

She'd never been primary on a murder before.

That alone was enough to give her palpitations. She didn't want to mess up something this big. One black mark on her record—aka Tony—could be forgiven. Two major mistakes would form a pattern of bad decision making. Not only would she not be able to win back her job in Philly, but no other department would seriously consider her either.

"I know he didn't do it." Captain Bing glanced at his brother, then back to Gabi. "But we have to run this the same way we'd do with anyone else."

Anyone else would be in cuffs already in the back of the patrol car, Gabi thought.

She filled her lungs with air, then squared her shoulders. "I need you to leave the crime scene, sir."

The captain frowned. "You don't have to do this alone. I just need you to be the lead investigator."

Yeah. The figurehead who goes down if there's a scandal.

She held the captain's gaze, could see her career sinking into the quicksand of office politics. "I'd appreciate it if you could wait outside."

The captain raised an eyebrow.

She stood her ground.

And a few seconds later, his stance relaxed, and he gave an approving nod. "Good. That's exactly how you should be handling this. I'll go and notify the victim's family. I already called the coroner."

He moved to the door, casting a last look at his brother before he stepped outside.

Only three people remained: the investigating officer, the possible perpetrator, and the possible witness.

Gabi addressed Doris first. "Were you here at the time of the shooting?"

Doris drew her robe tighter over her chest. "I came in after. I walked down because I thought I heard a shot."

"Did you see anyone?"

"Just Hunter."

Gabi looked at the man.

"I got here three minutes before she did." His voice was gruff, his eyes hard, his stance battle ready. "Cindy was already dead. Nobody else in the apartment. Didn't see anyone leaving."

Gabi turned back to her neighbor. "I'll have someone walk you up to your place. I'll come by later to talk."

Doris nodded and pushed shakily to her feet. She kept her gaze away from the bedroom.

Gabi opened the door for her neighbor without touching the knob. Chase had arrived at last. He was talking with Joe in the hallway.

Gabi asked him to walk Doris home, and Chase immediately took the old woman's arm.

Gabi turned to Joe next. "Would you mind bringing in my crime scene kit?" She handed him the keys to her cruiser, then, as he hurried off, she turned her attention to the front door, more specifically, to the lock mechanism.

No scratches on the wood, no damage to the metal components, no sign of forced entry. She stepped back inside and went to the windows that looked to the parking lot. Locked. No sign of tampering.

She turned and scanned the apartment as if seeing it for the first time. Hunter was smart enough to stay out of her way. He did stop pacing at last. He was leaning against the counter in the corner.

31

His place was the same as Gabi's one floor up, or almost the same, mirror image—a short hallway in the back with two doors, one to a bathroom, the other to the bedroom. She could see the corner of the bed from where she stood, simple pine, nothing fancy.

The living room had nicer furniture: leather sofa, ottoman, recliner, a big-screen TV. She noted the pink purse on the sofa and the army duffel bag on the floor. Both would have to be taken into evidence.

While she waited for the crime scene kit, she observed the possible suspect once again, now that she knew that he was *her* possible suspect. He was watching her, six feet and two hundred pounds of sheer intensity. He looked like a guy who could seriously hurt someone. Since he was a soldier, Gabi wasn't going to hold that against him.

"I'm Officer Gabriella Maria Flores," she introduced herself belatedly. "I'm in charge of the investigation."

He'd heard all that, but she wanted to say it again, in a tone that would tell him she meant it. *She* was in charge now, for better or worse. Having a brother who was the police captain wasn't going to help him. The sooner Hunter Bing understood that, the better.

Before Hunter could respond, Joe popped in with the crime scene kit.

"Thanks." Gabi took the plastic box. "Has anyone talked to the neighbors?"

"Storage on one side, empty apartment on the other," Joe said. "Want me to start the door-to-door?"

"I need you to stay here to keep out nosy neighbors and reporters."

She was issuing orders to a detective. Way weird. But Joe acknowledged her with a simple, professional nod.

Chase was coming back down the hall. "She's shaken but all right. What do you want me to do next?"

"You can start the door-to-door. We need to see if we can find anyone besides Doris Hastings who saw or heard something. I'll interview her personally in a minute."

Chase nodded and went off.

Gabi had to give it to the Broslin PD, they were easy-going guys and worked well together. No prima donnas, and no dirty officers either, from what she'd seen in her six months here.

32

She pulled a crime scene log from her kit and handed it to Joe. "Please make sure you have everyone from the PD who's been here tonight fill this out. Has anyone been inside the bedroom?"

"Not that I know of." Joe cast her a dubious look as if he thought the crime scene log was overkill. "The captain arrived first. He was in the living room when I got here. He told everyone to stay out."

She glanced back at Hunter, who was watching her intently, as if she was taking some kind of a test and he was trying to decide whether to pass her.

He'd probably called his brother directly instead of calling 911. Did that mean anything? Not necessarily.

If Hunter was guilty, who better to help cover up the crime than a police captain? On the other hand, if he was innocent, Hunter would still want his brother's help. Gabi was only sure of one thing: at one point, she was going to have to interview her boss. *Peachy great.*

She swallowed a groan and pulled back into the apartment so she could start processing her crime scene.

Her crime scene.

A little excitement glittered through her dread. She drew a measured breath. *Step one.* She placed the kit on the floor, and quickly dusted the front door for prints. She found fewer than she'd expected for a rental place, as if the door had been recently wiped clean.

When she finished, she turned to Hunter. "I need you to come over here."

He strode over with long, measured strides. He didn't remove his gaze from her for a second, didn't look toward the bedroom. The army had probably taught him to keep his eyes on the enemy. He was an opponent not to be underestimated.

She mirrored his earlier fight-ready position, standing with her legs slightly apart, even if she thought it unlikely that he'd tackle her. Even if he was guilty, this early in the game, he'd still think his brother was going to save him. "I'm going to do a pat down. Arms raised to the side, please."

His muscles flexed under the soft cotton of his shirt. The material stretched even tighter across his wide chest as he fully extended his massive arms. "I'm not carrying."

And any cop who made a habit of taking a suspect's word for that kind of thing was a dead cop sooner or later.

Carmen, the Philly officer who'd encouraged Gabi to be a cop and helped her realize that dream, had something she called Carmen's Cop Rules. Number one on the list was, *trust no one*.

Gabi leaned closer to Hunter, aware of where his hands were, how close she was to his knees. If he made a move, she was ready. But he stayed still.

He smelled like plain old soap, a clean, masculine scent.

She patted him down front and back, keeping it one hundred percent professional, refusing to be impressed by his physique. She focused wholly on whether or not he had any kind of weapon on him. Becoming distracted during a pat down was a good way to get killed.

Not a big fan of searching pockets, she left that for last, found nothing but loose change in his left pocket, a small black velvet box in the right. She opened the box, then cast an inquisitive glance at him.

He stared back at her without a word.

"I'm going to have to bag this as evidence," she said, and then went ahead and did.

His eyes were throwing cold sparks by the time she finished.

"Do you have any firearms on the premises?"

The muscles tightened around his mocha eyes that had entire storm systems brewing inside them. "In the bedroom, on the floor next to the bed. An older-model Beretta."

"Registered to you?"

"Yes."

She noted that information and, again, did her best to withhold judgment. The victim was his girlfriend, had been shot in his apartment, with his weapon. Still, she needed to keep an open mind. She had to go into this investigation with as few preconceived notions as possible.

"I didn't touch the gun," he said. "I found it there when I came in. It should be in the wall safe. I don't know who took it out or how."

"We'll see." She scanned his hands. "Are you sure you didn't touch the weapon?"

"I almost grabbed it when Doris came in. She startled me." He blinked, looking bewildered for a moment.

Doris was decidedly inquisitive. Gabi wasn't surprised that the old woman would investigate. "Okay. I need to test for gunshot residue.

Hands out front, please."

Some PDs tested for GSR at the station. She liked keeping a few tabs in her crime scene kit. The sooner the suspect was tested, the less chance for contamination.

GSR was mostly burnt and unburnt particles from the explosive primer, the propellant. It contained lead, antimony, barium, and some other elements, all easily identified in a lab.

She pulled a couple of contaminant-free adhesive tabs and applied them to each of Hunter's hands, peeled them off after a moment, and bagged them separately. They'd be sent to the lab in West Chester for the SEM Test—Scanning Electron Microscopy. The lab would check the elemental profile for GSR, tell her whether or not Hunter had been anywhere near the murder weapon when it'd been fired.

Hunter shifted on his feet. "I washed my hands," he said as if he just now remembered.

Gabi watched him closely as she considered his revelation. Her instincts prickled. "Why would you do that?"

"I had blood on my fingers. I checked for Cindy's pulse." He looked away from her for the first time. "She didn't have any."

Okay, so the GSR would likely come back either negative or inconclusive. "Why not call 911 right away?"

"Instinct, I guess." He looked back at her. "I'm trained in battlefield first aid. I saw that she'd been hit and jumped to help. Habit."

Sounded reasonable. But his hand washing was also awfully convenient. "So you came in after the murder."

"Yes."

"Did you hear the shot on your way into the building? Did you see anyone leaving?"

"No." Every muscle in his face and neck tight, he rubbed a hand over his right eye. "Must have happened just minutes before I pulled up outside. When I came in, she was still bleeding." He choked up on the last words.

Gabi considered the scenario as he told it. Gunshot. A minute or two later, Hunter pulls up, unaware. He's young and quick—out of the car, up the front steps, down the stairs to the lower level, down the hallway, into the apartment.

Doris heard the shot, but she's slow. Maybe she takes a minute to think about whether to investigate. She puts on her slippers, her robe,

35

pads down the hallway, very carefully down the stairs, down the basement-level hallway all the way to the back.

Hunter *could* be telling the truth. He could have arrived at the building after the murder, but still beat Doris to the apartment.

But he could just as easily be lying. Maybe he'd come in, had an argument with the victim, shot her, was in the process of figuring out how to get rid of the body when Doris walked in.

The timing worked both ways.

Carmen's Cop Rules #2: *Miss nothing.*

Gabi glanced at the front door. "How did Doris get into your apartment?"

Hunter blinked. "The door was open when I got here. Cindy had a key." He paused, then went on, the grief in his voice more pronounced now. "I didn't think much of it. Didn't lock the door behind me as I came in. Got excited when I saw her purse on the couch. I just rushed forward."

He rubbed his eye again, as if trying to rub away the images he'd seen.

Gabi squashed the twinge of sympathy that had no place in a murder investigation. She stepped over to the door and stuck her head out. Joe was still there. "Could you please come in and stay with Mr. Bing for a moment?" she asked him.

She went back to her crime scene kit, bagged and tagged the victim's purse, tagged Hunter's duffle bag, then carried the kit to the bedroom. Before she stepped inside, she glanced back toward the kitchen.

Hunter was watching her, his eyes dark wells. The hard set of his jaw said he wasn't a fan of her working method. Resentment came off him in waves.

She could live with that. She wasn't here to make friends. Her job was to make sure the guilty didn't go free—regardless of how well they were connected.

Her cell phone rang. Gregory was reporting in. The kid was full of pizza and home safe. She told him to keep her number and call if he needed help again. Then she put away her phone, filled her lungs with air, and opened her crime scene kit.

The bedroom was the same as hers one floor up, white walls, tan carpet. Hunter had country furniture that'd probably come as a set from one of the Amish stores up on Route 30: a simple five-drawer pine dresser against one wall, two matching pine nightstands with matching lamps against another. A plain pine bed sat between the nightstands, king-size.

The body sprawled on the blood-soaked mattress, a gruesome tribute to violence. Most of the blood still glistened red, but some patches were already turning black. Nobody had accidentally stepped into the pool on the floor, no helpful footprints.

Figuring out who'd spilled that blood fell to Gabi now. And she had to figure it out fast. She didn't want to find herself in the middle of yet another media spectacle.

Chapter Five

Cindy Simme's cowboy-boot-clad feet hung over the edge of the bed. She'd been standing facing toward the hallway when she'd been shot, and had fallen back. She still had her coat on. No hat.

One small hole in the middle of the forehead. A good chunk was going to be missing in the back. Gabi could see skull fragments and some gray matter on the sheet.

A familiar anger punched through her, the feeling that no matter how hard she worked, how hard all the police worked, they couldn't stop all the senseless deaths. Death was always faster.

Way too young to die. Not that she hadn't seen younger, teens and toddlers even. She used to live and work in a minority neighborhood, in a place where death was faster than anyplace else.

A black man who lived in the inner city in a high-crime area had a life expectancy twenty-one years shorter than an Asian woman out in the suburbs. Hispanic men didn't fare much better. In some inner cities, the life expectancy was closer to that of Africa than the rest of the US.

She had reason for knowing those statistics. They included her brothers.

She wanted to go back to the Twelfth to make a difference. She wanted to save kids from ending up in body bags.

Where she'd come from, violent death was accepted as a normal part of life. Funeral homes had special plans catering to gangs that included gang colors and extra security. And still people shot up viewings—part of normal, everyday business. Nobody got outraged.

But here in Broslin, a young woman's murder was going to be big news, a shock to the town. Here, a resolution was going to be demanded come hell or high water. Cindy Simme would be a high-profile case even if it didn't involve the police captain's brother.

None of that was good news for Gabi.

She reached for her recorder, dictated the parameters first: name, date, time, location, listed all people who'd had access to the crime scene to the best of her knowledge. Then she moved on to the specifics of the crime, her first observations.

"Victim is Cindy Simme, female, in her late twenties." Joe had said twenty-seven, but until Gabi confirmed, she wouldn't record that. "Likely cause of death, gunshot wound to the head. No sign of struggle."

She walked to the window, checked it without touching anything. "No sign of forced entry at the front door or the windows."

She catalogued as many details about the victim, the crime scene, and the crime itself as she could, then turned off her recorder and scanned the room in general, hoping for some clues about Hunter.

The sparse furniture was good quality, the bedroom masculine but pretty neat. Closet closed. Dresser closed. She opened both with a minimum of contact, found nothing but clothes stacked in military order. No sign of anything having been disturbed.

No sign of burglary in the room in general. But behind the slightly askew dresser, the safe that Hunter had claimed was supposed to keep his gun locked away stood empty.

The Beretta 92, a decent semiautomatic pistol, lay on the floor.

She walked back to the kitchen. Joe was guarding the door from the inside. Hunter was once again leaning against the counter, still wound up, his eyes still full of anger.

"Did you move the gun?" she asked.

"I told you I didn't touch it." Impatience laced his voice.

"When was the last time you saw the weapon?"

"The last time I was home on leave eight months ago."

"Who else has the safe combination?"

"My brother and Cindy." He rocked on the heels of his army boots. "She had a key to the apartment. I told her she could hang out here if she ever needed to, since she lives with her parents. I told her the combination to the safe because I keep some cash in there too. If anything happened to me in combat, I wanted her to have it."

"How much?"

"Over six grand."

Gabi hadn't seen the money on Cindy, but it would fall to the coroner to fully inspect the body. The killer could have taken the cash. Or Hunter could be making it up to throw her off the scent.

"Do other apartments have safes?" Hers didn't.

"My brother let me put one in. Since I'm gone for long stretches of time and I own a weapon."

She watched him for another second, then went back to the bedroom, grabbed her camera, and began snapping pictures. She recorded the scene without number tags first, then with. She was careful not to go too close to the body or interfere with it in any way.

She found the bullet, embedded in the wall behind the bed. She left it there for the time being.

Every once in a while, she glanced back at Hunter. He was pacing again. Carmen had a theory that if you left a suspect waiting, the innocent tended to pace and stay agitated. The guilty ones sat all calmly, sometimes even pretending to nod off. They were trying hard to show that they had nothing to worry about.

Hunter hadn't yet sat for a second.

Gabi finished with the photos and rolled some video of the bedroom. She was wrapping that up when Joe called out. "The coroner's here."

Dr. Evelyn Koppel was in her midforties, short and round, square glasses, black hair, coffee-color skin that was mostly covered up by protective gear. She must have suited up out in the hallway. She sailed right in. "Officer Flores."

"Dr. Koppel."

They knew each other from when the captain had sent Gabi to the coroner's office a month ago to follow up on a suicide case.

"So this is my victim," the woman said, taking in the room. At a crime scene, the coroner was the highest authority.

Although, from what Gabi understood, since this coroner's office covered an exceptionally large territory, sometimes Captain Bing's team processed the entire crime scene and the coroner stayed at her lab, waited there until the body was brought to her.

Not today. This was going to be a no-holds-barred investigation.

Two assistants came in next, in their twenties, neck tattoos, goatees. One of them had those weird round metal piercings in his ears that made big holes.

Gabi introduced herself to them before turning to Dr. Koppel. "I already recorded the crime scene. Let me know when I can remove the murder weapon."

"I need to snap a few pictures first for my own records," the woman said without taking her eyes off the body.

They each had their own role to play. The coroner's job was to establish the cause of death. The investigator's job was to figure out who killed the victim.

Gabi left Dr. Koppel and her team to their task and walked back to Hunter. She stopped less than two feet from him, legs apart in a power stance, eyes unblinking. "I'm going to take you in for questioning."

She'd known she would from the first minute. This was not the case to leave her t's uncrossed and her i's undotted.

Resentment flared in his eyes, his shoulders tensing another notch. "Every minute you waste thinking I did this is a minute the real killer is using to get away."

"Then it'll be best if you cooperate fully. That'll speed things up, I promise."

"I imagine it would be easiest to pin this on me. You wouldn't have to look any further. Is that how you do it in the city?" he challenged her, ready for battle.

"I'm not interested in easy. I'm interested in the truth, Mr. Bing." She stepped another step closer, daring him to make a move. She needed to establish who was in charge here, so he'd remember when he was sitting in the interrogation room across the table from her. "Time to go."

Cuffs?

Judging by the hard look in his eyes, he knew exactly what she was thinking.

In the end, she just jerked her head toward the door. She didn't want him to think she was intimidated by him.

Even if she was, maybe just a little.

Carmen's Cop Rule #3: *Reveal nothing.*

Joe stepped aside. "His first night home from service and you're going to make him spend it in a holding cell?"

Normally, officers didn't question each other's judgment in front of the suspect. But she understood that Hunter was different. He was part of the family at the station, more so than she was.

She liked and respected the men she worked with at the Broslin PD, hated the idea that this case might bring tension to her working relationships with them.

"Doing my job. You'd do the same." She marched Hunter by Joe.

She was going to work the case by the book. All the t's most definitely crossed, all the i's dotted. And not with smiley faces. "I'll be back in a minute. Nobody gets access to the apartment but the coroner's people."

She walked Hunter out to Mike at the front door. At least Mike hadn't gone to high school with Hunter. "Can you take him back to the station? I'll be in later to question him."

"No problem."

He looked drawn. Whatever he'd eaten was doing a number on him.

"Maybe you should go home afterwards," she suggested.

"It's not that bad. I'll come back."

He nudged Hunter as they all walked out. "Hey, did you hear that the Energizer Bunny was arrested?" Mike paused for effect. "He was charged with battery."

Gabi rolled her eyes.

Hunter groaned. "You're a regular standup comic."

Mike puffed out his chest. "You never know. It could happen someday."

A greasy-haired, short-necked, thirty-something guy ambushed them at the bottom of the steps, snapping photos, blinding them with the flash. One of the local reporters. "Are you arresting him?"

Gabi said, "No comment."

"Can you confirm that the victim is Cindy Simme?"

"No comment."

"Can you confirm that she was murdered? Was she raped?"

"No comment."

"Who do you think did it? Is Hunter Bing a suspect?"

"I can't discuss an ongoing case. If you want a press release, go see the captain." Gabi marched Hunter to Mike's cruiser and put a hand on the top of his head as he ducked into the back of the car. His dark hair was springy, tickling her palm.

He said nothing, but the muscles stood out in his neck. He had to be in shock, at least partially, but he was furious too. His silence came from a tremendous amount of self-control. Plus enough smarts to know that anything he said could be used against him.

He hadn't fallen apart, not from the death of his girlfriend and not from being taken in for questioning. Some people broke down babbling once they were in the back of a police cruiser. Gabi would have been surprised if Hunter had.

She advised him to get a lawyer, closed the door, then watched as Mike plopped behind the wheel and drove away.

She walked back into the apartment building, ignoring the reporter who, now that Mike wasn't guarding the front door, followed her right in, peppering her with questions.

Joe stopped the guy outside the apartment. "Restricted area."

And Gabi shut the door in the guy's face.

One of the coroner's assistants was coming from the back. "You can take the gun now."

The bedroom still looked like she'd left it. The only difference was that the victim's hands had plastic bags over them to preserve any evidence that might be under her fingernails.

Gabi bagged and tagged the Beretta while Dr. Koppel, standing to the side, was busy taking notes.

By the time Gabi walked out of the apartment, the reporter was gone, probably off to track down the captain. She went to check in with her neighbor upstairs. Doris's memory of the evening wasn't going to get any sharper than it was tonight.

They sat at the kitchen table. Doris gripped her teacup as if it contained some miracle elixir that could turn back time. Of course, the cup probably *did* hold some elixir, eighty or so proof. Gabi wasn't going to criticize, under the circumstances.

The small apartment had a certain old-world elegance with its Queen Anne chairs and the doilies under the fine china. Doris talked about British porcelain manufacturers like others talked about beloved family members, but Gabi could never get the names straight.

Doris set her cup down. "Are you sure I can't offer you some tea and biscuits?"

Caffeine might be good. "All right." Gabi nodded, not expecting to see her bed tonight. "If you're sure it's not too much trouble. How are you doing?"

"Better than that poor woman." Doris moved to the counter and picked up a new teakettle patterned with the British flag.

Her apartment had more British novelty items than the gift shop at Buckingham Palace. Not because her taste ran that heavily to patriotism, but since people knew she was British, they kept giving her things wrapped in the Union Jack. Of course, she was way too polite to hide any gift away in the back of a cabinet.

Gabi slid her recorder to the middle of the table. The clock on the microwave showed close to midnight. She didn't want to keep her neighbor up later than absolutely necessary. "I'll record this if you don't mind. You're the only witness so far."

"Of course, dear."

"Did you know the victim?"

"Only by sight. I saw her a time or two, coming around when Hunter was home on leave." She poured tea into a flowery cup then brought it over, along with a matching saucer. "I don't think we ever talked."

"How well do you know Hunter Bing?"

"I see him when he's home for leave. Polite young man. He'll hold the door. Once he carried my groceries up. I don't hear a peep from downstairs when he's home. Not the type to blare the telly." She smoothed her robe down with an unsteady hand as she sat.

"Could you tell me what happened tonight?"

Doris picked up her own cup and sipped her tea for a moment. "I was watching an old Sherlock Holmes rerun. I heard a shot, and at first I thought it was on the show. But Sherlock didn't react, and then I thought, oh dear, that sure sounded like it might have come from downstairs."

"Do you remember what time?"

"The show was about to end, so a little before seven. I put on my robe. I knew Hunter was coming home." She hesitated. Sipped. Cleared her throat. "I thought maybe he dropped his gun. I wanted to make sure he wasn't hurt."

"Did you see anyone as you were going down the stairs?"

"Nobody. I went down and saw his door open a crack. I knocked. Nobody said anything, so I went in. Hunter was in the bedroom. I think I startled him."

"Did he have a weapon in his hand?"

"No."

"Did you see any blood on him?"

"On his right hand. I thought he was hurt, then I saw the young woman on the bed." Doris gripped her teacup. "I had to sit for a minute."

She'd taken it well, all things considered. Gabi reached over to pat her hand, then caught herself. The town was rubbing off on her. She was having tea with old ladies and bursting into displays of affection. What next, greeting people by name on the street?

"What did Hunter do?"

"He went to wash up, then he called the police."

"Did he go back into the bedroom?"

"No. He waited with me, made sure I was all right. He was in shock, I think. We both were. We didn't speak. Then Captain Bing came. The others were a minute or two behind him."

Gabi nodded. Made sense that they would arrive at the same time. They'd all been at the same party. "Did they go into the bedroom?"

Doris gripped her cup. "Nobody did. Captain's orders. He wouldn't even let anyone inside the apartment. He called the dispatcher and asked for you to be sent, even before he asked Hunter what happened."

"What did Hunter tell him?"

"He said he came home, found Cindy on the bed, the gun on the floor." The old woman's frown deepened into lines that for once made her look her age. "You don't think he'd do something like this, do you? He's such a nice young man."

"We'll see what the evidence says."

"Handsome too." Doris shot a speculative look at Gabi. "The kind of man who could make a woman's heart sing with one look."

Doris was the expert on that. She had loved and mourned her husband, but was now active in the dating scene at the senior center. She certainly had more dates than Gabi.

"Virile," the old woman added.

Gabi didn't want to think about Hunter's virility. She didn't disagree with Doris, but her focus had to be on whether the man was innocent or guilty. "Is there anything else you can think of? Anything you saw or heard?"

But after several seconds of staring into her cup, Doris sighed. "It all rattled me rather more than I'd like to admit, I'm afraid."

She did look shaken and tired, eyes drooping, shoulders hunched, very different from her usual graceful, ladylike posture.

Time to let her go to bed.

"I'd like to go over everything with you again tomorrow," Gabi said. "Maybe you'll remember something new. If you remember anything before I can stop by, please write it down and call me."

She thanked Doris, then left her to catch some sleep if she could.

It might not be easy. Some things could never be unseen.

On her way out, Gabi checked via radio how Chase was doing with the door-to-door. Almost finished. Unfortunately, none of the tenants he'd questioned so far had heard or seen anything.

Doris's apartment was directly above Hunter's, so she was closest, technically. Since Hunter's was a basement apartment, nobody lived below him. The end unit he rented shared walls with one other apartment on that level, but that stood empty, according to Joe. The basement level was mostly underground, so that muffled sound considerably.

At seven p.m., at the time of the shooting, people had been eating, talking around the dinner table, or watching TV. If they'd heard the pop of the gun, they put it down to someone knocking over a chair above or below them or a car backfiring in the parking lot. A gunshot wasn't the kind of sound people around here expected to hear, so their brains simply didn't go in that direction.

Gabi checked the emergency exit in the back. The green metal door opened to a narrow back alley that housed the garbage containers. The alley created a wind tunnel effect, sucking through frigid air from one side of the building to the next. She didn't think people ever hung out here. Not even smokers. If the killer used this exit, the chance for a witness was slim.

She went back in. Mike had returned while she'd been outside.

"Hunter's in holding." He started up the staircase next to Gabi. "I'll help Chase finish the door-to-door."

"Thanks. I appreciate it."

The coroner's assistants were coming up with the gurney, a black body bag strapped in place. Gabi strode over and held the front door for them, then followed them outside.

She stood aside as they loaded the body into their black van. "Is Dr. Koppel still here?"

"She's gone back to the office," the guy with the pierced ears said, lifting Cindy's weight easily.

"Any idea how backed up she is?"

He gave a one-shouldered shrug. "I think she actually caught up tonight before we got the call on this case."

First piece of good news today. "You think I might have some results before noon?"

"Yeah. Sure."

She left them to their work and checked out the front entry. Bright light above the door, but no cameras. In Philly, a person couldn't take two steps without being recorded, but comprehensive surveillance hadn't yet caught up with Broslin.

She scanned the parking lot that looked like every other apartment building parking: older-model cars, heavy on pickups that single guys preferred in the country. Dozens of people drove in and out every day. Unless the killer dropped his business card with a confession stapled to it, they weren't going to find any clues here.

Joe was coming over. "They're done in there. Did you want to go back in?"

"I still have to dust for prints." She'd left that for last, since the dust tended to cover everything.

"I can do the sweep out here, front and back." Joe flipped on his flashlight. "Then I'll do another in the morning when I can see better."

He wanted Gabi to move on to the questioning, so Hunter could be released sooner rather than later. But whatever his motives were, Gabi appreciated the dedication. "Thanks."

She hurried inside and began dusting for prints. The safe had been wiped clean, which gave her a good indication that she'd find the same with the murder weapon. Plenty of prints on the furniture, but she had low expectations. The killer had clearly cleaned up after himself.

She dug the bullet out of the wall behind the bed, bagged and tagged it. 9mm, the kind the Beretta would fire. Then she sealed up the apartment, waved good night to Joe as she strode to her cruiser.

The snow had nearly stopped. Only a few large flakes were floating from the dark sky. The houses and businesses all decorated to the nines only added to the Christmas wonderland effect. As she drove past Broslin Square with the gazebo that sparkled with lights, she felt like she was in a snow globe.

Anyone else would have thought, *everything perfect*.

But all Gabi felt was *trapped*.

Chapter Six

With the glaring lights of the holding area, Hunter felt like he was under the interrogation spotlight already. He was the only "guest" in the back of the police station. The other two cells stood empty.

As if his grief, shock, and outrage weren't enough to make his head spin, his brother's quietly spoken words hit him like a hand grenade blast.

"What do you mean Cindy was cheating?" he demanded. If this was all a bad dream, he hoped to hell he was about to wake.

He'd kept his cool with Officer Hardass, but now, alone with Ethan, the last of Hunter's composure was fast disappearing. "Why in hell wouldn't you tell me before?" He ran his fingers through his short-cropped hair. "I showed you the ring."

Ethan stood outside the bars, his forehead lined with deep furrows. He seemed to have aged years since the party. His expression full of remorse, he shoved his hands into his pockets. "I thought I had to give Cindy a chance to come clean. If she'd made a mistake but owned up to it, asked you to forgive her... It was between you and her."

Hunter swore darkly. Then he remembered the odd way his brother had been acting at the party. So this was why.

"I'm sorry," Ethan said.

Hunter swore again. He had a hard time processing the past couple of hours, not the least that he was behind bars. How the hell did he get here? He was in Broslin. War and death were supposed to be behind him. His mind had been flying a hundred miles an hour toward the new life he'd been fantasizing about, only to crash into the brick wall of hard reality.

He was innocent, but plenty of innocent people sat in prison right this minute. The circumstantial evidence could bury him.

And that wasn't even the worst part.

Cindy is dead. Killed.
She'd cheated.

While he'd been off to war and Cindy had been sending him those e-mails and little care packages, she'd been sleeping with another man.

"Who?" He growled the single word.

Ethan's face twisted as if he'd rather eat broken glass than say the name, but he said it anyway, his voice filled with cold anger that was the opposite of Hunter's hot fury. "Cameron Porter."

Hunter stepped back from the bars and dropped onto the bench. He rubbed his hand over his eyes, trying to bring up the man's face. *Blondish hair, too perfect teeth.*

Cameron Porter worked at Charlie's car dealership down by Route 1. Or at least he had when Hunter had last seen him.

"I bought a car from him. The blue GMC I had before the truck. A fucking used-car salesman?"

Ethan's eyes filled with sympathy. "He's moved up to managing the dealership. He's Charlie's right-hand man."

"Always been a brown-nosed piece of shit."

"Rich piece of shit now," Ethan said. "Lives in a mansion in Brandywine Estates. Drives a BMW."

Hunter swallowed the bitterness creeping up his throat. "So Cindy wanted a mansion. That's it?"

Ethan cleared his throat. "I notified her family."

Hunter leaned back against the wall, his chest tight. He liked Cindy's parents. "How did they take it?"

Kathy and Matteo had always treated him like family. His mother had died in a car accident when he was eight. His father was a drunk—the best thing that could be said about him was that he stayed out of his sons' lives. For most of his life, Hunter had only Ethan, but even Ethan was always busy.

Starting in high school, Ethan had worked two or three jobs so he could kick in for the bills. He kept that work ethic even when he made captain at the PD. He saved and invested in real estate.

After his mother's death, Hunter had never known a sit-down family dinner until he started dating Cindy. She had parents and grandparents and uncles and aunts and cousins, a big, boisterous family, good, churchgoing people.

Matteo and Kathy had been married for thirty-two years. They lived the life Hunter had planned to live with their daughter.

"Are you sure about Cindy and Porter?"

Ethan wouldn't meet his gaze. "Saw them a couple of times, parking in the middle of the night by the reservoir."

Hunter's hands tightened to fists. The reservoir was a known local make-out spot. Sometimes more. He'd driven by there at night before and seen cars rock. Hell, he'd parked there with girls in high school and had rocked his first car, a 5.0 Mustang, a few times. He'd had some fun times in that car, an '87 coupe, the quintessential drag car—light body, small frame, serious power. He'd missed the Mustang more than he'd missed those girls.

He wondered how much Cindy had meant to Porter.

"I'm sorry," Ethan said again. "She didn't deserve you."

"She didn't deserve what she got either." Hunter's voice came out sounding rusty. "I wish she told me she was that lonely."

He'd been ready to spend the rest of his life with her, and she was cheating. Hell of a thing was, he grieved her death regardless. "The thought of us together, building a family, was what kept me going these last couple of years."

He didn't know how to erase that all of a sudden.

He drew a slow, deep breath. "Jesus. The way she looked on that bed. I'm never going to forget as long as I live."

That dark image hung heavily in the air between him and his brother. They'd both seen it. They would both have to live with it.

"It's motive," Ethan said quietly.

The cheating. Right. Motive for murder.

Officer Flores would definitely think so. Hunter stared. Maybe others would see it that way too. He'd come home, found out Cindy had been cheating, and he lost it. "I would never have hurt her."

"I know." His brother's gaze was steady, his voice sure.

Hunter appreciated that. "On the other hand, I could definitely hurt Cameron Shithead Porter." He was itching to pound his fists into something, and Porter seemed like the perfect target. "You think I'll be released after the questioning?"

"You will if I have anything to do with it." Then Ethan's sympathetic gaze morphed into a hard glare as he continued. "But if you go within a hundred feet of Porter, I'm going to toss you back behind bars myself."

Yeah. Hunter let the fantasy go. Showing violent tendencies while he was being looked at for murder probably wouldn't be the smartest thing.

"What's the new cop's story?"

A lot of what was about to happen to him depended on the officer in charge of his case. Before Ethan had called her to the crime scene, he'd mentioned that she used to be a Philly cop, but nothing beyond that.

"We had an opening six months ago," Ethan said now. "She applied. Her career ran into a snag in the city. She's here for a fresh start."

She seemed the no-nonsense, follow-the-rules type. Her career had stalled, which meant she was here to prove herself. Putting her boss's brother away for murder might do the trick. It'd make her reputation as a straight shooter who wasn't afraid of going after anyone or anything.

Ethan flashed his big-brother look. "You don't talk to her until the lawyer gets here."

Hunter nodded. He wasn't stupid. He hadn't hurt Cindy, but he knew how it looked. Means, motive, and opportunity—he was three for three. He was a district attorney's wet dream.

He sat there and thought about that as he waited.

In the end, the new cop hell-bent on busting his ass arrived at the same time as the lawyer, Paul Welty—a gaunt, harried guy with a rumpled tie who looked like he was working on his third ulcer. He asked for time to consult privately with his client and received it.

Hunter knew him only by sight. Bottom line: Ethan had called him in, and that was good enough recommendation.

Hunter started with "I didn't do it."

"And we'll prove that," Welty declared with full confidence, opening his fancy leather notebook. Then he reached into his pocket, came up with a roll of antacids, popped one into his mouth, and talked around it. "Let's start at the beginning. Alibi?"

Hunter shook his head, then rolled into his story, but their tête-à-tête didn't last long. He didn't have much to say.

When they were done, Officer Flores led them to the conference room for the questioning. At least it wasn't the interrogation room with the one-way mirror that they used for serious suspects.

Hunter checked her out while she set up the recording equipment on the long table between them. He'd been too shocked to fully inspect her at the apartment.

She was nearing end of shift, but her uniform was clean and crisp. She wore her straight, dark brown hair in a strict bun at her nape, not a strand out of place. No makeup, not that her large brandy-color eyes needed any. Nails strictly trimmed, no nail polish.

He'd never met a woman who tried to hide her femininity as hard as she did. Trying to fit in as one of the boys at the station? Good luck. Wasn't going to happen with her curves. The more she tried to hide it, the more she radiated some undefinable female allure.

She was hot, no doubt about it, those legs, boobs, and lips a serious triple threat. He wondered if that made her life as a cop harder or easier. Harder, he decided, since she was doing what she could to downplay her looks instead of enhancing them.

She had a small mole at the corner of her lips that he watched as she recorded the date, time, case number, and names of everyone in the room. Then she looked up from the recorder and at Hunter at last.

He held her no-nonsense gaze and firmly stated, "I didn't kill Cindy Simme," for the record.

Officer Hardass didn't seem impressed by his declaration. Although nothing about her looked like the average beat cop, her eyes did have the ability to harden in a blink, turning her gaze into a lethal weapon. "When was the last time you saw the victim alive?"

First time heading a homicide. She'd push extra hard. But she didn't fully know what she was doing, no experience. He was her bird in the hand. Easiest for her would be if he was guilty. First suspect, nabbed at the crime scene, case closed in a jiffy. She would want to look good on her first case. In her head, he was probably already wearing orange overalls and sneakers without laces.

Shit.

Army rule #1 was to always have a plan. Hunter's current plan was to cooperate fully so he could be eliminated as quickly as possible. "The last time I saw Cindy was when I was on leave. Eight months ago."

"Could you recount the events of yesterday evening for the record?"

He began with his flight back home, how his brother had picked him up at the airport, had dropped him off at the apartment so Hunter could wash up before going over for the welcome home party. Talking was easier than sitting there thinking about all the circumstantial evidence piled against him.

"I arrived at the party around five thirty. I was waiting for Cindy to show up. Then I checked my phone and saw I missed a call from her, from the landline at my place. I figured I'd drive over." He put his phone on the table. "You can check my phone records."

"Will do," Flores assured him in a cool tone that said she didn't need his advice on how to conduct her investigation. "Why do you have a landline when you're not home?"

"Ethan had the phone turned on for me. Phone, Internet, cable. Comes as a package."

She thought for a second, couldn't find fault with that, so she moved on. "Who was at the party?"

He listed as many names as he could remember.

"When did you leave?"

He tried to think back. "Around six thirty. Maybe a little later."

"Can anyone confirm? Did anyone see you leave?"

"Dakota Riley," he said with a rush of relief, grateful now that Dakota had followed him outside.

But would that be enough? Even if she could remember his departure to the minute, he didn't think time of death could be pinned down with exact precision. The coroner would establish time of death as a range, say, six thirty to seven.

Hunter was at the crime scene minutes after the murder. Cindy's blood was still flowing. As far as timing went, he was pretty sure he was screwed.

Even though Officer Flores was recording the interview, she took the trouble to write Dakota's name down on the sheet of paper in front of her. "Did you stop anywhere on your way home?"

"No. I drove straight to the apartment."

"What happened when you got there?"

He'd told her before, but now he told her again.

How his stiff fingers had come away covered in blood after checking for Cindy's pulse, a familiar, impossibly bright red he'd seen plenty of times before. Death's own color.

He'd just stood there, couldn't catch his breath, couldn't conquer the utter disconnect—flashbacks to battlefield scenes, to the crumpled woman in the hallway in that Afghan village. The woman's blood and Cindy's blood swirled together in his mind, the two images juxtaposed over each other.

As he'd stood there in his bedroom, for a startled second he'd thought he could hear the Chinook coming, only none of that made sense, because he was home in Broslin, and this was Cindy.

Things like this weren't supposed to happen here.

His brain hadn't been able to process the gruesome sight on his bed.

"It was surreal." He'd thought he might be having a PTSD hallucination. "As I reached for my phone, I saw the gun on the floor, and I recognized it."

That had snapped him out of his disconnected state with the force of a grenade blast. Then the loose floorboard in the middle of his living room creaked. He'd spun around, expecting to see the killer.

"Then Doris came." With pink curlers in her hair.

Everything had felt utterly unreal. Hunter still felt disconnected.

Maybe he *was* going crazy. Some guys did. After getting out, they couldn't handle the transition back to normal.

Except, Flores—looking at him expectantly—was real, and the lawyer by his side was real, which meant that Cindy's death had to be real too.

"How about the ring in your pocket?" Flores asked.

A full-carat kick in the gut.

He cleared his throat. "I was going to propose." For a moment, he hesitated, not sure how to say what he needed to say.

She immediately caught the change in his demeanor. "What is it?"

The words tasted bitter in his mouth. "Cindy was having an affair."

Flores's eyes focused on him sharply. "When did you find out?"

"About ten minutes ago. My brother just told me."

She spent a moment digesting that. "Do you know who she was seeing?"

"Cameron Porter, according to Ethan."

She wrote down the name. "You know him?"

He nodded.

"Was Porter at your party?"

"No."

"When was the last time you saw him?"

He had to think. "Couple of years ago."

"How long has he been having a relationship with the victim?"

Betrayal and disappointment twisted his gut. "How the hell should I know?" He swore in silence, then reined in his frustration enough to say, "Up until a few minutes ago, I didn't even know that Cindy was seeing him."

Flores kept her face neutral. "How was your relationship with the victim? Difficult? Any arguments? Did she resent that you were always away?"

Apparently, she did. Not that she'd ever said anything.

"We were fine. Called. E-mailed. Yeah, she wanted me home." But Cindy had never acted like his absence was a huge issue for her, a deal breaker. He should have asked more questions, paid more attention to what she needed.

"Did she ever ask you to quit the army?"

"No, but I wasn't going to reenlist. I already made that decision. I was going to tell her last night." When he proposed. The thought twisted the invisible knife stuck in his gut.

Officer Flores pushed on with the questions, grilling him, sometimes asking things she'd already asked, worded differently. She didn't let up until the lawyer finally protested and reminded her that his client wasn't under arrest, he was cooperating freely.

Around three in the morning, Flores decided to give them a break. But no matter how hard the lawyer fought, she refused to release Hunter and locked him up again instead, pointing out that she could hold him for a full forty-eight hours without charging him.

The cheating was big, Hunter thought. In her mind, he was probably already convicted.

At the apartment, shocked and angry, he'd reacted with a pushback. He'd antagonized her, which had been stupid. He hadn't cared at the time. He'd expected her to look at him for the murder, but he also hadn't been that seriously worried.

Now he was.

The cheating could bury him.

Chapter Seven

"No prints on the murder weapon, wiped clean like the safe," Gabi reported to the captain who'd hung around at the station for an update. At four in the morning, both of them were dead on their feet.

"I'm sending the Beretta for ballistics," she continued. "Neither the victim's purse nor Hunter's duffel bag has anything of interest. I plugged in the victim's cell phone. Three calls made yesterday: her parents, Cameron Porter, and Hunter Bing. Two calls received: her parents and Cameron Porter. I'll talk to them later today."

The captain gave a somber nod, then pushed a few sheets of paper toward her across his desk. "My written report. Let me know if you have any questions."

Submitting a report was standard operating procedure for the first responding officer on the scene.

She skimmed the pages, then looked up. "You should have told me about the affair, sir."

She wasn't sure if she should read anything into the fact that he hadn't. The captain hadn't wanted his brother to find out about the infidelity in interrogation. Okay, so she could see that. But it was about as much interference as she was willing to allow in her case.

* * *

By nine in the morning, working on four hours of sleep, Gabi was checking in with Doris, but her neighbor hadn't remembered anything new.

Next, Gabi drove to the victim's parents' house. They were home, along with Cindy's Aunt Ruth who'd flown in from Ohio that morning. The Simmes were destroyed, as expected. They showed Gabi photos, assured her through tears that Cindy had been a perfect angel. Of course, even mothers of serial rapists usually said the same.

Kathy Simme, wrapped in desolate black, told Gabi she'd talked to her daughter Friday afternoon. Cindy had been nervous about something. Kathy had thought her daughter was just excited about seeing Hunter again after all this time, but now she wasn't sure.

Gabi asked dozens of questions, but none of the answers provided any clues, only made the Simmes cry. She wasn't going to get any workable clues here. Aunt Ruth, a couple of years younger than her sister, walked Gabi out while the parents comforted each other.

Gabi turned back from the threshold. "Anything to add?"

The short and stout woman gave a teary-eyed smile. "That girl lived for love. She could win anyone over. Lord knows, we've had our differences, but she won me over too."

"What differences?"

The aunt moved to draw back, but Gabi repeated, "What differences?"

"It was a long time ago. Just a teenage girl's fantasies."

"What did Cindy fantasize about when she was a teenager?" Gabi asked in a voice of authority that law-abiding citizens often responded to.

Aunt Ruth sighed. "About my husband. Chad was very handsome. All the young girls mooned over him." She crossed her arms. "That was all. Harmless fantasies, nothing more to it. Cindy was an only child, used to getting all the attention. When my brother-in-law got promoted to a more demanding job and my sister was sick for a while, Cindy made up stories to get back some of that attention she was losing."

"What stories?"

The woman hesitated, her arms folding tighter around her. "She thought Chad was interested in her. She daydreamed about them doing things, then confused her fantasies with reality. Of course, nobody believed her."

She shook her head. "I was mad at her for a while, I'll admit. But then Chad died, six years ago, and we made up eventually. She was my youngest niece." Tears flooded her eyes as she finished.

Gabi thanked her, then walked back to her car.

So Cindy might have been molested by an older family member who was now six years gone. Gabi hated the idea on principle, but even if it happened, hard to see how that would have any connection with yesterday's murder.

She drove to the station, tired, but early for her shift.

The building was much smaller than PD headquarters at the Twelfth Precinct, a lot less crowded and a lot more sane. At the Twelfth, at noon they'd still be processing the prostitutes and junkies they'd picked up overnight. The Broslin station was at peace, only Leila the dispatcher at the front desk. At the moment, Gabi could appreciate calm.

The captain's office stood empty. He was probably out investigating on his own. Or still sleeping. He'd left the station at the same time as Gabi this morning.

Leila caught her looking. "He's at the new mayor's office."

The dispatcher was a tough single mom of three teenage boys, the least small-town, home-sweet-home, apple-pie person Gabi knew in Broslin, the kind of could-have-been-an-inner-city-girl type Gabi appreciated. The woman had a serious shoe fetish. Black patent leather pumps with studs and spikes today.

"Today's the first day of the Special Response Task Force," Leila said. "The mayor wants the captain there every day until they have everything figured out. It's about some decommissioned military equipment they're giving out to police departments now. The mayor wants it all."

The tone of her voice made Gabi ask, "The captain doesn't?"

"He doesn't think we need armored vehicles." Leila rolled her eyes. "We don't have anyone trained to drive them. We can't afford the upkeep. Anyway, you drive one to serve a warrant, you still have to get out to go to the door."

Which would render the whole armored protection moot. Gabi nodded. If she'd ever seen a place that didn't need armored vehicles, it was Broslin.

"It's all political." Leila sorted through some printouts. "If the captain can't convince the mayor to forget it, we can kiss our budget good-bye. There won't be room in it for anything but the upkeep of the new stuff we'll be getting and never using." She paused. Then a wistful smile crossed her face. "On the other hand, maybe we'll lose funding for the extra dispatching coverage."

While Leila was pragmatic to a fault, Robin Combs, the second-shift dispatcher, was into all things mystical. Leila hadn't taken kindly to the new-age spirit showing up at what she considered *her* station.

Robin had feng shui-ed the place to within an inch of its life, including a foot-tall lucky bamboo on the front desk. Could be why things were more peaceful around here, Gabi thought, not that she believed in feng shui.

Her mother had run enough scams for Gabi to never trust anything she couldn't touch. *Everything's a scam,* had been her mother's life philosophy. Gabi didn't completely disagree. She'd thought Tony was real, but at the end, he'd turned out to be just another scammer.

"Hunter?" she asked.

Leila's face softened. "Passed out, poor guy, the last time I checked. He's one of the good ones. I can't tell you how many times he's fixed my car, or fixed something in the house for me."

Gabi walked back to holding. Could the man everyone liked drill a bullet between his girlfriend's eyes when he got mad at her?

He was sleeping soundly on his back on the bench, his arms folded under his head.

His dark hair was too short to be mussed. His clothes were wrinkled, but he didn't look much worse for wear. His biceps bulged enough to roll back the sleeves of his T-shirt. His wide chest rose and fell with every breath.

Most people looked vulnerable in sleep. Not Hunter. His strength was evident in every inch of his well-honed body. His arms were steel cords of muscle, the soft material of his T-shirt molded to the ridges of his flat stomach, his muscular thighs stretching the material of his camouflage pants.

He was like some great, slumbering beast. *Poke at your own risk.*

His legs were crossed at the ankles. He slept with his boots on, at the ready.

No doubt, ready to leave.

But could she let him?

Ninety-nine percent of the time, the most obvious suspect turned out to be the perpetrator. Most crime was pretty straightforward, nothing like the labyrinth of false clues and sudden revelations on prime-time TV. You saw a guy with a gun running from the scene of a robbery, he was your guy, usually.

You saw a man, *his* girlfriend killed in *his* apartment with *his* weapon...

If they were at the Twelfth, instead of being held for questioning, Hunter would have been arrested already.

She didn't have an iota of doubt that the man in front of her could kill. But had he killed Cindy Simme last night? Gabi wasn't feeling it.

Means was solid. He had access to the gun. Motive was questionable. He claimed he hadn't found out about the cheating until this morning, but he could be lying. And she wasn't sure about opportunity. The timing was iffy. She wanted more solid proof before going for an arrest.

As Joe had said, Hunter was just returning from serving his country. He deserved some small benefit of the doubt. He was in custody. That was enough for now. He wasn't going anywhere.

She let him be and strode back to her desk. Before she talked to him again, she wanted to have more information, more facts, more ammunition. She would have dearly liked to catch him off guard with something, even if she knew that catching a man like Hunter off guard wasn't going to be easy.

Gabi was turning on her computer when Mike strolled into the station.

He came over, still pretty pale. "Need any help? The captain said if I have time, I can assist."

"How's the stomach?"

He flashed a ghost of a smile. "I'll never eat tuna fish again. Hey, do you know how fish go into business?" He was joking again. That had to be a good sign. Maybe he'd live. "They start on a small scale." He grinned.

She rolled her eyes, but she couldn't help a smile. Mike was all right. "I'd love some help."

His grin went double-wide.

She got it. With all the detectives at the PD, neither of them would have gotten anywhere near a murder investigation if not for all the conflict of interest in this case.

"Cindy had an affair with Cameron Porter." She watched as Mike's eyes widened. "But I want to wait with talking to him until he gets out of work." She could exercise some discretion and wait until he got home this afternoon. No need to put him in an uncomfortable situation in front of his boss and coworkers.

"And I want to talk to Dakota Riley to see if she'll confirm the time Hunter left the party. But I want to lay some groundwork first." The more information she had, the better questions she could ask. "Why don't you grab a cup of coffee while I check my e-mail, then we'll get started."

While Mike walked to the back, she ran through her in-box, had nothing from the coroner, so she called the woman's office but found the line busy.

She had Joe's report. Nothing useful had turned up in the front parking lot or the back alley, neither during last night's sweep, nor this morning.

Next she began the report on the door-to-door, but Mike was coming back, and he summarized it for her.

"Nobody saw or heard anything suspicious. Chase and I figured the killer probably isn't another tenant in the building. Someone heading up the stairs would have been seen by Doris Hastings. We couldn't find anyone on Hunter's floor who'd been home alone. Half the people were out, either at work or just out for Friday night. The other half had girlfriends or buddies there with them to provide an alibi."

She made room for him by her desk. "Let's run a background check on the victim."

"You won't find much," Leila said as she walked by on her way to the break room. "She's a kindergarten teacher. Lived here all her life. Not so much as a parking ticket,"

Leila proved to be right. Cindy Simme had a clean record. Except for her college years in Philly, she'd worked and lived locally her whole life. Prior to her teaching position, she'd worked at a deli, Charlie's Subs. Nothing terribly exciting, nothing that would explain how she'd become the target of a killer.

"We'll interview her supervisors and coworkers," Gabi told Mike, then ran a background check on Hunter next—also squeaky clean.

She checked her e-mail again. "I put in an inquiry to Hunter Bing's commanding officer before I went home this morning. We should have a response today. Maybe there'll be something there. A history of violence in the army."

Mike shook his head. "I doubt it."

Gabi called the coroner's office again. The line was still busy. She pushed her chair back and stood. "All right, let's go see Dakota Riley. How do you feel about swinging by the morgue on the way?"

Mike turned a shade paler, but then squared his shoulders. "I'm in."

She bit back a grin. If the tables were turned, she'd have to be dead and cold not to want to be involved in every step of the investigation.

An e-mail pinged into her mailbox, and she turned back for it. "Hunter's service record." She scanned it quickly. "Promoted several times over the years, even received a medal. No disciplinary action. His CO can't say enough good about him."

Mike didn't say *I told you so*, but she could read it on his face.

"How was Hunter in questioning?" he asked on the way over to West Chester.

"Kept his cool." But she hadn't missed the anger bubbling just beneath the surface. Could she see him going ape shit on someone who'd betrayed him? Yeah. Pretty easily.

"From what you know of him, can you see him committing violence against a woman?" she asked Mike.

"No. He's a good guy. When I moved to Broslin, he was home on leave. Precious days, right? He spent one full weekend helping me move in. Offered his pickup to truck furniture in from the stores in West Chester. I got a fourth-floor apartment. He helped me drag everything up. He didn't know me from Adam. He just happened to hear from his brother that I needed a hand moving. He would never have hurt Cindy."

Gabi tapped the steering wheel. "Over half of all murdered women are killed by the man in their lives. Cindy cheated. Hunter just returned home from the service, hadn't had time to readjust to civilian society. He's been in the army for twelve years. He's used to solving problems with weapons." She paused. "Maybe he was drinking at the party." *Damn.* "I should have made him take a test."

Mike glanced at his watch. "Way more than twelve hours passed. Forget it." Then he added, "He didn't look drunk."

And he hadn't smelled like alcohol when she'd patted him down, but she should have thought of testing him anyway. She'd been too startled by suddenly finding herself heading a murder investigation.

The brick building of the coroner's offices on Market Street looked as clinical from the outside as it was on the inside, the roof gray and shaped at an angle like a coffin lid.

The strong smell of disinfectant mixed with more sinister odors inside, and Gabi took shallower breaths, then tried to breathe through her mouth, but it didn't help any, so she resigned herself to the momentary discomfort as she waited to be acknowledged by Dr. Koppel, who was working on the victim.

White tile covered the floor and the walls, all the way up to the ceiling. A half-dozen stainless steel examining tables lined up in the middle, a scale hanging from the ceiling next to each. A dozen metal storage units with glass doors held instruments and chemicals in carefully arranged order on the shelves.

Dr. Evelyn Koppel glanced up at last from the body that lay stark naked and stiff in death, the skin grayish. The incisions had been made, but the internal organs hadn't yet been removed for weighing.

The doctor's forehead furrowed. "How can I help you, Officers?"

Mike backed out. "I need to check on something in the car."

Gabi stepped closer. "Just wondering if you have anything yet. I'd be grateful for any preliminary findings that you could share."

The doctor gestured at the body on the stainless steel slab. "Cause of death, gunshot to the head. Nine millimeter. Consistent with the weapon found at the scene. She died instantly. No gunpowder residue on her face, so the shooter was standing at some distance. No other injuries. No defensive wounds. Doesn't seem like she was in an altercation prior to being shot. No tissue under her fingernails."

Gabi swallowed her disappointment.

"No evidence of vaginal trauma," the doctor went on. "But I did find traces of semen. The victim had intercourse in the hours leading up to her death."

Bingo. "I'd like the DNA on that semen as soon as possible."

"One more thing." Dr. Koppel turned back to the body, her voice softening a shade. "She was about two months pregnant."

Gabi blinked. *Cameron Porter?*

She'd screwed up the breathalyzer test. She had to be extra careful going forward. So she asked for DNA from the fetus.

Mike was waiting for her outside, leaning against her cruiser with a hand pressed against his middle.

"So there's this coroner in cross-examination at a trial," he said as he went around the car to get in. "The attorney is really drilling him. *If you didn't take the victim's pulse and didn't listen to his heart, how could you confirm him dead?* The coroner says, *Well, I had his brain in a jar, but hey, he could be out there, practicing law somewhere.*"

Gabi shook her head. Leave it to Mike to have a joke for every occasion. "How are you doing?"

"Stupid stomach bug," Mike said. "Anything on the victim?"

"Let's go see Dakota Riley. I'll fill you in on the way."

Chapter Eight

Hunter knew the dream by heart. The same images came back night after night to haunt him.

He was hurrying down a dark hallway when a shadow jumped out in front of him and he caught the glint of a gun. He fired, the shadow crumpled, and he could see the face of a young woman. Blood spread on the ground, a black puddle in the darkness.

He normally woke at this point, but this time the dream went on. The woman's face turned into Cindy's. Then the lifeless body at his feet turned into J.T. Grief sliced through Hunter like shrapnel. He was too late to save anyone. An overwhelming sense of guilt drowned him.

The sound of squeaking metal startled him awake, and he rolled to a standing position, grappling for his rifle, his brain thinking he was still overseas. A confused moment passed before he came back to the here and now—a holding cell in Broslin.

He dropped back down to the bench and shot a bleary-eyed look at his brother, who stood in the open cell door, watching him come awake. "You got anything against people sleeping?"

His brother raised an eyebrow. "It's two o'clock in the afternoon."

Hunter ran his hand over the stubble on his jaw, took a moment to appreciate that, among all the tragedies, his team had *not* been too late to save J.T. His buddy was home in Tennessee. *Alive.* Unlike the burka-clad woman and Cindy.

Ethan jingled the key ring in his hand. "I'm springing you."

"Am I cleared?"

"Not yet. Let's take a break anyway."

Hunter flashed him a dubious look. "Are you sure you want to go up against Flores?"

"Hey, who's the boss here?"

"Leila," Hunter deadpanned and made his brother laugh.

But even as Ethan laughed, concern sat in his eyes.

Hunter didn't want anyone to worry about him. "Slept like a dead possum."

"I don't see how."

Hunter worked up a tired smile. "No incoming enemy fire, and this bench is a hell of a lot softer than a pile of rocks on some Afghan hillside. Warmer too."

His brother stepped back from the door. "You can shower at my place before we head over to the diner."

"What if Officer Hardass wants to question me again?"

Ethan lifted an eyebrow. "I wouldn't talk like that in front of her, if you know what's good for you. She's tougher than she looks."

And she looked plenty tough, Hunter thought as he pushed to his feet. Officer Flores had a story. Since she was investigating him, he wanted to know what made her tick. But asking his brother would be useless. Ethan wouldn't discuss any personal information about an officer of his.

So Hunter asked a general question. "How did the guys handle a female partner?"

"Nonissue. She's good at her job. That's the only thing that counts around here." Ethan hesitated. "The wives and girlfriends were a little nervous at first."

Hunter could see why. Officer Flores was difficult to ignore from the male perspective: tall, long-legged, nicely curved. "Is she single?"

"As far as I know. But nobody here looks at her that way. Harper might have, but then he went on leave."

Harper and Mike were the only bachelors left at the Broslin PD, and Mike had been hopelessly in love with Joe's sister, Amber, forever. The other guys had found their matches and settled down in the last couple of years.

Hunter followed his brother through the station. Nobody there but Leila, who gave him a hug.

Outside, his brother's cruiser waited. This time, Hunter got in the front, last night's events swirling in his mind: Cindy's death, the news that she'd been unfaithful, the fact that he'd been held for questioning. He hadn't been charged, but he knew how it all looked. His apartment. His girlfriend. His weapon.

Hunter watched the lights and decorations on the houses they passed, the Christmas-postcard scenes around him. Last night, they'd felt like a welcoming embrace. Today, he felt utterly disconnected. "How fucked am I?"

Ethan grunted. "I'd say foreplay stage."

"Ever seen anyone convicted on circumstantial evidence alone?"

"Once or twice." Ethan's jaw clenched as they took the winding country road that led to the Bing homestead. "The jury felt things went past reasonable doubt. That's not going to happen here."

"I have no alibi."

"Doesn't mean anything."

"If I'd driven faster, I could have made it home five minutes earlier. I drove slow, enjoying the feel of being home, having everything around me be safe and familiar. And I was trying to figure out what to say when I got to her, how to ask her."

"You're not going to prison," his brother said gruffly.

Hunter stared out the windshield. "You trust Officer Flores?"

Ethan didn't think about it. "I trust all my people. They wouldn't be at the PD if I didn't."

They pulled up the driveway, stopped in front of the house, in the spot where Hunter had briefly argued with Dakota the night before.

"If Dakota hadn't stopped me, I would have gotten to the apartment sooner. Maybe I could have saved Cindy."

Ethan got out of the car. "We'll figure out who did this, and he'll be brought to justice. Don't do the *if* game. It'll drive you crazy." His voice was off a shade, his shoulders stiffening.

Hunter winced. Man, he was stupid. "Sorry, bro."

Ethan's first wife, Stacy, had died in a home invasion. Come to think of it, under very similar circumstances as Cindy.

Hunter froze by the car, his blood running cold. "You don't think Stacy's case could be connected to Cindy's, do you?"

No connection seemed possible. Stacy's killer was dead. And yet—

Ethan's mouth tightened to a nearly invisible line. "Beyond the similarity of the murder, there's no connection. Stacy's case is closed. That's all finished. I finished it myself. This is something else."

Shouldn't have brought it up. Ethan had probably already thought of the possibility. *Okay.* Stacy's killer was dead. Ethan was right. This was something new here.

They stepped inside one after the other, as glum as a funeral procession.

The house sparkled. Sophie must have stayed up half the night to tidy up. She struck Hunter as an exceedingly capable woman. And pretty and kind. And obviously in love with his brother.

Hunter looked around for her.

"She's at a friend's house," Ethan said. "Jack Sullivan's wife, Ashley. She's having a baby."

Huh. "Didn't have Jack pegged as a family man."

"Father of two any minute now. He adopted Ashley's little girl already. They're doing some home-birth thing." Ethan shuddered. "Best not to think about it."

The dogs greeted them with wild, slobbery enthusiasm, a whirlwind of wagging tails. Mango, the orange cat, watched the scene with a superior air from the back of the couch. The disapproving look on her face said Ethan and Hunter should have made an appointment before coming over.

Ethan let the dogs out back. The cat took one look at the frozen landscape and stayed where she lay.

Hunter went upstairs and showered, changed into clean clothes that Ethan had set out for him. The faded I LOVE BROSLIN T-shirt with the letters made up of various mushrooms fit fine, the jeans a little wide in the waist, but nothing a belt couldn't fix.

As he padded down the stairs, his brother looked up from his phone. "Main Street Diner? Pizza Palace?"

Hunter paused on the last step. "I'm fine with leftovers from the party."

"Plenty of that." Ethan headed for the fridge. "I'll grab a quick lunch with you, then I'll have to go back to the mayor's office. We're negotiating new equipment," he said without any enthusiasm.

Hunter walked to the kitchen island. "Are you going to be one of those PDs with the fancy SWAT team and tanks?"

Ethan sneered as he put a platter of deviled eggs on the slab of granite in front of Hunter with one hand and a bowl of meatballs with the other. "Some of us don't feel the need to hide behind a tank."

Hunter stuck his chin out. "Oh yeah, tough guy?"

He couldn't count how many tumbles on the floor had begun with those words when they'd been kids. But now both of them just grinned, some of the tension leaving the kitchen. Hunter grabbed an egg. God, it was good to be home like this, talking trash with his brother. "Anything new from Flores?"

Ethan slid onto a barstool. "Couldn't tell you if there was."

Hunter shoved the deviled egg into his mouth, picked up another. "She better be looking at Porter."

"I'm sure she'll get to him. But Cindy wasn't killed at Porter's apartment with his gun," Ethan said quietly.

Right. Flores was probably busy trying to find proof that Hunter was the killer. Frustration kicked through him. Focusing on him was a waste of time. But there was nothing he could do about it.

That things could get this messed up in such a short time seemed impossible.

"How did Cindy's mom take the news?" Cindy was especially close to her mother, Kathy.

"Like you'd expect." Ethan dropped the meatball back into the bowl as if he'd suddenly lost his appetite.

Hunter too had trouble swallowing the second egg and didn't reach for the third. "I should stop by."

"No."

His gaze cut to Ethan. "You think they think I had anything to do with it?"

His brother shrugged. "By now, probably half the town knows you've been held for questioning. The family is in deep grief. They're not thinking straight. Give them a day."

He slipped off the barstool. "Most real murder cases are not some big mystery like on TV. With a little poking and all the new lab tricks available these days, we usually get a fair idea who the perpetrator is within the first day or two. This won't drag out long," he promised as he walked to the door. "The beer is in the cooler in the garage. Plenty more food in the fridge. You make yourself at home. Relax."

After his brother left, Hunter gave relaxing a try. His restlessness won in the end. He grabbed his phone, turned it back and forth for a second or two, then called J.T. He'd promised himself he would check up on the kid. But J.T. didn't pick up.

Hunter ate a few more eggs, then put away the tray and made himself coffee, drank it standing in front of the sliding glass doors that looked to the open fields. His gaze hesitated on the gentle rise he'd picked out last night for a house to live in with Cindy.

The welcome home party seemed a million years away. His stomach clenched; pressure built in his chest.

He stared blindly at the snow-covered fields, and the weight of Cindy's death hit him so hard that he had to lean his forehead against the cold glass. He could see her again, lying lifeless in a pool of blood on his bed.

He grieved in silence. They had a hundred little connections between them, even if her dreams for the future were different from his.

She *had* acted different lately. The e-mails had slowed. The last time he'd been home on leave, she'd been distracted. She hadn't had as much time for him as usual, but he'd accepted that she was busy with work. She'd been getting her kindergarten class ready for a play.

And now she was gone.

He couldn't find it in him to be truly mad at her. But some Neanderthal part of him wanted to be mad at someone.

Cameron Fucking Porter.

Hunter's free hand clenched into a fist. He swallowed the last of his coffee, let the dogs back in, then walked out of the house to Ethan's pickup that sat in the driveway. Keys behind the visor.

Hunter drove around town blindly for a while before he ended up at Cindy's parents' place against his brother's advice, a fifties ranch home on a quiet street. Half a dozen cars crowded in the driveway, probably relatives who'd come to offer support.

He wanted to do the same. He *needed* to do the same.

He parked by the curb, then loped across the lawn, rang the bell, and waited.

Cindy's Aunt Ruth opened the door. She froze for a second before she called over her shoulder, "Kathy, you better come out here."

Kathy Simme appeared a minute later, her eyes red and swollen with dark circles under them. She wrapped her arms around herself when she spotted Hunter. She didn't step outside and didn't invite him in.

Hunter couldn't even imagine what she was going through. "I'm really sorry for your loss. I can't believe she's gone."

Her mouth snapped into a tight line, cold anger glinting in her swollen eyes. "Why aren't you in jail? I thought you were arrested."

He winced. "I was in only for questioning."

"Cindy knew this was coming." A sudden sob escaped her, then her expression turned hard and cold. "She told me she was nervous about seeing you last night. You will burn in hell for this, Hunter Bing." And with that, she slammed the door in Hunter's face.

He stood there staring at the door stupidly, feeling gut-punched. Then he finally caught something Kathy had said.

Cindy had been nervous?

Maybe she'd meant to tell him about the affair.

He wanted to ask Kathy some questions, but he wasn't going to get any answers here today. Kathy didn't want him here, and he had no right to intrude unwanted. Cindy's parents needed time—Ethan had been right—to take the jagged edges off their pain.

Hunter strode back to the pickup and slipped behind the wheel, fighting grief, anger, and disappointment. If Cindy confessed last night, he wouldn't have taken her confession well. But he wouldn't have hurt her, dammit.

He stared at the house where he'd once belonged, had been treated like family. But when Cindy's father came to the front window and closed the curtains, Hunter started the pickup and pulled away from the curb.

He drove around town aimlessly. He had no idea how he ended up at the used-car dealership.

At least a hundred cars crowded the lot, balloons and ribbons everywhere. Cameron Porter's smarmy smile beamed on a billboard that advertised the best deals in the state.

A squat building sat in the back, its whole front wall glass. As Hunter rolled into the lot, he could see Porter standing in the middle by a desk, talking with a young couple.

The bastard was here, smiling, business as usual, while Officer Flores was out there somewhere looking for proof against Hunter. Hunter found the thought difficult to swallow. His grip tightened on the steering wheel.

He wasn't going to go in. He *wasn't* going to go in.

And then he did.

Chapter Nine

Since the captain wasn't picking up his phone, probably still with the mayor, Gabi left an update on the coroner in his voice mail.

Then she and Mike caught up with Dakota Riley at the local spa where the young woman worked the reception desk when home from college on breaks.

"Hunter seemed confused." The girl kept biting her bottom lip, glancing away, then back. "One minute he was flirting with me, the next he was pushing me away. I have no idea what got into him. He's not like that normally. He's a great guy, you know. Just got hooked by the wrong woman."

She sighed as theatrically as an actress on a daytime soap. Her long-suffering look said she thought she was the right woman for Hunter.

Gabi couldn't blame her for being attracted. Hunter was a very attractive kind of guy. Since he was a suspect, Gabi couldn't consider him that way. But she could understand if Dakota got hung up on him a little. Or even a lot.

"Do you know what time he left the party?"

"A little after six thirty. He kind of snuck out, but I saw him."

Maybe he thought he could kill his cheating girlfriend, then sneak back in without anyone noticing, and have the perfect alibi, a hundred people swearing that he'd been with them all evening, celebrating.

"Are you sure it was six thirty?"

"I looked at the clock on the wall because I was thinking, like, why was he leaving so early. I went after him to ask what was wrong." Dakota flashed a coy smile. "Then we were, you know, kind of embracing."

A detail Hunter had left out. "Did he tell you where he was going?"

"To Cindy." Anger sparked in the girl's eyes. "She was a total bitch. I know she's dead and all that, but she was. She was totally cheating on him. I saw her with Cameron Porter." She stuck out her chin. "I told Hunter. He needed to know, don't you think? He's a hero. And he's like so hot. He's a man, you know? I'm tired of stupid little college boys."

Gabi made some noncommittal sound as her brain buzzed. So Hunter might be interested in Dakota. And he, in fact, had known about the cheating before he'd gone to see Cindy. That he'd lied about when he'd discovered his girlfriend's infidelity didn't look good for him.

Dakota gave an exasperated huff. "I mean, what did he ever see in Cindy? She was totally old. Like twenty-seven. I couldn't believe that he'd leave me to go to her."

Gabi flashed the girl a sympathetic look that said, *hey, we're just two chicks talking about stupid guys who don't know a good thing when they see it.* "What did he do when you told him?"

Dakota pouted. "He rushed off."

"Men. What can you do, right?"

Dakota got into the whole women-of-the-world-come-together spirit, and began talking about her past with Hunter, a bunch of infrequent, accidental meetings on the street, turned into elaborate adolescent fantasies. She was convinced that they were having a relationship, and even now, Hunter was just taking time to recover from the shock of his cheating ex before coming for Dakota.

The more she talked, the more Gabi suspected that the relationship thing was wholly invented. But no matter how hard she pushed Dakota, the girl didn't deviate from insisting that she *had* told Hunter about Cindy's infidelity before Hunter left the party.

That new piece of information kept floating to the forefront of Gabi's mind on her way back to the station with Mike. "All right, so one big step forward. Hunter knew about the cheating before he drove to the apartment."

"He still didn't do it," Mike said stoically.

"We'll see." She'd meant to let Hunter go after another round of questioning, but now she wasn't sure. "Motive, means, and possibly opportunity." *Shit.* "How pissed will the captain be if I arrest his brother?"

"The captain doesn't roll like that. You do what you have to."

"Do you think I'm wrong about Hunter?"

Mike rubbed his side. "Yep."

But she couldn't factor in Mike's vote of confidence, which stemmed from friendship and loyalty. She absolutely couldn't factor in the captain's anger or lack thereof. And she couldn't factor in the fact that if Hunter wasn't a suspect, she'd be attracted to him.

She stifled a groan. What was she, stupid? And yet there was something there, on a level that had nothing to do with rational thinking, just plain, idiotic chemistry.

When they got back, Mike offered to go and start interviewing Cindy's coworkers, so she dropped him off by his cruiser, then she walked inside to question Hunter.

Leila, on the phone, waved at her, covered the receiver. "Ten-ten by Route 1 at Charlie Heinz's car dealership." Then she said into the phone. "Thank you, ma'am. An officer is on her way."

Fight in progress. Gabi turned tail.

The first thing she saw when she pulled into the dealership was Captain Bing's green pickup. Since she knew that the captain was with the mayor, she had a really bad feeling about this. She jumped from her cruiser and ran for the building that was wrapped in a giant red Christmas bow.

People loitered outside, looking in through the large windows at two men who were exchanging punches in the showroom. Hunter Bing and, presumably, Cameron Porter. *What the hell?*

She'd gone out of her way to be helpful to Hunter, held him for questioning only instead of arresting him. *So he talks his brother into letting him out and comes here? Seriously?* She burst in, going to a hundred on the pissed scale in a second flat. "Police. Stop!"

Hunter kept going, but the other guy looked happy to see her, lips swollen, hair disheveled. He tried to ease back, but Hunter wouldn't let him. At least neither man had a weapon.

They knocked over two dozen or so three-foot car-pipe candy canes that had been tied into a bunch with ribbons. The metal made a horrendous noise clattering on the tile.

"Step away from each other," Gabi snapped at them.

But, instead, Hunter put Porter in a headlock. *Not bad.* She didn't approve of the move, but she appreciated the smooth skill with which it'd been executed.

Porter, who had the body of an office worker as opposed to the body of a warrior like Hunter, shot Gabi a panicked, pleading look, and she grabbed her baton and swept Hunter's feet out from under him in one sudden swipe.

He went down with a surprised look but barely hit the floor before he bounced up and swirled to face her, and for a moment, she wasn't sure if he was going to tackle her. He didn't, but he stood his ground, chin down, breathing like a bull in the arena.

Violent energy sparked in the air. He was all fury, all on, all trained killer. Reaching for her gun would be a sign of weakness, so she didn't. It would also be an escalation, and she wanted to deescalate.

He could have been on an action movie poster, pumped up, fury boiling in his eyes, quintessential warrior. He held her gaze, then, after a long moment, he reined himself in at last, dropping his shoulders even as his square jaw remained tight-set. He raised his hands, palms out. "I'm done."

"I hope so." She shoved her baton back into place.

Cameron Porter had scampered to a safe distance, finger-combing his fashionably cut hair and straightening his clothes.

"This criminal—" He glared at Hunter with blistering indignation.

Hunter growled in warning.

"Sit," Gabi snapped out the single word and pointed at two chairs at a safe distance from each other. "Both of you. Now."

But instead, Porter pushed on with "I want to press charges for assault. I want you to arrest this man."

She narrowed her eyes.

And Porter obeyed at last with a long-suffering grunt, rubbing his jaw.

"You too," Gabi told Hunter, glad to see the murderous intent dimming in his eyes. She wasn't afraid of going up against him, but she was glad she wouldn't have to.

He dropped into the chair and stared at her with insolence. His gaze held plenty of anger, and even grief still, and beyond all that she caught traces of a more complex look of... *lost*. That nearly got to her, but she shook off any budding sympathy.

She was so not going to get suckered into feeling sorry for him.

She didn't have to ask who'd let him go.

She drew a deep breath and dropped her shoulders. The best way to diffuse a situation was to present a calm demeanor and appear to be in complete control. Which she was. If either of the idiots as much as moved, she was shooting their dumb asses.

"Want to tell me what happened here?" She addressed the question to both men.

Porter blew air through narrowed lips in a self-righteous huff. He had a thin but defined mouth, almost aristocratic looking. "He busted in and attacked me like a madman. I *am* pressing charges. You need to put this criminal in cuffs, Officer."

Hunter shot a dark glare toward Porter, his lips moving against each other for a second as if he had plenty to say, but he was fighting it. Maybe he'd belatedly found his self-control. Good for him.

"Murderer," Porter muttered, awfully brave with Gabi standing between them.

Hunter shifted in his seat as if thinking about going for another round.

"All right." Gabi had just about had it. "I'm taking you both in."

She gestured for Hunter to stand. "Hunter Bing, you're under arrest for assault." She Mirandized him good and proper.

Porter was grinning with satisfaction one minute, went back to whining the next. "Why do I have to go in?"

"To make a statement."

He seemed satisfied with her answer. No doubt he couldn't wait to list all his complaints. She checked her dislike of the guy. She didn't like the idea of Porter stealing Hunter's girlfriend while Hunter was off risking his life for the country, but she couldn't let her personal opinion of Porter's character influence the investigation.

"Hands," she said to Hunter, and reached for her handcuffs.

She didn't much like him at the moment either. She wasn't impressed by guys who solved problems with violence. "You make one move, and I swear I'll beat you with a candy cane."

Hunter held her gaze, the angry heat dimming in his eyes. Then his lips twitched, and he held out his hands. "Abuse of power by candy cane?" He shook his head. "This country sure changed while I've been away."

God help her, he had a sense of humor. She bit her lip so she wouldn't smile while she cuffed him.

She took him by the arm, his bicep large enough so she couldn't close her fingers even halfway around it. She escorted him out. Porter followed them. Gabi let the manager sit in front, put Hunter in the back—seemed smarter not to have them sharing a seat.

From the corner of her eye, she caught a cruiser coming up the road. Chase. He pulled in and walked over.

Gabi nodded toward the people still outside the building. "Any chance you could take statements?"

"Sure." Chase drew up an eyebrow at Hunter cuffed in the backseat. "There's no reason to go hard on him. He didn't do it."

He meant the murder.

She kept her cool. "If nobody minds, I'm just going to go by the actual evidence."

Chase rubbed a hand over his face. "I don't like the sight of him in cuffs, but I know you have to run things this way. If he ends up in court, there can be no doubt that no favors were given. We're all glad we weren't picked for this." He flashed a rueful smile.

She nodded, relieved. She liked the people she worked with. She didn't want this case to mess that relationship up with resentment.

But Chase said, "If you need help, you call me."

Feeling a little better about her day, she thanked him, then got into her cruiser and took the men in. They didn't say a word on the way. Maybe they'd found the brains they'd misplaced earlier.

When they arrived at the station, she put Porter into the conference room, then booked Hunter and escorted him back to the holding cells, leaving him with an "I'll deal with you later."

"I'm sorry," he said.

That stopped her in her tracks and had her turning back.

"I shouldn't have gone to see Porter. My brother's going to kill me."

She watched him dispassionately. "Nobody is going to kill anybody on my watch."

"I don't usually act like this big an idiot."

"Any reason you save it for when I'm on duty?"

The corner of his mouth turned up for a second, but the repentant expression remained on his face. "I'm sorry I caused trouble."

His attitude threw her. For one, it didn't fit with his earlier combative mood. Two, she was used to people in lockup ranting and raving, threatening with their lawyers or the media, or whatever powerful friends they had.

She tried to look at him without bias. Truly, if he'd wanted to really hurt Porter, Porter would have been dead before she'd gotten there. Hunter had spent twelve years in the army. He was more than capable of mopping the floor with a used-car salesman.

He'd been pissed, violent even, but had exercised control. He'd pounded his frustration out on Porter, but stopped well short of seriously hurting him.

None of that mashed with the image of a man who got mad at his girlfriend, pulled a weapon, and shot her point blank in the head.

"We'll talk about this when I come back," Gabi told him, and walked away in the hope that his reunion with common sense wasn't just a brief affair but a permanent relationship.

She glanced back from the door. He was watching her with the baleful expression of a tragic hero from a dark story.

She refused to fall for it.

As she returned to the conference room, Porter broke into a litany of complaints, but she cut him off with "Did you know that Cindy Simme was pregnant?"

His ruffled hair had been combed back into smooth order while she'd been gone. He probably carried a comb in his pocket.

He paled at her words, but other than that, not a single gesture betrayed distress. While Hunter was tightly controlled passion, all manner of emotions simmering under the surface, Porter had a colder quality to him.

Gabi could more easily see him for one cold, calculated shot between the eyes. "How are you with guns?"

"Never shot one in my life." He fussed with his silk tie. "Do you think I should get one? For self-defense?"

"No," she said. "You didn't answer my question about Cindy's pregnancy."

Several seconds passed before he gathered himself, manicured hands tightly clasped on the desk in front of him. "I'm not sure what you're implying, Officer. I'm here to press charges."

"We'll get to that." Her interest in the assault was secondary. Her first priority was the murder case. "How long have you been having an affair with Cindy?"

He reached up to loosen his tie. "That's nonsense. I just got engaged to Mandy Heinz last week. We are a very happy couple."

Gabi paused a beat. "Charlie Heinz's daughter?"

He nodded. "June wedding."

"I need you to tell me where you were last night between six and seven."

The blood rushed back into Porter's face. "I didn't kill Cindy, for heaven's sake." He pressed his already narrow lips into an even tighter line. "You talk to Hunter Bing about that. Or is his brother using you to make sure Hunter gets away with murder?" His tone suddenly had an edge to it.

Her blood heated, as always when someone accused her of corruption.

"Your alibi for the night in question, please," she said with extra care.

He shifted on his seat. "I was home."

Convenient. "Witnesses? Were you with your fiancée?"

Porter huffed at her. "This is ridiculous."

"Are you saying you were alone?"

"Me being alone at night doesn't mean I killed Cindy."

"But you were seeing her."

The look of hate and outrage he shot her was nearly the same he'd been regarding Hunter with earlier.

When he still wouldn't confirm the affair several seconds later, she pushed on with "I've ordered a DNA test on the fetus."

His Adam's apple bobbed as he finally lost his nerve. His gaze turned pleading. "Mandy can't find out about this."

Not a word on how terrible he felt about Cindy or the baby.

"Why don't you start at the beginning and tell me everything?"

He shifted in his seat. "I met Cindy at the hot air balloon festival. We were both alone, went up in the same basket." He cleared his throat. "We quickly discovered that we had a connection."

"How about your fiancée?"

"I love Mandy," he rushed to say. "Cindy was an unfortunate mistake. You have to understand."

She understood nothing about men like him. "Did you know that Cindy was pregnant?"

"No." He met her eyes straight on.

"When did you last talk with her?"

"Last night. She said she had a few things to take care of, then she'd come over. She wanted to talk to me." He blinked. "I guess I fell asleep waiting for her. In the morning, I figured she'd gotten caught up in whatever she had to do. I was running late, so I thought I'd call her from the office when I got in. But as I walked in, people were talking that she'd been murdered." His voice faded on the last word.

"Exactly when and where did you talk to her last night?"

"She called me around six."

"From her cell?"

He nodded. "The connection cut out at the end. I couldn't call her back. Her battery must have died."

"Did you see her yesterday at all?"

"No. We don't usually meet on Fridays." His tone turned sheepish. "I have a standing date with Mandy, but yesterday she went to the opera with her mother. That's why I told Cindy that she could come over."

"Did you see her the day before?"

"We were running a special midweek sale at the dealership. We were swamped, ended up staying open late. I was beat by the time I locked up. And then Mandy wanted to talk about the wedding."

He clasped his hands on the table. "Look, both Cindy and I are busy people. We hooked up when we could. It wasn't a regular thing. She was lonely. I didn't want to let the opportunity slip by. In a couple of months, I'll be married. Why let a free ride go to waste?"

A prince among men. "Are you sure you didn't meet with Cindy Simme at all for the past two days?" she asked again.

"That's what I just said."

Yet the coroner had found sperm. And if Porter was lying about not seeing Cindy, what else was he lying about?

"Did Cindy know that you and Mandy got engaged?"

He clasped his hands tighter. "I was waiting for the right time to tell her."

Or the opportunity to get rid of her.

"What do you know about safes?"

He stared. "The dealership has one. We keep checks and cash in there until it's time for the armored car pickup."

"How do you open it?"

"With the security code."

"Could you open it if you didn't have the code?"

"Of course not. That's the whole point. You need the combination to open the lock."

He didn't look like a professional safecracker. Then again, what did she know about him? Just what he'd shown her today, and that was that he had no morals whatsoever. He got a woman pregnant while asking another one to marry him. And, if he could string those women along all this time, he was obviously a fairly good actor.

Maybe he'd known about the pregnancy. Cindy and the baby were in the way of a wedding that was going to considerably increase his net worth. Charlie Heinz was a local business czar. Porter was about to marry an heiress. He had a comfortable setup at the dealership. He was the boss. He already had a lot and stood to gain more.

He definitely had motive, and then some. As for means... Could he open Hunter's gun safe? Then there was opportunity. He didn't exactly have an alibi.

Gabi added interviewing his neighbors to her to-do list. Maybe one of them had seen him leaving around the time in question. Investigative skills or not, nothing beat getting lucky, Carmen used to say.

Carmen's Rules #6: *Get lucky.* Which included making your own luck. You put yourself out there every day, ran down every lead, gave luck a chance to find you.

But Porter's neighbors would have to wait. First, Gabi wanted to talk to Hunter.

Chapter Ten

Hunter sat back on the bench in the holding cell and let his head drop against the wall. He sure hadn't pictured his homecoming like this. He'd been home for two days, and he'd been tossed into a cell twice.

And he had a feeling his day was about to get worse. Officer Gabriela Maria Flores was pushing through the door and marching toward him with her long-legged stride like a winter storm.

Immaculate uniform, dark hair in a tight bun at her nape, she was one tough operator. He wasn't entirely comfortable with the two of them being on opposite sides of an issue like, say, murder.

"I don't think you're particularly stupid," she said without preamble, obviously not a woman given to meaningless niceties. "You're the prime suspect in a fatal shooting, and the second you are released from questioning, you commit assault? Run down for me what you were thinking."

Not much. But he wasn't about to admit anything to Officer Long Legs. He shrugged.

"Guys will be guys, right?" Her voice dripped with undisguised disgust. "You know what? I don't even want to hear any excuses."

The tone of her voice bothered him, that she would think he was a no-good loser. He'd been off his game for the past couple of weeks. It'd all started with the rescue op on that Afghan hillside. He couldn't forget the young woman he'd shot by accident. Her face kept coming back to him in his dreams, the way she went down like a broken doll.

Finding Cindy dead in his bed had brought everything back, made everything worse. Cindy was a whole other layer of grief and guilt and anger.

"I'm not going near Porter again. I swear. You don't have to worry about that. I promise."

Flores's eyebrows rose. "What? No excuses?"

"There's no excuse for stupid."

Some of the pissed-off she'd come in with evaporated from her face and stance as she unlocked the cell door. "I need to get your statement about the assault. We'll go over to the interview room." She paused. "Are you hungry? Thirsty?"

He wasn't either, but nodded anyway. If he ate, he could drag out the time he spent with her. He needed to convince her that he wasn't a criminal, or a complete jerk.

She slipped the cuffs off her belt. "Are you going to do anything else stupid today?"

"No, ma'am."

She put the cuffs away, then took him by the arm as she led him to the interview room. She had long, slim fingers, her grip firm. She smelled like shoe polish. He glanced down. Yep, her boots were gleaming.

He liked her orderliness and that she strove to do everything as well as possible. He appreciated competence in a woman as much as in a man. She would have done well in the army.

He hadn't been her greatest fan at the beginning. Hard to appreciate someone who was looking at him for murder. He'd given her a hard time. Then again, he hadn't really been thinking straight.

But, as he'd told her, he was done with being stupid. He couldn't afford to act like an ass, and he didn't want to. He needed to get his act together. And he needed to stop thinking of her as the enemy. Her competence was his best chance for coming out of this mess clean.

As Flores marched him up front, Leila flashed him a sympathetic look from behind the copy machine. She was balancing on crocodile-skin stilettos with five-inch heels.

"Could we have a couple of hoagies and some soft drinks?" Flores asked.

Leila closed the copier. "No problem. They'll take about twenty minutes to deliver."

Flores paused. "What do you know about Charlie Heinz?"

"Rich as God. Pretty much thinks he's better than everyone else."

"How about Mandy Heinz?"

"She's his only kid. Why?"

But Flores didn't respond. She looked thoughtful as she thanked Leila, then walked Hunter into the interview room.

His lawyer, Paul Welty, was waiting for them inside.

Officer Flores was all right, Hunter thought again. She'd waited to question him until he had representation. She must have called the guy herself, since Hunter hadn't done it. He'd figured the assault was an open-and-shut deal. He'd hit Porter. He wasn't going to deny it.

Flores plopped a recorder between them and turned it on, identified him and herself, the lawyer, added the date and time. Then, holding Hunter's gaze with steady intensity, she said something that nearly knocked Hunter off his chair.

"Were you aware that Cindy Simme was pregnant?"

The air left his lungs in a whoosh, his mind scrambling to bring back the image of Cindy on his bed. He'd been focused on her injury. He tried to think back, but he couldn't remember her belly.

His gut twisted. "How far along?"

"Eight weeks."

He drew a ragged breath. *Jesus.*

The lawyer stepped in with "Do you need a couple of minutes? We can ask for a break."

But this wasn't something a couple of minutes could fix, so Hunter shook his head. He wanted the interview to be over with.

"Did you know about the pregnancy?" Officer Flores asked again.

"No. She never said anything." Not over Skype, not in e-mail.

Would she have last night, if she hadn't been killed? Was this why she'd come to his place instead of the party? Maybe Cindy had wanted to talk to him in private. A pregnancy wasn't the kind of secret a person could keep forever.

No way to tell in hindsight how he would have responded. For sure, he would have been angry at the betrayal, but he couldn't be angry at this point. She was gone, along with her baby. The utter, senseless tragedy of that was incomprehensible.

"Why?" he asked. "What possible motive could anyone have to kill a pregnant woman?"

"Maybe the pregnancy caused problems for the killer. Or the killer might not have known that she was pregnant. Maybe the pregnancy wasn't relevant to the murder whatsoever."

"Are you looking at Cameron Porter?" Dark thoughts chased one another around inside Hunter's head. "Maybe he knew Cindy was coming to see me and he showed up at the apartment. Or maybe he followed her. They could have argued. Cindy took the gun out of the safe because she felt threatened. Then Porter grabbed the weapon from her."

Flores gave a noncommittal nod. "I'm looking at every possibility."

Yes, she would. She'd be thorough. Which allowed Hunter to take a mental step back, gain a little perspective. "I don't know if I can see Porter doing that kind of violence. He's a twerp, but that's far from being a cold-blooded killer."

She considered his opinion. "Everyone has their snapping point. Everyone has something they'd be willing to kill for."

Maybe so. He'd certainly killed for his country. He turned his full attention to the woman across the table from him. "What would you kill for?"

Her response came without hesitation. "To protect people."

They probably had more in common than either of them realized. He'd always been clear on the fact that as an opponent, she wasn't to be underestimated. But she'd also make a formidable friend. If he could get her on his side.

Or maybe she was on his side already. She was on the side of truth, and the truth was with him. Certainly a new way to think about the situation.

She redirected the interview with "Why did you assault Cameron Porter?"

"Alleged assault," the lawyer objected.

She fixed Hunter with a hard look. "Here's the tricky part. You're trying to convince me that finding out your girlfriend was cheating didn't incite you to violence, that you're a man in control of your emotions. But by assaulting Mr. Porter, you've just proved the opposite."

"I shouldn't have gone to the dealership." Easy to see that in hindsight. "But I did, and then I saw the bastard, and in the heat of the moment, I just went for it."

Her eyes narrowed. "Like you went for Cindy in the heat of the moment? Freaking cheater. Just like a woman. Bitch had to die."

"No." Hunter knew what she was doing, pushing him, trying to make him slip. "I would never have hurt Cindy. And I'm sorry about Porter. That won't happen again."

"You claim you didn't know about the cheating when you went back to your place last night."

"I was going to propose," he said through his teeth. Flores had found the ring in his pocket. She had to know what he'd been planning.

"We have a witness who says she told you about Cindy's infidelity at your brother's house, and you stormed off directly after."

"What witness?" Then it clicked. "Dakota." *Shit.*

He tried to remember what the girl had told him. "Look, Dakota was hitting on me." Oh God, he remembered it now. *"Did you think she waited for you all this time?"*

He drew a deep breath. "I thought she was making stuff up in desperation. I forgot it the second I walked away from her."

His mind had been too full of the future he'd been planning. He simply hadn't allowed reality to intrude into his fantasy. Then he'd walked into his apartment and, in a split second, reality had exploded in his life like a land mine, tore his dreams apart, left him in pieces.

Officer Flores watched him. "Have you ever had a sexual relationship with Dakota Riley?"

"No. Jesus. She's a kid."

Flores measured him up for several seconds. "Are you going to go near Porter again?"

Hunter rubbed his sore knuckles. He would say it as many times as he had to. "No. I regret doing it the first time."

The burst of violence hadn't fixed anything, hadn't brought Cindy back. He'd just made everything worse. "I'm not even really jealous of him anymore. I swear."

All the frustration and anger over Cindy's death had exploded in his head earlier. But the truth was, he was angrier at himself than anyone else. He should have checked his phone earlier, should have driven back to the apartment sooner. "I'm done with Porter. If Cindy wanted him instead of me… Look, it's not his fault. I'm not going to go after him again."

"Are you sure? Because the judge is going to ask my opinion before he sets bail."

"I give you my word." He held her gaze. "Are you going to look at Porter for the murder?"

"I'm going to fully pursue all avenues of investigation."

Leila brought in their lunch, enough for the lawyer too. Officer Flores kept up with the questioning while they ate, circling mostly around the murder, even if Hunter was technically in for assault at the moment. To be fair, the two were connected.

They went over the timeline again. Where he'd been, at what time, from the moment he'd gotten off the plane in Philly. Then his relationship with Cindy. How much did they talk, what they talked about. Did they fight?

His lawyer added some halfhearted objections, but he didn't have much to do. Officer Flores kept the interview reasonable and professional. She might be on her first homicide investigation, but she was doing a good job.

Which earned Hunter's grudging respect. He appreciated her competence. He also appreciated her long legs and dangerous curves. But she *was* investigating him for murder. Fantasizing about the woman naked was stupid. And he'd just promised her that he would smarten up. So he was going to cut back on the fantasizing part. Probably.

* * *

Gabi had Sunday off, but she went to talk to Cameron Porter's neighbors anyway. Court wouldn't be in session until Monday, so Hunter would have to sit out the weekend in holding while he waited for his bail hearing. In the meanwhile, she had plenty to investigate. She didn't drag Mike in on his day off. He needed to rest and get over his stomach bug.

Mike had already interviewed Cindy's coworkers. Shocked by her murder, they'd all told him the same thing: Cindy was a nice person and a good teacher. They all knew she was going out with Hunter, but nobody was aware of her seeing anybody else.

Since Cindy's coworkers yielded no clues, Gabi hoped Cameron Porter's neighbors would have something for her.

Mini mansions lined up one after the other in the fancy development. Nobody had a bad thing to say about Porter, but they didn't have a good thing to say about him either. They knew about his relationship with Mandy Heinz. Nobody knew about Cindy Simme. He'd been able to keep that relationship a secret.

On the night in question, two of the neighbors remembered him being home. They remembered the lights on, his BMW in the driveway. One woman—big lips, big boobs, big diamonds—recalled Cameron Porter taking out the trash just before seven, at the same time when she let her purse dog out to tinkle.

Gabi crossed Cameron Porter off her list with a little

disappointment. He'd had excellent potential. Part of her had wanted Porter to be the perpetrator. She didn't want Hunter to be the bad guy in this. And not just because it'd be easier for her if she didn't have to arrest her boss's brother for murder.

She liked that Hunter had admitted being stupid about Porter. It was a hopeful sign for a man when he could admit being wrong. Tony never had. Not even when he'd been caught red-handed with bribes, not when all the other allegations had poured in.

Gabi drove out of the development but pulled into a strip mall parking lot to think for a minute. Most murders were committed over love or money. With all the cheating going on, Gabi was betting on love in this case. A crime of passion, in a way, murder over love and betrayal.

Porter was out. Hunter was still on the list. She had enough circumstantial evidence to put a case together against him. But the more time she spent with him, the more her instincts said he wasn't the type to shoot a pregnant woman in the head. He was already under arrest for assault. He wasn't going anywhere. She wanted to wait for more proof, one way or the other.

Hunter-Cindy-Porter. Then Gabi thought, *Mandy Heinz.* Mandy was linked to this too. Maybe she found out that Cindy was having an affair with her fiancé.

Gabi called in to Leila. "I need an address for Mandy Heinz, daughter of the guy who owns the used-car dealership, Charlie's." And then something else occurred to her. "Do you know Charlie's Subs?" According to her file, Cindy had worked there before becoming a kindergarten teacher. "Is it the same Charlie?"

"Yep. Old man Heinz owns a bunch of places." Leila paused, then rattled off the Heinz mansion's address.

Okay, so the victim worked for the father of the woman whose fiancée she was sleeping with. Did that mean anything? Didn't have to. Small town—few job opportunities. And Heinz had a number of businesses.

Gabi drove to the old estate in the middle of twenty acres of parklike setting, where Mandy lived with her parents. The young woman was home but heading out to a charity meeting, something about a steeplechase.

Impeccably dressed in supple leather riding boots, designer pants that hugged her lean figure, and a matching brown leather jacket,

Mandy Heinz was nothing but grace and manners. If Gabi's unexpected visit was an inconvenience to her schedule, Mandy didn't show any hint of it.

Instead, she called for the help and asked for tea to be served in the orangery. Gabi followed her to a fancy greenhouse attached to the back of the mansion where the Heinz's overwintered their lemon and orange trees.

"I love having tea in here." Mandy smiled with true pleasure and a glint of girlish excitement in her sparkling blue eyes. "Makes me feel like I'm on a picnic in Italy."

The greenhouse was heated just enough so they could take their coats off and be comfortable, but the temperature lingered several degrees below that of the house. To imitate what the Mediterranean would feel like in winter, Gabi suspected. They had to keep those trees happy.

The silverware was real silver, the china something her neighbor Doris would have had heart palpitations over. The napkins were fabric. Which, as far as Gabi was concerned, defied all logic and practicality.

For a moment, she felt like she should be wearing white gloves and a fancy hat. Then she tugged her uniform straight and reminded herself that she was here in an official capacity.

"I need to ask a few questions, if you don't mind. I won't take up a lot of your time."

"It's about Cindy Simme, isn't it?" Mandy's smile never left her face, but a flash of distress came into her blue eyes.

Gabi stirred her tea. "Did you know her?"

"Just by sight. We weren't friends."

"Did you go to school together?"

"I didn't go to school here. I went to Villa Maria Academy."

Private school all the way. "When was the last time you saw her?"

"At the decorating of the gazebo on Broslin Square three weeks ago. I'm on the committee that raises funds for town decorations for the various holidays. Cindy and some of the mothers were out with her kindergarten students to help. They do that every year before Christmas. Some of the elementary school classes too, depending on their teachers."

"Did you talk to her?"

Mandy sipped her tea, swallowed slowly. "I only stopped by for a few minutes to make sure everything was going as planned. She was busy supervising the children."

Gabi hesitated, not sure how to word the rest of her questions.

Mandy preempted by asking, "Are you here to ask me about my fiancé's friendship with Cindy?" Her voice barely trembled on the word "friendship."

"Were they friends?"

Mandy sipped again. "You tell me."

Gabi neither denied nor confirmed. "Do you know if Cindy had any enemies?"

"I didn't know her well enough to answer that question." She paused. "If she had any enemies, I wasn't one of them, if that's what you're asking."

"Not everyone would be so understanding about her fiancé's friendship with another woman."

Mandy's face morphed into a careful mask. "Cameron suits me. My father is ready to retire. He wants his businesses to stay in the family. He's what you call a micromanager, has to constantly check on everything. He's not going to be able to let go unless he has someone he thinks can fully handle things. Cameron is the most effective manager we've had. He could take over all the businesses, not just the dealership, and make them all successful."

"And you?"

"If my husband handles the business, I'll be free to pursue my own interests."

So by marrying Porter, Mandy was buying her own freedom in a roundabout way. Her father could have chosen worse for her. She understood that and accepted it. They would have a prenup that'd make Porter toe the line. She'd have control.

Gabi didn't pretend that she completely got how these things worked in high society, but if she was looking for a crime of passion, she didn't find much passion here. It was almost as if Mandy thought herself too civilized for that kind of thing.

The woman's discreetly tinted lips twisted. "Look, all his life, all my father ever wanted was a son. He's old-fashioned that way. Now he gets his son, and I will no longer have to feel the weight of his disappointment that I wasn't born a boy. I can't become his son, but I can give him a son. And then everybody will be happy."

Gabi thought how, looking at the mansion from the outside, she'd pictured the family to be just as grand and perfect as the house. But they were almost as dysfunctional as her own had been in the bowels of Philly.

"Were you at Hunter Bing's party Friday night?"

Mandy's name wasn't on the list, but Gabi couldn't be sure that the list was complete. She'd gotten the impression that people were coming and going.

A fond smile turned up Mandy's lips. "I was at the Delaware Opera with my mother and two of her friends. *Aida*. Outstanding performance."

"Is Mrs. Heinz home by any chance?"

"Up in New York with my father. They're visiting an old friend. I don't expect them back until Monday night, probably pretty late."

Gabi watched her for a moment or two, letting her instincts kick in, listening to what they had to say.

Mandy Heinz was too soft-spoken, too controlled, too polite for a crime of passion. Too smart. She wouldn't risk the life she had just to remove Cindy Simme from her path. She would have found a more sophisticated way than murder to deal with a rival. If, in fact, that rival had bothered her, which didn't seem to be the case.

Gabi thanked her for her time and got up to leave.

As they walked out, Mandy stepped into a spacious sitting room that opened from the main foyer. "Let me grab my purse."

Gabi peeked in after her and checked out the huge fireplace, the expensive, chunky, masculine furniture. An ornate mahogany gun cabinet stood in the corner with at least a dozen gleaming hunting rifles. Hunting trophies decorated the walls, everything from wild turkey and deer to a brown bear showing some serious teeth, interspersed with portraits of military men from Napoleon to General Washington.

Mandy flashed an indulgent smile. "My father's little man cave."

They walked out of the house together.

Hunter-Cindy-Porter-Mandy. Gabi reconsidered the love square as she got into her car.

Porter had alibied out, and Mandy would alibi out too. Hunter Bing was back to being the sole suspect, with the trifecta of motive, means, and opportunity—a perfect package.

Then the grinding gears in Gabi's brain spit out another name: *Charlie Heinz.*

She perked up behind the wheel. Heinz had his little empire at stake. He'd handpicked his successor, and his very accommodating daughter had gone along with the choice. Then he found out that Porter was having an affair. Heinz might have taken that as an insult to his daughter, an insult to himself. Heinz had plans for Porter. Maybe the old man wasn't the type who put up with cracks in his plans.

And since Cindy had worked for Heinz in the past, she knew him. He could have followed her to Hunter's apartment. If he showed up at the door with some excuse, she would have let him in.

Gabi started up the car and headed down the long driveway. As soon as Charlie Heinz got back from New York, she was coming back to talk to him.

Chapter Eleven

Hunter caught his first lucky break on Monday morning. The judge in West Chester had an opening in his schedule if they could get there in the next thirty minutes for the arraignment. Officer Flores drove Hunter over, told the judge he wasn't considered a flight risk, which kept the bail manageable. The lawyer took care of the paperwork.

Hunter thanked his lawyer for his help, then followed Flores across the street to the parking garage. She'd offered him a ride back since he needed to pick up his wallet and phone from the station.

"Thank you for speaking up for me in front of the judge."

She turned, cool gaze, hot curves, all long legs. The winter sunlight revealed highlights in her dark chocolate hair. The way she looked in her uniform, a couple of businessmen passing by were taking a second look, and a third.

She didn't seem to notice. "Just to be clear, I didn't speak up for you because you're my boss's brother."

"Never thought that for a second."

"If you were anyone else, I would have done the same."

He nodded. He was beginning to see why his brother had hired her. Being above reproach in her conduct was important to her. She had clear ideas on what was appropriate and inappropriate, and she kept on the right side of the line.

He was starting to like her, which made him feel guilty as hell, unfaithful to Cindy, which was nuts in a way. He didn't know how to feel about Cindy. The way it looked, his relationship with her had been in his head for the past eight months. She'd moved on without remembering to tell him.

"I'm just saying that I appreciate that you can take an unbiased view in the assault case, even when you're still looking at me in connection with murder. Which I didn't do. Anyway, I appreciate the fairness," he told Gabi.

"Then you're welcome." She pushed the call button for the parking garage's elevator. "By the way, Cameron Porter alibied out. I'm only telling you this so you don't get it in your head to pay him another visit. If you come within a hundred feet of him, you're going to see my fair nature disappear."

Porter alibied out. Hunter waited for more, but she stayed silent.

"When can I have my apartment back?"

She unlocked the car. "I need to check with the DA first, make sure he has everything he needs. If he's set, I don't have a problem with releasing the crime scene."

He got in next to her and thought about the way the apartment had been when he'd last seen it, tried to imagine what would be waiting for him. He made a mental list of all the things he'd need to do.

She turned on the radio. Christmas music filled the car. She turned it off with a groan.

"It's not going to turn you into an elf if you listen," he promised and liked the smile that played at the corner of her lips, wiggling the small mole that kept drawing his attention.

She glanced at him. "Do you believe in Christmas?"

"I do," he said without hesitation.

"Even after all you've seen and done overseas?"

"Especially because of that. Do you?"

"Believe in Christmas?" She kept her attention on the traffic, merged. "I don't know. I've never really seen it beyond the commercial part. Where I'm from, Christmas was basically hokey window displays."

"That's just sad."

"My mother used to say Christmas was a sucker's game."

Which made him really wonder about her mother. "Did you like living in Philly?"

"It's where I belong."

Was there a note of hesitation in her voice? He wasn't sure. "Why?"

"I was born there. I can relate to it. I learned how to be a cop there."

"Was it a family thing?" Mike was fourth-generation cop. Some families were like that. Same with the military.

93

But she gave a bitter laugh at his suggestion. "I learned from a tough Philly cop, Carmen Morales. She taught me the rules."

"What rules?"

"Rule #1: Trust no one. Rule #2: Miss nothing. Rule #3: Reveal nothing. Rule #4: Question everything. Rule #5: Eye on the clock. Rule #6: Get lucky. Rule #7: Trust your instincts."

Good rules to live by. "The army has rules too."

"I bet."

She was usually as tightly wound as the strict bun at her nape, but now her posture relaxed. She obviously missed her district and the people she'd worked with. He could relate. During his twelve years in the army, he'd missed Broslin every day.

And now he missed the guys he'd served with, the brotherhood, the camaraderie.

"Can I take you to lunch?" He was hungry.

"No." The response came without hesitation.

"You're giving me a ride."

"Doing my job."

"I'm trying to get you to like me. I think the person who's investigating me for murder should get to know me better."

"Because to know you is to like you?"

He grinned.

She shook her head. "You know what kind of people cops like?"

He waited.

"People who stay out of trouble," she told him.

"Believe me, going forward, that's on top of my to-do list."

She drove in silence for a while before saying, "Tell me about Cindy."

He drew a deep breath, his light mood disappearing. "Sweet. Kind. Petite little thing. You looked at her, and you just wanted to save her."

"From what?"

He thought. "I don't know. But she brought out the protective instincts. She wouldn't have hurt a fly. She loved little kids. Loved her job. Patient." She'd been patient with him, waiting without complaining. Or so he'd thought. He shook his head. "Maybe I didn't know her as well as I thought I did."

"How did you meet?"

"At a party. She just finished college. I was home on leave. We were both celebrating."

"Was she a party girl?"

"No. Her friends dragged her out. Later, when we were seeing each other, when I was on leave, we mostly stayed in. She was always working on some special project for the kids. I got good with the glue gun, helping her."

"Sounds sweet as homemade apple pie."

"She was. And she could bake them too."

Flores waited several beats. "So how do Porter and the pregnancy come into this picture?"

Beat him. "Is it possible to have a relationship with someone and not know them at all?" When he wasn't grieving, he was angry. When he wasn't angry, he was feeling stupid for not knowing somehow that Cindy hadn't been happy.

"It's possible. Believe me," Flores said with feeling.

She sounded like she was talking from personal experience.

"You have quite an army record," she said out of nowhere, maybe to turn the conversation from a topic that was hitting too close to her.

"I liked the army. For the most part, I think I was good at it."

"Good shot?"

"Best in my unit." No reason to lie. And she probably had his full army record already.

"The killer has to be a hell of a good shot," she said. "Someone untrained making a shot like that, chances are one in a million. People who know their way around guns aim at center mass. With a big target, they'd have a good chance of success. Not too many shooters can pull off a bullet between the eyes." Her gaze cut to him. "Could you?"

He'd committed to going with the truth, so what the hell. "Probably."

She didn't say anything for a while, so he felt compelled to add, "But I didn't." He rubbed a hand over his scar. He'd gone down in a barrage of bullets that day. He'd fired off his entire magazine.

He turned to Flores. "You know how you have cop rules? Like I said, the army has rules too. One of them is, anything worth shooting is worth shooting twice. At the very least, double tap. One to the head, one to the heart. But mostly, we have the rifles. We don't worry about counting bullets. Ammo is cheap. Life is expensive."

She thought on that for a few seconds. "You want me to look for someone who's a good shot but not army trained."

He gave her the truth, once again. "As long as you're not investigating *me*, I'm happy."

She snorted. Thought some more. "One shot, people in the building would think it's a car backfiring. A barrage of bullets, and more people than Doris would have come investigating. Maybe the guy is a good shot, *and* smart." She looked at him again.

"But just because I'm a good shot, and smart, not to mention devilishly good-looking, it doesn't mean I'm him."

That finally got an actual laugh from her. He found that he liked the sound of her heartfelt laughter.

"Watch out with that ego," she said as she pulled up in front of the station. "Carrying around something that large could cause spinal injury."

After he retrieved his wallet and cell phone, Officer Smart Mouth offered to drop him off at his brother's place.

He was going to ask her in for a cup of coffee, but her radio went off, and she drove away to put the fear of God into whatever unsuspecting criminal crossed her path next. Hunter almost felt sorry for the poor bastard.

Only Sophie was at home at the log cabin, standing by the stove when Hunter walked in. The dogs rushed to greet him, outdoing each other in begging for ear scratching, which he handed out freely. The orange cat ignored him from a distance.

"How did it go?" Sophie asked cautiously as she stirred something.

"I'm out on bail."

"Who was the judge?"

"Judge Gardner."

She nodded. "He knows your brother. I think they're on good terms."

Hunter didn't want to think about his brother. Ethan had stopped by to check on him several times over the weekend, never missed a chance to chew him out for messing with Porter. He'd been pissed. Hunter had been glad they had the bars between them.

Sophie turned off the gas, then moved over to the coffee pot, made them each a cup, brought it over to the island, and sat next to him. "Any new developments in Cindy's case?"

Hunter let his shoulders slump. Thinking about the developments felt like a punch in the gut. "She was pregnant. Eight weeks. She was having an affair with Cameron Porter."

Sophie choked on her coffee, set the mug down, and stared at him, her eyes filled with compassion. "Do you think he killed her?"

"He has an alibi."

Sophie slid off her chair and hugged him hard and long. "Cindy didn't know what she had in you." She pulled back. "You didn't deserve to be betrayed. I'm sure you're angry at her. And grieving at the same time. That has to be confusing."

"I'm not angry at her," he said without thinking, then paused. Okay, that was new. "I *was* angry when I first found out about Porter."

Angry enough to go and beat up the guy. Or maybe that was just about his general frustration over his helplessness in the case. But the fury had drained out of him with the scuffle. He was no longer mad. And he wasn't inconsolable with grief either. He mourned Cindy, but not as a man would mourn the woman who was the other half of his soul.

"I'm not sure if I was ever truly in love with her," he surprised himself by saying.

Sophie raised her eyebrows as she sat back on her chair.

He rubbed his hand over his face. "Maybe I was just in love with the idea of coming home to someone and starting a family. Lonely soldiers are always talking about coming home and what we'd do when we got here."

He drew a slow breath. "I was never here for her. I can't blame her for looking for love from someone else."

"She had a right to love anybody she wanted, but she should have told you as soon as her feelings changed." Sophie sat there next to him, a comforting presence, not a hint of judgment.

"My brother is lucky to have you," he told her. "When I look at him look at you, that's love. I don't think I ever looked at Cindy that way."

"You'll find the right woman." She patted his knee.

"Maybe I'm not the kind of a man who can do the love thing."

"You become that kind of a man when you find the right woman." Sophie went back to the stove, poured half the chicken soup into a container. "I'm taking this over to Ashley. Plenty more left. Help yourself."

"Tell Jack I said congratulations," Hunter said. "I hope baby and mom are okay." Then he added, "Boy or girl?"

"Girl. They're doing really well. Still picking a name. The big sister, Maddie, wants either Cinderella or Belle." She grinned. "I don't think you'd recognize Jack. He turned into a puddle of mush."

After Sophie left, Hunter showered and shaved, borrowed some fresh clothes from Bing. He was padding down the stairs when his phone rang.

J.T. was on the other end. "Yo, bro. How is it going?"

"Just got out of jail."

"Drunk and disorderly? Celebrating your homecoming?"

"Mostly just disorderly. What's up in Tennessee?"

J.T. grunted. "Lost the job, about to lose the apartment. It's a giant clusterfuck. I'm about to move back with my parents. What am I, twelve?" He sounded glum, the opposite of the goofy kid he'd been before his captivity.

"It's temporary," Hunter told him. "If it makes you feel better, I'm staying with my brother."

J.T. paused before saying, "I'm thinking about moving up to Alaska. Work on the oil pipeline, ice road trucker, whatever. I could drive up there."

"Stop in on the way. We'll catch up," Hunter offered, unsure whether a state that was dark for three months every winter was the right place for someone who was depressed. "Alaska will be different from Tennessee."

"I like the sound of different. I ain't scared of grizzly bears."

"Says the guy who never met one."

"You got me there."

They shot the breeze for a while, mostly Hunter trying to cheer J.T. up. He didn't say anything about Cindy. J.T. had enough troubles; he didn't need anyone dumping more bad news on him.

After they hung up, Hunter's phone rang again. Officer Sexy Voice.

"Your apartment has been released. You're free to go back there."

All business as always. He tried to picture what kind of man she'd go out with. Someone tough as nails. She was a strong woman, she wouldn't put up with a weak man for a day.

"Thank you." He used to think that she was a hard-ass cop, but that wasn't it. She pushed when she needed to, but she hadn't gone after him nearly as badly as she could have. She was keeping an open mind, hadn't arrested him yet for the murder. She'd spoken up for him with the judge on the assault case. Because of her, he was out on bail and could sleep at his own place tonight. "I appreciate the help."

"I'd appreciate a confession," she deadpanned on the other end.

"Not going to happen."

"I didn't think so."

"Do you really think I killed Cindy?" For some reason, it mattered.

"Rule #3: *Reveal nothing*." Then she asked, "Do you need contact info for a crime scene remediation company?"

He knew what that was, people who cleaned up after murders or when somebody died at home and wasn't found for a while. "My brother should have it."

"I'm sure he does. You have a good day." She hung up on him.

She was probably busy. Hopefully busy investigating Cindy's murder and clearing him.

Since Sophie's chicken soup smelled delicious, he had a bowl of that, then let the dogs out and gave them fresh water before he walked across the fields to the construction site. The workers were mostly local boys. He knew a couple, caught a ride into town with Howie Peters.

Howie barely looked at him, broke out in a sweat trying to come up with something to say that didn't involve Cindy or the murder investigation. Too late, Hunter remembered that Howie and Cindy had gone to school together, been friends.

"How soon do you think the construction will be finished?" he asked the guy to lead the conversation to something that would set Howie at ease.

"We have to be out of here in four months. That's the final deadline. The crew has another project right after this in Wilmington." He shrugged. "We'll make it. We're on schedule."

Howie rambled nervously about the economy and the slowing of the construction business, how a hard winter was predicted that would make everything even worse.

Hunter appreciated the ride, but he was glad when it was over.

The yellow police tape was still up over his apartment door. He ripped it off and walked inside. Then the smell hit him, and he had to cover his nose with his hand.

The aftermath of a massacre. Images flooded his mind from his first two tours when his unit had been in Afghanistan to fight, unlike the peacekeeping mission they'd been tasked with his last tour. God, he was sick of blood.

He breathed through his mouth as he went through and opened all the windows, then stood in the cold, bracing air rushing into his apartment. After a few minutes, he could breathe a little easier. But he went outside to call his brother.

"I'm at the apartment. It's been released."

A moment of silence came through the line. "You should have said something." Ethan's voice held concern. "I wanted to go with you. Want me to come over?"

"It's not like I haven't seen blood before. I'm thinking about gathering up everything and taking it out to the dump in the back of the pickup. I don't want the crime scene cleaners. I can handle it."

"You need a special license to transport hazardous materials." Ethan switched to his cop tone. "And they need to be disposed of properly as hazardous waste."

Because nothing could ever be simple. "It's just blood."

"All bodily fluids and human tissue are classified by law as hazardous waste. I'm going to text you a number. Call it. They'll be in and out in a couple of hours."

Hunter thought about the conditions inside, the fact that a team could get the job done twice as fast as he could alone, the fact that he didn't want to get into any more trouble with the law. "Fine. Okay."

He must have caught the remediation crew on a slow day, because they were there in an hour, three men and a woman, coming from Philly. They acted like they were all family. They were professional, polite, fast.

The youngest guy, in his early twenties, looked excited to be there, maybe his first time. When he casually mentioned to Hunter that they had putty knives in the toolbox because brain matter hardened to the consistency of cement after a couple of days, Hunter told them to call him when they were done and drove over to the gas station to grab himself a drink.

He sat in his pickup and thought about where he was in his life. The murder case didn't look good. The forty-eight-hour mark had come and gone, and he was still the only suspect. He hadn't been arrested for the murder, but he figured he was close to it.

Flores was a good cop, but this was her first murder case. She'd want to produce results. And she had only Hunter.

Circumstantial evidence, but plenty of that. His gun, his apartment, his girlfriend. His *cheating* girlfriend. And he could have been there at the time of the murder. The DA would say he had been.

And what alternative could the defense attorney offer?

None. No other suspects.

Hunter finished his soda and chucked the empty bottle to the back. He'd just spent his weekend in a cell. He couldn't imagine being locked up for twenty years.

Flores had her cop rules, but the army had rules too. First rule: Always have a plan. Second rule: Always have a plan B.

His original plan had been to cooperate and wait for the truth to set him free. That hadn't happened so far. He needed to come up with a plan B.

Run, he thought, as much as he'd hate to do that to his brother. He could go to Alaska with J.T. At the moment, that sounded pretty good compared to staying and taking his chances.

Question was, how much did he trust Flores? Did he trust her to find him justice?

Chapter Twelve

Gabi took care of a small fender bender she'd been called to, filed her report, then shrugged into her coat once again and drove to Captain Bing's place. Nobody seemed to be at home, but she hadn't come to visit. She wanted to time the drive from the farm to Hunter's apartment, at about the same time that Hunter had done it.

She had double shift today. She didn't mind. She wanted to progress her murder investigation.

On the first run, she drove leisurely from the Bing homestead to the apartment building and came up with twenty-two minutes. On the second run, she raced as fast as traffic would allow and was five minutes faster.

Next, she timed how long it took to get out of the car, lock it, and walk to Hunter's door. Two minutes flat, if she hurried.

Gabi walked up a floor next and knocked on Doris's door.

Her neighbor greeted her with a sincere smile and offered a cup of tea.

"Thanks. Maybe later. I was wondering if I could talk you into an experiment," Gabi said. "Would you mind walking down to Hunter's place and let me time it?"

Interest sparked in Doris's eyes. "Of course not. I know what you mean. Come in. We need to start in the bedroom. You want to start with me putting on my robe and my slippers."

She led the way and reenacted the whole incident, even got into bed and turned on the TV.

"So I heard the shot." She nodded toward the TV. "I waited a bit to see what Sherlock and Watson had to say about that. Then I turned off the telly to see if maybe the shot came from somewhere else. Then I convinced myself that it did."

She pressed her lips together for a moment. "I didn't mention this before, but my Chester, God bless his soul, had some friends who took their own lives after they returned from the service. Once that popped into my head, I couldn't just stay up here watching Sherlock as if nothing had happened. I had to go and check."

She slipped out of bed and tugged on her robe and slippers, shuffled through the apartment, took the time to lock the door behind her.

Gabi timed everything. She followed the old woman down the hallway. Two minutes passed between when Doris had "heard the shot" and reached the top of the stairs. But things slowed down at this stage. Doris had to hold on to the railing. She had to stop to steady herself a couple of times.

"Dratted blood pressure." She pursed her lips. "Stairs make me dizzy."

Once downstairs, she didn't walk as fast as before. "I slowed down a bit here. I was wondering if I misheard. If I was sticking my nose into something I shouldn't. I was thinking it's not very polite to knock on someone's door to ask if he might have tried to shoot himself, is it?"

Doris's trip to Hunter's door clocked in at a full seven minutes.

"Are you sure you didn't see anyone coming or going?" Gabi asked.

Doris sighed. "My memory is so bad these days, I feel as if my mental notes are written with invisible ink. But I do remember this. The gunshot shook me up, you know, brought things into focus."

Gabi helped her neighbor back upstairs and promised to come over for tea later. First, she wanted to work a little more on the case.

The timeline didn't add up. She didn't think Hunter had enough time to commit murder. According to her calculations, Doris had just missed Hunter in the hallway. He'd been maybe a minute or two ahead of her.

But since everything turned around on minutes, Gabi couldn't be sure. She was swallowing her frustration over that, heading to her car in the parking lot, when she glimpsed a spark of light in the bushes next to the building. It wasn't seven p.m. yet, but dark already this time of the year, otherwise she wouldn't have noticed that small dot of light.

When she reached within three or four feet, she could smell the pot, could see two bodies moving in the brush.

"Police," she called out. "Come out with your hands in the air."

She heard some furious swearing, and the dot of light disappeared. A teenage boy, eighteen or so, stepped out first. He stood so he would shield the girl—about the same age, short blonde hair, glasses, high school sweater—hiding behind him.

"We were just talking. Weren't doing anything," the boy protested.

Gabi watched the girl, who wouldn't meet her eyes. "So I'm not going to find a half-smoked joint if I check behind those bushes?"

The girl's face crumpled. "You can't tell my parents. Please. They'll kill me."

"One joint," the boy begged. "Pot isn't even illegal now in most states."

Some states. But Gabi didn't correct him. She waved them off. "Don't do it again." She wasn't going to bust them and mess their lives up for half a joint.

As they made grateful promises, her phone buzzed. She checked it. The low-battery warning blinked right above the time: 6:55.

"Hey!" She stepped after the kids. "Come back here."

They walked with shoulders dropped, chins down, as if they were going to their execution.

"Just a question." She relaxed her body language to set them at ease, even as excitement rushed through her. "Do you come out here a lot?"

The girl looked at her feet. "Just during the week. When Tommy gets home from his after-school job at the Pizza Palace, I tell my parents that I'm going down to get the mail, and I hang out with him a little."

"Were you here last Friday?"

"We didn't see anything about the murder," the girl said immediately.

Her boyfriend shifted on his feet.

Gabi focused her full attention on him. "How about you, Tommy?"

"Nuthin." He fidgeted.

"Maybe I should take you two in, then we could talk under more comfortable circumstances. I don't want you to rush. I want you to have time to think."

The kid's face turned red.

Gabi softened her voice. "If you saw something, it'd be best if you told me. A murder investigation is kind of a big deal. It's not something you'd want to mess with."

"I didn't see anyone strange, I swear." Tommy hesitated. "I think I might have heard the gunshot."

Gabi stilled. "Are you sure?"

The kid shrugged. "We were kissing. I just thought a car backfired." He shrugged again, miserably. "But when I heard that a woman was killed, it made me wonder. You know?"

His girlfriend's eyes went wide. "I didn't hear anything."

"Did you see anyone leave right after the shot?" Gabi asked Tommy.

"No. We were kind of saying good-bye at that point. I would have seen if anyone ran down the stairs. We look around good before we come out."

Made sense. They wouldn't want to be discovered.

Gabi glanced toward the building. So nobody came through the front. The killer most likely left through the emergency exit. And nobody had been out there, in the dark, windy alley, to see.

"Did you see anyone go in?"

This time, the girl spoke first. "A soldier guy. He wore camouflage pants. I think he lives in the basement. I think the woman who was shot was his girlfriend or something."

Tommy was nodding. "He came maybe two minutes after that pop."

"After? You sure?"

"Yeah. Hundred percent."

Exasperation cut through Gabi. "Why wouldn't you say something when the police went from door to door?"

The girl's eyes begged for understanding. "If my parents found out that I was out here with Tommy, I would be like grounded forever."

Gabi stifled a groan. A teenager's degree of self-involvement could not be underestimated. Hunter might have been arrested, even gone to prison, all so this one wouldn't get grounded.

All the sympathy she had for the star-crossed lovers evaporated on the spot. "I'm going to need the both of you to come in with your parents and make an official statement." She pulled out her notebook. "Full names and apartment numbers."

The kids reluctantly gave that information, but protested having to go in.

Gabi raised her index finger to quiet them. "The sooner the better. I'm heading back to the station right now. If you don't come clean to your parents and come in within the hour, I'm coming back. One way or the other, we'll be making this official."

* * *

Hunter drove around town and thought about Cindy, tried to see their relationship from her side, what it must have been like to be left behind, always waiting.

He'd had this rosy mental picture of coming home, what their lives were going to be together. But those were just a blind man's dreams. He'd been blind all these years as far as she'd been concerned.

"I'm sorry." He said the words out loud in case her spirit was hanging around. "I forgive you whatever needs forgiving. And I'm sorry too."

The dark weight in his chest eased a little.

Somehow he ended up by the library, and on impulse, he went in, picked up an armful of books, mostly sci-fi and a techno thriller. He needed something to occupy his mind, and he preferred reading to watching TV. Most of the prime-time shows were about crime and violence, and the news was the same. He'd had enough of that for a while.

Tonight, he was in the mood for peace.

He also stopped by the town's only department store and picked up two pillows and a new comforter, new sheets. The boxed-up Christmas cookies by the register looked good. He tossed a couple into the cart.

To hell with running away. For one, his brother would kill him. Two, he was pretty sure Flores would track him down anyway. That thought tugged up the corner of his lips for some reason.

While he waited in the checkout line, the remediation people called to let him know they were finished. A lot faster than he could have done the job by himself. He was grateful that his brother had talked sense into him.

When Hunter got back, the cleaners walked him through the apartment to make sure that everything had been done to his satisfaction, then the small crew left.

His windows were still open, the strong scent of disinfectant in the air. His dresser had been dragged out to the living room. His bedroom was empty—no bed, no nightstands, no lamps that used to sit on the nightstands. Even the carpet had been ripped up, including the padding, and new plywood had been put down in patches.

He'd thought they would take the sheets, probably the mattress and just shampoo the carpet. But the cleaning crew had done a lot more than he'd expected. He appreciated that. He didn't want to come face-to-face with a blood splatter when he least expected it.

That thought brought another. Who cleaned up the blood *he* had left behind? He'd spilled enemy blood on the rocky Afghan soil. Who'd scrubbed up the blood of that Afghan woman in the village?

Guilt tore through him, restlessness filling his body. He pushed the dresser against the wall in the living room so he wouldn't bump into it coming and going, but then he had nothing else to do after that.

He called his brother. "How do you feel about me replacing the carpet in the apartment?"

"I have people to do that."

"I need something to occupy my time," Hunter said quietly.

A moment passed. "Fine. Make sure you get a receipt. I'll reimburse you later."

After they hung up, Hunter closed his windows, then searched for carpet stores on the Internet, found one in West Chester that was running a sale. He could drive over tomorrow and order what he needed. He thought about picking up a bed at the same time. Or not. He could go without a bed for a night or two, sleep on the couch. No sense in setting up a bed if he'd just have to disassemble it and drag it out of the bedroom to install the carpet when that came in.

He showered, dropped to the couch, and picked up a book, but couldn't get into it. He wondered what Officer Flores was doing upstairs. Then he decided to go up and see. He'd seen her name on her mailbox, so he knew her apartment number.

Standing in front of her unit, he almost changed his mind. Then he ended up knocking.

She answered the door barefoot, in exercise shorts and a tight top with spaghetti straps. His gaze ran up her long legs, over her trim torso, tripped over her generous breasts, then settled on the fine sheen of sweat on her chest. He'd probably interrupted her nightly exercise routine.

He'd only ever seen her in uniform before. The intense wave of lust caught him off guard. After the day he'd had, lust was the last emotion he'd expected to have to deal with.

"I stopped by earlier," she said. "You weren't home. I was going to walk down again later. We have two witnesses who can put your arrival at the apartment building *after* the gunshot."

"Yeah?" He felt his face split in half with a smile. "For real?"

"For real."

He reached for her without thinking, picked her up, and swung her around in the hallway. He might have whooped.

Then he caught himself and set her down. "Sorry."

She raised an eyebrow, but she was smiling as she shook her head. "Forgiven. This once. Don't do it again." She watched him for a second. "How are things downstairs?"

* * *

As the smile immediately disappeared from his face, Gabi could have kicked herself for asking. It had been the first time she'd seen Hunter happy.

He's no longer a suspect.

She didn't want to analyze why she liked that idea so much. She stepped back. "Want to come in?"

He immediately stepped forward.

Maybe he needed to get out of his own place for a while. As a soldier, he was probably used to blood, but a death this personal still had to be difficult. She wasn't sure she'd want to sleep in that apartment if she was in his place.

She moved to her couch and grabbed her Broslin PD T-shirt from the back, pulled it on, deliberated for a moment if tonight was the night to break her own rules. What the hell.

"I was about to toss some frozen burritos in the oven. Want some?"

His stomach growled. "That'd be great." A glint came into his mocha eyes. "You know, I could grow to like you, Officer Flores."

"For frozen burritos?" She bit back a smile. "Anyone ever tell you, you shouldn't fling around affection so cheaply?"

The glint remained. "Do you prefer when guys play hard to get?"

And for some reason, his teasing voice sent butterflies fluttering in her stomach.

Oh, sweet chimichanga, if she looked at Hunter Bing that way for even a second, she deserved to be called stupid. So he was no longer a suspect. But he was still her boss's brother.

She led him into the kitchen. "Word of warning, I'm not much of a cook. I bought the stuff on a closeout sale. Food poisoning isn't completely off the table."

He glanced around, his eyes widening a little when he looked toward her bedroom.

She winced, but resisted the urge to jump and close the door. He was staring at the poster above her bed, an image of Annie Oakley with the quote "I ain't afraid to love a man. I ain't afraid to shoot him either."

He raised a dark eyebrow at her as he turned, his lips twitching.

She so wasn't going to comment. The poster had been a gift from Carmen.

Gabi decided to reroute Hunter's attention by opening the box of frozen burritos, showing him the contents. "See? Nothing fancy."

"I'm used to MREs."

"That's the dried food in the little packets that never go bad, right?"

"Meal Ready to Eat. Basically they dehydrate food into something that looks and tastes like a piece of cardboard. You're supposed to reconstitute it with hot water, but in reality, half the time we're not allowed a fire to avoid enemy detection, so we just chew on the cardboard."

She tried to imagine that as she turned on the oven. "Let's not throw the *cardboard* word around until you taste this."

She dropped four burritos on a cookie sheet and slid them into the heating oven, then set the timer. Next she grabbed some sour cream from the fridge. She put the blue tub on the middle of the table. "Sour cream covers a multitude of sins."

"Amen."

She stepped back to the fridge. "I got water, milk, or soda."

"Soda is good." He looked around again. "How long have you been living here?"

"Six months."

"How do you like it?"

She shrugged. "The lease won't let me install a chin bar in the bedroom door."

"I can talk to the landlord about that," he offered. "Where did you live before this? I mean, which part of the city?"

"Southwest Philly. Twelfth District."

His eyebrows shot up. "Rough neighborhood."

"Some of it."

"How do you like Broslin?"

"Too quiet."

His lips twisted. "I wouldn't mind it a tad quieter."

Right. His homecoming hadn't been the most relaxing. He'd probably expected it to go a lot differently from the way it had, an unexpected murder, then becoming a suspect.

But he was no longer a suspect, and he was in her apartment. He was the first man in her apartment since she'd moved here. Why had she invited him in? Why had he come up? She tried not to read too much into that.

His girlfriend was gone, his brother was busy being a newlywed, his apartment was busted. He was only here because he was lonely. Gabi relaxed. He probably missed the camaraderie of his unit. She still missed her team at the Twelfth.

"So Broslin is not your thing?" he asked.

She shrugged. "When I first got here, I thought all the small-town sweetness looked fake. Almost like a movie set. People kept stopping me on the street to welcome me, and I kept waiting for someone to break script."

He smiled. "I bet the paper ran something about you once your hiring was confirmed. A new cop is big news in a small town. People were probably admonished to make you feel at home."

She shook her head with some amusement. "I would have felt more at home if they shot at me."

Hunter's eyes turned somber as she said that, and she could have kicked herself once again. She was making jokes about being shot? Really? She scrambled for a sharp change of subject.

But before she could think of something, he said, "Thanks again for releasing the apartment. I could stay at my brother's place, but I don't want to interrupt all that loving bliss."

"No problem. The DA had no objections. We got everything we needed."

"It's good to be home. Even under the circumstances." He paused. "I'm putting in new carpet tomorrow. Once I'm done, nobody will be able to tell that anything ever happened there."

But he would never forget, not for a minute, Gabi thought. *How could he?*

He'd held up well after Cindy's death, had stood up to questioning, but tonight there was a touch of vulnerability about him. Gabi wasn't used to fuzzy feelings, but she was seeing him in a different light suddenly. She'd lost enough people, both friends and family, to know that no matter how it happened, that kind of loss was never easy.

To distract him, she grabbed on to the next neutral subject she could think of. "So want to give me some heads-up on the Christmas parade? It's my first small-town Christmas. The sweetness might send me into diabetic shock. I'd feel better if I was prepared."

"We have an outstanding parade. The best." He puffed out his chest. "What do you have in Southwest Philly?"

"Drive-by shootings."

She winced. *Way to go, stupid.* How could she say *shooting* again? She was seriously off her game around Hunter.

But a smile tugged at the corner of his lips. "You're a cop. People like the PD around here. They might even put you on a float."

"Not if I still have my service weapon."

He flashed a full grin. Then, as he watched her, the grin disappeared little by little, and his eyes turned somber. "I thought about running."

"For mayor?"

He held her gaze. "Away."

She stared. "When?"

"Tonight. Before I came home. I didn't want to go to prison for a murder I didn't commit."

She opened her mouth to protest, but he cut her off with "Tell me you've never seen anyone wrongly convicted."

She snapped her mouth shut. "So why didn't you run?" she asked after a second.

The smile he flashed was almost boyish and wickedly attractive. "I decided to trust you, Officer Flores."

She wasn't sure what to do with those words. "That's a hell of a lot of trust for an officer working her first murder case."

"It's not like my life was hanging in the balance or anything," he said in a wry tone.

Then he asked her about her job back in the city, and she shared a couple of stories. Then the oven beeped, and she served dinner. While they ate, she asked Hunter about his time in the service.

Trading war stories was kind of nice, the most dinner entertainment she'd had in a while.

When he finally stood and thanked her for the food, saying good night, she was surprised to realize that she wouldn't mind if he stayed a little longer.

She thought about Hunter as she tried to fall asleep, and thought about the case. Cindy was connected to Hunter, Porter, Mandy, and, in an indirect way, to Charlie Heinz.

Hunter wasn't the killer. She was grateful that her instincts had proven her right on that.

But then who shot Cindy? She had to be missing something. Somebody in this tangle of relationships had to be connected to the murder.

She considered Porter again. Financially, he had the most to gain. By marrying Mandy, he'd be taking over the dealership, then all of Heinz's businesses eventually. Cindy had been in the way. The motive was fantastic, but he *had* been seen at home at the time of the murder. Could the neighbor woman who'd seen him be lying? Could she have seen someone else? But why would someone else be taking out Porter's garbage? And the driveways were close enough together that neighbor would have known if it wasn't him.

Gabi moved on to Mandy once again. Her mother was in NY with her father, but Gabi had called the other two friends who'd been at the opera with them, and they'd confirmed that Mandy had been there the entire evening.

Charlie Heinz, however, had not gone to the opera Friday night. Because he'd had other plans? Gabi wondered what Heinz would do if he found out that his future son-in-law was cheating on his daughter. What if he'd decided that Cindy was jeopardizing his carefully set-up plans for succession?

He was coming back from New York tonight. Gabi was going to see him first thing in the morning.

Chapter Thirteen

Gabi rose early so she could get a good run in before she began her shift. After that, she drove straight to the Heinz mansion. The maid informed her that Mr. Heinz was at his country club.

Gabi drove over, spent twenty minutes arguing that as a police officer, yes, they had to let her in whether Heinz was playing squash or not.

By the time she gained admittance, Heinz had finished his squash match and was having a continental breakfast in the main dining room, at the best table, right in front of the fireplace.

The six-sided dining room overlooked the snow-covered golf course. Floor-to-ceiling windows, wide-plank hardwood flooring, elaborate antique furniture; the paintings on the walls were by famous local artists, even one by Ashley Price Sullivan. A ten-foot Christmas tree towered in the middle, so overdecorated Gabi could barely see the green. The tree sparkled as if the ornaments were all Swarovski crystal. On second thought, they probably were.

Heinz looked completely at home in his surroundings, wearing an impeccable three-piece suit, drinking coffee while reading the *Wall Street Journal*. His hair grayed at the temples, giving him a distinguished air. He was in his sixties, but fit. Every time the waitress passed him, she smiled extra hard. Heinz had his head buried in the paper. Maybe he thought the waitress was beneath his notice.

In addition to Charlie's Great Rides, the car dealership, he also owned Charlie's Suds, a car wash, Charlie's Subs, a deli, and Charlie's Storage—according to the quick online search Gabi had run on him.

When she stopped at his table, he immediately stood to greet her and gestured for her to sit. "Coffee? Anything to eat?"

He was as unfailingly polite as his daughter, but beneath the surface veneer, his eyes were cold and calculating.

A waitress appeared, standing at attention, eagerness to please shining through her.

Gabi sat, aware how out of place she looked in her uniform. "I'll take coffee. Black. Thanks."

Heinz nodded as if the waitress needed his approval. He kept his gaze on Gabi. "Welcome to Broslin. I understand you're the new officer. I was hoping to meet you at the Christmas fundraising ball I put on for the Broslin PD every year. Right here, in fact."

He pointed up. "In the second-floor ballroom. Captain Bing is a good friend of mine. I'm surprised he didn't just call to let me know you needed my assistance."

All those words just to say *I can end your career with a word.*

Gabi sat unflinching. "I'm the primary investigator in Cindy Simme's murder case. Would you mind if I asked a couple of questions?"

His smile turned slightly patronizing, as if he said, *If I minded, you wouldn't have been let in.* "I've heard, of course. Very unfortunate. I didn't personally know the young lady, although, as I understand, she worked for one of my businesses at one point."

Gabi took out her notebook. "I'd love to have specifics on that."

"The manager at Charlie's Subs called me yesterday, in case I wanted to do something for the family. The sub shop, of course, will be sending flowers. I thought I'd donate a certain sum to the school where she taught, to benefit the children who lost her. They might need some counseling or, at the least, a little distraction. I can't imagine them coming back to the classroom after the Christmas break and missing their teacher. Terrible."

His voice and facial expression were that of a campaigning politician. He said all the right things, but Gabi couldn't connect to him on any level.

He pushed the *Wall Street Journal* to the middle of the table and drew his coffee closer. "I'm not the type of person who likes drawing attention to himself. I spend a considerable amount on advertising my businesses, but in my private life, I appreciate privacy."

He glanced around at the handful of other diners, a few of whom were watching. "If you need to talk to me again, I don't think the police car and uniform are necessary. I'd be happy to take you to dinner in the city and talk as friends."

The waitress arrived with coffee. Gabi thanked her, then focused back on Heinz. "I understand you're a hunter."

He smiled. "Nothing better on a crisp November morning than being out in the woods. Clears the mind. The only way it could be better would be if I had a son to take with me."

His gaze dipped from her face to her body. "Do you hunt, Gabriella? I have a great little hunting camp on the other side of the reservoir. You're welcome any time."

She drank her coffee to give herself a moment. "Could you tell me where you were on Friday afternoon between six and seven? I ask everyone I'm interviewing regarding the case."

His eyes narrowed a fraction, even as his smile never wavered. "Friday-night poker with the mayor and two councilmen." He gave her the names.

It had to be the mayor and two councilmen. *Who else?*

Of course, just because Heinz had an alibi, it didn't mean he hadn't hired someone to do his dirty work for him. He could certainly afford help. He had motive. And with his connections and money, he would expect to get away with murder.

But that theory, like all others before it, got snagged on the murder weapon. How would Heinz, or his hired man, know the code to Hunter's safe?

"I met your daughter the other day," Gabi said pleasantly. "I understand congratulations are in order. I'm sure you're excited about the wedding."

She was watching him closely for a reaction, but couldn't be sure if she saw a momentary shadow in his eyes or just imagined it.

"My daughter's happiness is my number one priority."

Sure, that sounded reasonable. But with all the tools at his disposal, how far was Charlie Heinz willing to go to ensure that happiness?

Gabi watched him for another moment then finished her coffee and pushed her chair back. She didn't have enough to seriously question the man. She had what she'd come for, an alibi and a good feel for the type of person he was. Would he go to extremes to protect his personal interests? She was pretty sure he would.

He lifted an inch or two from his chair in an old-fashioned gesture. "I enjoyed meeting you, Gabriella. I understand you had some trouble at your previous job. I hope nothing like that will happen here in Broslin. You'll find that we're a very welcoming community for people who know how to fit in."

She let the subtle warning glance off her. "Thank you for your cooperation, sir."

As she walked out, she dug into her pocket and handed a five-dollar bill to the waitress by the door. "For my coffee." She didn't want it to go on Heinz's tab.

She strode across the pavement to her cruiser, ignoring the inquisitive glances from people who were arriving. So Heinz knew about her past. Of course, the twenty minutes she'd waited for security to admit her was enough to run a quick web search on his phone.

She didn't have time to fume about that. On the way back to the office, she caught a domestic violence call. Since Mike was the only other officer on duty and he was in the middle of a shoplifting arrest at the supermarket, Gabi detoured and took care of the broken-bottle-wielding wife who was threatening her husband with castration.

Gabi took the wild-eyed woman in, put her in holding to be kept until she sobered up. The equally sloshed husband didn't want to press charges, so that was that.

Then she called the captain at home and gave him an update over the phone, cleared stopping by the mayor's office with him. She got the go-ahead, so she drove over to the municipal building.

Luck had her running into the mayor on his way out, on the front steps. If Charlie Heinz was impressive, the mayor was twice as distinguished, tall, blond, the smile of a dental model and the charisma of a movie star. Gabi found herself smiling back at him before either of them even said a word.

"Mr. Mayor, could I have a moment of your time, please?"

The smile only widened, and he turned to her with a rapt attention as if she was the only person in the world. "Anything for one of our fine officers," he said with as much enthusiasm as if they were surrounded by reporters.

He was good. She could see why he'd gotten elected.

"One quick question. Can you confirm that you were with Charlie Heinz last Friday between six and seven p.m.?"

"Poker night," he said with a fond expression. "It's a standing date. Just us boys, blowing off some steam."

"Thank you, sir."

"No problem at all. Is there anything else I can help you with?" His tone was absolutely genuine, as if his only job was to make her life easier.

The guy was going to be governor one of these days. This kind of political polish was plain wasted in the small town of Broslin.

"That's it," she said. "Thank you, sir."

"Keep up the good work, Officer." His blinding smile flashed once more, then he hurried on to the black BMW SUV waiting for him.

Gabi drove back to the office. She'd already run a background check on Hunter; now she ran one on Cameron Porter, Mandy Heinz, and Charlie Heinz as well. There had to be something somewhere, a clue. But if there was, it wasn't a criminal record. Her database search didn't turn up any brushes with the law. She'd never seen three people so squeaky clean.

While she was signing out of the database, the coroner called.

"I had both the fetus and the sperm inside the victim DNA tested per your request. Sample A and Sample B have only a 0.5% chance of being related. Whoever had intercourse with the victim on the day of her death wasn't the baby's father. The lab ran both samples against the criminal database. Neither came back as a match," Dr. Koppel said.

Gabi thanked the woman. Wow. So Cindy had been having affairs with two different men.

But what did that mean for the investigation?

Option One: The baby was Porter's, who had an alibi. But the sperm guy could still turn out to be the killer.

Option Two: The baby wasn't Porter's, but the sperm was. In that case, the baby's father might be the killer.

Option Three: Neither the sperm, nor the baby was Porter's, which meant there were two other men in the picture, one of whom could be the killer.

Bottom line was Gabi needed Porter's DNA so she could figure out which of the options she needed to investigate further.

She made the call, gained Porter's agreement, and headed over to the dealership. She discreetly collected the DNA sample in the back office with a cheek swab, then drove it to the lab in West Chester.

By the time she finished her daily paperwork, her shift ended. But even after she got home, she kept thinking about the murder case.

She had no information about the one or two unidentified men Cindy had been seeing, so she set that aside for the time being. She reconsidered Mandy and Charlie Heinz, who were rich enough to hire someone to do the killing for them. Sadly, Gabi didn't have enough to ask for a warrant on the Heinz's financial records. And even if she did, both Mandy and Charlie Heinz struck her as smart enough to use untraceable cash reserves.

The case bugged her on many levels: the murder of a pregnant woman, the framing of a soldier returning from war. This was her first murder case, and she refused to fail.

When her doorbell rang, she went to answer, thinking Doris was coming to ask her over for tea. But when she opened the door, a fully decorated Christmas tree greeted her.

"Hey." Hunter stuck his head out from behind the tree, grinning. "Thought maybe you could use some Christmas cheer. I noticed last night that you haven't started decorating yet." He walked right in with the glittering monstrosity.

In his other hand, he carried a casserole dish, which he explained with "My turn to provide dinner."

Chapter Fourteen

She'd never had a Christmas tree. Her parents hadn't been the type. The closest they'd come to celebrating the holidays was her mother selling fake gift cards and sending out donation requests from bogus charities. Gabi wondered what Hunter would think if he knew that she came from a family of hardened criminals.

He was still grinning at her. Being cleared in the murder had made a big difference in his demeanor. He looked younger. Sexier, if that was possible.

He held out the tree for her. "Gift from the owner of the Country Store. I got another one from Eddie Gannon."

"Guy who drives the town plow?"

"He moonlights at the Christmas Tree Farm around this time of the year, if we don't have too much snow and the town plow isn't needed."

She didn't reach for the tree, just stood there, trying to decide how to handle this. "Everyone wants to make sure you have a great first Christmas back at home?"

He nodded. "But I can't fit two trees into my apartment."

She blinked as he stepped forward and placed the casserole on the kitchen table, then went and stuck the tree in the corner of her living room. He plugged in the lights. Colored bulbs blinked on and off in some kind of a coordinated pattern. The man was a steamroller.

He flashed her a pleased look. "It came with lights. Can't make it any more convenient than that."

"I wasn't planning on decorating."

"You better not let anyone in Broslin find out about your anti-Christmas tendencies. You don't want the intervention that would follow, believe me. Don't you miss the magic of Christmas of your childhood years?" he asked in a teasing tone.

She snorted. "I was just thinking that we never had a tree. But, actually, one year my brothers and I strung an overgrown marijuana plant with popcorn."

Hunter raised an eyebrow.

"We were proud of our handiwork too." She was suddenly transported back twenty years to the disheveled row house with all the hidey holes in the floor boards. "We were young enough to think that if there was a *tree*, there might be presents under it in the morning. Instead, our father beat us black and blue for messing with his side business."

There, the truth was out. But Hunter didn't react with judgment.

"So no good childhood Christmas memories?" he asked with a hint of sadness.

"Not that many." *Christmas or otherwise.* None, really, but she didn't want to sound like a whiner, so she kept quiet.

He nodded toward the tree. "Want me to take it back?"

The tree had been a kind, neighborly gesture. She could be polite about it. "How hard could it be to unplug the lights and just ignore the damn thing?"

A wry smile tugged up one corner of his lips. "That's the Christmas spirit."

Since she no longer considered him a suspect, she allowed herself to think, for the first time without guilt, how incredibly hot he looked. She liked his warrior body, his general no-nonsense attitude, his sense of humor, that mischievous glint that came into his eyes from time to time.

But she didn't really know how to relate to him. Until recently, their relationship had been cop to suspect. Now? She wasn't sure.

She stepped into the kitchen and checked out the casserole dish. Why would he bring her dinner?

She didn't want to think too much into the gesture. Maybe he couldn't handle eating dinner downstairs all alone, thinking about Cindy.

Gabi cast one last glance at the blinking tree in the corner, then removed the cover from the dish, along with the sticky note that said: *Lasagna. Thank you for your service.*

She pushed the food into the microwave. While it waltzed around on the turntable, she grabbed two plates. Doris always brought out her best china for guests. Gabi's choice was chipped or unchipped.

She could afford new dishes, but she hated wasting time on shopping.

Hunter slid onto a chair, sniffed toward the food. "I have a dozen more in my freezer. I think my brother stocked them, then forgot to tell me in the upheaval."

"People dropped them off at the station."

"I figured. I'll ask Leila for the names. I need to thank the cooks."

He leaned back in his chair, relaxed, his long legs stretched out in front of him. And she found that she liked this new, easy-going version of Hunter Bing.

His eyes focused lazily on her and held a little too long, as if maybe he too liked some things about her. The thought made her skin tingle.

Then the aroma of the food hit her and made her salivate. A sense of hominess filled the apartment suddenly. She wasn't at the point yet where she could admit that it was nice to have Hunter come up, but she could allow that she didn't hate it.

She grabbed a bottle of water for herself from the fridge and soda for him. Then the microwave dinged, and she retrieved their steaming dinner, set it on the middle of the table, found a scooper thingy in the back of the silverware drawer.

"Go ahead," she told Hunter as she sat.

He piled food on his plate, then passed the scooper. "Thank you, Officer Flores."

"Considering that this is our second dinner together, I think we can move on to Gabi."

He smiled.

She didn't mean to smile back, but her lips tugged up anyway. Then her stomach growled in the silence.

The lasagna smelled and looked mouthwatering piled on her plate, the red sauce glistening under the lights, mixed with the gold of gooey cheese.

Heaven, she thought as she dug in. She savored the mesh of flavors, close to moaning. "So what would I have to do to get the casserole treatment around here?"

Hunter grinned at her. "Break a leg?"

She glanced toward the window, and he laughed.

And it hit her what a transformation her apartment had gone through in the past fifteen minutes. She had a Christmas tree brightly blinking in the corner, the kitchen enhanced with the aroma of amazing food, the place filled with the sound of male laughter. All of that courtesy of one Hunter Bing.

"Arrest anyone today?" he asked.

"Beat up anyone today?"

"Very funny." He ate another forkful. "Any news on the case?"

She did her best not to show how frustrated she was with the lack of progress. "Still working my way down the suspect list."

He raised a dark eyebrow. "There's a list now?"

"Kind of."

"Sounds encouraging. Any imminent arrests?"

"A couple of people have motives and means, but they all have alibies."

"Like Porter?"

She nodded. "Then again, they could have hired the job out. But I'm having a hard time seeing that in Broslin. In some parts of Philly, sure. You need a hit because, say, you're on parole, you ask your cousin or someone else in the gang, a recruit. No big deal. But where would a person go in Broslin to find an assassin?"

"Doesn't feel right," Hunter agreed.

"That's what I think." She went for another bite. "And Cindy wouldn't have let a stranger in. No sign of forced entry. Either the killer came with her, or she let him in later. No defensive wounds. The gunshot came as a surprise. There wasn't some big argument where they fought and wrestled for the weapon."

"How did the Beretta get out of the safe?"

"I don't know. Here is the problem: Cindy knew and trusted the guy, or woman, enough to let him or her in, enough to be alone with him or her. But then why get the gun out of the safe?" Gabi shook her head. "If you're worried about someone to the degree that you need a weapon to face them, easiest thing would be to just not let them in. The weapon is a stumbling block for me. I'm going to focus on what I know for sure, and I'll come back to the weapon later."

"So Cindy knew the people on your list?"

"Yes," Gabi said.

She was still stuck on the love-square thing, Hunter, Cindy, Porter, Mandy, plus Mandy's father. Cindy knew Porter was going out with Mandy; she had to. The whole town knew. She didn't know about the engagement, but she knew about the relationship, although maybe she'd convinced herself that Porter would leave Mandy for her. Cindy and Mandy were at the gazebo decorating. So yes, they knew of each other, and they knew each other.

Charlie Heinz claimed he didn't know who Cindy was, but he could be lying. Cindy would almost certainly know who he was. He was the big man in town; probably most everyone knew him. Cindy had worked for one of his businesses. He would have come in to check on things. Even if he thought the employees were beyond his notice, the employees would have paid attention to him. He was the big boss, the owner.

"Trouble is," she said between bites, "I'm not sure if any of the people on my list are the type to kill." Mandy was too detached for a crime of passion. Porter was too much of a wimp. Gabi had seen him fight. Physical violence wasn't his thing. And Heinz...

She wasn't sure about Heinz. He was a good shot, for one, had to be with all those trophies. But his alibi with the mayor was rock solid. All of her suspects' alibies were.

"My suspect list is crap," she admitted. "Alibies all around, and I think they're the wrong type of people for something like this. It takes a special type to kill a defenseless woman."

Hunter had stopped eating and set down his fork. He held her gaze, his mocha eyes filled with intensity. He watched her in silence, his lips flattening, then relaxing, then flattening again.

She stopped eating too. "What is it?"

The muscles in his face grew taut. His gaze deepened, darkened. "I killed a defenseless woman."

Oh shit.

She did *not* see this coming. Was he confessing?

But those teenagers had seen him arrive *after* the shot sounded. Could they be mistaken?

Gabi pushed her chair back, her mind reeling. She had *never* been this wrong. Then her brain whispered, *Tony.* Okay, so maybe she was the worst judge of men that ever lived.

"We should probably continue this at the station. You should call your attorney."

"Overseas," he said. "On my last mission."

Relief flooded her. Way to give her a heart attack. "That happens in war," she said evenly, not missing the tortured tone of his voice.

He hung his head for a second before looking back up. He kept looking at her, and she could see him thinking, reliving the moment, struggling with it.

He dropped his hands to his knees. "Wasn't during war. We were there for a peacekeeping mission. Someone from my unit was kidnapped. Once we found out where he was being held, we went in after him." He paused.

She waited him out.

"J.T. was held in a small village. We moved in, in the middle of the night. A civilian stepped into the line of fire."

She pulled her chair back to the table. "You can't control that kind of thing."

Guilt thickened his voice. "Can't I?"

"Is there anything you could have done differently?"

"I could have not shot when she jumped from her bedroom."

"And if instead of her, an enemy combatant jumped out and you hesitated?"

"I wouldn't be here." He sounded matter-of-fact about the possibility of his own death. "We wouldn't be having this conversation. Which doesn't negate the fact that shooting her was a serious error in judgment."

She reached for a sip of water. "We all make serious errors of judgment."

After a moment, curiosity entered his expression. "Not you, Officer Everything-by-the-Book."

Especially her. She closed her eyes for a second. She didn't want to talk about Tony. So she just said, "I almost arrested you for murder."

The corner of his mouth turned up a little. "How close did you come?"

"I had my hands on my cuffs a couple of times."

"I'm glad you gave me the benefit of the doubt," he said with feeling.

"I arrested you for assault."

"I deserved that."

She was pretty sure that was the first time she'd heard those words from someone she'd arrested.

She liked how candid he could be, how he'd just drop his guard. She liked his honesty. She wasn't sure if she wanted to like him quite as much as she did.

She must have had a look of consternation on her face, which he then misinterpreted, because he said, "Whether you're a fan of Christmas or not, you must miss your family around the holidays." He thought she was homesick. "What does your family think about you moving out to the boonies?"

"No family."

"What happened to them?"

"What's with the interrogation?" She raised an eyebrow. "Who's the cop here?"

"Just making conversation."

Her family wasn't conversation material. But with the time he'd served overseas, she figured his life hadn't been a cakewalk either. So she ended up saying, "Greek on one side, Spanish on the other. Although, usually everyone assumes I'm Mexican. Mother took off after my youngest brother, Miguel, was born. Cops were after her. She was a scam artist. We never saw her again."

Everything's a scam, her mother used to say. She only had the one rule; she wasn't a layered person like Carmen. Various scams were her bread and butter. There were smart people like her, she believed, and all the rest were suckers to be fleeced.

Tony had convinced Gabi that what they'd had was real. And then he turned out to be a scam. She supposed that made her a sucker.

She drew a deep breath. "Actually, my heritage is fully criminal. On both sides."

Hunter said nothing, no judgment on his face.

"My father worked at the shipyard, rotating shift," she said. "He grew weed as a hobby, but his main income came from grand larceny. He'd tip off his buddies about certain shipping containers, let them in the shipyard for a cut. He ended up dying in a workplace accident. A crane dropped a load on him. They had to put him in the body bag with shovels."

"Jesus."

She had no idea why she was telling Hunter any of this. Maybe to distract him from his own troubles. She never talked about her family.

"I'm sorry," he said.

She shook her head. "When I found out that he was dead, all I felt was relief that he wouldn't beat us again." It was her brothers' deaths that had broken her heart.

"My oldest brother, Roberto, was forced into a gang. They pick you, you don't get a choice. It's not like you can say, no thanks, and walk away," she paused, struggling with the memories.

Hunter waited her out.

"Roberto was killed at nineteen," she finished, then picked up the pace, wanting to be done. "Alejandro, my middle brother, died from a batch of bad drugs." She swallowed. "A cop shot Miguel, my youngest brother. He was sixteen, delivering illegal weapons. They asked him to open the trunk of his car. He pulled a sawed-off shotgun from under his seat. Didn't get a chance to shoot it."

Hunter kept watching her. "How did you end up with the police?"

"One of the officers who were there when my brother was shot kept tabs on me, Carmen Morales. She helped out if I was in a bad spot. One time, she bought me a tank of gas so I could keep going to work. It held me until payday. Before her, I thought cops were the enemy. Then I started to see the good she was doing in the neighborhood. I decided I wanted to do that, and she helped. She used to say, *the world needs strong women.*"

She hoped she was becoming one of those.

Hunter watched her in silence. After a while, they went back to eating.

"Hey," she said when she glanced at the Christmas tree and it reminded her of the ten-footer she'd seen that morning. "The suburbs are rubbing off on me. I went to the country club today."

"Thinking about joining?"

"Not for a million dollars."

"That's about what it'd take." He smiled. "So what did Charlie Heinz have to say?"

"How do you know he was the one I went to see?"

"I ran into an old high school friend this morning. She's a waitress at the country club now. She said Charlie looked at you as if he wanted to eat you for breakfast."

Small-town grapevine. Great.

"I told her you'd get stuck in his throat," Hunter added with a glint in his eyes.

She wasn't sure how she felt about the compliment. In the end, she decided to take it in the spirit with which it was given, and gave him a smile.

He smiled back, his sexy lips snagging her gaze and making her own lips tingle. There was something about the man that made a woman sit up and take notice. No wonder Dakota had a crush on him.

A new idea popped into Gabi's head. "How fast did you drive to the apartment from the party?"

"Not fast." He narrowed his eyes as if trying to figure out what she was getting at. "I was enjoying being back in town, how pretty everything looked, the Christmas decorations." His mouth twisted. "I was nervous about the ring in my pocket, trying to put together what I was going to say, how I was going to say it."

"Could someone leaving the party after you cut ahead of you? If he or she took another road. A short cut."

He blinked. "Maybe. I guess, someone riding hell for leather could have beaten me by a few minutes."

"A few minutes were all the killer needed."

His gaze sharpened. "Are we talking about anyone in particular?"

"Was Dakota upset enough about you choosing Cindy to do something stupid?"

Chapter Fifteen

Hunter wasn't buying into the Dakota theory. She was a kid, he thought as he lay on his couch later that night, trying to sleep.

Yeah, Dakota might get jealous, but murder? He didn't think so. The murder seemed like a setup. In his apartment. With his gun. The murder weapon wiped clean. Hunter got the impression that whoever had killed Cindy wanted him to take the rap for it.

Dakota might have wanted Cindy out of the way, but if Hunter went to prison, what was the point of removing the rival? He still wouldn't be available.

He'd told that to Gabi, but she still insisted on investigating Dakota fully. She would. She was the type to keep going until she conquered whatever stood in her way. He had to respect that.

He'd enjoyed having dinner with her. Gabriella Maria Flores was an interesting woman.

He'd been reluctant to leave her, but she had work in the morning, while he could afford to sleep in. And maybe if he stayed longer, she would have gotten the wrong idea. He didn't want to give her the wrong idea. Did he?

She was hot, he was a man; not being attracted would have been impossible. That gleaming dark hair tempted a man to find out what it would look like released from its tight bun. She had toned, endless legs. Her lips were distracting, especially that teasing mole in the corner. She could give a dead monk a boner.

But he wasn't looking for a quickie. He'd come home to become a family man. He still wanted that. He preferred the homemaker type, wanted a woman who lived for her family, sweet, loving, good cook, feminine. Cindy had fit that ideal to a T, winner of half the baking prizes at the Mushroom Festival.

Bitterness doused the flickers of sentimental memories. He couldn't think of her without thinking of the cheating. Hunter shifted on the couch, trying to settle in. He needed something to occupy him. He'd buy carpeting in the morning, and he'd install it himself, he decided. The work would give him something to focus on instead of thinking endlessly about Cindy and driving himself crazy.

He needed to get a bed too. But suddenly the apartment felt transitory. He didn't want to move back to the bedroom. Renting from his brother had been convenient all these years, but maybe he was ready for his own place.

The apartment suddenly seemed alien. He'd spent so little time here, his army cot was more of a home to him. Suddenly he missed the barracks, missed his team. He wondered how J.T. was doing in Tennessee.

He slept fitfully and woke early, drove to West Chester, and ordered his carpet, then drove over to the old Bing homestead, took a dirt road through the back of the property, and walked some, went up the small rise where he could envision his own log cabin.

He could see fruit trees and a vegetable garden. He liked how in the small villages in Afghanistan, people grew most everything they ate. He'd definitely get a dog. A cat too. And maybe chickens.

Which made him think about food, which made him think about dinner with Gabi. Which made him think about Gabi's new theory again, about Dakota. He did his best to remember Friday night, every word he and Dakota had exchanged. She'd seemed upset but not deranged, certainly not homicidal.

He ran through their last conversation again, caught something he hadn't remembered before. He yanked his phone out of his pocket and dialed.

"Hey, I was thinking about Dakota," he told Gabi on the other end. "I told her I was going to pick up Cindy. I didn't tell her where. She had no way of knowing that Cindy was at my place."

"Okay." Gabi paused. "Actually, I was just calling around to guests at the party. Eddie Gannon saw her go out, then come right back in a few minutes later. She stayed for another twenty minutes after you left. I think we can cross her off the list."

When they hung up, Hunter felt nothing but relief. Dakota was a good kid. He didn't want her to get tangled up in a murder investigation.

He looked around, figured out which direction he'd want his living room window to look. Toward the woods. When he stepped out to his back deck, he wanted to see nothing but nature. A house began taking shape in his mind.

Something a lot like Ethan's place.

That thought stopped him.

He would have to make sure he lived his own dream, not his brother's. He had looked up to Ethan when they'd been young, the whole big-brother thing. Then he'd left for the army at eighteen and being a soldier became his identity. Now here he was, close to thirty, his own person at last, and for the first time, he had to figure out who he really was and what he wanted.

He'd already made a mistake with Cindy, blindly following some fantasy. Maybe the log cabin on the farm was another fantasy that didn't truly belong to him.

He shoved his hands into the pockets of his jacket. A slight breeze blew across the field, cold but not freezing. No snow today. He tilted his head up to soak up some winter sunshine, closed his eyes for a minute.

He had two things to figure out in the near future: where he wanted to live, and what he wanted to do for a living. He'd thought about becoming a cop, but now he discarded the idea. He wanted peace in his life. Maybe a physical job. Maybe something outside, moving around in the fresh air.

He walked over to the construction site, Hope Hill Acres.

He talked to the construction manager and found out pretty fast that he'd have to look for a job someplace else. They had enough workers for now, and work had slowed for the winter anyway.

The crew boss told Hunter to come back in the spring. He also said he'd had two other applicants already that morning. Arnie Martin was selling his gas-station-slash-car-repair-shop in town, or closing it if he could find no buyer. Some of the junior mechanics were jumping ship.

Hunter thought about the gas station with the tidy mechanic shop in the back of the lot, the good-sized apartment on top. Didn't sound like a bad investment, as long as the price was reasonable. He could have his own business instead of a job, live in the upstairs apartment. No urgency to build a house, really. He wasn't bringing a bride home anytime soon.

His mood soured by that thought, he walked back across the fields to his pickup, then drove around to Bing's place, hung out with the dogs since, according to a note on the fridge, Sophie was helping her friend out with the new baby.

Hunter wanted to talk to his brother, run the idea of Arnie's gas station by him. Something like that would definitely require either a loan or an investment partner or possibly both. Ethan had a good head for business.

But when Ethan walked through the door with thunder on his face and said, "Someone just shot the front windows out of my cruiser," Hunter forgot all about his entrepreneurial dreams.

He came out of his seat. "What?"

"At the turnoff to the driveway. I was on the radio to Leila, signing off for the day, letting her know I'd be home if there was an emergency. A bullet came through one window, went out the other. Missed my head by an inch."

Ethan turned around and pointed out the open front door at his cruiser. The two front windows were shattered. He moved to go back out, but Hunter caught up with him and grabbed him by the arm. "Better stay inside."

"Probably a stray bullet from a hunter." Ethan frowned. "That shouldn't happen. The whole property is posted. We have too many people around here. Too many animals." His expression darkened. "It could have been Sophie."

A misguided hunter. Ethan would think that. He lived in Broslin. Hunter's first thought had been *sniper.* Ethan was more likely to be right in this case, but still. "Why don't you call it in and have the guys comb through the woods?"

Ethan shook his head. "I'll go out there and look around. Reckless discharge of a firearm is a crime. Someone needs a good talking-to. I can handle that without backup."

Hunter moved into his path and blocked the door. "You're the police captain. You've put away your share of idiots. Somebody could be holding a grudge. Maybe the bullet wasn't an accident. At least let me come along."

His brother considered him for a few seconds, then reached for his radio and called in the shooting.

Chase and Gabi showed up within minutes. Ethan filled them in.

Chase headed out immediately, but Gabi hung back, a look of

fierce concentration on her face. Hunter couldn't look at her without thinking he wanted her. Her fault entirely. No man on earth could resist the way she looked in uniform.

She was tough and sexy at the same time, the blue fabric molded to her curves. Hunter thought he could definitely develop some uniform fetish if he spent a little more time with her.

She was watching Ethan as if considering whether to say what was on her mind, but then went ahead with it. "Do you ever go into Hunter's apartment while he's deployed?"

"I do," Ethan said. "I check to make sure he doesn't have a water leak or bugs. I like knowing that the place is fine for him when he comes home."

"People around town know he's your brother."

Ethan flashed a where-is-this-going look.

She straightened her spine, which pushed her boobs out, which didn't make it any easier for Hunter to concentrate. "What if the bullet in the apartment was meant for you, not for Cindy?"

Then she pushed on with "Cindy arrives, turns on the light. Somebody sees it from the outside, knows the captain goes in there all the time for maintenance. The killer sneaks in, shoots before he realizes it's the wrong person."

"With my weapon?" Hunter shook his head. "How? While getting the gun, wouldn't he have realized that it was Cindy in there and not Ethan?"

"Good point." Gabi thought some more. "But I still think the two shootings could be connected. Cindy being shot Friday, then the captain being shot at today seems too much of a coincidence. We haven't had a shooting since I've been working here."

"The car windows were likely an uncoordinated deer hunter," Ethan insisted.

Hunter wasn't so sure.

Then the phone rang, and Ethan picked up, the tension on his face doubling as he listened. "Thanks for letting me know," he said and hung up, turned to Hunter.

"Dad's in the hospital. Someone ran him off the road an hour or so ago over in Avon Grove. His car rolled. He broke his left arm. They're putting a cast on. He'll be ready in an hour. I'll go pick him up when we're done checking the woods here."

Hunter tried to digest the news. What were the chances that both his brother and his father would be involved in accidents the same morning? Something that could have proven easily fatal for both. The day was turning pretty accident-prone for the Bing men.

"Sir, what if the shooter is someone who wants not only you but your whole family?" Gabi echoed Hunter's thoughts. "Maybe he was going for Hunter at the apartment, got Cindy by accident. Then tried your father. Then you in the driveway." She held up a hand in a *wait* gesture. "Cindy doesn't lock the door, expecting Hunter. The guy think it's Hunter in there, pushes his way in. Cindy gets the gun, the guy grabs it away from her..."

Ethan was back on the phone already. "How is it going? How much longer do you think you'll be over there?" He listened. "Call me when you're ready, and I'll come pick you up. Stay in the house until I get there. Is Jack home?" He nodded at the answer. "Good. Tell him I said to keep an eye out." He listened. "No. Everything's fine. I'll tell you later."

He hung up, didn't need to say he'd been talking to Sophie.

He called Joe next and asked him to go over to Jack's place and hang out in the cruiser outside. Then he listened while Joe said something on the other end. Judging by the way his eyebrows were knitting together, Joe wasn't showering him with good news.

"All right," Ethan said at the end. "You keep me up to date on the developments. I'll rework the shifts." Then he hung up, looked at Hunter and Gabi. "Mike's in the hospital with acute appendicitis. He's having emergency surgery tonight."

Which meant the department was another man short.

"Is he okay?" Gabi asked with a concerned expression. "He thought it was a bad batch of tuna."

"They'll fix him," Ethan said with enough gruffness that Hunter knew he was worried.

"Anything I can help with?" Hunter offered.

"Stay out of trouble," Ethan told him. "All right. Let's go."

But instead of heading straight for the door, he turned toward the wall, pushed a framed poster of wild horses aside, and opened his gun safe, pulled an old Colt Detective Special, a six-shot .38 special snubnose revolver, and handed it to Hunter. "Just in case."

Hunter checked the gun. Fully loaded. He shoved it into the back of his waistband and pulled his shirt over it. He caught Gabi's eyes on him.

He was freshly out on bail for assault. She could have protested.

But the only thing she said as she headed for the door was, "Stay safe."

Obviously, she expected him to hide out at the house and let her and his brother protect him. "I'm not staying." He headed out behind her. "I'm going with you."

His brother turned back, squared his jaw. "The hell you are."

"The hell I'm not."

"You sit tight right here. You have a gun to protect you. There's no need for you to be out in the open, if you're a possible target."

"You're a target, and you'll be out in the open." He stopped in line with Ethan, almost toe to toe, the soldier facing down the police captain. The scales had evened out. They'd grown up. It was no longer big brother versus little brother.

Hunter did his best to sound reasonable. "Short of shooting me, there's nothing you can do to hold me back. Every minute we waste arguing about this is a minute we're handing to the shooter to get away."

Ethan swore under his breath. Then he shook his head as if what he was about to say went against his better judgment. "I'm appointing you as an auxiliary police officer for the duration of this case. You are to provide backup to Officer Flores and will work under her close supervision. If she says *jump*, you ask, *where is the trampoline?* Is that clear?"

Hunter knew it wouldn't be in his best interest to grin, so he didn't. "Yes, sir, Captain."

Chapter Sixteen

The captain teamed up with Chase. Gabi had Hunter for a partner as they spread out in the woods, circling the area where the captain said the shot had most likely originated.

She wasn't a big believer in coincidences. Three men from the same family coming in contact with violence within a couple of days definitely smelled fishy. Maybe in the inner city, something gang related, okay, she could see it. But not in Broslin. Something didn't add up, and since this all seemed to be connected to her murder investigation, she was determined to get to the bottom of it.

Hunter was pulling ahead, in full soldier mode, alert, posture ready for anything. He *was* a hunter. He'd been named aptly. Fully focused, every muscle ready, he was pretty impressive as he stalked through the woods like he owned them.

"Stay where I can see you," she told him. With all his military training, he was better on terrain like this, but she was still responsible for him.

Tracking wasn't her strong suit, although the inch of snow helped, made scanning for tracks easier. While she carefully inspected the ground as she moved forward, her phone buzzed. Cameron Porter.

"I want to drop the charges against Hunter Bing," he said as she picked up, without bothering with niceties.

She stopped. "Has anyone talked to you about that?" She didn't think the captain would go and pressure the guy, but she wanted to be sure.

"Mandy found out. Too many people saw the fight at the dealership. She told me I deserved a punch in the face. I'm to own up to my own part in all of this. She says if I do, she'll consider forgiving me. She's an angel. I don't deserve her."

Mandy was a pragmatic person. She knew if the case went to court, the reason for the fight might come out, show up in the papers, Gabi thought. "All right. Just come in and sign the paperwork, and that'll make it official."

She ended the call with Porter, then turned back to her search. She didn't want to call out to Hunter, who was now barely visible, a hundred yards ahead. She'd tell him when she caught up with him.

She searched for boot prints in the snow, froze her butt off before she found them. She crouched to give the prints a closer inspection.

Hunter saw her stop and immediately headed back. "Looks like what we're looking for." He scanned the ground in every direction while she called the find in over the radio.

When she finished, she remembered the news the footprints had made her temporarily forget. "Cameron Porter called. He's withdrawing all charges."

Hunter grinned. "Best piece of news I heard all day."

She narrowed her eyes at him. "There'll be no displays of any kind of stupid macho temper while you're assisting me with this case."

"No, ma'am." He was standing way too close to her.

She could smell the masculine scent of his soap. She raised an eyebrow, not liking the way his eyes glinted. "You better not be mocking me."

"I wouldn't dare. You're my superior officer."

She gave him her tough-cop look, doing her best not to stare at his chiseled lips. "And don't you forget it."

His gaze dipped to her mouth, then back to her eyes after an endless moment. "Permission to follow the tracks?"

Follow them where? She could only see the handful of prints right in front of her. The soil was rocky around them, the snow spotty, far from an even cover.

At her questioning look, Hunter pointed to the ground a couple of feet from him where a tiny pebble lay dirt-side up instead of shiny-side up like the rest.

"Permission granted," she said, and he began moving in that direction, scanning the ground, careful where he put his feet. The trees and some evergreen bushes soon hid him from her.

She stayed where she was to mark the original spot, shuffled in place to keep warm while waiting. She didn't want to mess up a possible crime scene. She was with Hunter on this one. She wasn't buying the careless-hunter theory.

For a case that was supposed to be open and shut—woman killed in boyfriend's apartment with his gun—things were certainly going all over the place.

The captain arrived first. He saw the tracks immediately, stopped at a safe distance.

"Large boots, likely a man," she reported. "Hunter's gone to track him."

"Won't be easy." The captain scanned the semi melted snow. "Our man kept to the rocks where he could."

She didn't enjoy being right. "A hunter wouldn't bother to hide his tracks, would he?"

Bing moved to the left and walked a few feet forward to a trampled spot behind some bushes. "This is where he stood."

Gabi looked back. Yes, someone could see the captain's house and driveway from there. She scanned the ground carefully. "He took the shell casing. Do hunters do that?"

The captain shook his head, an ominous look on his face.

As someone who'd lost family members to violence, she could sympathize. "I think we should set up protection for the family, sir."

Before the captain could respond, Hunter popped into sight, his long stride eating up the ground as he walked toward them. "The boot tracks end at the road. He had his car up there. No tire tracks. He was smart enough not to pull off into the mud."

The captain scanned the woods, eyes narrowed, the set of his mouth grim. They all knew the shooter was long gone, but Gabi kept looking too, anyway. Not a leaf moved, no sound of footsteps on dead branches, only the dull noise of cars moving in the distance on the highway.

"Let's go back to the house and come up with a strategy," the captain said, and radioed Chase to let him know he could return to the station.

The three of them walked back to the log cabin. The captain dragged up a metal detector from the basement. "Birthday gift from Sophie. She thought it might be fun to search for rusty bayonets."

"They had a revolutionary war battle somewhere around here," Hunter filled in Gabi on their way to the mailbox. Then he asked his brother if he'd found anything yet.

"If we find this bullet, I'll be happy."

And they did, digging it up in less than an hour, after the captain pretty closely guessed the trajectory.

"Forty-five caliber." Gabi held it out on her gloved palm. "A common caliber for hunting rifles." Had it found its target, the injury would likely have been lethal.

Judging by the look on the men's faces, they were thinking the same.

* * *

After Ethan sent Sophie out of state to visit her mother, the three Bing men took over the house.

Hunter had to accept that his father had slipped back into his old ways. The old man hadn't come to the welcome home party and wasn't happy to be here now where Ethan kept a close eye on his drinking. He was guzzling beer in the basement where he'd claimed an old couch, having declared the guest bedroom too fancy for his taste.

The day after the shooting in the driveway, Gabi popped in. Since they were having lunch, she joined them at the table at Ethan's invitation and opened her laptop, pulling up a spreadsheet.

"I took the liberty of compiling a list of people you put in prison, sir, who were released in the past six months. I gave weight to those with potential for deadly violence. I identified three who I think should be our top suspects. They're brothers."

Ethan's head dipped into a nod. "The Wilson boys. They'd do something stupid, if anyone would."

Hunter stifled a grin. Gabi could manage the heck out of a case. The more time he spent with her, the more he respected her. He'd always been into the sweet-as-peas, homemaking, pie-baking, mothering types, but something about Gabi's brisk efficiency got to him. A man couldn't help wondering what it'd take to make her lose that cool control. What she'd look like with her hair spread out on a pillow instead of tortured into a tight bun at her nape.

She was saying, "The two younger brothers picked up a couple of teenagers outside of town on a deserted country road and had themselves a party. John Wilson was convicted of rape and torture, released six months ago. Reborn in prison," she added. "Mark Wilson also went away for rape and torture, then knifed someone in prison, most likely, but it couldn't be proved. Released October second. Luke Wilson, the oldest, was in for murder even before the other two got there. He beat his own cousin to death in a bar fight. Released November tenth."

Ethan narrowed his eyes. "Last I heard, the brotherhood broke up. When John found God in prison, he decided he couldn't lie anymore. He provided information on his brothers. He got an early release, lives with his mother now as far as I know. The other two could never figure out who said what. Suspicion all around. I don't think they'd work together." He thought for a moment. "My best bet is that one of them is acting on his own."

He glanced at his watch. "I have to be at the mayor's office in twenty minutes." Then he glanced at Gabi. "You got this?"

"Yes, sir," she replied in a tone that said she was ready to ride herd on somebody's ass. Hunter was grateful that no longer meant him.

Ethan slid off the stool and walked to the basement door, opened it, called down, "We're off to work. I'll turn on the security system. You sit tight, all right? Stay inside."

Two succinct curse words floated up in response.

Ethan closed the door and flashed an apologetic look toward Gabi.

Since Gabi was driving, Hunter had nothing to do, so he pulled out his phone and tried J.T. again. He was worried about the kid.

Depression was nothing to mess with. Hunter had read some flyer on the flight back to the States that encouraged the soldiers to get help as needed. That flyer contained some startling statistics. The suicide rate among former servicemen and women was astronomical. On the average day, twenty-two took their own lives.

He was relieved when J.T. picked up.

The kid sounded as listless as before while they assured each other that they were both doing just fine.

"You know how I said I was losing my lease?" he said then. "I can't get another. Not with no job. The economy ain't the best in Tennessee. I'm leaving for Alaska tomorrow."

"Sounds like an adventure. You go up there and kick some polar bear ass." Hunter tried to lighten the conversation. "You still thinking about driving up? Flying might be faster."

"I need some quality time with my pickup."

A long stretch of road, mountains, rivers, and fields going by could be relaxing. Maybe some quiet time to reflect was exactly what J.T. needed, time to process all that had happened to him.

"A road trip sounds good," Hunter agreed. "Hey, maybe you'll have some adventures on the way."

"Anything could happen. What adventures are *you* chasing?"

"The adventures are chasing me." Hunter debated for a moment whether or not to say more. Then he went ahead with "I think my family is being targeted by someone."

"Like VA scams?"

"Something else." Hunter paused. "You know that girlfriend I told you about? She's been killed." Then he shared some of the other details.

"That's fucked up, man. I'm coming to see you," J.T. offered immediately. "I got your back, bro. You had mine, time to return the favor."

"You don't owe me any favors."

"I'm coming up anyway. I'm gonna leave right now."

Hunter tried to talk him out of it but couldn't, and gave in at the end. He'd been missing his team. And J.T. probably needed a morale boost too, before setting out for the great unknown.

"Army buddy," Hunter told Gabi after ending the call. "Coming up to see me. Driving through on his way from Tennessee to Alaska."

Gabi glanced over. "Sounds like a long drive."

"I think it'll do him good." Hunter thought another minute or two about the kid. Maybe he could talk J.T. into sticking around until the rehab facility opened in the spring.

* * *

Gabi tried to adjust to the idea of Hunter in the passenger seat. He was too close. His shoulders were too wide. He was looking at her too much. She couldn't have been more aware of him if he was naked.

Now that he wasn't a suspect, she could admit that she was attracted to him. Who wouldn't be? He was so hot he could probably fry eggs on his pecs.

She wasn't sure how she felt about working with him. The whole setup reminded her too much of Tony.

Then Hunter smiled at her and her heart gave a little thud. She refocused her attention on the road. She was *not* going to fall for another partner.

His fresh, soapy, masculine scent filled the car. He smelled like he'd showered just before she'd arrived. She didn't want to think about him in the shower. Or what the two of them could do in a shower—

"So how come you're driving?" he asked.

"Because it's my cruiser," she snapped.

"Can I drive?"

"No."

"What if you get incapacitated?"

"I don't get incapacitated."

He might have been chuckling next to her. She didn't look to check.

They went to John Wilson's house first since he was the only one they had an address for. According to record, he'd promised, right in court during his trial, to someday settle up with everyone who had anything to do with him being put away. Captain Bing was at the top of that list.

A little old lady opened the door.

Gabi introduced herself and Hunter. "We need to speak to John, ma'am."

The woman's knobby fingers worried the edge of her apron. "Is he in trouble?"

"We just need to ask him a couple of questions."

"I'll let him know when he comes back. My brother owns a fishing boat in Jersey. They go out for a week at a time."

That didn't sound promising. "When did he leave?"

"He left here on Thursday. The boat went out Friday first thing in the morning. He called when they pulled anchor. He's a good boy now. He walks with the Lord."

Hunter glanced at Gabi. Gabi shook her head. It didn't look like they hit pay dirt here.

"Do you know where we could find Mark and Luke?" she asked the woman.

And they lucked out there, or at least halfway. Mrs. Wilson had an address for Mark, but not for her oldest.

"You be careful with them boys now," the old woman warned. "They still follow sin." She shook her head, a sad look in her eyes. "But I'm praying."

While Mrs. Wilson lived in a modest neighborhood of fifties' ranchers with her youngest, her middle son, Mark, rented in a different part of town. His street ran parallel to the railroad tracks, a row of duplexes from the twenties and thirties on tiny properties with no driveways or garages.

The street was so dilapidated, it almost made Gabi feel at home. She could have been right back in her old neighborhood in the city. She waited for the can't-wait-to-get-back-home mood to hit her, but it never came. Huh. Maybe Broslin was growing on her. She couldn't decide if that was good or bad.

Until now, Hunter followed her lead, no macho assertion of his manly strength, which she appreciated. But now as they headed up Mark Wilson's front steps, he moved next to her, trying to put himself between her and whoever opened that door.

She reached out sideways and held him back. "I don't need a living shield, but thanks."

Her hand was pushing against his rock-hard abdomen. His coat was open, so she was touching the soft material of his shirt, and could feel the ripple of muscles underneath. Heat rushed up her arm and spread through her body. The sudden, physical need caught her off guard for a moment. She snatched her hand away.

Heat burned in his eyes, amusement twitching at the corner of his lips. He stepped back, but not far. "If you do need anything, you let me know," he said inches from her ear.

The two of them as partners was possibly the worst idea in the universe. Gabi gathered herself and took the next step up, then rapped on the door. Nobody came to see what she wanted. She rapped again. Nothing. She called out, "Police. Open up."

Seconds ticked by in silence.

She turned to Hunter. "Let's go around."

He held her gaze as if trying to puzzle something out, but then gave a sharp nod and went left. Gabi went right, looking in windows. They met in the middle in the back, tried the back door with no better results than the front. Since they didn't have a search warrant, they couldn't do much more.

A neighbor stuck her head out as Gabi and Hunter walked back to the cruiser. "He ain't live here no more." She stepped outside, disheveled and gap-toothed, two different color socks on her feet.

"Thank you for letting us know, ma'am," Gabi responded. "Do you know where he might be?"

The woman wiped her hands on her stained muumuu. "Couldn't pay the rent. Moved in with his cousin down on Maple Street."

"Would you know the cousin's name, by any chance?"

But the woman shrugged, stepped back, and closed the door behind her.

Gabi called Leila over the radio. "Do you know who Mark Wilson's cousin is? Lives on Maple Street."

"I only know one Wilson on Maple Street," Leila said after a moment. "Donald. Minor idiot. He's been brought in a couple of times." Leila told them the address. "He gave up his dealer once to get charges dropped. He's a born weasel. He'll give up his cousin in a second."

But Mark Wilson wasn't at his cousin's house either.

Donald told Gabi they'd had a disagreement the week before, and Mark had left. With Donald's car. She got the impression that Donald was too scared to go after him. Gabi put out an APB on the car, then she went around with Hunter to visit Mark's known associates to see if he was hanging out with one of them.

They had no luck with that whatsoever.

The drive-around just ate up their day while Hunter's constant nearness made her frazzled. She didn't do frazzled, dammit. But trying to ignore Hunter's charms all day was exhausting. While he'd been a suspect, she'd suppressed any kind of attraction toward him. Now the dam had burst.

She had a serious crush on the guy. He made her feel like a teenager. She was a police officer, for heaven's sake. And she was awash with lust for him. She was no better than Dakota. She needed to get a grip.

"I'd like to take you to dinner," he said as they headed back to the police station so she could write up the paperwork.

"Thanks, but I can't."

"I meant later." His easy smile tickled something behind her breastbone. "I know you still have work to do."

"No, thanks." Then she asked, "Why?"

"Because you're an interesting woman, Gabriella Maria Flores."

That almost sank her. If he said she was hot or some other cliché men told women to get them into bed, she could have ignored him. But she liked the idea that he thought her interesting.

"You have a heart," he said next. "You're a good cop and a strong woman. I want to get to know you better."

"I've been down this road before."

"Gone to dinner with a man? I'd hope so, or I'd have to think the men in the city were all blind and stupid."

"I had a relationship with a previous partner." Big mistake. But Tony could be pretty damn persuasive. They'd spent night shift after night shift together. One thing led to another.

Hunter didn't seem discouraged. "I'm only in the position temporarily. I could be relieved of my duties tomorrow."

"No."

He watched her for a long moment. "I take it the relationship didn't end well."

"I'm dropping you off at home." She turned on their street since they were passing right by it. She wanted him out of her cruiser so she could think straight.

"What did he do?" Hunter asked.

She pulled into the parking lot and stopped the car. He made no move to get out.

She cleared her throat, kept her eyes on the steering wheel in front of her. "I trusted him. We grew up in the same neighborhood, knew the streets, knew the players. Cut from the same cloth. I thought." A small, bitter laugh escaped her. "Turns out he took money from criminals, from evidence too. He's done other things a cop shouldn't do. Bad stuff. I didn't know."

"I believe you."

She turned to him. "Why?"

"If you didn't care for justice, you'd have gone easy on me to score points with my brother."

"That's not how I work. But I was his partner, and his girlfriend, so I was painted with the same brush. Afterwards, whether you're dirty or not, all people remember are the accusations."

"So you came to Broslin to lay low."

"Yeah." She palmed her face. "Only to be handed a murder case where the police captain's own brother was the primary suspect."

"That's as high profile as you can get in Broslin." He grinned. "I'm glad you cleared up that little wrinkle." He reached for the door and got out at last, but then he leaned back in and said, "I had fun with you today, Gabi," as if they'd been on a date.

Then he closed the door and strode away. Even from behind, in jeans and a light jacket, he was clearly a soldier, a warrior. His strength was evident in every move of his powerful body. His body language said he was focused and alert. If a dozen ninjas jumped from the bushes, he would have been ready to take them on.

Okay, ogling time over. Gabi put the car in gear and drove away. But, despite her best efforts, she was still thinking about him all the way to the station.

Chapter Seventeen

As soon as Gabi walked in, she went to catch up with the captain.

"I find it suspicious that nobody knows Mark's and Luke's whereabouts," she told the man. "Almost as if they're in hiding."

"We'll find them." The captain nodded grimly. "I appreciate the effort."

"Just doing my job."

"I don't like the idea that my family is in danger because of me."

"Hunter strikes me like the kind of guy who can take care of himself."

"And between the two of us, we'll take care of my father." He spoke with confidence, but the worry was there in his eyes.

"I can keep going," Gabi offered. "I have nothing pressing. I don't mind putting in an extra couple of hours."

But he dismissed that with "I need to call around and get a bead on Mark and Luke. Let me see if I can scare up something."

He meant past informants, Gabi thought. "We'll start over tomorrow and get our guy."

"That's the spirit, Officer." The captain gave an approving nod. "Sometimes I get too busy to stop and talk, but I want you to know I'm glad you came to Broslin," he said gruffly before he went back to his computer screen.

Gabi felt a warm tingle around her heart as she walked to her desk to make sure everything was squared away. She liked working for the captain. She liked the whole PD, to be honest. They were small enough to be transparent. There was nothing underhanded going on, no abuse of power or any kind of dishonesty as far as she could see. Because the people were good. Captain Bing had put together a hell of a team, one she was proud to be part of. She was going to miss them when she left here.

She plopped behind her desk and brought up her e-mail. Saw the report from the lab. The baby's DNA and Porter's were a match. She called Porter to let him know. He thanked her in a wooden tone, then hung up on her.

On the way home, she kept wondering who sperm guy was, but couldn't come up with any decent theories. She stopped at the Main Street Diner for some mushroom pie, one of their specialties that was quickly becoming her favorite treat.

"And a little something for dessert. I promise you'll like it." Eileen, the diner's owner, slid two toffee-almond cookies into her bag. "There you go, Gabi."

Eileen had been calling her by name since Gabi had stopped in for coffee on her first day on the job. The older woman always had a smile on her face, her long graying hair in a French braid, her flowing dresses usually covered by an apron. Warmth and kindness radiated from her. Gabi suspected half the reason people came here was to get their mothering fix from Eileen.

And the cooking was beyond great. The glass display was an invitation to food orgasm. Gabi wished her neighborhood in the city had a place like this. She was going to miss the diner when she returned.

"Try this." Eileen pushed a cup in front of her. "Free sample. Mushroom ice cream. I'm already testing new recipes for summer."

Gabi didn't expect much, but she was prepared to be polite. At the first taste of the ice cream, however, she felt her eyes go wide while her taste buds danced the cancan. "Wow. You're good." She had another spoonful, then gestured at the diner with her empty spoon. "How did you end up doing this?"

She meant Eileen owning the place and running it all by herself, all the employees, the customers, the incredible amount of work and coordination, the sheer creativity.

The woman flashed a motherly smile. "The hard part was to believe that I deserved it. I spent a lot of years thinking I didn't want nice things, shouldn't want nice things, because I wasn't going to have them anyway. What's the point of wanting something you can't have, right?"

Exactly. Gabi nodded.

"Here is the secret." Eileen gave a conspiratorial wink. "We don't get what we deserve from life. We get what we take. And I think it's okay to take what you want, as long as you're not hurting anybody. Actually, if you're helping others in the process, that's the right way."

Gabi gave that serious thought while she finished the ice cream.

She didn't hate Broslin. She didn't even dislike it. If she wanted to be honest, the town was a really nice place to live. So why was she resisting it so much? Because deep down she wanted this life, but she didn't think she could ever have it, would ever deserve it?

She was needed at the Twelfth, she told herself. She belonged in her old neighborhood. *Don't I?* a small voice in her head wondered out loud for the first time.

Of course, she did. Gabi shook off any budding doubts, then thanked Eileen for the food, and drove home.

The wind picked up so she hurried in from her car, paused at the wall of mailboxes inside the front door. No mail for her. To the right stood the hallway to her apartment, in front of her the stairs that led down to Hunter's level.

The mushroom pie was enough for two days. *Or for two people.* She wondered if Hunter was here or had gone over to his brother's house. In his place, she would have stayed out at the log cabin. She wouldn't want to hang out in the apartment after what had happened there.

She felt bad for brushing off his dinner invitation. Maybe he just needed company, wanted to stay away from the bad memories that lived in his apartment.

She could give him the cookies, if he was home. The fewer calories she ate, the less time she'd have to spend at the gym. She walked down the stairs and looked down the long hallway, saw his door open a crack. Then he appeared in the door, carrying a hammer.

He was on full alert as soon as he spotted her. He hurried forward. "Anything wrong?"

She felt stupid for having come down. What was it that she really wanted? She decided she was too chicken to answer that question.

But she did have news. "The lab work came in on Cindy's baby." She hesitated.

"I can handle it. Porter's?"

She nodded.

He remained motionless for a long moment, and she watched as he absorbed the news, processed it. Then he rolled his shoulders.

"Okay."

He had accepted the past, she thought. The anger was gone. He still had the sadness, but he wouldn't rage again, wouldn't go after Porter again. He was moving forward.

Her gaze dropped to the hammer. "What are you doing?"

"I'm putting in new carpet." He swung the tool in his hand. "I need a bigger hammer. I think I have one in the toolbox in the back of the truck."

She turned around. Stopped. Lifted the paper bag of cookies. "Eileen's giving out free desert. You'll be burning more calories tonight than I will. I should leave this here."

He peeked into the bag. "Toffee-almond cookies?" He suddenly sounded like a little kid, his face brightening a shade.

He was ridiculously handsome. *Thud-thud-thud* went her heart. She handed him the cookie bag, then moved to go.

"Hey," he said. "I could use a hand."

She had no intention of hanging out with him. She had no idea how she ended up installing carpet, breaking only for mushroom pie and cookies with Hunter an hour later in the kitchen.

"I never knew carpets had to be stretched," she told him, proud of their handiwork. They had the padding down, the carpet cut and half of it already in.

"I learned that from Bing." Hunter swallowed the last of his share of the mushroom pie. "When he first got into the landlord business, he'd buy these hideous fixer-uppers, then put his heart and blood into them to make them livable before he rented them. I helped if I was home on leave."

She could see the two brothers working together. She wondered what her brothers would have ended up doing if they'd managed to grow up into adults smart enough to leave the criminal life behind.

The shadow on her heart must have showed on her face, because Hunter asked what was wrong.

She shook the gloom off. "I don't like having an unproductive day like we had today. I was hoping to have a solid suspect in hand by tonight."

"We've been very productive here, if that's any consolation." He reached out to snatch one of the cookies, his sexy lips curving into a grin.

And she suddenly wondered how those masculine lips would feel against hers.

They were sitting at the kitchen table. As she shifted, her knee touched against his. Electricity arced into her through that small contact point.

She moved her knee. She needed to distract herself. She grabbed on to a wayward thought that had been rattling around in her brain. "I've been meaning to tell you something, but I'm not sure how you'll feel about it."

He grinned. "You want me badly, and you're tired of resisting it?"

Heat flushed her face. She hoped he was just joking and didn't really know how close to reality he was hitting.

She sucked in her lower lip, then let it go. "I think Cindy might have been molested when she was a teenager."

Hunter's merry mood immediately disappeared, his eyes focusing sharply. He set the half-eaten cookie down. "Why?"

And Gabi told him what Cindy's Aunt Ruth had told her. The longer she talked, the more shadows gathered on Hunter's face.

She finished with "I'm not a psychologist, but I was thinking, if that's true, then maybe that's why she needed more than one man in her life. She might have felt guilty over what had happened with her uncle. Like it was her fault. She wanted validation from men, proof that she was still lovable."

Hunter dropped his gaze to stare at his half-eaten cookie. "You could be right," he said heavily. "I wouldn't have thought of that."

She gave a small sigh. "I know a thing or two about seeking validation from men."

Her hindsight was twenty-twenty. Too bad her foresight had been blind.

Hunter looked up with questions in his eyes.

She shrugged. "My parents broke the law; my brothers broke the law. I come from criminals. Then I became a cop. I felt like I had to work extra hard to prove myself. I still do. I wanted validation from the other cops. If they accepted me, that meant I wasn't a criminal like the rest of my family."

"Tony," he said after a moment.

She ran her index finger down the tabletop in a straight line. "He pursued me. And I gave in, even if it wasn't the best idea, since we were partners. But I think, under it all, I thought that if he wanted me, that meant he accepted me. And he was a cop. So there was that validation I craved."

"What he did wasn't your fault."

"But it was my fault that I didn't see what he was," she said. "A crooked cop." She shook her head. "I couldn't help what my parents had been. I was born into that. But I chose Tony. So what does that say about me?"

"That you're human," he told her. And he reached out to cover her hand with his, brushed his thumb over her knuckles before she pulled away.

Because it felt too good.

Because she thought she couldn't have it and didn't deserve it? Her earlier conversation with Eileen came back to her.

No. She had to pull away because starting anything with Hunter was a bad idea, Gabi tried to convince herself, but she wasn't sure if she succeeded.

Chapter Eighteen

Hunter had a hard time taking his eyes off Gabi once they were back to carpet laying in his bedroom.

"What are you doing for Christmas?" he asked her.

She was a hard worker. Smart too. She had keen insight. He found that he liked her sharp brain as much as her tempting body, maybe even more. He liked her courage too, on the job and otherwise. Remaking herself to be something different from her family had taken plenty of courage.

She hammered in a nail, ran her finger over it to make sure it wouldn't stick out. "Probably volunteer to work."

Because she had no family. Hunter felt bad for her. His father wasn't a prize winner, but at least Hunter had always had Ethan.

Gabi probably missed her brothers. Being exposed to death and violence didn't make a person immune to grief. He knew what it was like to lose close friends. Every one of those losses hurt.

As a soldier, that was the life he'd signed up for, the price of war. It seemed insane that those kinds of losses were going on here in the US, where people were supposed to be safe.

"I'm sorry about your family, your brothers," he said, respecting her for what she'd made of herself. She'd pulled herself up by her bootstraps, taken on a job where she could help others. "Do you think you'll ever go back to Philly?"

"As soon as I can."

He didn't like the idea of her leaving Broslin.

He held his hand out for the cutter, and she handed it over. They worked well together. He made the last cut, and then they were done at last.

She stood and wiped her hands on her pants. Her bun was loose, so she took it down and put up her mess of dark tresses into a ponytail, which she quickly braided into an orderly arrangement. She had dirt streaks on her face and a hammer hooked through her belt. She looked as hot as hell on fire.

For some of the guys he knew in the service, the coming-home ritual included hooking up with the first woman they found willing. But he'd never been like that. He shook off the X-rated images that Gabi inspired.

Her saying, "Now all you need is a bed," helped.

The words were a bucket of cold water thrown into his face. Suddenly he saw Cindy lying in a pool of blood on his old bed.

He moved out of the room. "I want to paint first."

She followed him. "If you want, I can help you with that too."

He stopped in the kitchen and turned to her. "I'm still trying to figure out how I can repay the favor for tonight."

"Not necessary."

Stray strands of dark hair curled around her slim neck. He resisted the urge to touch them.

"Let me take you to dinner tomorrow," he asked for the second time.

Instead of the instant rejection, this time she tilted her head as she considered his offer. Too long, he thought, and wasn't surprised when she said, "That's not a good idea. You're my partner. You're my boss's brother."

"Temporary partner. And Ethan won't mind."

"If people see us together, they might question why you were cleared so rapidly of the murder."

"Because two eyewitnesses cleared me." Yet he knew what she meant. She wanted to be above reproach while in Broslin. She was here to build her reputation back. Fine. He didn't want to mess that up. But she'd been here helping him for hours. He wanted to do something nice for her. "I saw you going for a run this morning. How about if I take you for a run?"

She raised an eyebrow, the gesture full of feminine sass. "I'm not a dog. I don't need to be taken."

He bit back a smile. "Where do you run?"

"Down to Route 1 on Main Street, then back. Ten miles round trip."

Ten miles was a long run for someone who wasn't in the army or some other kind of training. He wondered what she was running from. Tony's memory? The death of her brothers?

He shook his head. "Sidewalk running is no fun. Tomorrow morning, six a.m. I want to show you something." When she looked dubious, he added, "Unless you're worried that you can't keep up with me."

She flashed an *as if* look. "I'll be ready at six."

* * *

Gabi had no idea why she'd agreed to go for a run with Hunter. She stretched while she waited for him outside the next morning. If he didn't show soon, she was going to take off without him.

But by the time she pulled her ponytail tight and smeared on some lip balm, he was pulling up in front of the building.

He rolled down the passenger-side window. "Sorry I'm late. Spent the night at the farm."

Of course. To protect his brother and father if needed. "How was it?"

"Everything quiet."

She expected him to park and get out, but instead, he reached over the passenger seat and pushed the door open for her. "Hop in."

"Who drives to go for a run?" she grumbled, but she slid into the seat. She rolled the window up against the morning cold.

"You'll see," he said mysteriously.

He looked good, freshly scrubbed and bright-eyed first thing in the morning. In a good mood too, an easy smile on his face.

She didn't smile, as a rule, until she had her second cup of coffee at the station.

"Have you found your Christmas spirit yet?" he asked as they drove by Broslin Square.

The decorations were out of control. "This place would make Liberace feel underdressed." She nodded toward the gazebo. "It's not like I hate Christmas. I just don't get the hoopla. You put the decorations up, you take the decorations down. What's the point?"

"It's more than decorations."

She shrugged. "Not that I've ever seen."

They drove south out of town, into the woods, and parked on a patch of dirt he called a trailhead. As a city girl, she'd managed to avoid nature up to this point in her life. She would just as soon avoid it this morning, but she didn't want Hunter to think she was scared of a challenge.

They started with stretching. She tried not to stare. He wore a long-sleeved cotton shirt that fit him well, showing off plenty of bulging muscles. His black sweatpants clung to the most amazing male ass she'd ever seen. He bent to loosen his lower back muscles, then did a few squats.

She wished he'd get on with the running already, before she started drooling.

The day before had been warm enough to melt the snow, then temperatures dropped overnight, so the soil was firm instead of muddy, but still a mess of frozen dips and ridges of dirt.

"How is this better than a nice, even-surfaced street?" She cast him a dubious look. "I don't see the point."

He didn't seem perturbed by her doubts. "You will," he said, and finally took off down the trail.

She ran after him. *How bad can it be?*

For the first ten minutes, the whole nature thing was plain annoying, although the sight of him from behind helped to ease her pain. But the ground was uneven, littered by broken branches. Having trees all around was strange. And the narrow, winding trail allowed only so much visibility. She couldn't see far enough down the path to assess upcoming danger.

But at one point, she fell in rhythm with Hunter and moved together with him. Other than their footfalls, she could hear no sound. Not even birds. They were probably snuggled up in their nests.

The silence seemed empty at first, but by the time they reached the end of the first mile, she was beginning to find the lack of cars and people soothing. Lack of color too. The green of pines broken up with the drab branches of deciduous bushes and trees was pretty restful, actually. No billboards and shop window signs screamed at her.

When a fallen tree blocked the path, instead of slowing to go around, Hunter sailed right over it. So did she, and found the jump exhilarating.

"Faster?" Hunter asked.

She grinned. "Yes."

And she immediately realized he'd been holding back for her. His powerful body pumped forward, clearing obstacles, taking turns, handling inclines.

Running like this was different from her dreary slog on Main

Street that she endured so she could get to that second cup of coffee at the station. Running freely through the woods was amazing.

She didn't even mind when her lungs and muscles began to burn. The air was incredibly clean, the temperature brisk—just cold enough so they weren't sweating.

Only when they reached Hunter's pickup did she realize that they'd run a loop. She bent over, tried to catch her breath. "How long was that?"

"Thirteen miles."

A lot more than her usual routine, but she'd barely felt it. Because it hadn't been boring.

He stretched again, showing off an array of impressive muscles, then grabbed two bottles of water from the cab, tossed one to her. "What do you think?"

She drank. "I can almost begin to understand why people like the whole nature thing."

His laughter cut through the clearing. And then he snagged her around the waist with his free hand, moved her up against the side of the truck, and kissed her.

She was too stunned to react. By the time she caught up with what was happening, his warm lips were firmly settled against hers. His arm was snug around her waist, his hard body pressed against hers, his warmth seeping into her.

She felt dizzy for a second. *Probably from the long run.*

Then she felt tingly. She could smell his shampoo, some manly scent that got under her skin. Her blood was suddenly rushing in her ears. *Probably from the exercise.*

He dragged his mouth over hers, and her body responded with embarrassing eagerness. *Probably only because...*

Oh hell, who was she kidding?

She gave up reasoning and the need to think, and let her traitorous body lean against his as she capitulated.

He groaned deep in his throat, a sound of pure male need.

For a second, she could see them flinging their clothes to the wind and him lifting her up against the side of the truck, her legs hooked around his waist, his powerful body pounding into her.

Her belly clenched.

Nobody here to see.

But she ended up pushing him away.

He searched her face. "What's wrong?"

"We shouldn't be doing this." No matter how much her body ached for more.

"And when the case is closed?"

She moved away, opened the passenger-side door, doing her best to appear unaffected despite the disconcerting weakness in her knees. "We'll reevaluate."

"I'm not going to let this go," he warned. "We have something here. You know we do."

She didn't respond. She didn't want to lie by denying his words.

"You have another minute?" he asked once they were driving down the road. "I need to swing by the Methodist Church. It's on the way."

Now what he was up to?

"Relax," she told him. "It was just a kiss. Consensual. You don't need to go to confession."

He laughed out loud. "Methodists don't do confessions. I need to drop off something."

That something turned out to be a huge bag of winter coats, gloves, and hats—donations from Hunter, Ethan, and Sophie.

Gabi went with him to the back door of the church that opened to a simple storage room, nothing but tables lined up. Two sweet old ladies with blue hair sorted mountains of winter gear. They thanked Hunter for the bag almost tearfully.

"You'd think they got donated a kidney each," Gabi whispered on their way out. "Where's all that stuff going, anyway?"

"To the homeless in Philly."

She knew what he was doing—showing her the other side of Christmas, the side that went beyond the window displays.

Okay, so this part she liked. But if he expected her to break out in carols and start running around with an elf hat on her head, he had another think coming.

* * *

Gabi barely got to work when Donald Wilson came in to make a deal. He had two thousand dollars' worth of old parking violations in West Chester. He could probably remember Mark's whereabouts if those parking violations were erased, he suggested.

Captain Bing pulled some strings, and ten minutes later they had the address to a trailer owned by Mark Wilson's new girlfriend.

By then, Hunter was in too, so he rode with Gabi. Going out on a case with him when she'd just made out with him in the woods felt awkward. Gabi did her best to keep things extra super professional between them.

On the way over, she rehashed what they knew about Mark Wilson. Luckily, the drive to the trailer park was short. They found the beaten-down, blue single-wide without trouble.

Once again Hunter came up the steps with her, jockeyed for position. She fixed him with a look and stepped in front of him, pushed the doorbell, then stepped back. Smart move. The man who came to answer had a gun tucked into the front of his belt.

Gabi nodded toward the weapon. "You have a permit for that?"

Hunter slipped in front of her smoothly and placed his hand on his own sidearm.

Mark was in his midthirties, unwashed blond hair, his soiled shirt hanging on skinny shoulders, dark circles pooling under tired eyes. "I don't need no permit. All I need is the Second Amendment."

"Mind if we come in to chat for a minute?" Gabi asked, keeping it all friendly, stepping around Hunter. The smell of pot coming from the trailer nearly knocked her off her feet.

Mark spit. "You got a warrant?"

She remained calm and reasonable as she said, "Ever heard of an unwarranted search? I can smell the dope from here. Believe it or not, that gives me the right to enter."

Mark began with "Asshat," then went on to a string of more colorful words as Gabi pushed inside and disarmed him in one smooth move. Mark swore an extra row before yelling, "Police brutality!"

But his trailer park neighbors, if they heard, didn't rush to his aid.

Hunter went straight to the kitchen. "We're only here to ask a couple of questions."

A bong smoldered on the table, a bag of weed in clear sight on the counter. Mark grabbed the bong and the bag and shoved them into a half-empty kitchen cabinet.

"I'm not here to bust you for weed," Gabi told him.

Mark checked her out, his gaze hesitating over her boobs. "Wanna sit?"

"Can't remember when I got my last tetanus shot. Thanks anyway." She stayed between him and the front door. "Where were you Friday night between six and seven?"

Mark had to think. "Here. Home."

"Anyone here with you?"

"Nah. Not on Friday."

"You hunt, Mark?"

The guy shook his head with derision. "Sitting out in the woods, freezing my ass off? That ain't for me. Luke's the gun nut in the family. You want guns, go to him."

"So you don't own a rifle?"

"No way."

"How about a car?"

"Not since I lost my license. Can't afford to keep one if I can't drive it. I hitch rides from my buddies."

"Donald said you took his car," Gabi said.

"Borrowed it." Mark swore darkly. "Some nasty dudes took it from me. I owed them a spot of money." He scratched his head. "Donny's cool. He don't mind."

"You might want to ask him about that." Gabi watched the guy. "When did you lose the car?"

"Two weeks ago." He scratched his head. "Wait. No. Three."

"What kind of car was it?"

"Old-ass Honda. Red"

Okay. Not the dark SUV that had run Zechariah Bing off the road.

She looked around. If Mark did have a rifle, he didn't keep it out in the open like his weed. He had no alibi, but they had no tangible proof to link him to Cindy's death, the shooting on the captain's property, or running the captain's father into the ditch.

She watched closely how the guy related to Hunter, but didn't see any hidden anger or disguised animosity. He barely acknowledged Hunter. She had the strong impression that Mark had no idea who Hunter was and just took him for a plainclothes officer. She had a hard time seeing Mark with a deadly vendetta against the Bing family.

They questioned him for another half an hour but couldn't back him into a corner, couldn't make him change his story. Honestly, he didn't look smart enough to be that good an actor.

"Where's your brother Luke?"

He smirked. "Dunno."

"When was the last time you talked to him?"

"Can't remember."

Something about his smug tone made Gabi snap. She stepped up real close, got right into the guy's face. "Do you think it's a joke? One person's dead, another two could have been killed." She grabbed for her cuffs. "Guess what? I'm taking you in for the pot. Parole violation. Maybe sitting in a cell will improve your memory."

But taking Mark in didn't loosen his tongue, other than for swearing. Gabi decided to let him sit and stew for a while. She even gave him something to stew about. "I hear you had trouble in prison before you were released. Someone got killed. I'm sure his buddies are waiting for you. They'll be ready when you go back in."

While giving Mark time to rethink his strategy, Gabi went back out with Hunter, checking on people Luke Wilson had associated with in the past. But nobody knew where the guy was, or if they did, they weren't talking. The longer the day wore on, the more tense she became.

The reason she agreed to Hunter becoming her temporary partner wasn't only to have backup. If she was correct and the killer was after the whole Bing family, then Hunter was a target.

Every instinct she had screamed that there was going to be another attack.

She liked the idea of Hunter with her during the day, then hanging out with his brother in the evenings and sleeping over at the farm. She wanted him protected.

And because she believed he was in danger, their lack of progress frustrated the doughnuts out of her.

Hunter, on the other hand, stayed completely calm and, if anything, introspective. She kept catching him watching her. Sometimes with more than a little heat in his eyes.

She ignored that completely, even if those looks set something aflutter in her chest. She didn't care if an entire flock of butterflies established a colony in there. She still wasn't going to fall for her new partner.

She hoped the captain never found out about that kiss.

Chapter Nineteen

"I kissed your officer," Hunter said when his brother walked in the door that night. He didn't want to have this kind of secret between them. Especially since he fully intended to kiss Gabi again.

Ethan narrowed his eyes, patting the dogs that rushed to greet him. "Which officer?"

"Very funny." But Hunter grinned. Then he grew serious again. "I initiated, she stopped it. If there's anyone to blame, it's me."

Ethan raised an eyebrow. "What about Cindy?"

Hunter sank into one of the rustic armchairs in the living room. "Good question."

His brother came over and dropped into another chair, the dogs following to lie down at his feet. "Is this a rebound thing? Flores deserves better."

They were in agreement about that. "You're protective of her."

"I'm protective of all my officers."

"Shouldn't you be on my side?"

"I am. I'm making sure you're not making a mistake. Also, she's not one to stand for bullshit. You mess with her, she might shoot you. I don't want to lose her. We need her at the station."

Hunter couldn't help a grin. "Somebody shoots me, I thought you'd be more worried about me." Then his joking mood evaporated. "Too fast?"

His brother considered the question. "Only you can say."

Hunter nodded. The strangest thing was, Gabi was not at all his type. Maybe he'd been wrong about his type. God knew, he'd been wrong about a lot of things. "When I'm near her, it's like—"

But Ethan raised a hand and cut him off. "If it's all the same to you, I'd rather not hear details on how hot you are for one of my officers."

Good point. "She's working a case in which I was a person of interest. A case to which you and I are both connected." Now that Hunter spelled it out, he could see her point about acting with caution. "Is this going to be awkward? I mean if something happens between us." He was surprised by just how much he wanted something to happen.

Ethan watched him. "It'll be what you make it. We don't have fraternization rules at the PD. For one, she's our first female officer. Until now, I hadn't thought I needed to put something into the rule book."

"But just so I know, you have no objections?" Gabi's career was important to her. Hunter wasn't going to do anything to jeopardize her job at the PD. He wanted to see where things could go with her; he didn't want to cause problems for her.

But Ethan said, "None from me." And then he stood. "And for stressing me out with that kind of personal relationship talk, you're cooking dinner."

"I'm not staying for dinner. Unless you need me."

"Should be safe enough inside with my guns and my dogs. I'm more worried about you."

Hunter flashed a cocky grin. "Now that I know someone is out there, I'd like to see the guy get a drop on me." He pushed to his feet, grabbed his coat, ruffled up the dogs a little, then walked away.

He picked up a box of doughnuts on the way home. He swung by his apartment and grabbed a casserole from the freezer, then went up to Gabi's place.

When she opened the door, he held out his offerings. "I remember you mentioning a certain willingness to help me paint."

Truth was, he could handle the painting on his own. But he wanted her company.

She wore black yoga pants with a T-shirt, her dark hair in a loose ponytail that reached past the middle of her back. He liked her hair, especially when she let it loose a little.

She looked into the box. "Are you trying to bribe me with doughnuts? So cliché." She gave him the stink eye and made him laugh.

"Clichés are clichés for a reason. They work." He lifted the casserole dish up for her inspection. "I have other wonders.

Macaroni and cheese. You come down with me, and I'll pop this baby right in the microwave." He wiggled his eyebrows. "You know you want it."

She was biting back a smile, shaking her head, but then she took her keys from the lock inside and stepped out, locking her apartment behind her. "Only because I'm out of frozen burritos." She stepped forward, but he hadn't stepped back, so suddenly they were too close to each other.

The air seemed to thicken in the hallway. The fact that he'd kissed her that morning made his needs rush sharply into focus.

He wanted to take her back into her apartment. He wanted to take her, period. Instead, he leaned forward and simply brushed a kiss against her lips, infinitely more chaste than what his body was demanding.

He was prepared to leave things at that, but she swayed toward him a little when he began to pull back, extending the contact between their lips. He pushed her back against her apartment door, wishing his hands weren't full with doughnuts and the mac and cheese.

Her hands moved to his hips and rested there lightly.

He tasted her. Dammit, he wanted her so much he couldn't see straight.

But she made a protesting sound, and he pulled back at last. "I know. I said I'd wait."

"You're crushing the doughnuts," she told him, half laughing.

He glanced at the box. He'd crumpled the corner he was holding. "I can't believe you were thinking about the doughnuts."

"One, I'm always thinking about doughnuts." She stepped around him and started down the hallway, glanced back over her shoulder. "Two, women are great at multitasking."

He followed her downstairs. "Give me another chance. I guarantee I can kiss you until you forget about saturated fat and refined sugars."

She just shot another look back at him. He decided it was at least a *maybe*.

They ate half the casserole before they began painting, rehashing the case and all the clues they had, but they didn't come up with any brilliant insights. After dinner, they started taping around the door and window openings.

He enjoyed her company a great deal. Beyond the strong physical attraction, he plain had fun hanging out with her. She could work hard and joke around at the same time, didn't take herself too seriously.

"Picked out a bed yet?" she asked when they broke for doughnuts and milk finally.

His easy mood evaporated at the question. Every time he thought *bed*, he thought of Cindy. "I figured I'd wait until the room was ready for it."

She flashed him a thoughtful look. "You're putting off getting one."

He drew a slow breath. "Maybe."

"You think you'll ever sleep in this bedroom again?" she asked as she looked around.

The room stood empty, masking tape already in place, the edges painted, ready for rolling the rest of the paint. The professional cleanup crew had scrubbed the blood splatter off the wall, so no evidence of the murder remained at this stage.

Yet he could see it all with high-definition clarity. He hadn't made a conscious decision, but now that Gabi had asked, the answer simply slipped out, and he knew it was right. "Probably not."

She waited a moment before nodding, no sign of surprise on her face. "Where will you go?"

"I thought about building a house. Then I thought about buying Arnie's gas station." He needed to talk to his brother about that. With everything going on, he kept forgetting. "There's an apartment above the mechanic shop in the back. I'm going to have to do something for a living. Why not that?"

"Sounds like a plan. So you're definitely staying in Broslin?"

"There's no other place like it." He caught where her mind was going. "You're definitely going back to Philly?"

She nodded.

"What do you miss most about the city?"

"Familiarity."

"The more time you spend in Broslin, the more familiar it'll get."

"I'd feel guilty if I didn't go back."

Guilt was an old friend of his. He felt boatloads of it over the woman he'd shot in Afghanistan, over letting J.T. get captured in the first place, over Cindy's death. What did Gabi have to feel guilty about? He raised an eyebrow.

"I'd feel like I took the easy path," she said. "I don't want to leave my old neighborhood that needs me. I want to help people."

"Because the only way to help people is if you're an inner-city cop?" he countered. "Other people are no help whatsoever?"

"My family hurt people. I want to make up for it."

"What would they think if they saw you now?"

A wry smile twisted her lips. "Spit on me for turning into a cop." She sighed. "I feel guilty about that too. Like I betrayed my kind or something."

"That's a lot of guilt."

"I feel most guilty over the fact that I wasn't able to save my brothers."

"None of that was your fault. Not even remotely."

"I should have been able to talk them onto the straight and narrow path."

He shook his head. The ten-mile run every morning made sense at last. He had a feeling he'd just found out what Gabriella Maria Flores was running from so far and so fast.

"People do what they want to do. You can't much talk anyone into anything. You chose the right path because you wanted to. They wanted something else. You're going to have to let the guilt go, or it'll drag you down."

She watched him. "Can you do it? Can you let things go that happened overseas?"

"I hope so. Eventually." He had nightmares, but he'd only been home for a couple of days. He hoped with time the nightmares would fade.

"There are a million ways to do a lot of good right here in this town," he told her, and decided he was going to get involved in something at the earliest opportunity.

Maybe Gabi could too. It'd be a way for her to put down roots in Broslin. "You could join some ongoing efforts here. Eileen at the diner donates the leftover bakery goods to the battered women's shelter in West Chester every evening after closing. She could probably use help with loading and unloading. She also puts on a big Christmas-basket thing every year."

Gabi smiled at last. "I like her."

"I thought you didn't like anything about Broslin."

"I like Eileen."

"Sophie, my sister-in-law, got into adopting mutts and training them into search-and-rescue dogs. She adopted Peaches when she met my brother, and she just adopted Pickles. Do you know Sophie?"

"Met her a few times when she came in to see the captain. She's scary nice. She and Leila organized the police barbeque this summer like two four-star generals."

"I wouldn't doubt it." Hunter grinned. "Anyway, my brother is mentoring some troublemaker kid out at the farm. Got him a job taking care of the horses. Do you like horses?"

She raised an eyebrow. "I'm a city girl. Is this a trick question?"

He opened his mouth to rattle off other possibilities, but she held up a hand to ward off the rest of his list. "I get it. I can be anywhere and do good things."

"Yes, you can." He didn't want her to leave Broslin.

They finished the room in record time, then they washed up in his bathroom. He rubbed a spot of paint off her temple that she'd missed. And then he got lost in her brandy-color eyes.

"I'm going to kiss you," he warned. "And the only thing you're going to think about is that you want more."

And then he claimed her lips.

This time, he had both hands free. He put them to good use as he seduced her with his mouth. His fingers traced the curve of her hips, down then up, her slim waist, her rib cage, the curve of her breasts.

He ran his tongue along the seam of her lips, then, when a small moan escaped her, he swept inside. He loved the velvet heat of her mouth, the way her tongue danced with his. He was hard, his body pressed against hers.

He was in heaven, and he never wanted to leave. He didn't hold back. He wanted her to understand how serious he was. He wanted to push her past denial.

Then he forgot all that and got completely lost in her.

They were both breathing hard by the time he finally pulled away.

"Did you think about doughnuts?" His voice had been reduced to a raspy whisper.

"What? Who?" She looked at him dazed.

He wanted to lift her up onto the sink and take her all the way. Instead, he let her leave.

After she went upstairs, his place seemed empty suddenly. He thought about that as he ran to the store to pick up an outlet cover to replace one that'd cracked when he'd prepped the room for painting.

By the time he got back home, J.T. was waiting for him in front of his door, sitting next to his duffel bag on the worn-out carpet, his back against the wall, head hanging. His shoulders drooped. He was in BDUs—battle dress uniform aka camo pants and shirt—playing with a pack of cigarettes.

The he saw Hunter and smiled, but the effort was halfhearted at best. "Hey."

He was gaunt, even skinnier than when he'd been rescued. His thin smile couldn't disguise the bleakness in his blue eyes. Hunter sure as hell hoped the kid was going to get some kind of therapy and soon.

J.T. stood up.

Hunter clapped him on the shoulder. "How was the trip? I didn't think you'd get up here this fast."

"I just kept drinking coffee. Probably not enough. Got my truck totaled this morning." He shook his head.

"You okay?"

"Not a scratch. Got a rental." His expression turned somber. "Sorry about the girlfriend, man. Sorry about the other stuff too. I'm glad to see you're still in one piece."

"We'll find who's behind everything."

"I'm here to help."

Hunter unlocked the door and pushed it wide open. "Come on in."

J.T. dropped his duffel bag inside the door.

"Traveling light?"

"I don't know what's waiting for me up there. No sense hauling furniture." The kid yawned. "Man, I'm beat. You got anything to eat?"

"Macaroni and cheese. I'll need to reheat it." Hunter set a new goal. He wanted J.T. to be five pounds heavier by the time he left Broslin. "You can start on some doughnuts."

He handed the half-empty box from the counter to his buddy, then popped the casserole dish back into the microwave. "It's nice to have someone around from the old team."

Maybe he'd think less about Gabi.

"I miss the guys, stupid bastards," J.T. said in a wry tone.

"Messed-up shit. Over there, all you can think about is getting home. Then you're home and all you can think about is what the guys are doing. Wondering if everything worked out for everybody after they got back."

Hunter nodded, although he'd been too busy in the last couple of days to think too much about his army buddies. He hoped their homecomings had turned out better than his.

"Guess it didn't work out too well for you so far." J.T. dropped to the couch and put his feet up on the coffee table, then set the box of doughnuts on his lap. "So who's this asshole that's after your family?" He dug in.

Hunter sat in the recliner. "No idea yet. The police have a couple of suspects, but nothing definite. We figure it has something to do with my brother."

"The top cop?"

"It's probably some pissed-off criminal he's put away."

"I bet. I'm here now. We'll kick ass. Don't you worry."

J.T. had never been anything but confident. But the signs of his captivity still lingered. He didn't have his usual upbeat energy behind his words.

Maybe hanging out in Broslin for a while would do him good. Hunter didn't like the shadows behind the kid's eyes that hadn't been there before the Taliban had snagged him. "Do you have anything lined up in Alaska for when you make it up there? Are you sure you want to go up now? You could wait here until spring."

J.T. licked a spot of jelly off his thumb. "Chuck said I could stay with him in Anchorage until I find something."

Chuck Schur was another friend from their unit, a gentle giant, half Inuit.

"What's Chuck doing these days?"

"Drives a truck for now. He says he's never home anyway, so he wouldn't mind if I hung out at his place while I looked for a job."

"You think you'll give truck driving a try?"

J.T. shrugged as he stuffed the last doughnut into his mouth. "The freedom of the open road? Sounds good, doesn't it? What are you gonna do for a living?"

"Still trying to figure that out."

And he was trying to figure out more than work.

He'd been looking forward to J.T.'s arrival and was happy that his friend was visiting, but he wished it was Gabi sitting on his couch. As soon as he thought that, he felt guilty for thinking it. J.T. had come to help. So he said, "I'm glad you're here," which was God's honest truth.

"Yeah, me too." J.T. yawned, looked around. "Do you have any beer?"

* * *

Gabi finally caught a break in the case the next morning. Mark Wilson gave up his older brother in exchange for the PD overlooking his drug possession. Since the mayor's task force wasn't meeting for a change, the captain went out with Gabi to catch up with Luke Wilson at last, leaving Hunter to spend some time with an old army buddy of his who'd shown up the night before.

Luke lived in a basement-level apartment like Hunter's, except in a derelict building that looked as slummy as Gabi had ever seen in Broslin. The captain probably had previous experience with this guy because while he went to the front, he sent Gabi to the back. Since she didn't know which window to watch, she moved into the far corner of the narrow open lot behind the building so she could see the entire back wall.

As she ducked behind a collection of garbage cans, one of the ground-level windows opened, a fat little man twice Gabi's age squeezed out, and began running straight toward the lot on the right. The open area looked like a building had been recently knocked down there, construction debris standing in piles.

"Stop! Police!" Gabi dashed after him, her boots pounding on the frozen ground.

Luke was a lot faster than he looked. He zigzagged like a quarterback between the piles of rocks and dirt that lined the lot, heading for the chain-link fence.

Never going to make it.

But he had an escape route set up. He hopped on a pile of cement blocks, then from there he jumped on a plastic barrel, then hooked a leg over the fence and just rolled over the top, landing on the other side in a splash of mud. In a split second, he was up and running.

Did that just happen?

Gabi sprinted to catch up. She ran every morning, rain or shine, for this very reason. She had to be fast enough for foot chases.

Up the makeshift steps. Over the fence. She managed to avoid the rolling-in-the-mud part and landed on her feet. "Stop! Police!"

Luke had a getaway bike waiting, a rusty piece of junk half-hidden in a pile of trash. But the stupid thing worked.

She was close, less than ten feet behind him as he jumped on the bike. His butt didn't even touch the seat; he just shoved off and pedaled like crazy. His comb-over waved in the breeze as if mocking, *see ya later.*

She put every ounce of energy she had into an all-out dash, while the captain bellowed, "Stop!" from somewhere behind her.

Five feet. Four. Three. Gabi leaped on Luke, taking both the man and the bike to the ground. A searing pain bit into her shin. His knee connected with her head, rattling her brain. She rolled back, and as her vision dimmed, saw the bastard pulling a gun, aiming at the captain who'd just climbed over the fence and was down on one knee.

Her head swam, but she pushed away from the pavement and dove at Luke again, unbalancing him as his weapon fired. She felt the bite of the bullet on her neck a split second before they went down together.

Chapter Twenty

Hunter left J.T. to take a nap on the sofa. He drove by the station to see if his brother and Gabi were back yet. They weren't.

Leila was sitting at the front desk with a big brown envelope in her hands, mouth agape.

Since he'd never seen the woman speechless before, curiosity got the better of him, and he strolled over.

"What's that?"

She blinked. "DNA ancestry search. You send in a cheek swab and they tell you who you're related to, dead or living. As long as your relatives are in their database. But a lot of people are doing it now. It's some new fad."

He seemed to remember reading something online. "Yeah?"

"My youngest boy did it as a school project for biology. We found a couple of distant relatives we didn't know about. And, apparently, we're related to President Garfield." She dropped the envelope. "Frankly, I was hoping we'd find out we're distant cousins to Manolo Blahnik."

After Hunter left the station, he drove over to his brother's place to check on his father. The old man was rebelling. To make sure that he wouldn't sneak out and go to town in search of hard liquor, Hunter decided to stay.

He spent two hours chopping wood. He ignored his protesting back, stiff from spending the night on the floor in a sleeping bag. He'd given the couch to his guest. The physical labor helped to work out his muscles.

Hunter wielded his ax on the side of the house opposite from the woods. That should be safe enough. Anyone wanting to take a shot at him would have to come out into the open to do it, stand in the middle of the field. Hunter had his brother's handgun tucked into the back of his jeans. He was ready.

He worked up a good sweat by the second hour. Time for a break. He wedged the ax into a chunk of wood and went inside, grabbed a snack and a soda. He checked on his father downstairs. The old man was sleeping. Hunter was getting ready to go back out again when the mail came. Pete Kentner, the mailman, brought it up to the front door.

"Hey, I thought you might be hanging out over here. Sorry I couldn't come to the party," he said. "I'm glad you're home safe. Can't believe someone would smear a hero like you. What the hell is wrong with people? Thank God, nobody believed her."

Her who? Hunter wanted to ask, but Pete kept on talking as he was handing over the mail: bills, junk mail, and the *Broslin Journal,* all held together by a rubber band. "I just want to shake your hand. You're a hero in this town, no matter what anybody says."

"Thanks."

But before Hunter could ask who said what about him, Pete was already off with "I'm running late," and a wave.

Back in the kitchen, Hunter grabbed a cup of coffee and sat down with the paper, a biweekly publication that dealt with local matters. He caught his own picture on the front page then Gabi's a few paragraphs lower.

CORRUPT COP FRAMES LOCAL HERO, FAILS the headline said.

He read the article with his jaw clenched, an exposé that told of Gabriella Maria Flores's ruined career in the city. *Internal investigation on corruption charges. Acceptance of bribes. Misappropriation of evidence. False arrests and other misconduct.* It was bad. A lot worse than he'd thought. Tony, the stupid bastard, had dragged her right through the mud with him.

Hunter slammed down the paper and called the editor, told him what he thought of the article.

The attack on Gabi riled him up. Of course, if there'd ever been a woman who could stand up for herself, it was Gabi. But he cared about her, cared what people thought about her, cared that she'd be hurt when she read all that drivel.

He was about to call her to warn her when his brother came in with mud-streaked clothes and face.

"Flores got shot," he said instead of greeting.

Hunter sprang to his feet. "How badly?"

"She's well enough to insist on driving herself to the emergency room. As stubborn as you are." Ethan paused for a moment. Shook his head. "No hesitation, not a lick of fear, just jumped in front of the bullet. You should have seen her fly through the air to take Luke Wilson down."

Hunter sure as hell hoped the *Broslin Journal* would run *that* story. "Which hospital? West Chester?"

But Ethan shook his head. "You're not family. They're not going to let you back. You can check on her when she gets home later."

How long before she got home? An hour? Two? Worry and impatience buzzed through Hunter. He slid the newspaper toward his brother on the kitchen island, then tried to call Gabi, but she didn't pick up.

Ethan read the headline and swore under his breath. "She just saved my life. Wilson was aiming at me."

"You think Luke Wilson is our guy?"

Ethan grabbed a cold soda from the fridge and came to sit by Hunter. He took a swig. "He has a rifle that uses .45 caliber bullets. No alibi for Friday night or the afternoon when the cruiser's windows were shot out. A history of violence. And revenge is his religion. The reason he was in prison? He beat his own cousin to death for some small betrayal."

"Got the rifle?"

"Waiting for the search warrant."

Gabi got hurt. Hunter's thoughts kept looping back to that. "I should have gone with you two." He fired off a quick text to see how she was doing.

Ethan grabbed a sheet of paper towel and rubbed some dried mud off his face. "She doesn't need a bodyguard. She can handle the job."

Of course, she could handle the job. But Hunter couldn't handle the idea of her getting hurt.

But at last, his cell phone pinged as Gabi texted back. *I'm fine.*

Hunter relaxed a little as he watched his brother clean himself up. "Had a mud treatment for your complexion? You know you'll never be as handsome as I am, right?"

Ethan snorted, then balled up the paper towel and chucked it toward the waste basket, made a perfect shot. Next he rolled up the *Broslin Journal* and tried to do the same with that, but Hunter snatched the newspaper out of the air and shoved it into his back pocket for later.

"You missed a spot under your left eye." He pointed out a thumbnail-size dot of mud on his brother's face.

Ethan rubbed the dirt off with the back of his hand. "What do you want for dinner?"

"I don't think I'll be here for dinner tonight either. I'm going to check on Gabi, and then I want to spend some time with J.T."

"How is he?"

"I worry about him."

"Got a bed yet?" his brother asked.

"Haven't had a chance."

Ethan nodded. "I've been thinking about the apartment. You want a different unit?"

After a moment of consideration, Hunter shook his head. "I'll be moving soon, anyway. Still thinking about building something, maybe out here. Thinking about Arnie's gas station too. It's for sale." He paused. "How would you feel about the two of us going in as partners?"

Ethan rubbed the back of his neck for a second, narrowed his eyes as he thought about it. Then he finally said, "It could happen."

"I need to research it a lot more. How feasible it is as a business? What kind of return on investment we're talking about?"

"Bring me the figures when you have them."

"Will do," Hunter promised. "Anyway, if we go ahead with the station, I'll just take Arnie's old quarters on top of the mechanic shop. Plenty of room up there. The closer I am to the business, the better I can keep an eye on things. The apartment I have right now will work fine until then."

"What if the shooter comes back for you?"

"I know how to take care of myself. J.T. will probably stay a couple of days. Besides"—he grinned—"Officer Hot Lips is in the building."

Ethan shot him an amused look. "You better quit talking about her that way before she overhears. She's woman enough to kick your sorry ass."

"I know," Hunter said with feeling. He liked that about her. Go figure.

She was the polar opposite of the sweet, mild, homemaker type woman he'd always thought he wanted in his life. And yet, he couldn't stop thinking about her. Since he had a feeling his brother would rather not hear about any dirty fantasies that involved one of his officers, Hunter changed the subject. "Anyway, you got Luke Wilson in custody."

Ethan took a drink. "I still don't want you to let your guard down. I want Wilson's rifle first and the ballistics confirmed. I want to be one hundred percent sure that he was the shooter. I want a full confession on Cindy. We'll probably get it. Officer Flores will be conducting the interrogation."

Hunter grinned. "I feel bad for the poor bastard." He paused. "I suppose we'll find out how Wilson got my Beretta out of the safe."

"He worked at Arnie's as a car mechanic at one point. He's good with tools." Ethan finished his drink. "Robin will let me know when his lawyer gets there, and I'll go back in to observe the questioning."

The sounds of the television downstairs reached them.

Hunter nodded toward the closed basement door. "What are you going to do about the old man while you go into the station?" Since the shooting, they'd only left their father by himself when absolutely necessary.

"I'll take him with me. He'll probably want to swing by his place and pick up some clean clothes anyway."

"Let me know if you need help with him." Hunter slid off his chair. "I should get home. See about my guest."

He drove straight to the apartment building and found J.T. in the middle of his bedroom.

The kid turned as Hunter walked in. "This is where it happened? And you just came in and saw her?"

"Yeah."

"That's fucked up, man."

"It wasn't pretty."

J.T.'s face darkened as he nodded. "Bad shit happens, and then you live with it. That's what we're supposed to do, right?"

Hunter didn't like the dark, bitter tone in his friend's voice. He made them a couple of sandwiches and they ate in the living room, the TV on the sports channel, but the game was pretty lackluster. Afterwards, J.T. decided to go for a drive. He said he wanted to check out the town, but Hunter suspected he wanted to find a bar. All the beer Ethan had stocked for him in the fridge was gone.

Since Hunter had gotten sweaty while chopping wood at the farm, he showered and changed, then he walked upstairs to see if Gabi was home from the hospital.

She answered on the first knock. A palm-size white bandage covered the side of her neck.

Okay, that didn't look like nothing. His chest muscles pulled tight. "How are you?"

"It's barely a scratch. More of a bullet burn than a hit. I just had to have it properly disinfected, since we rolled around in the mud a little." She was smiling as if it'd been all fun and games.

She would think that. *Jesus.*

A couple of stray strands had escaped her loose bun. They were wet. She was probably fresh out of the shower too. She wore jeans with a soft white shirt that showed the outline of her bra.

The connection between them was palpable. Need buzzed through him, not the general need to get laid because, hey, he was finally home from the army. His need for her was specific and urgent. He didn't just want sex. He wanted Gabi.

And all she wanted was to be done here and to go back to Philly. Frustration punched through him. He stepped forward, dipped his head, and slanted his mouth over hers. God, she tasted sweet.

She relaxed into his arms. And then he gathered her against him more closely and kissed her properly.

She could have been seriously hurt. He kissed her until that unbearable thought faded from his brain. He kissed her until pretty much everything faded.

When he pulled back, she shook her head. "What was that for?"

"I was worried."

"You shouldn't."

"It's a free country. I worry when I want to."

"I meant you shouldn't keep kissing me. You're still my partner."

"It was an innocent expression of relief. And the case is practically in the can."

"The key word here is *practically.*" She shook her head again and let him in. "Where's your friend?"

"J.T. went out for a ride. He's restless. He needs help, but I'm not sure how to give it."

"Just be there when he's ready to talk."

Hunter nodded. "I want to thank you for protecting my brother," he said after a moment. They were standing between the kitchen and the living room. He reached up, feathering a light touch on her neck under the bandage.

She didn't step away. "Just doing my job."

"I'm grateful all the same." He paused. "You get the local paper?"

She flashed a quick, wry smile and did move away at last. "This might come as a surprise to you, but I don't have that deep an interest in bake-offs. I can offer the latest issue of *Guns & Ammo* if you need something to read."

What he wanted her to offer him sure as hell wasn't reading material.

He pulled the folded-up *Broslin Journal* from his back pocket and handed it to her. "You might want to read this."

* * *

Gabi gestured him to her couch while she sank onto the love seat and read the headline.

Her gaze flew to Hunter. "Has your brother seen it?"

Hunter nodded.

"Am I fired?"

A scandal among his officers was the last thing a police captain would want. Sure, he knew her story, but hearing her side at the interview was different from having a more darkly biased, sensationalized version splashed across the pages that called his judgment into question for hiring her and bringing her to Broslin.

Hunter had that take-it-easy look on his face. "My brother doesn't run the PD by what the newspapers print."

A small measure of relief took the edge off her panic. She put the paper down, couldn't stand reading the entire story that made her out to be a conscienceless, corrupt cop who, along with her partner, let criminals go in exchange for money, misappropriated evidence, then, while her partner went to prison, got off on a technicality.

Hunter leaned back, stretched his muscular legs out in front of him and crossed them at the ankles, making himself at home on her sofa. His gaze kept dipping to her bandage. She found it sweet that he worried about her.

"I called and asked them to correct their story," he said.

She stared. He didn't owe her anything. She hadn't gone easy on him. Why would he care enough to defend her? That he did said something about him and his own sense of justice.

"Thanks. I hate reporters."

"Want to talk about it?"

"About as much as I want to be shot in the head." But maybe he was looking for an excuse to talk, an excuse for not having to go back down into his apartment, where dark memories were waiting.

Her gaze skimmed the shadows under his eyes. He'd had a rough couple of days: a murder, locked up twice, attempts on his father and his brother.

"Hey," she found herself saying, "want to stay and watch a game?"

"Is the game still on?"

"Over, thank God. A snoozer. I have last week's taped since I was on duty. From what I hear, it should be worth watching."

He nodded.

She got up and headed to the fridge. "How about a beer?"

"I think you're the perfect woman." He grinned at her. "Except for that puzzling reluctance to kiss. We're going to have to work on that."

Chapter Twenty-One

The game was great and the conversation was even better, as far as Hunter was concerned. During the slow parts, they talked about the advantages of bolt-action rifles versus lever-action. And Hunter found yet another thing he liked about Gabi.

"You hunt?" Maybe someday they could go out together. He could fill Ethan's giant freezer in the garage with venison.

But Gabi shook her head. "Just like guns. They're simple. Dependable. Get the job done." She paused for a second before saying, "Charlie Heinz invited me to his hunting cabin. He's big on trophy taxidermy."

Hunter's back muscles stiffened. "What did you tell him?"

"No, thanks. As far as men go, I prefer unmarried. And as far as food goes, I prefer to think they grow it at the 7-Eleven."

No threat of her winning the pie-baking contest, he thought, but he didn't think less of her because of it. He liked the fact that she'd turned down Charlie.

Then the game picked up, and they both leaped off the couch at the same time to cheer when the Eagles won at the end.

All in all, they spent an evening together that was more pleasurable than he could remember having in a long time. When he finally got up, he was surprised to find himself reluctant to leave. She was as comfortable to hang with as any of his army buddies.

But he felt things for her that he'd never felt for his friends. He felt things for her he'd never even felt for Cindy.

He stood in front of her door, his hand on the doorknob. That little mole in the corner of her mouth was driving him crazy.

"Thanks for the game and the beer." He reached for her waist with his free hand, kept his gaze on hers as he pulled her slowly against him. His gaze dipped to her lips.

"Don't kiss me. I don't like it when you muddle my brain and make me question my professional objections."

"Then brace yourself. You're going to hate this." He kissed the mole first. Then he covered her full lips with kisses. Then he licked the seam because he couldn't wait to taste her again.

He pulled back, maybe an inch. "Tell me how this is a bad idea," he whispered against her lips.

She pressed herself against him, her breasts flattened against his chest. His entire body felt electrified, wanting, demanding more. He reached up to cup the back of her head, and angled his own to kiss her again. Then he deepened the kiss, explored the softness of her mouth. *This* was what he needed.

His body grew hard as his tongue danced with hers. His free hand drifted down from her waist to her firm, well-shaped butt and gathered her even closer to him, nestling his erection against her softness.

The quiet moan that escaped her throat was his undoing. He kissed her harder, his needs more demanding with every passing second.

His hand slid down her maddening curves, under her thigh, and he lifted her leg up, hooked it over his hip. That allowed his erection to grind against her soft center in the most delicious way. The sweet, agonizing friction just about killed him.

"We can't keep doing this. It's not right," she murmured against his lips and lifted her other leg, hopping up into his arms.

Her endless legs wrapped around his waist, lining up their bodies perfectly, and he shifted her so her back was against the door, the pressure of his body holding her in place.

That left his hands free, a strategic advantage. He reached up to unbutton her shirt, might have popped a button or two, which were quickly forgotten once he found bare skin.

She wore a sports bra, plain white, sexiest thing he'd ever seen. Her breasts were perfect—they didn't need any pushing up or being framed in lace. He liked the simplicity, the I-am-what-I-am vibe that she had in abundance. He dipped his head to the valley of her breasts and inhaled her feminine scent, rubbed his lips against her velvet skin.

Then he reached up and tugged down the elastic material of the sports bra, and her breasts sprang free, became accessible to him at last. He had no intention of waiting. He closed his lips around the nearest nipple, licked it, scraped his teeth over it, suckled it into a hard peak.

He moved to the other breast after a moment, working on divesting her of her pants all the while.

But just when he was nearly done with unbuttoning her jeans, her grip around his neck loosened. She gasped into his hair. "Okay. Seriously. I can't have sex with my boss's brother."

He growled a single word: "Quit."

But he left the last button alone. He lifted his lips from her breasts and kissed her again, with all the desperation he felt. She was right, they shouldn't be doing this. Not because his brother might disapprove, which he didn't, but because of how things would look for her. She'd cleared Hunter of the murder, then later it comes to light that they'd been having sex. She didn't need to be accused as a crooked cop again. He wouldn't do that to her.

He wasn't going to do anything that might hurt her. Someday soon—although not nearly soon enough—Luke Wilson was going to be tried and convicted. Case closed. Gabi was worth the wait.

He rested his forehead against hers. "I want you."

She drew her lungs full, which lifted her breasts, which nearly broke his resolve. "The frustration is mutual," she told him.

He let her down but didn't step away yet, couldn't.

She pulled up her bra and drew her shirt together. "You know, auxiliary officers don't normally get to do strip searches."

And they laughed together, both of them still a little breathless, their blood still rushing.

He stepped back at last.

She buttoned up what buttons she had left. "Now what?"

"Once Wilson's put away, things will be easier. It'll be abundantly obvious to everyone that I had nothing to do with the murder, so a relationship between us won't have any shadow of doubt hanging over it."

"What if I'm back in Philly by then?" She held his gaze.

"Then you won't have to worry about dating your boss's brother. I can be in Philly in an hour or so. You're worth the drive. And you're worth the wait." She was worth whatever it took to get her.

A soft light came into her eyes, accompanied by soft heat. She looked as if she might just step back into his arms again for another kiss. But if she did, he wasn't going to be able to let her go a second time. So Hunter reached back and opened the door, didn't turn back to her until he was standing in the threshold. "Good night, Gabi."

For the first time since he'd met her, her eyes held a trace of vulnerability. "Good night, Hunter."

He went back downstairs with a hard-on. Thank God, J.T. was still out. The apartment felt dreary suddenly. Being on the basement level had never bothered Hunter before, but now he felt like he was in some dark cellar, all the light just one floor above him.

J.T. came in half an hour later, walking less than steadily. He dropped to the couch and stretched out. "Nice little town. I found Finnegan's. Man, I'm beat." He closed his eyes.

Hunter rolled out his sleeping bag on the floor again, on the other side of the room, against the wall. He wondered how often his friend drank. Was this how J.T. handled the memories of his captivity?

Hunter stared at the dark ceiling. Spring and the rehab center seemed a long time away.

He closed his eyes, let the minutes tick by, his thoughts returning to Gabi. His phone buzzed on the coffee table. *Ethan.* Hunter took the call into the bathroom so he wouldn't bother J.T.

"Anything new?" he asked as he closed the door behind him.

"Not yet, but I got the search warrant and put a rush order in on the ballistics on Wilson's rifle. As long as some high-profile case doesn't come in, we should have the results tomorrow. I thought I'd check in with you."

"All is quiet on the western front. When is Sophie coming home?"

"Her mother needs some work on the house. She'll stay until the end of the week to supervise it."

"The old man's still at the farm?"

"Passed out already."

"Is he drinking with his pain meds?" They would have given him pills for his broken arm in the ER.

"Nothing I can do about it," Ethan said, his voice laced with frustration. "He's been doing fine. Then the anniversary of mom's death came, and he went over the edge."

"Maybe we should try again to talk him into rehab."

"Want to have your head ripped off, be my guest. I'm done with that fantasy. We can't make him get better if he doesn't want it."

Ethan was right. He'd dealt with their father up close and personal over the years, while Hunter saw the man maybe once or twice during each leave. "I hate to feel this useless."

A moment of silence passed on the other end. Then what might have been a groan. "If you want to, we can talk to him."

"If he goes away, I have combat pay. I can foot the bill. He shouldn't always be your responsibility."

"We'll figure out the finances, if he agrees to go."

They talked for another few minutes before hanging up, then Hunter climbed back into his sleeping bag again.

He dreamed about hunting with Gabi, naked. Didn't bother them any—not in the summer heat. The fact that summer wasn't deer hunting season didn't come up in the dream.

Morning dew glistened on her skin as she stretched on the soft grass of a meadow next to him, taking a break from all that deer stalking. Her dark hair spread out around her like fine silk. She had boobs that belonged in a Renaissance painting. Or his hands. He preferred the latter.

* * *

Since Luke Wilson's lawyer finally put in an appearance, first thing in the morning, Gabi sat in the interview room with him and his client, hoping that the questioning would go smoothly. She wanted to close this case like she'd never wanted to close a case before.

Because somewhere at the end of this mess, Hunter would be waiting for her. The thought brought a smile to her face, which earned a suspicious look from the lawyer.

She cleared her throat. Captain Bing was behind the two-way mirror. Since the investigation involved him and his family, he stayed out of the interrogation room, but he would be watching closely.

"Where were you Friday night between six and seven p.m.?" Gabi addressed the suspect.

"I don't have to tell you shit," Wilson said between his teeth.

The mud had dried on his clothes, but that didn't improve his appearance. He was bleary-eyed and bad-tempered, his comb-over sticking up every which way. The night spent in the holding cell hadn't been kind to him.

She asked after his whereabouts for the date and time when the captain's cruiser's windows had been shot out.

He sneered. "I was home, sleeping."

"Do you have any witnesses?"

"Your mother."

Wilson's lawyer cleared his throat. Not that the subtle warning held back his client any.

"This is police overreach," Wilson protested loudly. "Harassment. Watch if I don't press charges. Police brutality too. When you attacked me, I hit my knee. Maybe it's permanent damage. Maybe I'll never walk again."

She was tempted to remind him that he'd walked perfectly fine to the interview room just minutes before, but she didn't.

She held his gaze. "You shot at an officer of the law." At least once. He'd shot at the captain while they'd been trying to apprehend him, nicking her.

Wilson puffed his chest out. "You attacked me, and my gun went off by accident. I could have been killed." He looked at his lawyer. "This is a frame-up. Do something."

"Maybe we could skip the theatrics," Gabi suggested. "Right now, I'm looking at you for murder, two attacks with a deadly weapon and vehicular assault. How about we get serious for a minute?"

The lawyer asked for time and furiously whispered back and forth with his client. Finally, Wilson gave a reluctant nod, but he was scowling heavily.

"We want to make a deal," the lawyer said. "We'll disclose Mr. Wilson's whereabouts for the night of the murder so you can move on and focus on finding the real killer. In exchange, no punitive action will be taken against my client for what he might reveal."

"Give me a sec." Gabi went out, stepped into the next room.

The captain nodded. "Go for it."

She went back to the interrogation room, but stayed standing this time. "Okay."

So the lawyer told her at which bar Wilson had spent Friday night, gave names of people he'd been drinking with. Since Wilson was out on parole after serving time for beating his cousin to death in a bar, his parole stipulated that he wasn't allowed in establishments that served alcohol.

The lawyer reminded Gabi that she'd offered immunity.

She nodded. She was after a murderer. She couldn't have cared less about Wilson having a beer.

She left the men again, made calls, confirmed the story, then let Wilson go and that was that as far as that thread of the investigation went. To say that she was disappointed was a vast understatement.

Before she could figure out what to do next, she had to go out on a car-theft call that turned out to be an elderly woman not remembering where she parked in the grocery store parking lot. Gabi helped her find her car, then went to assist Joe with a traffic accident. No fatal casualties, but it still took the better part of two hours.

Broslin PD was a small department: Captain Bing, Harper Finnegan, Chase Merritt, Mike Morris, Joe Kessler, and Gabi. Six people, three shifts, two on the day shifts, one on the night shift, usually. Pretty thin coverage. Even thinner now that Harper was on leave, Mike still at the hospital, and most of Gabi's time was taken up by the murder case.

At a larger department, she might have been able to work the murder full-time. Here, she had to help out with other tasks as needed.

By the time she got back to the station, the ballistics report on Wilson's rifle was in. It confirmed that the bullet that had gone through the captain's windows didn't come from that weapon. No surprise there, at this point.

Her suspect list was empty once again. There had to be a clue somewhere. What had she missed?

She took over the conference room and spread out the case file printouts until paper covered every inch of the long table.

Hunter popped his head in. "Need help? I got plenty of time. J.T. got sloshed last night. He's not up for company." He took in her piles and stepped all the way inside, closed the door behind him.

Just looking at him sent her blood rushing. Ridiculous. They were at work. She was a professional. *Focus on the work.*

"Luke Wilson alibied out. We need to find something we missed." She picked up the handful of papers nearest to her.

Hunter did the same. He leafed through information. Minutes ticked on as they traded one stack of papers for another.

Then suddenly his head came up. "How about the guy Cindy slept with earlier on Friday? You said there was another guy besides Porter."

"We have no clues to the second man's identity. Cindy's parents weren't aware of Cindy dating anyone but you. The DNA we have from the sperm doesn't have any close matches in any of the criminal databases."

"How about other DNA databases?"

185

She raised an eyebrow.

"Those places people send their DNA to and get their ancestry? Leila did it." He started out in a rush of excitement, but it quickly evaporated. His lips twisted. "What are the chances that the killer is interested in ancestry research?"

She could have kissed him. If they weren't on duty, she might have. "As long as somebody even remotely related to the killer has sent in DNA, the database will give us his name. Then we contact that guy and ask if he has any relatives in Broslin."

"Would this be legal?"

"DNA collected at the scene of a crime is fair game for pretty much anything." She picked up the phone, dialed the front desk, and explained to Leila what needed to be done. Leila promised to get right on it.

Buoyed by the possible lead, fully reenergized now, Gabi went back to the question that became more and more important as they eliminated suspects. "So how did the killer get your gun? Could someone have guessed the combination to the gun safe?"

"Echo34," he said.

Okay, not something obvious like his last name or birthday or 123456. "Does it mean anything?"

"My basic training company. Nobody in Broslin would know. What if the killer picked the lock?"

She'd played that movie in her head before, but now she played it again. "So he picks the lock on the front door, comes in, cracks the safe, hoping for money. He finds some cash and the gun and takes both. Cindy arrives. The killer hides in the bathroom. Cindy goes into the bedroom. She gets on the phone to call you. The killer makes a run for it, Cindy screams, he turns and shoots."

"Why didn't Doris hear the scream?"

"Maybe she thought it was part of her Sherlock movie."

Hunter didn't look convinced. "So a master safe cracker picks my apartment to break into? I'm a soldier. What did he think I'd have? Why not break into a bank, or at least a mansion?"

"That's why I didn't seriously consider the burglary option at the beginning. But at this stage... Do you know any master safe crackers in Broslin?"

Hunter shook his head. "Ethan mentioned a spate of bank robberies a while back, but they used farm machinery to drive through the front window, then grabbed the money from the cashiers."

She'd heard all about that. *Bank robbery by tractor. Only in Broslin.* Gabi bit her lip. She was so not commenting.

"Do you think whoever this other guy was in Cindy's life is the one who killed her?" Hunter asked.

"I don't know. That would mean that the three incidents are not related."

"So either the mystery boyfriend killed her, and the cruiser's windows really were just a hunter, my father's accident just an accident, or the mystery boyfriend has nothing to do with the murder and the three incidents *are* related, in which case Cindy was probably collateral damage," he said in a tight voice. "Someone came for me and found her in my apartment instead."

"I think I like the theory that the three incidents are related. It's hard to believe in so much coincidence."

"So assuming it's the Bing men who are targeted... Someone wants to kill me, watches the apartment. He sees Cindy go in. He tells her he needs to see me for something and asks if he could come in to wait." He paused. "They're waiting, chatting, and at some point Cindy realizes that the guy is up to something. She grows uncomfortable and calls me, but I don't pick up." Hunter sat heavily. "She goes into the bedroom and grabs the gun. The guy takes it away from her."

A long moment of silence stretched between them.

Gabi broke it at last with "Then the following week, Captain Bing is shot at in his own driveway. The same day, someone runs Zechariah Bing off the road. Assuming that the three incidents are related and it's the three Bing men who are targeted, are we sure that the captain is the primary target?"

"He's the most logical choice. He routinely makes enemies among the criminal element. It's his job. The killer wanted to hurt my brother by targeting his family."

"But—" She lifted her index finger. "Likely suspects were identified and investigated. They cannot be directly linked to any of the three incidents at this point."

Hunter watched her. "You only went back six months when figuring out who was released with a possible grudge against my brother. Could be the killer had been out longer. Maybe you can go back and check again."

"Yes." She'd already thought of that, was going to do it next. "Then there's another possibility."

He waited.

"It's possible that the primary target is not the captain. It could be you or your father. In which case, we should be looking for a different kind of motive."

He stared at her, and she could tell that a million thoughts were flying through his brain all at once. "My father," he said. "He's been a heavy drinker for a long time. He gambles. He borrows money, then he doesn't pay it back. I wouldn't be surprised if he had enemies."

Loan sharks? A distinct possibility. She'd had some experience in that area from her old job. A lot of people in the neighborhoods she'd patrolled lived hand to mouth, had to take payday loans and worse to make ends meet.

"How about you?" she probed.

But Hunter said, "I haven't spent enough time around here to piss anyone off to that degree."

Still, now that she thought of it, she wanted to see that line of thinking to the end. "You're a soldier."

"I killed people, you mean."

"How many?"

"Too many."

"Do you remember exactly?"

His expression darkened. "I remember every one, what they wore, where we were, if they were running toward me or away from me, and the look on their faces when they realized they were dying."

The stark tone of his voice touched something deep inside her. The ones he'd killed, even if they were the enemy, had mattered to him. He wasn't a callous man. Human life mattered to Hunter Bing. In hindsight, it seemed strange now that she'd ever suspected him of Cindy's murder.

"Could someone want revenge on you for something?"

"And follow me home to the US? How would they know where I live? I just got here. How could they get a visa this fast?"

"People in Afghanistan have relatives in the US. Say, you killed someone over there, and they have a nephew somewhere here."

He thought for a moment. "How would they know I was the one they were looking for? It's not like we wear name tags to battle."

No. The theory seemed pretty far-fetched. But some wayward thoughts she couldn't pin down floated in the back of her head, something that had to do with Hunter. Something that filled her with worry.

"All right," Gabi said after a frustrated few seconds when she still couldn't pin down the source of her sudden unease. "Let's go see your father and chat with him about his enemies."

The case was all over the place. She couldn't make head or tail of it. She was grasping at straws, and she knew it.

Maybe all first-time investigators feel this way.

She wished she had more experience. She wanted to do her best. Not just for the victim, but also because Hunter was involved in all this.

On the way over to the farm, he asked to swing by the diner.

"Closed," she said as they pulled up. "The sign says. Why are they closed in the middle of the day?" She hoped Eileen was okay. "And why is the parking lot full?"

Hunter smiled mysteriously as he got out of the car. "You'll see."

He walked up to the door, knocked, and they were let in.

The place was full to capacity, as if every woman in Broslin had decided to hang out here today. The tables were loaded with stacks of food and baskets set out in an assembly line.

Eileen hurried over. She hugged Gabi. "Stupid newspaper article. Don't pay any attention to it. Nobody else does."

Then she pulled back and greeted Hunter, finishing with "Staying to help?"

"In the middle of a case. On duty. Sorry." Hunter pulled an envelope from his pocket and handed it over. "My brother said he already dropped off his. I wanted to make sure I don't miss the deadline."

"Thank you." Eileen took his face into her hands, and smacked a kiss on his cheek. "Definitely not too late."

Gabi checked out the table nearest to her. In addition to food, the baskets also contained crayons and a small stuffed animal. Others had toiletry kits instead of toys.

Eileen beamed. "Broslin Baskets. They go to single moms, some older people who are alone, injured veterans. We're a regular Santa's workshop this time of the year."

Gabi went for her wallet, pulled out as many bills as she could afford to give. "I don't have a check. I hope this is okay."

"More than okay." Eileen kissed her too, then hugged her again for good measure.

This must be what family love felt like, Gabi thought, and held on for an extra second.

Her mother would have said she'd just been suckered out of money, but Gabi didn't feel taken advantage of; she felt something completely different. She felt gooey and warm inside.

"I know what you're doing," she told Hunter on their way back to her car. "You're trying to show me the town Christmas spirit."

"Who? Me?" He acted all innocent.

"You're like the ghost of the past or the future or whatever, pretending I'm Scrooge."

They were at the cruiser, she on her side, he on his, turned toward each other with the car's roof between them.

A dangerous glint came into his eyes. "Gabi, if I ever show up in your bedroom in the middle of the night, believe me, it won't be to give you a morality lesson."

She felt the promise of that through her body down to her toes. But she said, "If anyone showed up in my bedroom in the middle of the night, I'm likely to shoot them."

He laughed as he shook his head at her. "Of course, you would."

Chapter Twenty-Two

They grabbed a couple of burgers from the drive-through at the edge of town. Since J.T. hadn't called to see about any afternoon plans, Hunter figured his buddy had found something to keep himself busy. Young guy, alone in the apartment, fresh out of the army—Hunter was betting on the porn channel.

While Gabi drove, Hunter thought about what he could do with J.T. for fun. Not cold enough for ice fishing on the reservoir, not enough snow for snowshoeing. Deer season closed mid-December usually. They had extended season, antlerless, for regular firearms in Chester County, he'd seen the sign on the door at the gas station, but that didn't open until the twenty-sixth, the day after Christmas.

They could go hunt for squirrels, raccoons, or foxes, he supposed. Better than sitting all day in front of the TV. Hunter decided to ask J.T. about it when he got back from talking to his father.

He wasn't looking forward to having Gabi and the old man in the same room. His father had a mean streak. Cindy hadn't been able to handle him at all. If they were out together and for some reason Hunter had to swing by the old man's place, Cindy would have him drop her off at her parents' house first.

"He's a morose bastard," he warned Gabi as they got out of the car.

But she flashed a smile that said she ate morose bastards for breakfast.

And he wanted to kiss her right then and there. Apparently, he was a total sucker for the whole tough-chick-cop thing. Or maybe he was just a total sucker for Gabi.

The old man wouldn't come up from the basement, not even to be interviewed by the police, so they had to go down.

The place was only partially finished, furnished with Ethan's old furniture, plus a TV and a small fridge, the beginnings of a man cave.

Hunter's father began with "I don't feel like talking. I was about to grab a nap. My arm hurts. I don't have to go to work. I can do whatever I want."

He worked construction, and his crew had just finished a project, hadn't been called for the next. Winter was hit and miss in construction, depending on the weather. As usual, Zechariah Bing spent his downtime in the bottle. And this time he would stay in there for a good while since he couldn't work with his arm in a cast.

"I only have a couple of questions," Gabi countered without heat. "It's nice that I can talk to you here and don't have to ask you to come to the station. I spend half my life there." She smiled.

The threat was so veiled it was barely visible. Yet the old man caught her meaning: either he talk here or she'd take him in. "Be quick about it."

Hunter was about to tell him to be polite, but Gabi shook her head barely perceptibly. So Hunter hung back.

"It's about the accident," she began. "Did you see the face of the man who ran you off the road?"

The old man rolled his eyes at her as if she was a terrible bother. "I already told my son the almighty captain that I didn't. Dark SUV. Tinted windows. I didn't have time to notice more. One minute he bumped me, the next my car was flipping."

"I don't suppose you saw the license plate."

"What did I just tell ya?" he snapped at her.

"Do you have any enemies?"

He shrugged. "Plenty of assholes in this world."

"Anyone in particular? Anyone threatened you lately?"

"My shithead boss, for one." He harrumphed. "Last day on the last job, he said he'd fire me the next time he caught me drunk. Not that I drink before work. He makes up that baloney so he can have an excuse for docking my pay."

Since he had half a dozen empty beer bottles on an old coffee table in front of him and he was obviously at least partially intoxicated, his words didn't exactly ring with veracity.

Gabi didn't challenge him on that. She didn't sympathize with the old man either. "Anyone else? You had a fight with anyone lately?"

"My bookie. I owe him money." He cast Hunter a disapproving look. "Not that my high and mighty sons would help a poor old man out."

DEATHWISH

Gabi shifted closer to him. "Did the bookie threaten you?"

"He said, if I didn't pay my debts, he was gonna rub me out. Shoot me, my wife, my kids, and my dog."

Hunter's ears perked up, but his father waved off any concern. "Dillard don't mean it. He always says shit like that. A talker, that one. I don't even have a wife, or a dog. Anyway, Dillard likes me."

Gabi considered for a moment. "I'll need his full name and information on where I can find him."

"Hell no. Where will I go to invest for retirement if you pigs put him away?"

She raised an eyebrow at Hunter.

"Ethan will know the guy," Hunter told her. His brother knew everyone in Broslin who engaged in criminal activity for a living.

"Who else?" she asked the old man. "Do you owe money to anyone else?"

"Girlie, people you owe money, they don't kill you. They know if you're dead, you can't pay them back."

"The man in the SUV didn't kill you," Gabi pointed out.

The old man took a moment to think that through, stroking the three-day stubble on his chin. "You might have something there. I might owe a small chunk to a certain moonshiner." He lifted up his hand in a protesting gesture. "Nope, I won't be telling you his name either."

But Gabi kept pushing. "Even if you don't think whoever ran you off the road really wants to kill you, you have to consider that your sons' lives could be in danger. And one person is already dead."

"I never liked the Simme girl. Stuck-up little bitch. My sons can take care of themselves. I raised them to be tough. They'll handle what comes their way."

His full confidence would have made Hunter feel good if he didn't know for certain that the old man's lack of worry stemmed from the fact that he didn't give a damn about his family. He held back a comment that his father didn't raise them, had been too drunk to raise anybody.

Gabi kept up with her inquiry, letting the insults roll off her, knowing what she wanted and pushing to get it. She wasn't threatening, wasn't overstepping her authority, but she didn't back down either, just kept going with single-minded determination that wore the old man down. By the end of the hour, he gave up protesting and just answered the questions, cooperating at last, even if glaring all the way. But he still wouldn't name names.

So Gabi explained to him that the captain would know the names of all the bookies in town and all the moonshiners. If the old man didn't give her specifics, she was going to take them all in. That would upset a lot of people, and they'd all be mad at the guy who caused all that big stink in the first place.

Wouldn't you know it, he suddenly remembered the names.

Gabi and Hunter went upstairs, but Hunter returned to the basement with food and water while Gabi used the facilities.

"That one doesn't rattle easily," his father said, looking up the stairs with a speculative glint in his eyes.

"You need to talk to her with more respect the next time." Hunter set the plate and glass on the table.

His father raised an out-of-control eyebrow that was bushy enough for rabbits to nest in. "You sweet on that she-wolf?"

"That'd be my private business."

The old man huffed. Then ended up shrugging. "She's a sight better than the other one. I'm looking forward to watching her put you in your place."

Hunter left him and drummed up the stairs.

Cindy had been an assumption. They got along great, so he assumed they'd make a good couple, could make a good future with each other. They never fought. No sparks—not in anger, but not really in passion either. Their lovemaking had been comfortable. He'd always thought that was because Cindy was a lady, restrained in bed as she was in everything, sweet, pliant. And he'd thought that was what he wanted. Only now, knowing Gabi, did he realize that things would never have worked out with Cindy.

He was almost thirty, and he'd never known the kind of blinding need he felt for Gabi. And, beyond the physical attraction, he truly liked her company. He respected her skills. He appreciated her sense of humor. He couldn't stop thinking about her.

He wasn't going to ignore those sparks, for starters. He was going to do whatever it took to help her solve this case, then he was going to seriously pursue Gabi until she admitted that she couldn't live without him.

"All right. Let's run down our new leads," she said as they got into her cruiser.

"The sooner, the better," he told her.

The moonshiner alibied out immediately. According to his wife, he'd been in the county jail for the past three weeks.

The bookie was harder to find. He wasn't at his home address. His wife claimed Dillard was out of state on a business trip, she wasn't sure where. Pure bullshit, but they couldn't exactly waterboard her to get the truth out of her.

Hunter's father didn't know where the bookie kept his office these days. He switched around often, and senior Bing hadn't had anything to invest in a while, so he hadn't kept up with the latest move. The bookie proved harder to pin down than a grasshopper on speed.

Hunter and Gabi kept searching until her shift ended, then decided to take a break and regroup the following morning. Gabi was going to work the phones a few more hours that evening to see if she could scare up a lead or two to get them restarted.

Hunter went home to J.T., who wasn't excited about the idea of hunting. Okay, maybe that'd been a bad idea. Someone with PTSD probably didn't want to be around too much gunfire.

They talked a while, mostly about Alaska. Hunter brought up all the good things he knew about the state: fresh air, open spaces, the beauty of nature. But J.T. didn't seem excited anymore even about going up north. He was just going through the motions. Which worried Hunter.

He decided to take the kid to Finnegan's. Rose Finnegan's cooking made everything better.

As luck would have it, Harper was tending the bar. A decent crowd filled the place. It looked like half the town was at Finnegan's. Hunter could barely see a table available.

Harper Finnegan normally worked for the PD as a detective, but he'd asked for a leave of absence to help out at the family business while his father was recuperating from a heart attack.

His face lit up when Hunter walked in. "Good to have you home, man. I'm really sorry about Cindy." He reached out, and they shook hands over the bar.

"How's your dad?" was the first thing Hunter asked. Harper's father was nothing like Hunter's. Sean Finnegan was as decent a man as they came. Tough too. If anyone could shrug off a heart attack, it was him.

"Complaining about the diet, but better every day. Anything new in the case? I hear you made auxiliary officer." He grinned. "I don't know if I should offer congratulations or condolences. If you need help with anything, you let me know."

"Gabi and I are handling it."

Harper lifted an eyebrow, catching that Hunter was calling Gabi by her first name, but he didn't ask any questions. He wasn't pushy that way, let people's private business stay private, which Hunter appreciated.

He introduced J.T.

"Welcome to Finnegan's." Harper shook J.T.'s hand too. "First drink's on the house."

J.T. grinned, apparently having learned nothing from the night before. "I like this place."

They got their drinks but stayed at the bar, reminiscing over old war stories. Hunter didn't ask J.T. about his days in captivity, but he did say, "There'll be a rehab facility opening here in the spring for people with PTSD."

J.T. immediately moved on to another subject. Nobody wanted to be the guy who got captured. Nobody wanted to be the one his friends had to risk their lives to rescue. Even if Hunter and the others didn't think of it that way, J.T. would.

Maybe they'd talk about it someday, but that day clearly wasn't today.

"So you're seriously getting a big-rig license?" Hunter asked. "You can do that here too. No need to go to the end of the world."

J.T. finished his first beer. "Chuck says I can get a license in Anchorage. That's where he did it."

"Not many girls up in Alaska. Don't men outnumber women ten to one?"

J.T. offered a shadow of his old smart-ass grin. "That's why I'll be taking long drives to the lower forty-eight."

He was trying hard to seem cheerful, said all the right words, kept a smile on his face, but Hunter could tell that the three months of his captivity weren't behind him yet. He still carried that heavy weight on his back.

Only one way to deal with the past, Hunter thought, one day at a time. He could cheer J.T. up while he was in town, starting tonight. He ordered them Rose Finnegan's famous potato soup and a roast beef sandwich with fries.

As Harper walked off with their order, Hunter half turned and caught sight of Gabi in the corner booth with her neighbor, Doris Hastings. They had two bottles of Guinness in front of them. Doris was laughing at something Gabi had said.

Hunter grinned. An odd couple, but in a way, their friendship made sense. Both women were tough as nails. Doris could easily have been Gabi's grandmother.

He was still watching them when a sleazeball meandered over and began chatting up Gabi. The guy—midforties, stained jeans, wrinkled shirt—waved his beer bottle around as he was saying something, gesturing too widely, laughing too loudly.

The idiot was clearly working some pickup line. The jealousy slicing through Hunter came so swiftly it made him blink.

Let her take care of it. But when the guy was still talking a couple of minutes later, Hunter slid off his seat. "I'll be back in a sec."

As he approached, Gabi grinned at the jackass. Okay, so she didn't feel threatened or annoyed.

Hunter stopped next to the table, then smiled at Gabi and Doris. "Hey." He flashed the man a cold look.

The guy flashed a cold look back. "I was here first."

"That means you'll be first to leave." Hunter put some steel in his voice and caught the amused smile on Gabi's face.

Doris's eyes shone extra brightly. She leaned forward as if she were watching a show at the dinner theatre.

Hunter knew he was acting stupid, but he couldn't stop himself. "I think you have someplace to be," he told the guy.

Who squared his shoulders like he was about to fight, but then raised his bottle to the ladies and slinked away.

"Howdy," J.T. said from behind. "Reinforcements are here."

Not that Hunter needed reinforcements, but he appreciated the sentiment behind the gesture. The two of them, Hunter realized, looked like what they were: trained killers. While jackass was stupid enough to take on one, he wasn't stupid enough to take on a team.

"Thanks, man." Hunter made the introductions, and they were invited to sit.

Which Hunter liked for about a minute, until he realized that J.T. was watching Gabi with a little too much interest.

"The guy was harmless," she was saying. "I was about to give him the brush-off."

Hunter was more than glad to hear that. He hadn't thought about Gabi going out and guys coming up to her. Now that he *was* thinking about it, he didn't like it.

She smiled at him from across the table. His gaze dipped to her sexy mole, then her full lips.

He wanted to lean over the bottles between them and kiss her, but he was pretty sure she wouldn't want him to do that here. He didn't want to cause trouble for her. She was an officer of the law, and a certain kind of behavior was expected of her in public.

J.T. said something and Gabi laughed deeply, sincerely, the sound of her laughter filling the booth and Hunter's chest.

He glanced at J.T. He loved the kid like his own brother, but he would be okay with it if J.T. decided to go on to Alaska sooner rather than later.

They stayed about two hours. J.T. had a few more beers, Hunter didn't. He was driving. Gabi didn't have a second Guinness either; she was the designated driver in her party.

"So the cop chick, huh?" J.T. asked as they walked into the apartment. "What about Cindy?"

"It's complicated."

J.T. shook his head. "I guess. I mean, hey, good for you."

"It's not that I didn't love Cindy," Hunter tried to explain, having a hard time believing they were talking about feelings. "I just didn't love her the right way. I didn't know what the right way was."

"When you find the right way, you know it," J.T. said pensively, which made Hunter wonder if he had a girl in Tennessee and if so, why he was driving away from her. Hunter could pretty much guess. Sometimes it was hard to come home and go back to a relationship. People changed.

But they'd had all the relationship talk two guys could handle for one day, so he didn't ask for details.

He fell asleep thinking about the murder case. He was looking forward to working with Gabi again the next day. *Time to pin down that bookie.*

Chapter Twenty-Three

Since the captain knew the local players and they knew him, he figured it'd be best if he partnered up with Gabi the following day. They drove around, looking for Dillard, following leads that came apart at the touch like spider webs.

"Would he resort to violence?" Gabi asked as they left the guy's house for the second time, a very nice federal-style home in a small development. He had a wife and three kids in college. The wife still wasn't cooperating.

"He has a record," the captain said. "Aggravated battery. And people graduate from small crimes to big crimes. It's the natural progression of things, unfortunately."

"Still, taking out the police captain and his family. That's a big step for a bookie."

"More like organized crime MO," the captain agreed.

"I didn't realize that kind of thing went on in Broslin."

"We have drugs, we have illegal weapons, at some level those tie to organized crime, although we see the bottom layer here in town, the little guys, the sellers." He rubbed his neck. "Doesn't mean someone isn't moving in under the radar."

If someone *was* moving in, what better way to clear the way than to take out the captain who was known for being tough on crime and investigating criminals aggressively? Okay, so that'd be motive. Yet another one.

That she couldn't even pin down the motive for sure at this stage of the game drove her crazy. The whole case kept shifting like quicksand. There was something here she wasn't seeing.

"Maybe the bookie is moving up in the ranks, wants to be a

regular crime boss. Taking out somebody who owes him sends a signal that he's tough. Taking out a police captain and his family sends the signal that there's a new boss in town. His rivals might just bend the knee instead of fighting him."

The captain bobbed his head from side to side as if trying that on for size. "Instead of fighting every petty criminal, it's a show of strength in one fell swoop, three deaths instead of dozens in a prolonged turf war. Maybe." But he didn't sound like he was buying it.

"We need to find him." Gabi hated the idea of either the captain or Hunter being in danger. And, as ornery as their father was, she didn't want to see him dead either.

She didn't want crime taking Broslin over. The town needed to stay the way it was. Because—okay, fine—it was a pretty nice place to live. She didn't want Doris to be too scared to go for a walk. She didn't want people robbing the diner for cash or demanding protection money from Eileen.

At one point, when Gabi hadn't been looking, the town had grown on her, dammit.

Hunter too.

She stifled a sigh. He kissed like a champion. She found it difficult to go ten minutes without thinking about his kisses, and how she wanted more. Which needed to stop. She felt guilty just having those thoughts in her head while sitting next to the captain.

But at the bar last night... The memory of Hunter rushing up to save her still put a smile on her lips. He looked pretty hot when he was in protective mode. Not that she needed saving. But she found that she liked that he cared. She didn't even mind Doris's teasing on the way home.

But if Hunter was protective of her, she felt equally protective toward Hunter. The bookie had to go.

She turned to her boss. "What was the last time you had to talk to Dillard?"

Captain Bing considered her question as they drove out of the development. "I haven't seen him in a while. He hasn't been an issue this fall." His forehead furrowed. "Maybe he has his new office out of town. I already know all his tricks. Could be he decided to move over a jurisdiction or two where he can fly under the radar for a while before they get wise to him. I'll call around."

She hoped the search would be quick. But even while she was thinking about the case, she was also wondering if Hunter would show up again that night for dinner.

"Hunter is a good man," the captain said, out of the blue.

"Yes, sir."

"You're a good woman."

"Thank you, sir."

And then he didn't say anything else.

Her eyes rounded. *Holy smokes.* Did the captain just refer to her relationship with his brother? And was that an approval?

* * *

While Ethan was out with Gabi, Hunter spent the day at the farm with J.T., babysitting his father, his patience wearing thin. He was more of a man of action. He wanted to be out there investigating.

He decided to make himself useful in other ways, tried to cheer up J.T. They talked about the old days and played video games Ethan had stocked for some kid who worked at the stables. Ethan was mentoring the boy, trying to make something out of a troublemaker.

J.T. beat Hunter in the games—he'd had a lot more practice—then helped him chop more wood. Ethan and Sophie would be set for a couple of years.

When Hunter and J.T. were throwing some balls for the dogs later, Hunter pointed out the rehab facility, mentioned the spring opening again. J.T. didn't react. Hunter showed him the spot where he was thinking about building a house.

"That's good, man," J.T. said, but a shadow crossed his face.

Maybe he was thinking how nice it was that Hunter had all this land in the family while he had no place to live, no job, going up to Alaska just so he could keep living. Suddenly, Hunter felt like an ass, like he'd been bragging.

J.T. turned toward the house. "How about a beer? Might as well drink up now. I'll have to dry out once I'll be driving around the clock, right?"

And Hunter nodded. He didn't think now was the time to bring up J.T.'s drinking.

They hung out at the house until Ethan came home, then took off. They picked up dinner from La Cocina, a nice little Mexican takeout place, to give the casseroles a break.

J.T. checked out the row of Santas in sombreros that decorated the counter. A couple of people came over to say hi to Hunter.

"You have a good setup here," J.T. told him as they were coming out.

"I know." Hunter put the bag of burritos on the back seat. "And I appreciate it. You could stay, you know? The town is pretty welcoming."

But J.T. said, "Nah, man. I'm just stopping in. Then I'll be on my way."

They drove home in silence, but once they settled in, Hunter approached the subject they'd been so studiously avoiding. "I know you're physically recovered, but do you still have nightmares or anything?"

J.T. stared at him for a moment. "Yeah."

"How bad was it?"

"Bad."

"They hurt you."

J.T. opened his mouth to say something, but then just shook his head. "I'm gonna grab a shower."

He didn't want to talk about the past. He wanted space.

"All right," Hunter told him. "While you're in the shower, I'm going to step out for a minute."

J.T. gave a shadow of a grin. "Hot-chick-cop neighbor with the porn-star boobs?"

Hunter grinned back. "Maybe."

"You need backup, I'm your man." The grin turned a little more real.

"The day I need backup with a woman, you have my permission to shoot me." Hunter glanced at the counter, where several packages of La Cocina's authentic burritos waited.

"Why don't you take up a few and have dinner with her?" J.T. suggested.

"I thought I'd have dinner with you later."

"Are we buddies or what? Let's not do the whole *guest* shit. If I had a choice between a hot chick and you, no contest."

Hunter smiled as he nodded and reached into the bag for one of the packages. "I'll be back in a bit."

Then he left J.T. to his shower and went upstairs.

Gabi answered the door on the first knock, as if she'd been waiting for him. She wore exercise pants and a T-shirt that molded to her breasts.

"What's that? It smells good." She checked out the bag.

"Fresh burritos."

Her responding smile boosted his heart rate.

She went to the kitchen, and he followed, had trouble looking at anything but her butt. Then she glanced back, and he gathered himself at last, put the food on the table, but before she could reach to the cabinet for plates, he snagged her by the waist and pulled her to him.

"I missed you today."

"I'm a very busy professional woman. The safety of this entire town is in my hands," she deadpanned.

"As a citizen of this town, I feel like I should be doing something to express my gratitude."

"Change the oil in my car?" she suggested.

"Maybe a more personal expression." He dipped his head closer.

She cast him a dubious look. "Unplug the hair from my shower drain?" A smile hovered over her mouth. Even her sexy mole seemed to mock him.

"How about this?" he asked as his lips closed over hers and he backed her against the kitchen cabinets.

Her scent, the feel of her in his arms, the taste of her heated his blood. She kissed him back with the same passion. Nothing demure about her.

Her tongue dueled with his, his body already hardening. Who was he kidding? He was hard as soon as she opened the door.

She had a smaller bandage on her neck than the day before, this one tan, the color blending into her skin.

He kissed all around it. "How is the injury?"

"It was nothing when I got it, it's nothing now," she said, her tone distracted.

He loved her tough core. Why had he ever thought that sweet and dainty had been his thing? This was what he needed, what he craved, a woman who'd match him in every way.

He knew without a doubt that when he finally talked his way into her bed—may that moment come sooner rather than later—there'd be nothing careful or sweet and restrained about their lovemaking. He could feel his balls turn blue just thinking about her under him.

He deepened the kiss. She snuck a hand under his shirt, glided her fingers up his skin that drank in her touch.

A minute was all he could take. She was driving him crazy. He grabbed her wrists, pulled her hands above her head, held them there with one hand while his other one got busy with her shirt.

This time, she had on a lace bra. Looked new. For him?

Hot need shot through his body. *Front clasp. Thank you, Jesus.*

He loved that she was the kind of woman who'd think in practicalities.

He unsnapped the clasp impatiently, swallowing a groan as her left breast fell into his hand, right where it belonged. He tasted the right one, licking slow circles around her nipple, and enjoyed seeing her squirm. When he sucked that hard nipple into his mouth, she growled his name.

He guided her to the couch. "This isn't why I came," he gasped out as they tumbled to the cushions.

She looked at him, her face heated, her eyes questioning.

She was so beautiful, she made his heart hurt. "I just wanted to share dinner." Then he added. "But now I want to see more of you."

"How much more?"

"Preferably all of it."

"Is this a soldiers-must-conquer thing?"

"It's an I-want-you-because-you-drive-me-crazy thing."

"I do what I can." She flashed a grin, then her eyes grew serious when his fingers danced down the button of her jeans.

Then, just when he thought he had the upper hand, she executed some police maneuver and flipped him so she was on top.

"Hey," he protested.

"Don't make me get out the handcuffs."

Damn if that didn't make him harder. He reached to his own pants. "I need to get some room down here."

She swatted away his hand. "It's my couch. I'm the boss here." And then she unbuttoned him.

He sprang into her hand, and she laughed. "Aren't you eager?"

"I'm a soldier. I try to be, at all times, ready for anything."

She laughed again, pretty much the best sound he'd ever heard. But then she grew serious. "Are we really doing this? Nothing has changed. You're still my partner. You're still my boss's brother."

He could see the need in her eyes. He knew what he wanted, but she had to want it too. "We're off duty. There are no rules against fraternization at the Broslin PD. You say the word, and I'll disinherit my brother. Who needs the smug bastard?"

She grinned. "Actually, he might be okay with us. We had some kind of a talk today. I think." Then her grin faded. "But I'm still going back to Philly, as soon as I can."

"It's not the other side of the world," he suggested reasonably.

"I'll be working odd shifts. You'll be a gas station owner with a business to run. Whatever happens between us tonight can't go anywhere. It'd be over before it started. It's not just the distance in miles. We live in different worlds."

He liked her in his world. "I want you. Whatever I can get."

"Tonight, then," she said after a long moment as heat crackled between them. "One night, and then we both forget about it."

He wasn't stupid enough to promise that. Instead, he pulled her down to him and claimed her maddening lips. Denial was a common thing. People had to work through it at their own pace. Gabriella Maria Flores might not know it yet, but he was hers, and she was his.

His strategy for the mission was incredibly simple: he'd gain ground where he could, and he would never give up any ground he'd gained.

Chapter Twenty-Four

Gabi made a point not to be stupid about her life. Growing up, she'd hated her circumstances, which was why she'd sweated blood to rise above them. She prided herself on making good choices— okay, except Tony, but everyone was allowed one mistake. She wasn't going to mess up like that again. So how did she end up on the couch with Hunter?

She couldn't figure it out, not with her brain shutting down, one window going dark after the other. Her body took over. She swam in a sea of pleasure. In a few seconds, nothing existed but his masculine scent surrounding him and the feel of his hands on her heated, sensitized skin.

She was lying under him again after some slick military maneuver, and he was undressing her. She was helping him. Shirt came first, then her only sexy bra, flung across the room. She'd gone to the store to pick up a package of sports bras, walked by a display of these, thought of Hunter, and she'd dropped the lacy thing into her cart before she could think too much about it.

Bra already forgotten, he was working on her pants, and he kissed every inch he bared, from her waist to her knees, then to her ankles, then her toes, one by one. He laid a path of kisses down one leg, then up the other, then he placed a long, lingering kiss at her center, through her panties. She was already wet for him.

Not that he hurried. All the impatience he'd shown earlier seemed to have evaporated. Doris could have crocheted a pair of panties in the amount of time it took Hunter to remove Gabi's.

She squirmed under him. "I though they teach speed in the military."

"When warranted. There are times that call for careful

deliberation."

"You're going to deliberate me to death," she warned, just as he finally parted her hot flesh, a move that immediately silenced her.

But he didn't touch her further. He blew on her clit.

She nearly jackknifed off the couch. He pushed her knees up until her heels touched her butt, then he pushed her knees out until she was spread wide open just inches from his face.

And then he just looked.

Good grief. What was there to look at?

"Touch me!" she snapped when she couldn't stand the suspense any longer. "Touch me, you torturous bastard. That's an order."

He laughed deeply and heartily. "And what are you going to do if I don't?"

"I'll arrest you."

"I think that's what they call an abuse of power." His eyes glinted darkly. "But the idea of handcuffs does have considerable merit."

He pressed a finger against her clitoris and held it steady, kept up a gentle pressure until it seemed that all her nerve endings were moving to that one spot. She tried to squirm, but he wouldn't let her, his free hand holding her hip down.

Then he suddenly lifted his finger, and blood rushed to her aching nub as it swelled with desire. The most devilish grin came over his face. Then he flicked her throbbing clit, the sharp sensation sending her tumbling over into a mind-bending orgasm.

Her body was still floating in the stratosphere when her cell phone rang in the kitchen.

Hunter stopped with a questioning look.

She groaned. "That's work."

He let her up, his hard length straining toward her, a sight incredibly difficult to leave behind. But she wobbled out to the kitchen to pick up the phone.

Hunter came after her, hugged her to his naked chest from behind and kissed the back of her neck, nestling his enormous erection against her naked butt as she tried to focus on the captain on the other end of the line.

"Just got a call with the bookie's whereabouts. He's over at the Pink Penguin, a mile on the other side of the Delaware border. Apparently he's renting a room as his new office."

Gabi was already tugging on her clothes.

"Local police will assist in apprehension. I'll meet you there," the captain said.

"I'm on my way, sir."

She had her pants on at last and, after she hung up, she shoved the phone into her pocket, then scrambled after her bra and her shirt.

Hunter caught the urgency and was getting dressed too, having trouble pulling up his zipper. "Did I hear someone say Pink Penguin?"

She hadn't realized her phone was that loud. "What's that?"

"A cat house. Technically a bar-slash-club, but pretty much everyone knows they have girls upstairs."

She raised an eyebrow. "Have you ever been there?"

Her muscles stiffened as she waited for the answer. She so didn't want to be disappointed in Hunter. During Tony's trial, it'd come out that he'd taken sexual favors from prostitutes in exchange for looking the other way.

But Hunter said, "As teenagers, my friends and I spent considerable time fantasizing about the place. Then we grew up to be smart enough to know that real men don't buy women."

* * *

Gabi couldn't believe how civilized the place looked. The Pink Penguin was a Victorian mansion with a sprawling bar on the bottom floor that included a number of pool tables and large-screen TVs as well as quiet corners with comfortable couches. Two sets of stairs led to the second level, a large, curving one in the front, and a smaller staircase in the back.

"Servants' stairs," Hunter said behind her. "From back in the day."

She took his word for it.

She tuned out all the squealing from the girls and the swearing from the patrons. The local PD were processing people downstairs while the captain headed up in the front and Gabi and Hunter climbed the back stairs. She had her gun in hand.

Gloria, the owner, a woman in her fifties who looked like an aging movie star—great figure, overdramatic makeup—ran after Gabi and Hunter. "You can't go up there." She tried to block their way. "Please don't do this. You don't know the kind of friends I have who protect my business."

Gabi brushed her aside, gently but firmly.

But Gloria wouldn't quit. "Let's go back down and make some phone calls. It'll take one minute. You're making a big mistake."

Gabi and Hunter ignored her. They kept going.

They'd checked downstairs already, found Dillard's office empty. But from the nervous way the proprietor was behaving, they'd concluded that the man they were looking for was somewhere on the premises. Maybe taking a "break."

Gabi reached the top first, just barely caught a glimpse of the back of a girl hurrying into the last room at the end of the hallway. Hair in a ponytail, tank top, short shorts. No more than five feet tall, very slim, very young.

Red carpet covered the upstairs hallway, the lights turned down low, the smell of incense and perfume in the air. Gabi counted a dozen rooms, some with their doors closed, some open.

The captain appeared at the top of the front staircase, pointed up. The stairs continued to the third floor. Gabi nodded. She and Hunter would take this floor, and the captain would take the next one above them. As he started up, she moved to the first closed door to her left and rapped on it. "Open up. Police."

Hunter stayed close at hand, ready to provide assistance.

Loud swearing came from inside, the voice male, but when the door opened a crack, a woman stuck out her head. Gabi pushed in while Hunter stayed in the hallway, in case anyone in one of the other rooms decided to make a run for it.

She ignored the scantily clad blonde whose lingerie probably cost more than Gabi made in a week, and focused on the middle-aged man hurriedly dragging on his suit pants by the bed. Too tall and too fat. He didn't match the photo the police had of the bookie.

The room was clean, blinds drawn, just the bedside lamp on, silk bed linen, large mirrors everywhere. Glasses of wine on the nightstands. This setup had to be a lot more comfortable than standing on a street corner and turning tricks in a dirty, dark alley, the way it was done in the inner city.

The woman smiled at Gabi. "Want to join in, honey? No charge. I like girls in uniform." The smooth voice, the smile, the eyes were nothing if not beguiling. "I can make you real happy."

"If you want to make me happy, quit this job and find an honest occupation," Gabi told her, then pulled back out.

She moved on to the next door, Hunter grinning at her.

"Open up. Police."

She found the same situation as before. Except in this room, the guy was in his eighties with two women who couldn't have been past college age.

The third room netted a hairy little man with a transvestite. The transvestite didn't bother to hide the his-and-her parts, wiggled them for Hunter. The customer called Gabi a bitch and threatened her.

Gabi didn't have time to stop and squabble with him. She moved on, and the fourth bedroom produced the bookie at last, along with a lot of lace and leather. Dillard's "lady" friend was wearing the leather. Dillard was wearing the lace.

He was a clean-cut guy otherwise, distinguished looking once they let him put his suit back on. He could have passed for a school principal.

"It's a misunderstanding. It's not what you think it is," he assured Gabi confidently.

He was so convincing, if she hadn't seen what she'd seen with her own eyes, she would have been tempted to believe him.

"We'll sort it out," she promised.

"I want my attorney."

She slapped on the cuffs. "You can call him from the station."

They stepped out of the room, and Gabi saw Gloria in front of the door at the end of the hall. Almost as if Gloria was protecting that one room in particular. The glimpse Gabi had caught before didn't sit well with her. Maybe she'd just seen a petite woman go into that room. But it also could have been a young girl. From the back, she looked thirteen or fourteen.

She handed the bookie to Hunter. "Would you mind taking him downstairs? I want to check one more thing." Then she headed down the hallway.

"No!" Anger flared in Gloria's eyes. "There's no need for this."

"I'm taking a look just the same." Gabi stopped in front of her. "Step aside, please."

Gloria's anger shifted to fear. "I can't let you go in there."

"I can put you in cuffs and have the local cops take you in. Step aside." She reached for her cuffs.

And then Gloria moved at last, distraught. "It's all my fault. He shouldn't even be here today. It's not his day. Please don't make a thing out of this." She was beginning to sound scared.

Gabi tried the door. Locked. Whoever was in there had probably heard the commotion in the hallway and decided to play it safe.

"Police," she called out. "Open up!"

No response.

"Police. Open up!" She pulled her weapon.

She had no interest in the Pink Penguin beyond the bookie, but if Gloria had kids working for her, that was something Gabi couldn't overlook.

"Wait." Gloria caved, probably not wanting her door shot up. She pulled a master key from her pocket and unlocked the door. Then she gave Gabi one last try. "You don't have to go in there. You're going to regret it."

Gabi pushed right in.

The girl she'd seen earlier *was* just a girl after all, a high school kid. She'd changed since she'd come in. Now she was wearing a short-skirted Catholic school uniform.

But that wasn't the most disturbing sight that greeted Gabi in the room.

In the corner, hastily pulling on his pants, stood the Broslin mayor.

He looked a lot less distinguished and charismatic than when she'd talked to him a couple of days ago. His eyes darted around as if he was trying to figure out how to control the situation.

"Out," he snapped at Gloria at last, zipping up his pants. "Close the door behind you."

He shoved his shirttail into his waistband, shook his head at Gabi. "This is not what it looks like, Officer." He echoed the bookie's words, the standard refrain of criminals caught in the act.

Gabi said nothing. She was too disgusted for words.

He stepped closer. "I was curious. Nothing happened. No report is necessary. Believe me, I learned my lesson."

Whether to escalate this or not was up to the local cops, their jurisdiction. Gabi turned to the kid. "What's your name?"

"Vicki."

"How old are you?"

"Listen," the mayor cut in.

But Gabi fixed him with her best kick-ass cop look. "I can ask some questions here, or I can ask them at the station."

"Eighteen." The girl stuck her chin out. "I'm legal."

"Are you in school?"

"Dropped out two years ago," she said defiantly. "I don't need that shit."

"Are you from around here?"

Vicki shot her a look of hate. "From Jersey. And I'm not going back either. You can't make me."

A problem for social services. Then Gabi remembered Gloria muttering something about this not being the mayor's regular day. "What's his regular day?" she asked the girl on impulse, not even sure why.

"He's nice. He's not doing anything bad. It's a free country. You shouldn't stick your nose where it doesn't belong." The girl's voice heated with each sentence.

"What's his regular day?"

"Friday. What do you care?"

"Why is he here today?"

The girl grimaced. "My boyfriend is getting out of prison next Friday. Gloria said I could take the day off to go pick him up."

So the mayor had to reschedule his weekly visit.

Gabi's instincts prickled. "Was he here last Friday?"

"You don't have to answer," the mayor cut in, a twinge of desperation in his voice for the first time.

Gabi kept her eyes on the girl. "Actually, you do. Here or at the station."

The girl shrugged. "So he was here. So what?"

"What time?"

"We usually meet at six."

Behind her, the mayor sank onto the bed.

"What time did he leave?"

"Eightish, I guess."

Gabi radioed down to Hunter. "Would you send up a local cop? Thanks."

She opened the door, and when she saw the officer at the top of the stairs, she turned to Vicki. "All right. Off you go." She handed her out the door, hoping social services could help her, although if a teen wanted to run away, nobody could do a damn thing.

She closed the door and focused on the mayor again. "Do you want to tell me about this poker party you didn't have last Friday?"

"I want my lawyer. You're going to lose your job over this,

Officer. Think very carefully."

"Friday night. That's all I want. You're not under arrest here for anything. Yet."

He looked around, his gaze settling on his expensive suit jacket on the chair by the door. It probably held his phone.

Gabi stepped in front of the chair, blocking it. "The only thing I'm interested in is Friday night."

"It's poker night," he said at last.

"Do you ever play poker?"

He thought for a long moment, measuring his options before shaking his head.

"You come here on Friday nights."

He nodded.

A picture began to emerge in Gabi's mind. "How about the others? Heinz and the two councilmen?"

"They spend time with their girlfriends."

So the men provided mutual alibis for each other for the wives once a week, a neat arrangement. "Who are the girlfriends?"

"How the hell would I know?" He stood. "I'm not saying anything else."

Gabi had all she needed. "You stay up here."

He sat back on the bed, smart enough to understand that it wasn't in his best interest to go downstairs and show himself to a dozen police officers.

Gabi left him, went down, found the captain. "You might want to check out the last room at the end of the hallway on the second floor," she told him. She didn't want to say more. There were others around them.

The captain raised an eyebrow, but then started up the stairs.

Chapter Twenty-Five

Gabi looked around, caught sight of Hunter coming in through the front door.

"Dillard's in the backseat, ready to go," he told her as he walked up to her.

"Let's go, then."

She said nothing on the ride back about the mayor since Dillard could listen in. But once Dillard was in lockup, she told Hunter what she'd found out in that last room at the end of the hallway.

"So Charlie Heinz has no alibi for Friday night," she finished.

"And Cindy worked for Charlie's Subs before she started teaching," Hunter added, the two of them in the conference room, all the files spread out on the table.

Gabi thought back to everything she knew about the man. "He's a good shot. Big-time hunter."

"And he lied about his alibi. That has to mean something, right?"

She considered that. "Not necessarily. He's having an affair. He'd go the distance to cover that up. If his wife got wind of it, she could take him to court for half of everything he's got." And he had a lot. Which meant a lot to protect.

They fell silent for a while, looking at the sea of files as if they expected the answer to leap out any second like a playful dolphin.

Hunter broke the silence. "But why would Heinz go after my father and my brother? If the three incidents are connected."

"To lead us in another direction."

"Or those incidents could have been just plain accidents."

"Maybe." Hunter's father getting run off the road, she could see as an accident. The captain's car being shot at, not so much. Whoever had squeezed off that shot had taken too much care, picking up the shells, covering up his tracks. That hinted at something sinister.

"Heinz has plenty of rifles." She'd seen at least a dozen in the display cabinet in his trophy room.

"Do we have enough for a search warrant?"

"I don't know. But I'm going to try anyway."

She took care of the paperwork, then went to question the bookie while they waited to hear back from the judge.

Regardless of the new information they had on Heinz, the bookie too still had potential.

Among all the people she'd interviewed so far, Dillard was the one she could most see pulling off something like the crimes she was investigating. Bing senior was one of his clients who owed him money. The bookie had a demonstrated past rife with violence against those who'd tried to shortchange him. He might have gotten off on technicalities before, but Gabi swore that wouldn't happen this time.

"Did you know Cindy Simme?"

The guy watched her, measuring his words as he said, "She taught my kids in kindergarten."

"How well did you know her?" Well enough so Cindy would let him into the apartment? What if the bookie showed up, told her he needed to talk to Hunter about Hunter's father owing money?

The man shrugged. "All three of my boys had her."

Gabi questioned him for another hour. No alibi. He had opportunity, means, and motive. And he was someone Cindy knew. She might have let him in so the neighbors wouldn't see him waiting outside, to spare Hunter from embarrassment.

Gabi told the guy to lawyer up, she was keeping him for further questioning, then she strode out and put in a search warrant request for his place. Once that was sent off, she went back to the conference room.

Hunter was gone. Hopefully, he'd gone for coffee and would bring her a cup too. She sank into the chair at the head of the table and fingered through the file in front of her, trying to line up all the mismatched clues in her head so they would form a believable, logical story. They stubbornly refused. It was the weirdest case she'd ever seen.

The captain popped his head in, saw her, came in, and closed the door behind him. "Interesting find in that last room at the Pink

Penguin."

"What are we going to do about it?"

"Not much we can do. The girl is of legal age. She denies having been paid. We can't prove it. No exchange of money was witnessed," he said with distaste. "I knew there was a reason I didn't like this new mayor." He shook his head. "On the other hand, I don't think we need to worry about him messing with our budget. The special task force meetings are over."

Gabi's gut burned. "She's seventeen."

"I hate it as much as you do. But today, there's nothing I can do about it." He paused. "Guys like that, they don't stop. He'll do it again, he'll get caught again." His gaze hardened. "And, believe me, next time our distinguished mayor messes up, I'll be ready."

She did believe him.

She updated him on Heinz. "I'm going to talk to him again. Will that make trouble for the department?"

"That's not for you to worry about. You do your job, I do mine. If I have to replace the annual fifty grand his police ball and silent auction bring in, I'll find a way to do it. We're not the kind of PD that trades favors."

She was seriously starting to like her new boss and new PD. "No, sir."

As the captain left, Hunter came in with two cups of coffee. Gabi updated him on the Dillard interview. Then they spent an hour trying to piece the clues together, but even with Hunter's help, no clear picture emerged.

The two search warrants came back at the same time, approved for Dillard's place, denied for the Heinz mansion. Gabi left Hunter with the files, then asked Joe to go and collect any rifles he might find at Dillard's house.

She went to the Heinz mansion, would have preferred to go with a warrant, but she'd do what she could without one.

Heinz was the only one home from the family. The maid showed Gabi to the trophy room. A dozen pairs of glass eyes seemed to follow her as she stepped in.

Heinz stood by the window in a pose resembling the Napoleon painting on the wall. He turned in a measured move, gave her a measured look. "How can I help you, Officer?"

"You can start by telling me where you were Friday night from six to seven."

"At a poker party with the mayor. I believe he's confirmed already."

"He just unconfirmed it.'"

"That's not possible."

"I'm standing here telling you it is. Maybe your girlfriend can give you another alibi."

He reached up and loosened his tie. Caught himself. Dropped his hand. His voice tightened as he said, "We're done talking here. I'm not going to say another word unless my attorney is present."

The interior designer's fee for the room might have been more than Gabi's annual salary, but she refused to be intimidated by his tone, his posing, *or* his attorney. "Tell him to meet us at the station."

But instead, Heinz called the mayor, talking in hushed tones. Then he called the captain and had a rapid, heated conversation. Apparently, neither man told Heinz what he wanted to hear, because the third call went to his lawyer at last. Then Heinz insisted on going to the station in his own car and not in the cruiser. On this, Gabi decided to accommodate him.

She walked him back to the interrogation room instead of the conference room. Only because the conference room was full of case files, but he didn't have to know that.

The lawyer was there before she could offer Heinz a cup of coffee. Money could buy a lot of things, including speed.

"Where were you Friday night between six and seven p.m.?" Gabi asked again once they all settled down, this time with the recorder on the table between them.

"At home, alone," Heinz bit out the words.

"Not with your girlfriend?"

"I don't have a girlfriend."

"Anybody see you at home? The staff?"

"They don't live on the premises. Since my wife and daughter weren't home, dinner was not required. I sent everyone home early."

"What did you do?"

"Read a book."

"If you're not seeing anyone, why the ruse with the poker party?"

"Look," he snapped. "It wasn't some big conspiracy. We did have poker parties. Then about six months ago, someone in the group met a woman. He called to say he wouldn't be coming that night, but could we cover for him if his wife asked."

"And the others?"

"Eventually, they saw the opportunity inherent in an arrangement like this."

"Including you?"

But the lawyer interrupted with "What is the point of this questioning, Officer? Even if my client had an affair, and we're not admitting anything like that, it wouldn't be a crime."

"But there *was* a crime committed that night," Gabi countered. "Murder."

"My client had nothing to do with that."

"That's what we're here to determine." She kept her attention on Heinz. "How did you feel about Cameron Porter cheating on your daughter with Cindy?"

The man's gaze hardened. "Mandy's and Cameron's private business is between them."

Gabi said nothing. No way could Heinz stay out of something like that, not when he was a compulsive micromanager who had to have a hand in everything, solve everything himself. He'd even found a husband for his daughter. She hadn't even been allowed to do that for herself.

"Did you ever confront Cameron?" Gabi asked.

"No." Heinz huffed. "Everybody makes mistakes. He's the best manager I've had. As close to having a son as I'm going to get. He's an ambitious man. Too smart to be making mistakes like this, mistakes that could jeopardize everything. I knew once he was married, he would have ended any unwise relationships."

Gabi decided to take the man in another direction next and asked him for an alibi for the afternoon when the captain had been shot at and his father run off the road.

Heinz had to think. "I was hunting. I saw an enormous fox while deer hunting a few weeks before by Broslin Creek. Missed it then. I thought if I could find it again, it'd look nice stuffed."

"Witnesses?"

"You can ask the beagles. I took a couple of bitches with me. They weren't much help."

"You have a number of rifles."

"What of it?"

"Would you surrender them for ballistics?"

Here the lawyer protested again, and Heinz said, "I'm going to go with my attorney's advice, Officer."

He didn't look worried. He wasn't rattled. He clearly thought he was above being questioned by the likes of her. He kept frowning at her as if he considered having to answer questions in an interrogation room an insult.

While Gabi was taking notes, he pushed to his feet.

"Are we done here?"

Gabi stood too. "I need you to stick around a little longer. I'll be right back."

She met the captain outside. He'd been observing. She had to give it to him, despite the fact that the case involved his family, he tried to stay out of it, had stayed impartial, had not put any pressure on her.

A thoughtful look sat on the man's face. "What do you think?"

"Between Dillard and Heinz, Dillard is the known criminal," she said.

"But?"

"Something about Heinz bothers me. I don't know what."

"It's called instinct. Don't brush that aside."

She nodded. Carmen used to say the same. Carmen's Cop Rule #7: *Go with your instinct.*

Leila hurried over. "House fire on Bindery Road."

"I'm on my way." The captain strode off.

Gabi walked over to the conference room. Hunter was there, waiting, going through files for the hundredth time.

"Let's just focus on what we have on Heinz," she told him.

Hunter dropped into a chair, looking at her. "Cindy was a threat to Heinz's plan for Cameron Porter and the future of his businesses."

"And Heinz likely knew Cindy, even if he denies it. He's a micromanager. According to his daughter, he's constantly checking up on everyone. He visits his businesses all the time."

"He's a seasoned hunter. He could have probably made that head shot at that close range."

"He has plenty of rifles. He could have easily shot out the captain's windows, missing him on purpose. He didn't want to kill him. He just wanted to misdirect the investigation."

"And my father?" Hunter asked.

"Could have been Heinz too. The guy owns a car dealership. He could easily borrow an SUV. Or the accident might have been a true accident, the timing a coincidence." Gabi paced down the length of the room. "If we had a warrant, we could run ballistics on his rifles. We need that. All we have now is a bunch of circumstantial evidence."

"That didn't keep you from throwing me into a cell," Hunter said, but he kept his tone teasing.

She wished she could throw Heinz in a cell. Her instincts went off every time they were in a room together, but she couldn't prove a thing. And without a warrant, she wasn't likely to find proof. So she went back to the interrogation room to let Heinz know that he was free to leave.

* * *

Gabi began the next day in the conference room with Hunter, trying to regroup. But they no sooner began than Leila popped into the room, balancing on the impossible heels of her pink fur boots. She was smiling from ear to ear, carrying a handful of printouts. "The ancestry DNA report is back."

Gabi's ears perked up. "Does our sperm guy have any relatives in the database?"

"Mandy Heinz. Ninety-nine percent probability that the submitted DNA came from Mandy Heinz's father." Leila handed over the papers, then headed back to her ringing phone.

Heinz was having an affair with Cindy.

The thought blew Gabi's mind for a moment, but then she was grinning. "Now we're going someplace."

Hunter didn't seem to share her excitement. He sat heavily, his face a mask of conflicting emotions. He'd known about Cindy's multiple relationships, but finding out the identity of the second guy still had to be a punch in the gut.

"You okay?"

He nodded.

Her heart ached for him. She wished she could think of something to say to make him feel better. But they were on the job. She had to get moving.

"I have to go and bring Heinz back in."

She could have asked Hunter to go with her, but he looked like he could use a moment to digest this latest development privately. And she wasn't sure she wanted him in the same car with Heinz. He hadn't responded well to Porter. "I'll be back. You stay here. See if we missed anything in the files. Every tiny bit of evidence against him would help."

She hurried out and had Heinz in the interview room in less than an hour, along with his lawyer, who was protesting and flinging around accusations of police harassment the whole time she was setting up the recorder.

She ignored the guy, focusing on Heinz. This was it. Maybe the most crucial moment in the entire investigation. She had to get this right.

She sat straight, filled her lungs, relaxed her muscles. "How long have you been having an affair with Cindy Simme?"

Heinz came out of his seat, his eyes shooting fireworks. "That's absolute nonsense. I don't have to listen to this." Then he snapped at his lawyer. "Get me out of here. What in hell do I pay you for?"

Before the lawyer could say anything, Gabi slid the papers she came in with across the table toward him. "We have DNA evidence."

While the lawyer scanned the papers with a tightening expression, she turned to Heinz. "You had sex with the victim on the day of the murder."

Heinz dropped back into his seat. His face was a set mask that would have served him well if he actually played poker on Fridays. "Your lab made a mistake."

"I don't think so," Gabi said. "But we can certainly run the results again."

The lawyer looked up at last. "If you obtained my client's DNA illegally, we're going to fight that tooth and nail. We provided no sample. You had no permission."

"We didn't need permission. Mandy Heinz provided her DNA for an ancestry search site." Gabi explained the rest.

"There are serious questions about the legality of what you've done, Officer," the lawyer warned. "When I'm done with you, you're not going to have a job left. I'm going to make sure that evidence will not be admitted in court."

Heinz smirked at Gabi and threw his shoulders back, confident, and Gabi felt the case slip away from her.

She went with the only thing she had. "Were you aware that Cindy was pregnant? She was two months along." Porter's, but she didn't have to disclose that.

Heinz stared, his poker face dissolving, a stricken look coming into his eyes.

"A boy." She twisted the knife. "Cindy was two months pregnant with a little boy."

And then Heinz's composure crumpled. In a few seconds, he went from all-powerful to a broken man, his face ashen. "Why didn't she tell me?" Even his voice lost its strength.

His lawyer jumped in to remind him to say nothing, but Heinz waved the man off.

"A boy?" he asked Gabi.

She nodded.

The man closed his eyes. The muscles in his face drew together as if he was in physical pain. "I didn't mean to kill her," he whispered.

The lawyer protested again, but he had to know the case was lost. The admission was on tape.

"What did you mean to do?" Gabi asked Heinz, keeping her voice soft.

"Talk sense into her." Heinz folded his fingers on top of the table and stared at his hands. "She was a lonely young woman. She just wanted to be loved." He looked up into Gabi's eyes. "She initiated the relationship, about a year ago."

Gabi didn't say anything.

After a while, Heinz continued. "A few months ago, I found out that she was also seeing Cameron. I had a talk with her. I offered her a hundred grand to move away."

"What did she say?"

"She cried. She told me that I was the only one she loved. She was leaving Cameron." He closed his eyes. "I'm becoming an old fool. I believed her."

"And then?"

"On Friday, she called me from work. She asked me to meet her at Hunter Bing's apartment. We met there before. She had the key. It was a convenient place. No hotel check-in, no credit card record." He closed his eyes again. "We had relations."

"And then you shot her."

"She wanted a million dollars." He shook his head. "We got dressed; she made the bed, then just started in on the money. I told her she was crazy. I don't have that kind of cash floating around. She pulled the gun on me."

"From where?"

"The nightstand."

"Then what?"

"I talked sense into her. I talked her into giving me the gun."

"And then you shot her."

"No. I started to leave. I didn't realize until then how messed up she was. It shook me up. I tend to be a better judge of character."

He fell silent for a long moment before continuing. "She pulled out her phone, said she was calling my wife. She said it's the money or she'd tell everyone."

His shoulders dropped until the man seemed to have collapsed in on himself. "I got angry. I would have given her everything she needed. And then she lied, then tried to bleed me dry, then threatened to destroy my family. I pointed the gun at her to make her put the damn phone down."

Gabi waited.

"She laughed," Heinz said. "She kept dialing."

"So you shot her."

The lawyer cut in. "Don't answer that."

Too late, Gabi thought.

Heinz was lost, didn't even seem to hear the comment. "I didn't mean to shoot. I don't even remember pulling the trigger. I just wanted her to stop dialing." He covered his face with his hands.

"Did you take money from the safe?"

"She took it originally," he said in a listless tone, dropping his hands back on the table. "I grabbed it before I left. I thought maybe it'd point to burglary if the money was missing."

"And then you attacked the captain and his father to toss more false clues into the mix."

He blinked at her. "What are you talking about?"

"Running Zechariah Bing off the road."

Heinz stared at her blankly.

So maybe that *had* been an accident, Gabi thought, and asked, "Why did you shoot at Captain Bing's cruiser?"

But his lawyer protested, bringing up the Fifth. And Heinz recovered enough to shut his mouth at last. He seemed to realize that he'd just confessed to murder. But it was a situation where he could claim self-defense—Cindy had pulled the gun on him first. He could claim crime of passion, reacting to blackmail, or that the gun had gone off by accident. If his attorney was as good as he was expensive, he could work the charge down from murder one to manslaughter. Heinz wasn't going to add assaulting an officer of the law with a deadly weapon.

But Gabi had enough for a search warrant at last. One of the man's rifles was going to tell her everything she needed to know.

She read Heinz his rights, then grabbed the recorder. "I'll be back in a minute to take you back to holding."

But she turned back from the threshold. "One more thing," she said. "Cindy's phone was dead. She wasn't calling your wife. She was bluffing." And then she closed the door behind her.

Hunter was waiting outside the room. Gabi filled him in. She could see as fury filled him, dark anger. His powerful body vibrated with emotion. He was like he'd been at the dealership with Porter, but she didn't think he'd lose it again, not that way. He made no move toward the door.

She put a hand on his arm. "It's over. I have Heinz on tape. He's going to pay for this. Why don't you go home? Hang out with J.T. for a while. I'll see you later."

Hunter took her hand, ran the pad of his thumb over her knuckles. He held her gaze as he nodded once, then strode off.

She called the captain and gave him an update, then filled out the search warrant request and sent it in. Then she booked Heinz and took him back to holding.

After that, for the first time in a week, Gabi finally relaxed.

She drove home, satisfied with the day's work. Her first murder case and she'd licked it. She was pretty sure the captain was going to give her a glowing recommendation.

The road back to Philly should be clear.

So why wasn't she more excited?

All she could think about was Hunter.

* * *

Hunter wasn't in his apartment when Gabi got home from work—probably out with J.T.—but he showed up at her place that evening. Just in time. She'd been about to go down to see how he was doing.

"Thanks for everything you did for Cindy," he said, standing in front of her door. "The investigation couldn't have been in better hands."

"I bet you didn't think that when I dropped you in that cell."

He gave a rueful smile, his expression lightening a little. "Maybe not at that particular point. But then I learned to appreciate your investigative method."

He reached out, pulled her into his arms, and kissed her softly, tenderly.

She let him in. "How are you dealing with what happened this afternoon?"

He moved to the living room. "Went for a run. It gave me a chance to think. Then I went out for a while with J.T. He's still at Finnegan's, didn't want to come home. I didn't feel like staying. I don't think getting drunk's the answer."

He dropped onto her couch, leaned forward. He looked tired. "What was wrong with her? You think all this came from Uncle Chad?"

She hesitated for a moment, but then she nodded as she sat next to him. "Maybe. If Cindy was molested and nobody believed her, that had to leave some pretty serious scars. She had a hole inside her that no man could ever fill, and then she got herself in trouble. She might have found out that Porter was marrying Mandy. She decided to blackmail Heinz so she'd have money for the baby."

"Why not try to convince Heinz that the baby was his?"

"She was smart enough to know that Heinz would ask for a paternity test."

"And she couldn't tell me the baby was mine because the timing wouldn't work." Hunter closed his eyes for a second. "If she asked for help, I would have helped anyway."

They sat in silence.

"Frozen burritos?" she offered after a little while.

But he shook his head. "Maybe later. I came up because I want to show you something." He gave a ghost of a smile. "It's something Christmassy, so prepare yourself."

She was ready to roll her eyes, but then thought he could use a little Christmas cheer today, so she nodded. "I'll gird my loins."

His smile improved a shade. He stood and held his hand out for her.

He took her to the gazebo at Broslin Square, where a Christmas concert was in progress—a first for her. They walked up and stood in the back.

She'd thought before that the decorations on the gazebo were ridiculously overdone, but now they seemed appropriate for the festive event. The singers were all teenagers from Chester County Children's Homes according to the sign hanging above the choir.

Gabi knew what group homes were. They took difficult teens that foster parents had trouble with. But rough life and rough behavior aside, the teens sang like angels. A piano provided accompaniment, the player another teen.

The crowd, most of Broslin, listened with shining faces to an amazing rendition of "Silent Night." Gabi recognized some of the people: Eileen, Pete the mailman with his mother, and at least two dozen others.

She had never been a fan of the Christmas music that poured from the radio nonstop for three long months this time of the year, but this was something different—raw, personal, real. The more she listened, the more her heart quieted.

Even Hunter relaxed next to her. He took her hand. By the third song, she had her head on his shoulder. They were connecting somehow, in this unlikely moment. Pressed together, she felt almost as if they were one person. On some level, it was more intimate than when he'd had her naked on the couch.

Snow began falling gently, the snowflakes slowly twirling on their way down, as if dancing to the music. People oohed and ahhed. She was in a Christmas postcard, Gabi thought, or in a Christmas movie, the kind that she'd catch on the Hallmark Channel and channel surf over while rolling her eyes.

Tonight, everything felt different. She felt as if some indefinable thing had clicked into place in her heart. She snuggled closer to Hunter. He pressed a kiss at the corner of her mouth, on the mole she liked to pretend was a beauty mark.

The choir began singing "O Come All Ye Faithful." People listened without a sound, transported. A small basket made its way around. Before her mother's voice could have said in Gabi's head, *here we go, donations, the scam part*, Gabi saw that the basket contained candles. Both she and Hunter took one.

Then she moved to hand the basket to the young girl next to her, maybe fourteen, in a wheelchair. The girl's knitted hat had slid askew, and Gabi could see that she didn't have any hair. The girl was too weak to reach for the basket, so her mother grabbed a candle for her.

Gabi wondered what kind of cancer she had.

Then Hunter nuzzled her neck. "Thanks for being here with me."

They stood hugging, listening, under the stars, in the gently falling snow, until the choir leader stepped up to the microphone to announce that the next song would be the last.

"Please light your candles, and sing 'O Holy Night' with us," she invited the people. "And feel free to close your eyes and send all your Christmas wishes and prayers up on the wings of this song. Merry Christmas, Broslin!"

At the ends of the rows, candles were lit, then the light passed on from one person to the next. The musical accompaniment died away, nothing but the voices of hundreds of people floating up to the sky, trading places with the snowflakes.

Since Gabi wasn't sure what to pray for, she prayed for the girl next to her. And when she opened her eyes, she could see that the girl had hers tightly shut, nose wrinkled, mouth moving as she was praying for all she was worth.

Then her eyes popped open, and she caught Gabi watching. She smiled. "I was praying for those kids up on stage to all find a home by Easter," she said. "Aren't they great?"

And Gabi thought, *maybe this is Christmas.* Maybe tonight, here, she had seen it. Or, at least, caught a little glimpse.

Chapter Twenty-Six

Hunter stood in the middle of the owner's suite above the mechanic shop behind Arnie's gas station. The place was twice as large as his current apartment. He could hear the faint noises of traffic on the road and then, a minute later, the church bell.

He'd spent the day running errands, then finally ended up here. Arnie had given him a key.

He walked to the window and looked out at the houses, the cars, the people. The surroundings weren't nearly as serene as out at the farm, but he liked all the movement. He'd grown used to being surrounded by people in the army. He liked being in the middle of the action.

As it turned out, Arnie had a buyer for the gas station already, but that buyer didn't want the mechanic shop or the apartment above it. And without the gas station, Hunter could actually swing the financing on his own.

He could see himself here, keeping on the employees, hiring a few more mechanics to replace the ones who'd already left. He'd be part of a team again. His team. He'd be providing a service to the town. People would stop by. They'd chat. His mind painted a picture, and he slipped into that picture with surprising ease.

Reclaiming the old Bing homestead was a good dream, but it was Ethan's dream. Hunter could have been happy out there, but he was pretty sure he was going to be happier here. He liked being in the middle of things, liked having a team around him. He was looking forward to connecting with the people of the town on a daily basis.

Still, it was a big decision.

At least the Pizza Palace was within walking distance. Since neither he nor Gabi liked to cook, that might come in handy.

Something had happened between them the night before at the

concert. A connection had formed on some basic, primal level. She felt so incredibly right in his arms. He couldn't imagine another Christmas without her.

He'd wanted to go upstairs with her after they'd gotten home, but J.T. was back from his bar hopping so drunk he couldn't stand up, so Hunter took care of him instead.

In the morning, Gabi had gone to work while Hunter stayed home. His stint with the PD was over. He was going to miss investigating with her. They'd just have to spend more time together outside of work. He definitely wanted more of her.

He pulled out his phone and dialed her number. She should be getting off work right about now. "Hey, you got a minute?"

"Everything okay?"

"I need a feminine opinion."

"Men are only after one thing."

He grinned. He liked her weird sense of humor. "I don't know if I can argue with that." Since getting up this morning, he'd thought about her naked at least a few dozen times. "I'm at Arnie's gas station in the apartment. Do you have a few minutes to come over?"

She only hesitated a moment. "Sure."

She was there in ten minutes, her long legs encased in jeans, a soft, button-down shirt under her jacket.

He kissed her as soon as he let her in. Lingered over her lips. It took effort to pull away. "Let me show you around."

She smiled. "Lead the way."

So he showed her the cavernous living room open to the kitchen, the one good-size bedroom, then the two smaller ones, one of which Arnie had used as his home office. The place stood empty save the large rocking chair Arnie must have forgotten.

"What do you think?" He was surprised by how much he wanted her to like the place.

"Are you buying this?"

"Maybe."

"I thought you'd be building next to the captain's house."

"I think I like it in town better."

"Me too." She gave a wry grin. "I don't think I could take all that country all around me. There are horses and cows and stuff."

"The mind shudders."

She looked around again. "It's roomy." She pointed to the far corner. "You could put a weight bench over there."

She was the only woman who'd think of that as her first interior decorating choice. But he loved that about her. "Chin bar in the bedroom door?"

Her eyes lit up. "Definitely."

He moved closer and took her hands. Then he leaned forward and brushed his lips against hers.

She shook her head with a smile. "Is this why you wanted me to come over? A booty call?"

Heat rushed to his groin at her mentioning the possibility. "I wouldn't turn it down if you were offering. But mostly I was hoping I could talk you into helping me lay new carpet and paint."

A quick laugh escaped her.

"My brother released me from my duties as an auxiliary officer. I was only appointed for the duration of the case. The case is closed. No more conflict with that."

He drew her closer. Then closer yet, until she was snuggled tightly against him. Then he dipped his head and buried his face in the curve of her neck. He loved the sweet, womanly smell of her skin.

He walked his fingers up her back under her coat, touching, rubbing, then back down, and he curved his hands around her tight ass and cupped her to him. He was hard already, his erection straining to be encased by her softness.

Not that she was soft in many places—she had the lean body of a fighter—but she was soft where it counted.

He lifted her up and backed toward the oak rocking chair, lowered himself into it without letting her go, without separating their lips. With her sitting on his lap, he only had to dip his head a little when he was ready to move on from her mouth to her breasts.

As he kissed a path down her throat, she tossed her head back. He shucked off her jacket, then nuzzled his face between her magnificent breasts. Then he clamped his teeth around the top button of her shirt, ripped it off, and spit the button across the room.

The sweet, proper, homemaker of a woman he'd always thought he'd wanted would have been appalled. Gabi laughed. She gazed into his eyes with delicious anticipation. He finished the buttons with his fingers, since his mouth was otherwise occupied on her velvet skin.

She had the lacy bra on.

His voice thickened. "Nice."

Her smile hesitated. "I bought it with you in mind. Is that stupid?"

His erection twitched between them. "It's very, very commendable. A truly excellent idea. If I had the authority to give out medals..." He kissed around the lace as she shrugged out of her shirt. Then he ran his hands up her sides and moved them to the front, popped the clasp, and brushed the lace aside, freeing her to him.

She slipped off the bra too, and then linked her hands behind his neck. He leaned forward and went to his feast.

She had firm, high, full, glorious breasts. Truly prize-winning boobs he could have spent the rest of his life playing with.

He wanted her. In every way. "Let me take off a layer."

She helped him tug off his sweater. Then the camo T-shirt he wore underneath.

Skin to skin. He knew no better feeling in the world.

She combed her fingers through the smattering of coarse hair on his chest, caressing him. Then she did something with her thumbs to his flat nipples.

"Pants. Off." His voice turned hoarse. "Now."

She executed an acrobatic move that would have earned a standing applause in a circus or a medal at the Olympics, and was back on top of him, completely naked, in less than thirty seconds.

A man could fall in love with a woman like that.

She unbuttoned his jeans, then he lifted his hip so she could push the denim down below his knees, along with his boxer shorts.

Almost there.

"Condom in the back pocket." He'd been carrying one around for days now, just in case.

She reached back and retrieved the foil packet, tore it open. She sheathed him in latex, then positioned herself above him. He gripped her hips and guided her slowly onto him, pushing up at the same time, deeper, deeper, deeper—all the way to the hilt.

She was hot and tight and ready.

They both had to catch their breaths once he was fully inside her. He let her decide when to start moving, let her set the pace. She found just the right rhythm. And as pressure built in his balls, he used his firmly planted feet on the ground to set the rocker into motion, taking the sensations to the next level.

Her eyes widened as he rocked deeply into her.

He dragged her head down and kissed her. She kissed him back with wild passion. She truly was his match in every way.

But he couldn't think too deeply about that, since her muscles began contracting around him, squeezing his erection, and he exploded into an orgasm that robbed him of both breath and speech.

When she finally collapsed on him, he held her against his heart, breathing hard, body spent, mind boggled.

Several satiated minutes passed before she pulled back. "What are you smiling about?"

"I'm buying the place."

* * *

Gabi drove home, grinning all the way. *Hunter.*

He'd gotten under her skin but good. She wasn't sure she'd be able to pry him out of there. She wasn't sure she wanted to.

He'd stayed at the apartment. Arnie was coming over so they could talk numbers. She figured Hunter would do well. He was a good negotiator. He was good at pretty much everything as far as she could tell so far.

How close she felt to him made her wary. They hadn't known each other that long. Yet she felt she knew him. She'd seen him under the worst circumstances. Betrayed. Falsely accused. In danger of losing his freedom. She'd seen him when things were at their hardest.

How he acted under those circumstances revealed a lot about a man.

They had something between them. And she wanted whatever it was that they had.

She changed her clothes, then stopped over to check on Doris, stayed for a cup of tea.

Doris watched with a speculative look and a pleased little smile. "Love looks good on you, Gabi."

"What love?" She wasn't ready to discuss that. She wasn't sure if she was ready to admit it to herself.

"You're glowing," Doris said and toasted her with spiked tea. "When you find love that makes you glow, you don't let it go. I moved all the way across the pond for it."

The conversation unnerved Gabi. Later, when she went back to her own apartment, she couldn't find her place. She started cooking, which meant that she was really out of sorts. She didn't have much in her fridge, but enough for pasta.

The rotini was cooked, the sauce simmering, when someone knocked on her door. She thought it might be Hunter, coming home from the negotiation, so she hurried to open up and find out how that went. Instead, she found J.T. with a sheepish look on his face.

"I'm hoping you could help me with something." He ducked his head. "I've been mooching off Hunter for the last couple of days. I want to do something nice for him before I leave. I was out driving around and saw this Amish furniture store. Good, solid stuff. I thought I'd pick something for his new place."

She waited.

"I'm a guy." He ducked his head again. "I need help."

She opened the door wider, showed him her apartment—spare, haphazardly furnished. "Are you asking me for advice with interior decorating?"

He shrugged. "You're a woman. You must have the gene somewhere in there."

"If it's there, it's hidden deep." She laughed. But she didn't have it in her to say no. Not when it was for Hunter.

"Hang on." She stepped back into her apartment, hurried to the kitchen and turned off the stove. Then she grabbed her coat on the way out. She already had her wallet in the pocket.

"You know when he's coming home?" J.T. asked as they got into his blue Chevy pickup.

She'd been home for at least an hour. Hunter should be close to done with his negotiations. "I'm guessing any minute."

J.T. stepped on the gas. "We'd better hurry. I don't want him to see us and ask questions."

His gaze darted up the line of traffic. He drummed his fingers on the steering wheel while they waited for the light to turn. Then green flashed, and he shot down the street.

Broslin had one department store that had furniture, and two consignment shops, one dealing mostly in antiques, the other in repainted shabby chic pieces. They were all lined up on Route 1, but J.T. drove past them.

"Where are we going?"

He was focused on traffic. "It's a store up toward West Grove. Can't remember the name."

She let her head drop back against the headrest and tried to figure out what Hunter needed for his new place.

J.T. turned off on a side road. Gabi watched the fields and farmhouses go by. Then just fields.

"Almost there," he said and bent down, leaving one hand on the wheel while reaching down with the other and fishing around under his seat.

He came up with a SIG Sauer P226 and, in one practiced move, pointed it at her head.

Her service weapon was in a lockbox under her bed. Her off-duty weapon was in the locked glove compartment in her car.

Dammit.

Chapter Twenty-Seven

Hunter stood with his brother and Arnie in the apartment's kitchen, trying not to look at the oak rocker. After Gabi had left, Ethan stopped by to check out the place. Then Arnie arrived at last to discuss the particulars, and showed Hunter the finances.

The mechanic shop was still turning a profit, even with customers and some employees leaving because nobody knew how long they'd stay open.

"That'll be key," Ethan said. "To let everyone in town know you're taking over and not closing anything. You don't want to lose more customers."

Hunter nodded. A big sign up front and an article in the *Broslin Journal* would take care of that.

They talked some more, looked at more files, then Arnie left them there with the keys so they could walk through again.

"As soon as the business is back on track, I'm doing a full reno on the apartment," Hunter told his brother.

"I'll help."

Hunter nodded his thanks, then paused before continuing with "As soon as I'm done renovating, I'm going to ask Gabi to move in with me."

Ethan didn't think long about it. "She's good for you."

Hunter grinned. "Yeah." She *was* good for him. And in all this mess, he'd somehow fallen in love with her.

While he tried to catch his breath from that thought, Ethan's shoulder radio went off, and he had to go in, so Hunter stayed to lock up. He pulled his phone to call Gabi and ask her out to dinner.

She didn't pick up. Maybe she was in the shower. He was heading home anyway. Hunter put the phone away. He'd just go up to her place and check, maybe join her under the spray.

But his brother called before Hunter even pulled out of the

parking lot.

"Is Gabi with you?"

"No."

"I can't reach her. Wanted to tell her that ballistics are back on Heinz's weapons. The bullet that hit my windows didn't come from any of his rifles." He paused. "Also, Heinz's attorney called in. He found someone who saw Heinz out hunting that day, way on the other side of town. Gabi will have to confirm that."

"So Heinz didn't run Dad off the road and didn't come after you." Hunter tried to work through the implications.

"Doesn't look like it."

"Dillard the bookie?"

"That's another thing Gabi needs to know. Dillard thought we were still looking at him for murder, so he gave us an alibi at last. During the time I was shot at, he was in an altercation with a jockey."

"What kind?"

"Beating the guy up and setting his house on fire."

"So we still need to figure out who shot at you and ran Dad off the road."

"Right," his brother said. "And if this is a family thing, you're the only one who hasn't been attacked yet. Watch your back."

After they hung up, Hunter stayed in the car, thinking. He ran through everyone they'd already looked at and discarded. Had they missed anything? He wanted to go into the station with Gabi, look at the attack on his brother and father separately from Cindy's case, something they hadn't really done before.

He called her again. Still nothing.

Okay, if this was a family thing... Apparently, his father hadn't been the primary target. Both the bookie and the moonshiner were out. Hunter bounced back to his brother.

Who hates Ethan enough to want to hurt his father too?

It had to be an enraged criminal. They'd have to go through conviction records again.

A small thought nagged in the back of his mind. They'd looked at who could be after his father. They'd looked at who could be after Ethan. But they'd never really looked at who could be after him. He'd discarded that out of hand when Gabi had brought it up earlier in the week.

Because Hunter couldn't think of a damn person. But what if the attacks on his father and brother were to hurt him? Maybe the bastard was leading up to coming after Hunter at one point, wanted to rattle him a little first.

He glanced at the phone on the passenger seat as he drove toward home, impatient for Gabi to call him back.

Then the next thought hit him so hard, his knuckles turned white as he gripped the steering wheel.

If the shooter wanted to hurt Hunter, wouldn't he go after Gabi?

Hunter grabbed the phone and hit Redial. No response. He slammed his foot on the gas.

His mind churned furiously as he drove down Main Street. If the killer came into the picture because of Hunter, then who was he? An enemy following him to Broslin from Afghanistan seemed way too far-fetched. He would have spotted some Afghan dude following him around. Broslin wasn't that diverse.

An iceberg slammed into his chest when he realized that someone *had* followed him from Afghanistan to Broslin.

J.T. The buddy who was even now living in his apartment.

Except, J.T. had been in Nashville until after the incidents.

Except, Hunter had no proof of that other than J.T. saying so. J.T. could have been just down the road when he'd called and said he was driving up here. His truck had Pennsylvania license plates. *Shit.*

What if he hadn't started out in Tennessee? He hadn't crashed his own vehicle. He'd probably rented the pickup at the Philly airport when his flight had come in.

No. Hunter shook his head. J.T. couldn't betray him like that. Not even if J.T. was depressed. Not even with PTSD. You just didn't go after a team member like this.

Unless...

Unless, in J.T.'s mind they were no longer on the same team.

Did J.T. resent that he hadn't been rescued for three long months? It hadn't been for lack of trying.

Hunter thought back to the night when they'd finally gone in to get the kid. The house, the Taliban lookouts, the men interrogating J.T. Images flicked through his mind like on a movie reel.

They'd lucked out. J.T. hadn't been tied hand and foot, and he hadn't been injured so badly that he couldn't aid in his own escape.

Why hadn't he been tied? Why hadn't he been injured?

Hunter racked his brain. Three enemy fighters, the AK-47s

leaning against the wall.

Four AK-47s.

Shit.

He ran the reel again. Three rifles against the wall and one against the desk. *Did the fourth weapon belong to J.T.? Had he become one of them?*

Hunter played the reel, the shock on J.T.'s face, the momentary indecision. Then Hunter had killed two of the men while tossing his backup weapon to J.T. But in his shock, J.T. just stood there.

Before realizing all was lost and gunning down the last man.

Rescue had come; rescue had won. Other than martyrdom, what choice did J.T. have but to pretend that he was happy to see the rescue team?

Then the dash down the hall. The woman who'd burst from the room. The shot. Then running again.

Except J.T. hadn't run. He'd stayed back.

At the time, Hunter had thought he'd been injured. But later, at the field hospital, they hadn't found any serious new injuries beyond a healed over bullet wound he'd likely obtained when he'd been taken.

J.T. had stopped in that hallway because of the woman.

Whoever she was to him, Hunter had shot her.

His fingers tightened on the steering wheel. Words couldn't express the sense of betrayal and rage, the sheer disbelief that hit him as he ran through the events of that night in his mind one more time.

And then he thought of Gabi again, not answering her phone, and fear like he'd never known rolled over him.

* * *

Gabi had no idea why, but J.T. was driving her to a deserted area and he had a serious gun pointed at her. She only knew one thing: she had minutes to live.

She knew that hard, empty look in J.T.'s eyes. She'd seen it before, back in Philly when she'd been called to a shopping plaza shooting. The shooter had mowed down eleven shoppers, then stuck the barrel of his gun under his own chin as police surrounded him.

"That's the death-wish look," Carmen had said as the two of them had crouched behind a column. They couldn't do anything. The next second, the shooter had pulled the trigger.

J.T. scanned the fields, probably looking for a spot to pull over.

Her phone rang again.

He rolled down her window from his side. "Throw it out."

She swallowed hard, pulled the phone from her pocket, turned it off while pretending to drop it out the window, but instead, dropped it down her sleeve.

"Okay. It's gone. Don't shoot." She pretended to wrap her arms around herself like she was scared, but instead she unsnapped her seat belt and immediately plowed into J.T., knocking his gun up, then ramming her head into his solar plexus.

Of course, after that first moment of surprise, he fought to slam her back, the two of them straining against each other.

"Why?" she gasped out the single word, bewildered.

"He took what's mine. I'm taking what's his. I'm taking all of it," he shouted at her.

He was bigger, stronger, and had a good grip on his weapon, dammit.

Her one advantage was that he had to keep one hand on the steering wheel and one hand on the gun. The cab left no room for the kind of moves she'd learned in training, so she punched, scratched, tried to go for his face. He tried to slam the butt of the gun against her head to knock her out, but she bit his wrist, and he dropped the gun at his feet at last. He slammed his boot on it so she couldn't grab the weapon away from him.

He punched her in the chest, hard, and she lost her breath. He was too damn strong. She wasn't going to overpower him. She rode the blow to her car door, opened it, and dropped out of the moving vehicle.

She hit the ditch with a painful slam, got the wind knocked out of her again, rolled and rolled, staggered to her feet, and dashed for the stand of bushes just ten feet away. Then she darted into the woods behind the bushes.

She could hear the truck stop. The door opened and slammed shut.

He'd have his gun back in hand by now.

She ran faster, gasping for air.

She didn't pause for a moment to look back. J.T. had plenty of search-and-destroy training from the army. She wasn't going to give him a chance to put those destroying skills to use today.

The ground was uneven, but frozen solid at least. No path anywhere. She ducked around trees and bushes in the light of the full moon, jumped over broken branches.

She ran until her lungs and feet gave out, then collapsed against a boulder, in cover. Since she was a strong runner, she'd come a pretty good distance by then. She tried to listen for J.T., but she couldn't hear a damn thing over her own wheezing. Her heart beat hard enough to burst. Her hands were shaking.

She had to try three times before she finally succeeded at dialing Hunter.

* * *

Hunter was pulling up in front of the apartment when his phone finally rang, Gabi's name on the display screen. "Where are you?"

"It's J.T."

The way Gabi's voice shook made him see red. "I know. Are you hurt?"

"I'm safe. I got away from him. Where's your father?"

"At the house."

"Where's your brother?"

"Heading home. I'm coming to pick you up. Where are you?"

She gasped for air. "Go to your brother's place. J.T. lost it. He's really pissed at you for something. I got away. He's going to try to inflict some damage on you or somebody you care about. He'll go after one of you next. I'm safe. I swear." She hung up.

Hunter cursed, but then he whipped his truck around and called Ethan.

* * *

Bing senior stood in the open door of Ethan's house, one step inside the threshold, for once in his life looking completely sober, no trace of his usual cocky sneers. He paid no attention to the cat that sauntered out by him and disappeared in the hemlocks.

"He's got a gun on me," he called out as Ethan and Hunter pulled in, at the same time, and parked nose to nose, jumped out, and took cover behind their vehicles. "Don't call this in," their father pleaded. "If anyone else shows up, he'll put a bullet in my head."

"What do you want?" Hunter shouted the question, hoping to judge by the sound of J.T.'s voice where he was hiding.

But Bing senior responded instead. "He wants you to come in." And the old man backed away, as if on command. He stopped after five feet or so. "Toss your guns, phones, radios outside." Then he moved to the side and disappeared from sight.

Hunter checked the windows, blinds down with a few gaps here and there. J.T. had to be behind one of those gaps, watching. If they didn't obey, he could easily swing his weapon and start shooting at Hunter and Bing.

Hunter tossed his phone and weapon. Ethan stared at him for a moment, his jaw working, and then did the same, adding his police radio receiver from his shoulder to the pile gathering in plain view on the other side of the two vehicles.

Hunter moved forward, his head down as if in defeat, but in reality so J.T. wouldn't see that his lips were moving.

"Two against one. That's an advantage," he said under his breath. He didn't count their father since the old man had no training and was likely drunk, regardless of the sober look he'd presented for a moment. "And we both know the layout of the house. Any hidden weapons within easy reach?"

"Knives in the kitchen, baseball bat in the hall closet." Ethan barely moved his lips as he responded.

"Where are the dogs?" But even as Hunter asked, he reached close enough to hear Peaches and Pickles barking in the basement. He breathed a small sigh of relief. Could have been worse. They could have been dead.

Hunter moved forward, side by side with Ethan. The motion-detector lights lit up the front of the house, but the inside stood dark, a primordial cave ready to swallow them.

Then J.T. flicked on the light over the stove. He was standing in the kitchen, behind the kitchen island that would provide cover if needed, holding a SIG P226 to the old man's head.

"Move over to the staircase," J.T. ordered. He nodded at Ethan. "You go sit near the top." Then he nodded at Hunter. "You sit on the bottom."

They followed his instructions. When they were both sitting, separated by twenty or so steps, J.T. tossed them each a pair of handcuffs from his back pocket. "Cuff yourselves to the railing."

The railing was handmade from local hardwood, wrist-thick branches cut to size, stripped of bark, sanded and varnished, solid carpentry work. Sure, it could be taken apart, but not easily, and not in silence, not in a split second, which was all they'd get if, by some miracle, J.T. got distracted for a moment.

When Hunter hesitated with the cuffs, J.T. pressed the gun harder to the old man's forehead. Hunter didn't remember ever seeing his father this lost. The old man liked to pretend that he was still the boss of the family, that he could order his sons around, reprimand them as he wished. But now, his hands shaking, he looked to his sons to save him.

Hunter detached himself from the situation and measured his father up. The old man wasn't going to make a move. He was too scared. Good. Hunter didn't need a wild card.

He glanced at his brother at the top of the stairs. Ethan remained alert but relaxed. His body language seemed to say, *you take the lead, you know the guy.*

Hunter fixed his gaze on J.T. *SIG P226 in hand. Rifle on the shoulder. Knife on the belt.* J.T. had come to do battle. He hadn't been out drinking every time he'd driven off. He'd done some shopping.

"Why?" Hunter asked. He needed to gain time so he could come up with a plan.

"You took what's mine. Now I'm taking what's yours."

"What are you talking about?"

"You shot Aina." J.T.s face was a cold mask, but his eyes swam in pain. "I loved her."

"You were a prisoner."

"A hostage," J.T. corrected. "They needed someone to trade for one of their own. They didn't mean for anyone to get hurt, but you and I both fought too hard, and we both got hit when they took me. Aina nursed me back to health. We fell in love. We were married."

Hunter stared at him. *What?*

J.T.'s voice softened for a moment. "She took away the pain. She made me see things differently."

I bet. Hunter wondered if drugs had played a role. J.T. had been injured. They'd given him drugs and a pretty nursemaid, had manipulated his mind from day one.

"How much did you tell them?" Troop positions? The schedule of patrols? What else? Now the enemy's increased accuracy toward the end of their mission in the area made sense all of a sudden. *Jesus, J.T.* "What did you tell them?" he asked again.

J.T.'s gaze boiled with hate. "You killed her."

"By accident. You were there. You saw how it happened."

"She was innocent. Unarmed."

Hunter didn't bring up the phone that he'd mistaken for a

weapon. J.T. was in no mood for reason. He was getting more and more riled up. Hunter had to keep control of the situation until he could figure out how to change the balance of power.

"I love you like a brother. If I caused you any pain, I'm sorry," he said, taking full responsibility.

J.T. nodded. But he said, "I can't let you get away with it. She wasn't trash to be thrown away. She mattered. The man who killed her can't just walk away. Fair is fair. All I want is justice."

Hunter didn't disagree. He had taken a civilian's life. It had been reviewed by his superior officers, and he'd not been charged. He'd received no blame from the US military. But that didn't mean he didn't blame himself. He'd pulled the trigger—somebody had died. No doubt about that.

"I didn't mean to kill her," he said. "I wish that night went down differently." He met J.T.'s dark gaze head-on. "If I have to face the music for my actions, I'm ready. But my father and my brother have nothing to do with any of this. Let them go. Fair is fair. All you want is justice."

He paused but went on when J.T. didn't react. "You make me pay, you have your justice. You go beyond, and you cross over to cold-blooded murder. You don't want to tie Aina's memory to that."

"Don't you fucking dare say her name!" J.T.'s eyes bugged out of his head.

Keep him calm.

Hunter fell silent, gave J.T. time to settle down. He scanned the staircase, the kitchen, the living room, the hall closet with the baseball bat that might as well be a million miles away. He racked his brain for an escape plan.

"Were you ever in Tennessee?" he asked when the blotches of red finally faded from J.T.'s cheeks.

"I was on the next flight to Philly, right behind you." J.T. spat. "I wanted to take the girl you've been talking about. Then I found out that she was already dead." He swore. "Aina was everything to me. You took everything I have. Now I'm going to take everything you have. That's how justice works."

Hunter could think of several arguments against that last point, but J.T. was only interested in rage and revenge, not so much in logic.

He shoved Hunter's father over to a kitchen chair, while kicking a gym bag in front of him that had been hidden behind the kitchen island before. He made the old man sit.

"Hands back." He pulled two lengths of rope from his bag. And then he tied his captive to the chair, hands and feet.

While his attention was on that, Hunter glanced at his brother above him on the stairs. Ethan was surreptitiously reaching for his front pocket. Two fingers in, then out quickly as he was palming something.

J.T. turned toward them. Ethan slumped and glared as before. But when J.T. turned back to the old man to test the ropes, Ethan opened his palm wide enough so Hunter could see a small key.

Handcuff key. Of course, a cop would have one somewhere on him.

J.T. bent to the gym bag, pulled out a gallon milk jug, and twisted off the top. He moved to the bottom of the stairs, six feet or so from Hunter.

J.T. swung the opened jug toward Ethan at the top of the stairs. Liquid spilled as the jug flew over Hunter's head, the unmistakable smell of gasoline filling his nostrils.

The jug touched down, spilled more gasoline. Ethan had to pass the key to his left, cuffed, hand before grabbing for the jug, which was rolling by that point, gasoline spilling down the wooden steps. By the time Ethan righted the damn thing, three quarters of the contents had emptied.

J.T. laughed and hurried back to his bag, pulled another jug, and emptied the contents all over the kitchen. The old man coughed from the fumes. J.T pulled a third jug. The bag collapsed after that, empty. Not that three gallons of gasoline wasn't more than enough. Hunter watched, teeth grinding, as J.T. splashed the clear liquid all over the living room.

J.T. grabbed the bottle of cheap whiskey on the counter that must have come upstairs with the old man. Straining hard enough against the cuffs to bloody his wrist, Hunter watched in horror as J.T. poured the alcohol over his father's head.

Ethan gave up trying to hide the key and went at his handcuffs.

J.T. reached into his pocket and pulled out a lighter. But he didn't go to the door to escape the inferno he was about to create. He stood in the middle of the space, a deranged smile twisting his face.

He meant to kill himself too. He meant to die with them.

Hunter gave up on the cuffs and twisted his body to kick against the railing. The shock of the hard kick reverberated up the length of his legs, but the wood didn't budge.

Then Ethan was free at long last, tossing the key to Hunter, lurching down the stairs. Too late.

J.T. sparked the lighter. Blue flame danced at the tip of his thumb the next second. Then Hunter was free. But neither he nor his brother was going to reach J.T. in time. They were going to be too late.

Chapter Twenty-Eight

Gabi was waiting for J.T. to step back into her line of sight again. She crouched behind the door that led to the garage, watching the limited area she could see from the narrow gap. Gasoline fumes filled the house. She refused to cough.

Where in hell were Chase and Joe? She'd called the station on her way over. She'd been saved by the fact that she had her badge with her. The second she'd made it to Route 41 and waved at a car, the driver had stopped to help. She'd hitched a ride to the road behind the farmhouse, then cut through the woods in the back.

The click of the lighter came from the kitchen. She had only two options. Do nothing and J.T. would drop the flame, or make herself known in the hopes that she could distract him for a second.

She burst into the house, gun drawn, leaping forward. "Freeze! Police!"

J.T. spun toward her, distracted just long enough for the captain to throw himself on top of him, trying to trap the flame between their bodies. He managed to pin J.T., but only for a moment. Then J.T.'s hand shot out, and the lighter was still lit, touching down into a pool of gasoline on the tile floor next to them.

At the same time, Hunter vaulted over the two men. He reached his father and picked him up, chair and all, threw him through the sliding glass door with a crash, a superhuman feat Gabi only half saw as she dashed back to the garage. She grabbed the fire extinguisher she'd seen on her way in, then ran with the red tank to the wrestling men who were on fire in the middle of the burning kitchen.

She shot white foam at them as Hunter dashed back in and reached to pull them apart, his own shirt on fire.

"Out!" he roared at Gabi, but she doused him first, spending the entire contents of the extinguisher before she drew back.

Pain touched her feet as if she'd stepped into a hill of fire ants.

She glanced down. The bottoms of her trousers were burning.

"Out!" Hunter roared again. "Dammit. Please."

He knocked out J.T. Then he grabbed the coughing captain by the arm and was dragging him toward the busted sliding glass door.

Gabi was closer to the front door, so she darted that way, her lungs screaming from the smoke, her eyes burning.

She dove into the snow from the front porch, rolled around until the wet slush extinguished her pants, then she jumped up and rounded the house.

Hunter's father was still tied to the chair, lying on his side on the deck amid broken glass, bloodied but alive, looking around wildly. The captain was rolling in the snow on the deck a few feet away, doing a good job of taking care of himself.

Hunter was gone. Back in the house.

Sirens sounded in the distance. The dogs howled in the basement.

Gabi rushed to the basement window, looked through, saw the dogs at the stairs scratching at the door. She had her service weapon out the next second and shot out the narrow window, grabbed the weapon by the barrel, and cleared out the broken glass as the dogs ran over, wildly barking.

"Come on!"

They jumped, but the window was too high and their feet couldn't find purchase on the poured cement wall, nails scraping, scrambling. She slipped in without hesitation, shoved the old coffee table to the window—empty beer cans scattering—and the dogs knew what to do then. Up on the table, through the gap. The wood of the ceiling cracked and hissed as the house burned above them.

Gabi climbed the table, her boots, wet with snow, slipping on the wood. She grabbed on to the edge of the window frame, her bare palms on the broken glass, ignored the pain as she pulled, heaved, then she was out at last.

On the deck, the captain was untying his father and then helping him down the stairs. Gabi rushed by him toward the busted doors, ready to go in after Hunter, but he finally appeared, carrying J.T. on his back.

He staggered forward. "Go!"

She did, scampering back down the stairs, getting out of his way.

"In-ground gas tank," the captain shouted, shouldering his father forward.

They all kept on moving, didn't stop even when the sirens were coming up the driveway at last.

"Called the fire department from the garage," Gabi said as they could see two cruisers followed by two fire trucks.

In the end, that made all the difference. The arriving firemen were able to save the house from exploding.

* * *

One week later

Gabi was finishing her Christmas shift, cruising past the diner, when her old captain from the Twelfth Precinct called again. She'd volunteered for the first shift. Mike, recovered from the appendectomy enough to be back at work, had volunteered for the second.

"Have you thought about my offer?" the captain asked.

"Yes, sir."

"Good. As I said, we could use heroes like you in the department. I know there've been some questions before, but nobody is questioning you now. All that publicity with Broslin, that can be good for us too. It will reflect back on us when you come back."

Her name had been all over the papers. Captain Bing had very publicly credited her with saving the day. He'd told reporters if she hadn't shown up and provided that moment of distraction, four men would be dead.

She got fan mail now. No joke. She had a handful on the passenger side of her cruiser next to her. People sent her notes to the police department, including an entire third-grade class, whose homework had been to write a letter of admiration to someone local.

The kids mostly thanked her for saving the dogs.

Heinz was in jail in West Chester, awaiting trial for murder, bail denied. J.T. was in jail too. He hadn't been able to post bail. Turned out, he'd been drunk during the original attempts on the captain and his father; that was why he'd failed. But then at the farmhouse, he'd very nearly succeeded. Gabi didn't like thinking about that.

Despite of everything that had happened, Hunter kept visiting him.

"How soon do you think you can transfer back?" the captain of the Twelfth asked on the other end.

"I'm staying, sir."

The man laughed. "You're too good to be buried in a small town like that. We need you more here."

That played right into her guilt, but she'd figured herself out enough at last so she was able to deal with it.

"Sir, I think—"

But the man talked right over her. "You talk to your captain and set up the transfer. I'm going to arrange a press release for the occasion, so I'll need a date ASAP."

"I'm staying here, sir. But I appreciate the offer," she said, and ended the call.

Since she was driving by the gas station, she figured she might as well pop in to see Hunter. She'd helped with painting his new place, but then she'd gotten caught up in a couple of new cases, so she hadn't seen the apartment furnished yet.

She started up the stairs, heard voices, turned around to leave without being seen, but the door above her opened, and she was busted.

"Gabi." Captain Bing smiled warmly in welcome. Since the fire, they were on quasi first-name basis. He called her Gabi, but she still called him Captain Bing. She couldn't get used to Ethan.

The dogs ran by him and licked her, nudged her, wiggled all around her. She felt like she was standing in a barrel of giant, hairy fish. Really sweet, loving fish.

She made it up the stairs with some difficulty, scratching ears and patting backs.

The captain stepped aside as Sophie launched herself at Gabi.

"I'm so glad you're here." Big, long hug, like they'd been estranged sisters who hadn't seen each other in years. "I was just asking Hunter about you. I want to do something nice for you. I thought a spa certificate, but Hunter says a gift certificate for the gun range." She pulled back but didn't fully let Gabi go.

"Neither is necessary."

"You saved my husband and Hunter. You saved my babies." She gazed lovingly at the two Rottweilers that had nothing baby-like about them.

Gabi cleared her throat. "I don't expect payment."

"It's not a payment thing. It's a friendship thing. Whichever you pick—spa or gun range—we'll be going together. I hope we can be friends."

"I was about to call you." Hunter came to her rescue. "My family decided to surprise me with a home-warming-slash-Christmas dinner."

"Um…" Gabi was so overwhelmed by Sophie's warm welcome, she hadn't even noticed Bing senior at the table, who'd been half-hidden by Hunter and the Christmas decorations.

The apartment was a sea of green and red, decked out to within an inch of bursting at the seams. The tree was the least of it, nearly overshadowed by all the Santas, snowmen, reindeer, angels, candles. A string of snowcapped mushroom lights hung from the ceiling in the kitchen. Who did that? Most likely Sophie, Gabi figured, and then gave up any further grumpy thoughts. Nobody could think anything critical of Sophie. She was too sweet. Nobody could not like her.

Gabi drew back. "I don't want to interrupt." This was a family occasion.

Except the family was flashing identical don't-be-stupid looks toward her, and the dogs nudged her forward.

"I did the cooking." Sophie simply took her hand and drew her to the table. "I'm trying a new honey ham recipe. You have to try it."

Gabi was surprised to see that an empty chair waited for her next to Hunter.

"Let me pour you a drink," Hunter's father offered.

But before she could answer, Hunter caught her around the waist, pulled her flush against his chest, and planted a serious kiss on her lips.

She flushed red when he let her go, but nobody blinked an eye. The captain was dishing out food. The older Bing was pouring Gabi some red wine, although his own glass held water. Sophie was beaming at her from the other end of the table.

Gabi sat and ate, because she didn't know how else to react. But as the dinner progressed, little by little she did relax.

"How is the house?" she asked Sophie. Last she'd seen it, it'd been on fire.

"Fixed." Sophie grinned. "You can't even tell that anything happened. All the damage was surface damage. Thanks to you, the fire department got there before things could have turned for the worse. We only had to replace the floor and the stairs, the parts where the gasoline was spilled." She beamed with gratitude. "Since it's new construction, the beams weren't tinder dry. That helped."

Gabi tried to deflect another round of thanks, but they all toasted her anyway.

Her family hadn't had dinners like this. Dinnertime was busy time. Her mother usually worked the phones in the evening, the best time to catch people with her various scams. On the rare occasion that the family did sit down together, they all kept an ear open for the cops. Here, the cops were at the table. She was one of them.

The scene felt surreal. She suddenly felt like this was what she'd always wanted, without knowing it. Or maybe she'd never dared to admit. Hunter flashed her a sexy smile and claimed her hand under the table, and her breath caught a little.

A warm, gooey sensation spread in her chest.

Oh God, she thought, a little panicky now. She'd fallen in love with him.

That realization kept her in a daze through dinner. Which went relatively fast. Sophie kept looking between Gabi and Hunter, and suddenly announced, when they were barely finished with the tiramisu for desert, that she just remembered she needed to rush home to send a file to a client. She designed web sites for small businesses. She mumbled something about a Boxing Day special sale notice her client requested.

Bing senior decided to go with them, claiming he was in serious need of a nap after all the food he'd eaten. They all headed for the door all of a sudden.

But Captain Bing turned back to Gabi from the door. "The Broslin Women's League wants you to ride on the first float in the Christmas parade tomorrow."

Gabi choked on her tiramisu, which the captain took as a yes, and he hurried after Sophie, who was calling to him impatiently from the bottom of the stairs. By the time Gabi swallowed, it was too late to try to call him back.

She was alone with Hunter.

He pushed aside the tiramisu and was looking at her like *she* was dessert.

Her heart rate picked up.

He stood. "Want the post-reno dime tour?"

"Sure."

"The kitchen." He gestured toward the area to his right. "Living room."

Everything looked homey, his old furniture supplemented with some new pieces, simple, masculine, comfortable, a space where a person could relax.

He moved forward, and she stood up to follow him. He pushed the first door open. "Bedroom."

A king-size antique mahogany bed took up most of the room, two big matching dressers in addition to the his-and-hers closets, big windows that would let in plenty of light during the day.

Her gaze skipped back to the bed, and her skin tingled.

But Hunter moved on—big muscles shifting, distracting, brushing by her—and opened the next door. "The bathroom."

Like the bedroom, this too was light and spacious, a double shower instead of a tub. Practical. Everything was brand-new and gleaming.

She stared in wonder. "I can't believe you got this done in a week."

"My father works construction. They're in between projects, so his boss sent the whole crew over. They were working around the clock all week." He went on to the next room, opened it. "My home office."

Desk with a computer, chair, a wall of bookcases.

He paused, watching her face. "This place is closer to the station than your place."

She shot him a questioning look.

"In an emergency, a minute or two might make a difference."

She stared. Was he asking her to move in with him?

He grinned. "I'm asking you to move in with me." And then he opened the door to the third room that had no furniture, except for the infamous rocking chair in the middle.

He drew her to him. "This could be your office." His big hands cupped her butt, and heat sizzled through her. He kissed the mole at the corner of her lips.

She squirmed. "Do I get to keep the chair?"

"I insist." He had a devilish glint in his eyes.

He slid his hands under her shirt and went straight for her breasts, sending a bolt of need through her that left her knees weak. After a few moments of heavy groping, he tugged off the shirt altogether. Then he tugged off the rest of her clothes, leaving her in her bra and panties.

"Wait." He bent, took her badge, and pinned it to her bra, then stood back to examine her, heat boiling in his gaze.

She bit back a smile. "Is this some adolescent fantasy?"

He sighed appreciatively. "Officer Flores, I believe you're too sexy for your badge."

He stepped back to her again and kissed her. Then his fingers were under her bra, his thumbs rubbing against her nipples.

She kissed the scar at his temple. It scared her how much she needed him. But she said, "Watch those hands, mister. Don't make me get out the handcuffs."

His smile only widened. He leaned forward to nibble her earlobe and whispered into her ear, "You've been threatening me with those for a while now. I don't think you mean it."

She knew when she was being goaded. She didn't take out the cuffs. But they did make love under the Christmas tree.

Best. Christmas. Ever.

Then he picked her up and carried her into the bedroom, deposited her in the middle of the bed, and made love to her again. This time, handcuffs might or might not have been involved at last.

Afterwards, he gathered her against his amazing soldier's body, the two of them snuggled under his blankets. "I haven't slept in a bed since I got home." He kissed the top of her head. "But this is good. I love you."

"I love you too," she whispered.

And he kissed the living daylights out of her.

"So Bing and I were talking about something before you got here. It might interest you," he said a little later.

She waited.

"He's been mentoring a kid out at the farm. Boy raised by a single mom. Local troublemaker. He takes care of the horses now part-time. He makes some pocket money, plus he's too busy to get into trouble. It's working out. Bing thought the horses could use another couple of kids. I told him you might be able to hook up something with your old precinct, bring inner-city kids out for the summer."

She came up on her elbow, staring at him, excitement coursing through her. God, if her brothers had had something like that... "For real? The captain would do that?"

Hunter smiled. "Sophie seemed pretty excited about it, and my brother would eat rusty tacks if that pleased her."

"And I could be involved?"

"Ethan said he could use your help."

She kissed him, long and hard, with feeling.

He just kept smiling as she dropped back next to him, fitting herself against his body.

She rested her head on his shoulder, her hair loose and spread out behind her, her arm over him, her palm resting on his chest as his breathing evened.

The apartment glittered around them like some department store Christmas display. So maybe it had a certain quaint charm. A small-town Christmas wasn't the worst thing that could happen to a person, she decided.

Then she snuggled even closer to Hunter, feeling very much as if she'd found her place in the world at last.

"I believe in Christmas," she whispered against his warm skin.

And Hunter smiled in his sleep.